PRECIOUS TIMES

Linda Lenehan

ISBN 978-1-84753-691-4

Dedication

For my daughter Jodi

The Author

Linda Lenehan was born and educated in Southern Ireland, where she lived for most of her life.
She is now living in cheerful organised chaos on a farm in South Africa with her partner and teenage daughter.

The two girls had struck off together on a good note, much to the relief of Miss Helen. Earlier on, she had been a little unsure who to assign Cathy, as a 'first day partner' but Pauline had taken on that role herself and Cathy seemed more than happy with Pauline's self organised arrangement. During the morning, Miss Helen watched the pair huddle together like a new-found secret society and she knew that a strong friendship was being forged. Uncannily, she also knew that the friendship would deepen and last for many years to come. She was not wrong.

Can two women be friends all their lives?
No matter what!!

One

Cathy had been looking forward to this day for a long time. She was four-years-old and it was about to be her first real day at *St. Patrick's School.* She had met with her teacher Miss Spencer the previous week and she had been very kind to her. Cathy liked her immediately. She was about to enter Junior Infants, the youngest class in all of the Irish National School system.

Cathy's mother, Mary Corway, was against her daughter attending a national school. She wanted her to attend the *Little Sisters* on the Hill. Somehow, Cathy's father Jimmy Corway managed to persuade his wife to give *St. Patrick's* a chance. It was only down the road and actually a very good school. There was no need to fork out large fees for private schooling, just yet. His daughters' basic education would be catered for adequately within the portals of *St. Patrick's.*

When Mary was a little girl growing up in rural Ireland, a fancy education was regarded as a bit of a waste for girls. Generally, the overall opinion was that girls should be married before they were twenty and starting a family of their own.

Mary married Jimmy when she was 18 years old and was determined she was not going to have any sons at all. Two daughters and that was definitely that. Quite a difficult task to have set herself, especially since contraception wasn't permitted according to the Catholic Church - abstinence was supposed to suffice, although husbands were not to be denied their rights either. It was all very confusing, under no circumstances was Mary going to give birth to hordes of children. Her small family would be given all the advantages she had not been allowed to enjoy as a child.

Jimmy wasn't long out of his apprenticeship from the *Electricity Supply Board* when he decided that working for an employer all his life was not for him. Why make handsome profits for someone else? He applied and obtained a loan from the local bank and started up his own small enterprise, *Corway's Electrical Ltd.*

When Mary and Jimmy were first married, they lived in the small flat above his electrical shop; it was comfortable as well as convenient. However, as soon as Cathy was born, they knew they would have to move. There was no garden to speak of, and Jimmy's shop was situated on the main street in Shankill, about twenty minutes away from the town of Bray, not an ideal place to rear a young child. They both agreed that a house by the sea would be ideal. Mary thought it would be the perfect place to bring up their children and Jimmy agreed whole-heartedly.

Jimmy's business was young but sound and he had developed a good reputation from the outset, so the bank had no problem in granting them a mortgage. They searched high and low for their first real home. Eventually, a house in Newville Road just below the foot of Bray Head came on the market. It was a bit run-down and slightly above their price range, but they thought it had great potential. Moreover, if they lived sensibly, they could manage the repayments.

Three months later, when all the red tape had been taken care of, the family moved in. It was a red brick, four-bedroom house, approximately 30 years old, situated in a quiet and respectable area in the upper part of Bray. The garden was a shambles but Mary would fix that up in no time. Jimmy had the place completely rewired and they redecorated the entire house with the help of Mary's older and favourite brother Thomas. Thomas was a painter and decorator by trade. The kitchen was large and commanded a beautiful view of Bray Head. When they were at home, they spent most evenings in the kitchen planning a wonderful future together. They didn't have much furniture to speak of, so they only used the basic rooms; the rest would be taken care of when the finances permitted. The lounge and dining room wasn't important then, and there was no hurry. The bedrooms all had fireplaces just like the rooms downstairs. Mary wanted to remove the fireplaces in the bedrooms because she didn't want to be lugging coal up and down the stairs. Jimmy was reluctant to brick them up as he liked an open fire. He saw Mary's point and assured her he would do the lugging of the coal when it was necessary. They were happy. They had their first real home and they loved it. Initially, before Cathy was born, Mary helped Jimmy in the shop. Jimmy thought that rearing a child was a full-time job on its own and Mary agreed with him. Her place was in the home and she enjoyed it. Jimmy helped her a lot when Cathy woke at night; they took it in turns to feed her and change her nappies. Jimmy wanted to be an active part of his little daughter's life and not just a provider. He worked long hours and he was often away for days at a time, but at the weekend, he was a complete family man. On Sundays, weather permitting; they would stroll happily hand in hand along the esplanade. Jimmy wasn't the type of man to be too proud to push his little darling in her pram, he was proud to do it, and when Cathy gave him her first real smile, he was drunk with joy. Mary knew she had the most wonderful husband and daughter in the world. Jimmy knew he had the perfect family.

The big day arrived and Cathy's mother deposited her in a classroom filled to capacity, children everywhere, some of them crying bitterly and others laughing alongside wistful and pull yourself together mothers who feverishly worried about separation anxiety. General mayhem surrounded her. Her eyes tried to take in everything. Books, jigsaw puzzles, building blocks with letters on them, small blackboards with chalk, paints, crayons, and a huge table that had many strange items on it. This, she was told was the nature table. To Cathy it was a wonderful fascinating array of objects, some she had never seen before; a great treat for her young inquisitive mind.

Large lettering depicting the ABC's adorned the walls, battling for space with equally large pictures of numbers. A huge blackboard dominated the wall behind Miss Spencer's desk, and what a desk! It was filled with oodles of clutter, just like Cathy's little desk in her bedroom at home. Apparently, Miss Spencer was allowed to be untidy. It was just too much to take in all at once. The midmorning break provided more thrills when little cartons of milk and orange juice were dutifully passed around, along with sticky currant buns. Somehow, they tasted yummier than the ones Cathy ate at home. No swapping of lunches brought in by the pupils was permitted at all, but Cathy saw many little hands trading things around under the tables. No one noticed or seemed to care. School was fun. She was a big girl now. The morning passed in a flurry of excite- ment, meeting new children, remembering new names, distri- buting reading books, spelling books and of course, the endless trips to the toilet, which always had a queue waiting. However, *St Patrick's* was not to last long in the life of Cathy Corway – a little over five hours to be exact.

At the end of the school day, the bell rang loudly and all the children were told to line up in single file and walk, *not* run into the playground, where they were to wait by the gates. When the gates were unlocked, a host of relieved mothers gathered up their little fledglings with great gusto, delighted they were still in one piece. As there had been long queues in the toilets earlier, Cathy was bursting to go. Mary took Cathy's hand firmly, crossed the road and they arrived home in no time at all. Cathy shot up the stairs like a bullet and happily sitting on the loo, uttered four words loudly. "This is called a piss."

Cathy's father got an ear full that night, on and on about *I told you so* and *a crowd of hooligans*. She would not be attending *St. Patrick's* again. It was decided: *The Little Sisters* on the Hill was to be the school that Cathy would attend from now on. Fearful questions arose in Cathy's young mind. Were nuns real women? Nuns always wore long dresses and long veils that covered them from head to toe. They always had a prayer book welded to their hands; big wooden rosary beads straddled their middle bits. Nuns didn't seem to have a waist; everything just suspended itself with some kind of helpful divine glory. They didn't look like any of the other women Cathy had met in her young life. They always seemed to look sad; a far cry from Miss Spencer's smiling face. Cathy never asked for answers to these questions, not yet anyway. Something made her keep quiet; she thought she had caused enough trouble already.

***

Mary Corway made all the arrangements with the *Little Sisters* on the Hill and Cathy would start the following Monday. Beforehand, she had to accompany her mother on a long bus trip into Dublin to get her convent uniform, as no pupil would be allowed to attend classes without *The Uniform*. The whole affair involved the fitting of gymslips that were far too big, but *'sure she would grow into them in no time at all.'* There was a red sash for the waist that had to be tied somehow, sideways. Cathy was hopeful that it wouldn't transform itself into wooden beads in later years. And white long-sleeved shirts, that were to be worn at all times with the school tie. A blazer, also too big, with the school emblem heavily embroidered on the breast pocket. This seemed to have no other purpose but to show off what looked like two large birds having a very unpleasant argument.

Then there was one heavy grey wool winter coat with a belt and buckle, one silly grey beret with the same but smaller embroidered emblem of the fighting birds on the front, grey knee socks and the regulation black outdoor and indoor shoes. We also had horrendous grey school knickers with enough elastic in the waist and legs to hold up the *Golden Gate Bridge* for a year.

Sport was mandatory, even for the youngest pupils. The nuns insisted hockey and tennis were necessary to keep body, mind and soul healthy. These sports had their own set of regulation garments. For hockey, there was a grey wool skirt complete with an odd dividing piece dangling in the middle; probably to keep the grey knickers firmly closeted within their folds never to be glimpsed, even by accident. This skirt was always worn at knee length, along with a grey shirt and the embroidered fighting birds on the sleeve. Shorts were not permitted for tennis, but rather a white divided knee-length skirt and a matching cotton blouse sufficed. No embroidered birds. The final touch to this uncomfortable ensemble was the school uniform veil. It looked like a small section of net curtaining with elastic attached to it. This was worn while the young ladies were marched into chapel once a day, every day.

***

Along came the feared Monday morning, Cathy's first day at the Convent on the Hill. Mary cordially waited in the visitors' drawing room with her now petulant daughter clad in an ill-fitting grey mountain of woollen garments. The fighting birds perched in the correct places.

A short while later, Mother Anastasia Superior swept into the hallowed visitors' drawing room in a flurry of black and white robes, clanking keys, wooden beads and a huge armful of terribly uninteresting looking books. She was to remove Cathy from Mary's care and take her to her new classroom to meet her new teacher.

Maybe there would be another Miss Spencer waiting for her. Cathy knew the teachers in the convent were not all nuns.

For the first time since the episode in the loo the week before, Cathy laughed. *No, nuns were not actually women; they were really some sort of big floating penguins.* Cathy's father had read her a bedtime story the previous night about penguins. In it, they delivered the post, did little odd jobs, and were generally agree- able little characters altogether.

Cathy liked penguins. Maybe this school would be all right after all ...

Two

Cathy tried to skip along the corridor beside the Mother Superior. She had never been so close to a nun before and she had questions to ask, a lot of them. That was her first mistake.

The head nun informed her that she was to walk quietly at all times. She was to speak only when spoken to, and under no circumstances was she to run or skip anywhere.

Young ladies walked, ruffians ran.

3B Junior Infants.

Behind this door, 23 little minds were gathered. Their teacher, Miss Helen, told them they had a new little girl starting today so they were all to be nice and friendly and her name was Cathy Corway. Immediately all the pupils started asking questions.

"What's the new girl's name?" Patricia Ferguson asked.

"Patricia, her name is Cathy Corway," Miss Helen answered patiently.

"Miss Helen, why didn't she start on the big orientation day like we did?" Belinda Connell asked slightly confused.

"Cathy has attended another school, however, she has decided she would prefer this one instead," Miss Helen explained even more patiently.

That sounded important, this new girl must be special. None of them were new girls any more; they had been in school for a whole week already.

"Miss Helen, I heard my mammy say that Cathy Corway went to *St. Patrick's* and she did something pro ... pro ... pro- fane. It wasn't her fault, but what does profane mean? Mammy wouldn't tell me, she said I wasn't to concern myself with such matters," Fiona Murphy bellowed.

Miss Helen felt the stirrings of a tight knot fasten itself to the inside of her head. She enjoyed her job as a teacher and she thoroughly loved children. She had been educated in the same convent and she didn't want to smother her pupils. Miss Helen believed in opening up a child's mind, not closing it with draconian rules and regulations.

She believed every child was born with a blank tape that was continually recording and she wanted to fill those young recordings with happy memories. It was imperative to her that her students developed pleasant records from their school days. A few of the nuns agreed with her. However, the head nun definitely did not. Mother Superior was a staunch nun. She did

6

everything in the same way as it had been done since she joined the order as a young woman many years ago.

The classroom door opened and instantly there was a stunned silence. Mother Superior marched in with Cathy Corway in tow. Cathy Corway the profaner.

"Miss Helen, here is your latest charge, Cathy Corway. Cathy, this is Miss Helen, your teacher." Mother Superior turned and briskly marched herself and her wooden beads back out again.

All eyes were riveted on Cathy. Miss Helen walked up to her and took her gently by the hand. She had nice soft hands, hands Cathy didn't want to let go of. Everyone started speaking at once.

"What's your name?"

"How old are you?"

"Where do you live?"

"Do you want to sit with me?"

"Miss Helen, the new girl should sit beside me. I'm the eldest in the class you know," Pauline Dutton informed her teacher.

Miss Helen just smiled and asked Pauline to tidy up some of her clutter so Cathy could actually share the seat and table space beside her. Hastily, Pauline scooped up her belongings that were as usual scattered around her and piled them to one side. "Cathy, would you like to sit beside Pauline?" Miss Helen asked her quietly.

Without answering her new teacher, Cathy moved across the small classroom and sat down slowly beside Pauline, cautiously taking in her surroundings. Room 3B was different to Miss Spencer's classroom. There was no nature table. Miss Helen's desk was immaculately tidy. Immaculate, Cathy had learned that particular word that day, it was the way her mother had told her to keep her school uniform - she was to keep it immaculately neat and tidy.

The walls had pretty pictures of the ABC just like Miss Spencer's had. There were low shelves, which held storybooks. Other shelves displayed many different cardboard boxes, piles of paper, big fat crayons, and for some reason a tray with little white candles all neatly packed.

In one corner there was an altar to the *Virgin Mary*; it had a small red light in front of it, flickering gently. In the opposite corner, there was a smaller altar, which Cathy thought held a statue of *St Francis*. This one had no red light but it did have a vase of roses positioned to one side.

The blackboard wasn't black. It was green. *Was she to call it the green board?* All the tables and chairs looked like Miss Spencer's had, but they were all the same colour, green. Green board, green tables, green chairs. Cathy felt a little green herself.

The morning passed without any real disturbances. Without any real excitement either. There had been some strange noises in the passageway outside. At the time, Pauline whispered to Cathy, "That's only old *Sister Bernadette*. She's just chasing her pretend dog outside and his name is Scruffs. She thinks he's a bit naughty so she doesn't allow him indoors during the day." Cathy and Pauline just giggled.

The two girls had struck off together on a good note, much to the relief of Miss Helen. Earlier on, she had been a little unsure who to assign Cathy as a 'first day partner' but Pauline had taken on that role herself and Cathy seemed more than happy with Pauline's self-organised arrangement. During the morning, Miss Helen watched the pair huddle together like a new-found secret society and she knew that a strong friendship was being forged. Uncannily, she also knew that the friendship would deepen and last for many years to come. She was not wrong.

Three

1975

Junior Infants first term passed and so did the second and third. Senior Infants came and went and the new school year was about to commence. This year the girls had a new classroom and a new class name as they were now in First Class. They were no longer the babies of the school but they were not the seniors either. Nevertheless, First class was an important class; it was the First Communion Class. This meant they had to learn the Catechism in preparation for their First Confession and First Communion.

Cathy thought it was all quite boring really. The other girls avidly looked forward to wearing a beautiful white dress and a wonderful white veil with a flowering wreath attached, not just elastic.

Cathy didn't particularly like dresses or veils and her mother had given up trying to persuade her to dress nicely, to dress like a little girl should. Under no circumstances would Cathy wear the girlie stuff her mother was so enthralled about.

***

The Communion Day was a day Cathy wouldn't easily forget. Mother Superior wasn't impressed either. Father Muldoon was indifferent and old Sister Bernadette enjoyed herself enormously.

Special times had been organised for the girls in the school and town church. Lots of practising commenced, such as learning to genuflect in a ladylike fashion. Little girls had to learn to genuflect without showing any knickers. Knickers had taken on a new meaning to Cathy. They were something only her mother could see, and then only if absolutely necessary.

The Catechism was studied from cover to cover. They knew how to recite the Hail Mary and the Our Father backwards as well as forwards. The Commandments were forever imprinted in the young and impressionable minds. They spent what seemed like endless hours sitting in St Luke's Church while each and every one of them learnt how to confess their sins properly in a dark confessional booth.

Of course, there was never a priest in the confessional on the practice runs; he wouldn't be there until the 'real' confession which was held a week before Holy Communion day. A good job too, because Sheila Keating shouted a lot. The complete church and surrounding areas heard how Sheila had accident- ally murdered the family goldfish and blamed her sister. She also confessed that she told her brother to feck off.

One rule that had to be adhered to before any child received the Blessed Sacrament (according to Mother Superior) was enforced the night beforehand. No good Catholic could be allowed to receive Communion unless he or she had been fasting from midnight. It was this rule that caused the problems, Cathy and Pauline convinced themselves of this.

The day was bright and sunny. A total of 24 pretty girls, parents and relatives arrived at St Luke's for the ceremony. A long Mass in Latin commenced. Hymn after hymn was sung with shrieking but beautiful young voices, and nearly one-and-a-half hours later, they lined up in pairs in the aisle. Each child carried a spray of flowers, rosary beads and a little white candle. This was quite a lot to ask little, nervous young hands to handle.

'Ave Maria' thundered out from the church organ, and two by two, the Little Brides advanced towards the altar, where Father Muldoon was waiting for them. Each child genuflected without a pair of knickers in sight. Everything was going as planned and the whole congregation knelt down again.

Father Muldoon was about to give the first little girl her Blessed Sacrament when he was interrupted by a loud exclamation, "Jesus, Mary and Holy St Joseph, Bridie my Bridie she's on fire."

Sniff, sniff. Yes, there was a whiff of smouldering lace combined with a lot of unscheduled commotion coming from the altar.

Mrs Clark, a very large woman, thrust herself forward. She grabbed a huge vase of flowers and promptly emptied the lot over her daughter's head. Maybe it was the shock of the cold water. Maybe it was the congregation turning every which way they could to help, as almost every person in the sanctuary was hysterical.

Mother Superior deftly separated her charges, only to find Mrs Clark bent over her daughter Bridie in tears. Bridie was lying flat out on the floor unconscious, her knickers visible for all to see!

Dr Blake was summoned from somewhere at the back of the church to attend to the now bewildered Bridie (her knickers had been quickly hidden). Divine intervention again? Then, Father Muldoon just disappeared. He was later found propped up at the bar in Flemming's pub. Eventually the head nun decided that all the girls should go back to the convent until the unfortunate situation was sorted out and she deposited them in the school chapel with instructions to pray quietly. They were not a happy bunch of girls at all. They should be having the Communion breakfast in the nuns' dining room and visiting relatives. They shouldn't be back in the school chapel praying.

Pauline and Cathy were starving because neither of them had eaten anything since midnight. They knew the customary Communion breakfast was ready and waiting for them in the nuns' dining room, so why waste it? Hunger took over from better sense and they both left the chapel not bothering to ask any of the other girls along. They slipped quietly into the dining room where they shared a very pleasant breakfast with old Sister Bernadette and her imaginary dog Scruffs.

The old nun was very glad to see them; she had been waiting for quite some time for the Communion class to arrive. She wasn't able to cope with a large bunch of girls any more, so she was delighted that only two of them had turned up. During breakfast, she told them that Scruffs was old now, so she permitted him to stay indoors most of the time.

Most of the girls would say hello to Scruffs when they encountered him with the old nun in the corridors. They weren't bothered that he was invisible; he was just another part of convent life. They respected Sister Bernadette. She was too old to teach any more, but she was a fundamental part of their lives.

The girls who remained in the chapel tried to get on with what they were supposed to - pray. Sheila Keating did pray. She prayed very loudly, but it didn't resemble anything like what the Catechism held between its covers.

Belinda Connell decided there and then, she was going to be a pilot. Quiet, little Macy Thompson was convinced she was going to be a missionary of note. Fiona McLoughlin was just plain miserable.

Their day had not gone to plan and had been ruined, but they were children and children forget quickly.

Three weeks later, a somewhat subdued group of girls' received the Blessed Sacrament in a much less crowded St Luke's, without any mishaps. This time they were minus the candles.

Times were changing.

Four

1978

Cathy and Pauline hated school sports. They were now lively, adventurous ten-year-olds and had other pastimes in mind. For some time they had shared a collective passion for ponies and horses. Cathy wanted to learn to ride, it was her dream. When Cathy first approached her mother with her request for riding lessons, her mother was horrified. She told Cathy that sometimes the goings on outside the local betting shop were very distasteful indeed. She had visions of her daughter, in later life betting her savings away, on some three-legged nag. She kept these imaginings to herself, but she was adamantly against the idea from the word go.

Cathy always knew she could twist her father around her little finger when she wanted to, so she turned to him for help. Jimmy liked the idea of his daughter learning to ride; he liked the idea very much and he set about explaining to his wife that it would be good for Cathy. She would be out in the fresh air and it was good exercise as well. Murphy's Stables had a very good reputation and it was well within their budget.

Mary objected further on the grounds that Cathy might hurt herself. Jimmy reassured her she would be fine, carefully reminding her that Pauline had been riding for over a year already, and she hadn't hurt herself even once. Eventually, Mary reluctantly gave in; Cathy was allowed to attend the beginners' riding class at Murphy's Stables. She was over the moon with happiness and phoned Pauline to tell her the good news. Pauline was thrilled. She had actually fallen off on quite a few occasions when she first started, but Cathy's mum didn't need to know that. Mary would have preferred Cathy to spend more time in her ballet classes, which she had started when she was five.

Nothing comes without compromise and it was decided between the families that Pauline should attend ballet classes also. Ballet would be excellent for her deportment. She would be exposed to a milder and more refined way of life. Poor Pauline, she was continuously labelled a rebel without a cause, and Mary was sure it had something to do with the riding nonsense.

Mother Superior had to be consulted because with all the lessons, there wouldn't be enough time to pursue the sports set down by the convent, much to Jimmy's annoyance; Cathy was his daughter and he didn't understand why the head nun should have any say in this matter.

Surprisingly, the nun agreed that learning to ride was a good idea. Physical education was important to her and she conceded that Cathy and Pauline would have only one hockey, or one tennis lesson a week, as there were only a certain amount of hours in a day. Not great news to the girls' ears, but better than nothing.

From then on, twice a week, Cathy joined Pauline at Murphy's Stables and Pauline joined Cathy at Miss Smith's Dancing Academy.

***

Cathy adored the soft whinnies she received from the ponies when she approached them. They nuzzled her with sweet hay-filled breath and the conversations she had while grooming them, were beyond description. Her twice-weekly visits to Paddy Murphy's stables were the highlight of her life. To Cathy's surprise, she started to master the art of riding very well. Miss Smith, her ballet teacher, wasn't too happy about the idea of one of her pupils learning to ride horses, but she wel- comed her new pupil Pauline Dutton with open arms.

Initially, Pauline helped Cathy with her riding as much as she could, and Cathy tried to help Pauline with her ballet. Unfortunately, Pauline was like a thundering elephant in that area. It didn't bother Pauline, so it didn't matter. Pauline's mother Celia Dutton was also convinced that her rebel daughter would someday blossom into the next Dame Margot Fonteyn. She thought that ballet was exactly what was needed to develop a bit of refinement in her rebel daughter.

Five

Paddy Murphy was always firm but kind to his family of horses. He came from a long line of Romany people and had worked for most of his life around them. When he turned 14, he was taken on permanently at Blake's yard. Blake's was a reasonably sized hunting and racing yard.

Paddy worked hard and diligently. In return, he received a small but fair wage and he was permitted to ride Stubbs exclusively. The horse was a real winner in his day but he was now in semi-retirement. Stubbs would never be relegated to the factory as many of his predecessors were; he was far too valuable and loved. Stubbs gave the young fillies confidence, and put the young geldings firmly in their place. When the younger horses became fractious on an outride, Stubbs was ridden along- side them to prove that there were no real monsters in a par- ticular ditch or bush. At the time Stubbs was almost 23 and still going strong. Paddy idolised Stubbs and Stubbs idolised Paddy - a perfect union.

The owner of the yard, Captain Blake, rewarded Paddy's dedicated hard work by imparting his extensive knowledge in many equine disciplines to him.

Two years later at evening feeding time, Paddy gave his usual whistle for Stubbs to come in. He didn't come and there was no sign of him anywhere, so Paddy went to investigate. He found Stubbs lying down with a mouthful of uneaten grass in his mouth. At Paddy's approach, Stubbs lifted his head and softly whinnied, and with one long peaceful sigh, he went to sleep forever. His old heart just stopped. The Captain buried Stubbs out in the far paddock where he had spent the majority of his last years. Paddy was heartbroken. The Captain under- stood the bond the young man and horse had shared and he knew that something must be done. He suggested to Paddy that he should go over the water to his old friend and compatriot Peter Maguire, for a three-month stint at his riding school in Yorkshire. Reluctantly, Paddy went; he had never been away from Ireland before, he had never been anywhere.

Paddy stayed longer than three months, nearly 12 years in total. The Captain missed him sorely, but he was a kind man and he knew Paddy was happy.

Always ready to help anyone with anything, Paddy was noticed in the right quarters. He completed many courses in the art of saddlery and combined with this, he excelled at équitation. Paddy could handle a cross-country course with such ease, it was poetry in motion to watch. He was now 26, and he wanted to go home. He had completed his apprenticeship some years back, so he was under no obligation to stay. His longing took him home to Wicklow.

All things have the habit of changing, but Paddy wasn't prepared for the sight that met his eyes, when he returned to the Captain's yard. The large stable block was totally run-down. The gates creaked. The once emerald-green paddocks were now miserably overgrown. Ragwort sprouted everywhere, even from the now defunct chimney of what had once been his cottage home. Paddy's parents had moved to Kerry when he was 16, so the Captain had allowed him to stay in the small but cosy cottage, beside the main stable block.

What had happened to the horses? Paddy had heard rumours but regarded them as only rumours.

The Captain had never married, nor had he any family to speak of. His only family had been his horses and hounds, and, of course Paddy, who had been like the son he had always wanted. When Paddy was dispatched to Yorkshire and never came back, Captain Blake became depressed. He knew it wouldn't be fair to insist that Paddy return, but he couldn't find anyone to fill Paddy's shoes. Hence, he developed a reputation of being a difficult man to work for. Some hands came and some hands went, but none, according to the Captain, had the under- standing that Paddy shared with his horses. *Not a blasted one of them knew how to look after the hounds*. So the hounds were moved to the neighbouring manor house.

Captain Blake continued to hunt for a while and continued to train his racehorses, but his heart wasn't in it any more. He was just too old to cope without Paddy. Eventually, all the horses were auctioned off and the Captain became a recluse. His only regular companion was his housekeeper Mrs Byrne.

Paddy was shocked when he laid eyes on the Captain. The once tall, proud and elegant man was reduced to a gnarled, bent, blanket-covered heap lodged firmly in an easy chair by a huge log fire. Mrs Byrne was delighted to see Paddy. She told him that five years ago, the Captain had suffered a bit of a stroke and she also whispered that he was quite well really, just old and grumpy. Paddy refused to believe this and he app- roached the Captain with more than a tinge of anger. Cold, sad, hooded eyes looked up at Paddy.

"Yes, who are you? What are you doing here? What do you want with me? Mrs. Byrne, who on earth is this person?" Cap- tain Blake asked apathetically.

Then, recognition dawned in the old mans eyes, and Mrs Byrne was promptly dispatched for the whisky decanter.

"No, Mrs Byrne, we do not want a nice cup of tea," she was informed by a decidedly animated Captain. "Confounded woman, she's always trying to give me a nice cup of tea."

Paddy just smiled.

Long into the night, the two talked. They talked all through most of the next day as well. They had so much to say to each other, so many years to catch up on. Even after all that time spent chatting; they still had a lot to discuss. The Captain insisted Paddy stay in one of the guest rooms. Mrs Byrne was happy to have another person to look after. She was very fond of Captain Blake but she did get a bit lonely at times. She always had plenty of time for Paddy in the past, and believed he was a good sort.

Three days later, Mrs Byrne trundled into the Captain's bedroom with his breakfast tray. She pulled the curtains open as usual, but she didn't hear any of the usual caustic comments from under the bed covers. The Captain didn't stir. He had slipped away quietly in the night.

The always distant and suddenly concerned relatives made all the funeral arrangements. They buried Captain Blake three days later in the church cemetery. Paddy was beside himself with grief, he had just been reunited with his old friend and now he was dead.

He stayed on with Mrs Byrne to help her sort out the big house. Mrs Byrne had her own small cottage on the estate, where she had lived for over 40 years; the Captain had signed it over to her many years before his death. Paddy didn't want to be ungrateful to Mrs Byrne for her hospitality, but he had to consider his future. He was thinking of returning to Yorkshire, when he received a phone call from Mr Shaugnessy, of *Shaugnessy & Son*, the local solicitors. The solicitor asked Paddy to come and see him at two o' clock the following afternoon. He was a bit puzzled, but agreed. After the usual greetings, Mr Shaugnessy asked Paddy to sit down. He told him that Captain Blake had left his entire estate to him. He also informed him that this will, could not be contested, as it was made nearly twelve years ago.

"What exactly do you mean Mr. Shaugnessy?" Paddy was more than a little stunned.

"Well, Mr. Murphy, it's simple enough. Captain Henry Blake has named you the sole heir to his estate. You inherit everything, I mean *everything*, Mr Murphy."

Paddy was uncomfortable. Mr Shaugnessy's attitude was condescending and abrasive. He clearly did not approve of the late Captain's last will and testament.

"You seem to have fallen on your feet laddy. A nice tidy sum indeed," Mr Shaugnessy sniggered.

The hair on Paddy's neck bristled. Fallen on his feet had he? No, he had not. He had just buried the Captain, the only person in his life who had really believed in him. The first person who had ever encouraged him to do anything about his future. The first person who thought he had a future at all. He had just buried his dear friend, his mentor. Falling on his feet, had nothing to do with it.

Paddy just stared at Mr Shaugnessy. He stared hard at the weedy little man, who had sneeringly stated that Paddy had fallen on his feet. This solicitor had the emotions of a weasel. No, a weasel was better than this man; this man had no emo- tions at all.

"Now, Mr Murphy, there's a lot to do. First, the Captain's will must be filed in the Probate Office. Of course, I can handle that for you, but if you would rather use your own legal rep- resentative that would be fine by me. It's entirely up to you."

Paddy was having trouble taking in the fact that he had been mentioned in Captain Blake's will at all. Now, he was being advised that he could use his own legal representative. He didn't have a legal representative.

"I'll leave everything in your capable hands Mr Shaugnessy, thank you."

Paddy needed a pint of Guinness; he needed a glass or two of the hard stuff as well. He headed straight for Flemming's pub. All eyes turned to look at him when he opened the door of Flemming's. He didn't really notice any of them.

"Ah, Paddy, I heard you were back. Come over here and let me buy the new owner of Blake's a decent pint." This invitation came from Father Muldoon.

How on earth did the Father know he'd inherited Blake's? He had only just discovered this information himself, and that was less than an hour ago. *Word travels fast in small villages.*

Father Muldoon was fretting. That same morning the Arch- bishop had informed him, that he was about to get an assistant to help him with his parish. Father Muldoon was trying to figure out what he needed an assistant for. Hadn't he and Father Sheehan been administering to the parish together for ten years now, and perfectly well at that? They didn't need an assistant. His parish was getting smaller not bigger. The young ones all wanted to go off to far distant places. This generation of young ones had ideas beyond their stations. Well, that's what Father Muldoon thought. He had been in Flemming's for a while now, so every patron knew that a sermon was imminent. This was nothing new; they just nodded and turned back to enjoy their own pints. The population of the parish was actually growing. However, none of the customers in Flemming's was prepared to take the risk of informing the priest of that fact. In reality, Father Sheehan handled most of the work in the parish.

Paddy sat down at the bar beside Father Muldoon, and enjoyed more than one pint, and of course, more than a couple of tots of Jameson's whisky.

There was a lot more to the Captain's estate, than Paddy could have ever imagined. Apart from the big house, the stables and the land, (over 200 acres), there was another house in Brittas Bay. The Captain also had a healthy bank account. Money invested over the years, amassed to a total of just under £1.5-Million. Paddy knew the Captain had lived frugally, but, one point five Million!! That was an absolute fortune.

Many plans were about to be put in place, plans that would honour the Captain's memory. Plans the Captain would have approved of.

Paddy employed the services of a renowned firm of architects in Dublin, called Prentices & Co. Many weeks of discussions ensued, regarding the necessary building permissions and retention of building rights on the existing outbuildings. This was important, as Paddy was about to extend the yard.

The old barn was demolished and a new less backbreaking one erected. The existing stables needed to be totally refurbished as they had long fallen into decay. Two extra blocks were planned, one to stable ponies, and the other brood mares. Three feed rooms, two tack rooms and an office to round off the yard.

Paddy commissioned the building of an international indoor show-jumping arena. Above this, he planned a restaurant and bar, with large panoramic windows overlooking the main arena. This would afford his guests, the opportunity to watch the riders in action, while enjoying fine cuisine. A smaller indoor arena was built for everyday schooling, and regular riding lessons.

A full-size international dressage arena was also laid down. Only silica sand was allowed underfoot, as silica sand was ideal for schooling, this helped to protect the horse's tendons. *'No foot, no horse'* was Paddy's motto. In his mind, shale combined with shredded rubber, made the ground too heavy for any of his horses.

Another outdoor schooling arena was built near the main indoor one. This would facilitate the competitors warming-up their horses and ponies. Paddy was building what was to become, a nationally recognised equestrian centre.

He also planned an international cross-country course. He built this course himself, with the help of his apprentices. Time and knowledge was valuable to him and while the building of the cross-country fences continued, he instructed his lads on safety and style, and how riders should approach the course as a whole. Hunters and show jumpers held a special passion for Paddy. He had further plans to breed fine Irish Draughts, and many auctions later, he had purchased five young maidens and three proven mares. Three of these young maidens had the bloodline of the famous King of Diamonds flowing through their veins.

The paddocks needed special planning that only Paddy knew how to do. His people before him had instilled their vast knowledge of the healing powers of nature's herbs into him. A total of 100 acres of land was ploughed up and sown with different grasses, mainly rye. Rosemary, wild mint and wild parsley was also planted throughout the fields. The paddocks that the mares would graze in had raspberry bushes and other special herbs planted in the bordering ditches. Field shelters were built, with storage facilities for hay alongside. An adequate number of automatic watering stations were placed around these areas; which was fed from the estate's river via a simple but effective pumping system.

Paddy didn't move into the big house, instead, he chose to live in his old cottage beside the original stables. He modernised his cottage somewhat, but not much. His needs were simple. The big house was converted into a guesthouse, so visiting and competing guests would sleep soundly knowing their equine friends were nearby.

Mrs Byrne ran that side of Paddy's enterprise, with the help of her daughter Moira. At the time, Moira was fresh out of hotel school where she had passed all her final exams with distinctions and she was more than happy to accept the position offered. The prospect of working closely alongside her mother presented her with no problems at all, as the pair had always gotten along very well in the past.

When any maintenance had to be attended to, Mrs Byrne would summon Paddy. At all other times, his presence wasn't needed and Paddy didn't interfere. Between Mrs Byrne's housekeeping skills, (her cooking was legendary) and Moira's managerial skills, the guesthouse ran more than efficiently. Moira's main area was the restaurant and bar and she soon had both operations running smoothly.

Paddy managed the yard. The mother and daughter team managed the guests. Three riding instructors trained the children and adults, with two stable hands and four apprentices. Everyone had his or her place, and everyone was happy.

When the last area was finally finished, the gallops were given a facelift, but they would never be used again. Paddy no longer had any interest in bloodstock. Racehorses were wonder- ful creatures in their own right, but they held no real appeal for Paddy. Over the years, he had witnessed too many lives destroyed by bookies. He did not approve of gambling.

However, he did erect a plaque at the finish of the gallops. It simply stated:

In Memory Of
Captain Henry Blake
and
Stubbs

Six

"Pauline, for goodness sake, it's only a flipping ballet exam, no different from any of the others you have passed. All with high commendations I might add."

Cathy was a bit annoyed with her best friend. If anyone should be worried about a ballet exam, it should be Cathy, certainly not Pauline. Pauline was no longer the thundering elephant that she had been when she first started. The exams were scheduled for ten o'clock and quarter to eleven consecutively, the next Friday morning.

Both girls were now 13-years-old and First Year students in the convent senior school. The senior section was separated from the junior one, via a long divided driveway, with the main entrance situated on Putland Hill. The driveway to the senior school branched off to the left of the main house, and then it turned off again onto a pathway through a rose garden. At the end of this rose garden, there was a flight of concrete steps which led to the students outside door and locker room. Above the door was a large bay window, and on most mornings, Mother Superior liked to position herself at it, like a billowing sentinel supervising the arrival of her young ladies. If she happened to see one of *her* girls with a single item of the uniform out of place, there was hell to pay.

Initially, Cathy and Pauline had a good laugh between themselves about why it was called the outside door. *Maybe there was another secret inside door hidden away somewhere?*

On this particular morning, Cathy and Pauline were late. Nothing unusual about that, as Pauline was always forgetting something or other. Cathy swore she would be late for her own funeral. As they hurried along the road to school, they met one of the boys from the Christian Bothers College further up the hill. His name was John Clancy. Pauline smiled wickedly and said, "Morning, John, how's your gran, I heard she had a bit of a nasty turn last night?"

The turn John's gran had suffered was brought on because she had successfully completed a sneak attack on the kitchen pantry and raided the cooking sherry. This enabled her to have a great old time, subjecting the closest neighbours, to her constantly changing version of the famous old ballad *'Danny Boy'*.

Apparently, she enjoyed herself for over two hours before falling happily asleep in her armchair. Truth be told, the neighbours weren't bothered at all. The old woman was nearly 95-

years-young, so this infrequent disturbance was very minor to them. Most of them actually enjoyed her amusing renditions.

"Ah, she's fine now, just sporting a bit of a headache, that's all," John replied with a huge smile on his face. At that moment, John was very glad his gran had raided the sherry the night before. He had wanted to speak with Pauline about something important, something very private, for quite some time. He'd never really had the chance before.

Pauline was always down at the flipping stables or doing some- thing else. She was always rushing somewhere.

John had fancied Pauline secretly for as long as he could remember. When he watched her win the Junior Hunter Trials over at Murphy's Equestrian Centre last season, he thought she was marvellous. To John, Pauline was perfect and he shared her passion for horses. He retained a healthy sense of self-preservation around them. He was a bit scared at times; due mainly to his brother Michael, who was a working jockey with the Brien's racing yard, down at the Curragh in Kildare.

John had witnessed Michael taking some nasty tumbles over the years. Sometimes he thought his brother was crazy. That didn't stop John from joining the intermediate class at Murphy's though, as this was the only real time he got to see Pauline at all. John was a natural rider with a good seat and gentle hands, but he wasn't competitive. He knew he would never be in Pauline's league.

She was the kind of rider who rode to win, and John was content to stay in the background. As long as he could be around Pauline, albeit infrequently, he was happy. Now he had an opportunity to speak to her, and he wasn't letting it go.

"Pauline, can I have a bit of a word with ye, in ... in private? It won't take long." John couldn't believe his mouth had opened and he had actually spoken to Pauline. "Sure, what's up?"

Pauline looked John straight in the eye while she waited to hear what he wanted to say. She knew he was a bit clumsy when it came to girls, as he had tried to speak to her on a few occasions down at the yard, but he had always backed off. John became flustered as he felt the familiar heat rising from his neck upwards. He knew he was blushing.

"Oh, nothing is up," John replied looking down, shuffling his feet, and wishing wholeheartedly the ground would open up and swallow him.

"Well, if nothing is up with you, you'll have to excuse me, as I had better get on my way. I'm late for school again. See you later. Bye."

Pauline felt bad about being a bit short with him, but Cathy was glaring at her. Cathy had been in a peculiar mood for the last few days; she wasn't herself at all. Try as she might, Pauline couldn't get her friend to open up, about what was bothering her.

John Clancy was stunned, he'd missed his chance.

The under - 14s school dance was on the following weekend and he had wanted to ask Pauline to go with him. Now Peter Blake would get in there before him. He had to do something, and he had to do it quickly. "Pauline, Pauline, hang on a minute, will ye?" John knew he sounded desperate, but it was now or never.

"John, what is it? Just spit it out, I told you I'm late," Pauline was getting irritated and Cathy had just stomped off up the hill. "Well now, Pauline, you know our school dance is on next weekend?" John blurted out.

"Yes, I know," Pauline said abruptly.

John shuffled around once again. *Oh hell, this is difficult. I'm not stupid. I'm just having bad luck trying to think.*

"Pauline, will you, I mean, can you ..." he couldn't say what he wanted to say, the words were just stuck in his mouth.

"Go to the school dance with you John, is that what all this is about?" Pauline replied, feeling sorry she had been so sharp before because he was scarlet with embarrassment.

"Eh, yeah Pauline, would you?" John spluttered out completely astonished.

"Sure John, I'll go with you. Listen up now; give me a ring later on, about 7pm tonight, okay. Honestly I have to get to school, I'm already late. Bloody Mother Superior has it in for me. Boy is she on my case."

"I'll do that Pauline. I'll call you later. Yes, I certainly will," John said to Pauline's back as she rushed off. He was absolutely thrilled with himself. Pauline caught up with Cathy.

"What time is it?" Looking at her watch, Cathy announced, "It's nearly five-to-nine." Pauline decided not to respond to Cathy's acid tone. Sometimes silence was golden and this was one of those occasions, when she listened to what her head told her.

The sentinel wasn't in her usual position; the bay window was empty. Cathy was relieved because she wasn't wearing her uniform beret. Both of them clambered down the steps, changed their shoes, hung up their coats, and quickly prepared for class. Cathy had a frenzied search for her English homework. She could have sworn she had left it in Pauline's locker because hers was so full. "Fetch it later Cathy, if we're late for assembly again, the old bat will have our guts for garters."

Cathy didn't answer her; she just slammed the locker door shut and clattered up the back stairs, with quite a few other late stragglers. At the top, she composed herself and tried to proceed forward in a sedate manner towards the assembly hall. She donned her uniform veil in preparation for chapel. From 9.15 to 9.30 every morning, the entire senior school went to the chapel and supposedly made an effort to pray. Cathy and Pauline never bothered praying much. Usually they just knelt down and gossiped in whispered tones to each other; heads bent reverently forward of course. "What's up with John Clancy?" whispered Cathy.

"Ah, he just asked me to go to the school dance with him next weekend," Pauline whispered back. "What did you say?" Cathy said through gritted teeth.

"I told him I'd go with him." Pauline replied quietly, risking a brief and worried glance at her friend.

"For Christ's sake Pauline, you can't go. We have the fucking ballet exam on Friday morning and Paddy has the cross-country clinic on Saturday *and* Sunday. We promised him we would help, and we said we would stay over for the night to help Mrs Byrne out. You know she's short-staffed."

Cathy was on her feet now. She hadn't whispered the last statement to Pauline. She had shouted it at her. Then Cathy pushed her way roughly out of the pew, and ran from the chapel. All the other girls just sat shocked and open-mouthed. Pauline took a deep breath and followed her friend out, much to the consternation of Mother Anastasia Superior.

Cathy headed straight for her favourite place in the school grounds (the orchard). She thought she would be alone there. Effortlessly, she scaled the wall, as the gates were always locked, and plonked herself down underneath one of the apple trees. In the past, it was here, she and Pauline often resided when they were supposed to be having one of the school's three-day retreats. Sometimes they would just hide out under the old trees, avoiding the dreaded tennis or hockey lessons. If the gardener (Jamie) found them there, he would just turn a blind eye. He often had extended lunch breaks in the orchard himself, so a symbiotic relationship developed between them. *Scratch my back and I'll scratch yours,* was Jamie's favourite saying.

Sister Bridget, their English and History teacher was already in her classroom when her First Year pupils arrived. Cathy and Pauline were not in the class. English was their first period of the day, they should have been there.

The previous week, Sister Bridget had set her pupils some poetry homework. It was more of a competition really; the winner was to read her poem to the entire school, on the head nun's feast day. This was in ten days time, and there was always a school celebration on the feast day of Saint Anastasia.

"Good morning, girls … now settle down quickly, we have a lot to cover today." Sister Bridget announced to her students warmly.

The girls did settle down quickly, but the nun sensed something was amiss. She hadn't heard about the incident in the chapel.

"Does anyone know where Pauline Dutton is?" Sister Bridget asked looking around her classroom.

Pauline had won the poetry competition outright, and she wanted to congratulate her. Everyone stayed silent.

The nun looked around at her pupils again, and noticed Cathy Corway was also absent. She knew then, that something was wrong, but what?

Sheila Keating couldn't contain herself any longer, so she recounted the entire incident in the chapel to the nun, in great detail.

Sister Bridget listened to her tale, and when she was finished, she made a quick decision. *This matter has got to be dealt with promptly. It mustn't get any worse.* "Girls, I want you to sit quietly and review the chapter from 'The Merchant of Venice', the one we covered last week. Please excuse me, I won't be too long." The nun knew exactly where Cathy would be, and if her hunch was right, Pauline would be there too.

As she left, Fiona Loughlin muttered to no one in particular, *why should I read any of Shakespeare's stuff, he's never read any of mine?*

Jamie was making himself a drop of tea, and he got the fright of his life when Sister Bridget pulled open the door of his shed. The nuns never came into his shed. It was the only place he could be entirely alone. Jamie had a wife and nine children, so his home was always in a shambles, and there was never a quiet moment. His wife knew all about dental appointments, romances, best friends, favourite foods, secret fears, hopes and dreams. Jamie was vaguely aware of all the short, noisy people who lived in his home, and his shed was his sanctuary.

"Jamie, can I please have the keys to the orchard gate?" Sister Bridget asked briskly.

"Is there something wrong Sister?" Jamie had never been asked for the key to the orchard before, and he was a bit perplexed.

"No, nothing is wrong Jamie. Do not concern yourself. The key please, I've left my class unattended."

Scratching his head, Jamie found the key and handed it contritely to Sister Bridget. He continued to make his tea. He knew he would find out the reason for the sister's demand, at the 11am school break.

The head nun was disgusted at Cathy's outburst. She retrieved her file from the over-large filing cupboard, and found Cathy's parents home telephone number. She dialled and waited for someone to answer. There was no one home. She decided to phone Cathy's father at his office.

"Good morning, *Corway's Electrical*, how can I help you?" Sandra said politely. She was Jimmy's secretary and combined receptionist.

"I would like to speak to Mr Corway please," the head nun sharply requested.

"Certainly, who may I say is phoning?" Sandra enquired.

"Mother Anastasia Superior," the nun announced.

"Oh, hello Mother, how are you?" Sandra enquired even more politely. She had been a past pupil with the Sister's on the Hill until two years ago. She still remembered the unpopular nun pretty well.

"I am well, thank you for asking," the nun replied sharply. Sandra was not one of her favourite past pupils, and even now, the nun regarded her as a member of the fast crowd.

"Glad to hear that Mother, can you hold on for a moment please?"

"Yes, I will thank you." There was silence between the pair, as Sandra let her boss know that the head nun from Cathy's school was holding for him. He told her to put her through immediately.

"Mother, I am putting you through now, goodbye," Sandra said, relieved that she didn't have to hold any further conversation with the nun. *What a bitch* she thought. She knew from past experience, that when the school phoned, something was usually wrong. *Shit, what had Cathy done now? Jesus, Mary and Joseph, maybe she's had an accident.* Sandra squashed the impulse to listen in on the conversation, her boss hated eavesdroppers.

"Good morning Mr Corway. I'm sorry to bother you at your place of work," the head nun said to Jimmy, not sounding like she meant it.

"What is it Sister, is Cathy all right?" Jimmy enquired, slightly alarmed.

"Yes she is, and no she's not, Mr Corway." She didn't know where Cathy was at that moment, and she realised too late that she had been a bit hasty in making her phone call.

"Sister, please tell me what this is all about ... has my daughter had an accident?" Jimmy was usually a very calm man, but nothing was more important to him than his family's welfare.

"Mr Corway, I tried to speak to your wife first, but she is not at home," the nun told him acidly.

"Well, thank you for that observation and will you please tell me what this phone call is about?" Jimmy was getting annoyed; he didn't like the head nun one bit.

"Mr Corway, can you come to the school? This is not a matter to discuss over the phone, and will you please address me as Mother and not Sister."

Knowing he would get no further with the nun, he replied, "I'll be right over. Good bye, M-o-t-h-e-r."

Jimmy phoned his home but Mary wasn't answering.

"Sandra, I'm going to the convent, if my wife calls, please tell her where I am. No, on second thoughts, don't tell her where I am," Jimmy said to Sandra as he rushed through the front office.

"Sure Mr Corway, no problem. By the way, is Cathy okay?" Sandra enquired, genuinely concerned. She was fond of Cathy and she thought her boss was a good sort really.

"I don't know, that ... that fecking bat of a nun, won't give me any details, but it's probably nothing, so don't worry." Jimmy didn't believe there was nothing wrong. The head nun wouldn't have phoned him unless there was something wrong.

**

Sister Bridget's hunch was right. She opened the lock on the orchard gate, and entered. She heard Cathy and Pauline before she saw them. One of them was sobbing her heart out. She could see the two girls sitting under a tree in the far corner of the orchard. She walked up to them and said, "Pauline, please return to your classroom, I will deal with this matter. Now run along, there's a good girl."

"But, Sister ..."

"No buts Pauline, back to your class, now."

Pauline looked at Sister Bridget and then back to Cathy. "No Sister, I don't want to leave Cathy like this."

"Pauline, I will handle this matter, will you please obey my instructions immediately." The nun didn't want to have two girls in tears, but she wouldn't be undermined either. "Pauline, will you leave the orchard this instant, and go back to your classroom."

"Pau ... Pauline, please go, I ... I don't want you to get into any trouble, and I'm sorry I've been so horrible to you," Cathy gulped. She wasn't crying any more; she'd run out of tears.

"Cathy, it's okay," Pauline said putting her arms around her friend, and hugging her tightly.

"Pauline, will you do as you are told, please!" Sister Bridget ordered.

Pauline left the orchard reluctantly, via the gate and not over the wall. She knew she couldn't do anything more for her friend right now, not after Sister Bridget had ordered her to go.

"Cathy, come over here, come and sit on this bench with me," the nun had genuine concern in her eyes, and voice. "Would you like to tell me what is upsetting you so much?"

Cathy sat down beside her teacher. After a short while everything came gushing out, and Sister Bridget didn't interrupt her; she just sat quietly holding Cathy's hand, and listened. Cathy explained how she had overheard her mother, while she was talking to a doctor on the phone last week.

"Sister, she was very upset when she put the phone down. I asked her what was wrong, and she told me not to worry, she told me everything was fine. If she was fine, why was she so upset? We had a bit of a row about it. Then, she asked me to put the kettle on, so we could have a cup of tea and a chat." Cathy went silent.

The nun encouraged her to continue.

"She has to go into the hospital for an operation, and she's going in tomorrow." Cathy started crying again.

Sister Bridget was worried. She had never seen this pupil so upset before. "It's probably only something minor," the nun said trying to sound reassuring.

"It's not Sister, she told me all about it, and my mother doesn't treat me like a two-year-old, you know. She has to have a hysterectomy, and I think she has ca ... can ... cancer. My ... my ... dad, doesn't even know yet. Remember, Pauline's granny died of cancer last year." Cathy sat and stared in front of her, she was numb.

"Cathy, I want you to come back to the school with me."

"No, no Sister, I do ... don't want to go back to ... to the school, I want to go ... go ... go ... home," she spluttered through the tears.

"I understand, but you will have to get Mother Superior's permission, you know that."

"Can't you ask her for me?" Cathy pleaded.

"I'll ask her, but we must get back to the school now, I've left my class unattended, and heaven only knows what they are up to."

Sister Bridget and Cathy went back via the main house. The nun didn't want any prying eyes staring out of the classroom windows, to see Cathy in her present state. She wanted to protect her student's dignity.

When they entered the main house, she asked Sister Francis to make Cathy a cup of cocoa, and look after her until she came back. Spotting Mrs Cronin, who was one of the music teachers sitting in the lounge, she quickly explained that her English class was alone, and asked her to sit with them until she returned. She explained there was a matter of some urgency she needed to attend to. Mrs Cronin was only too happy to oblige and didn't ask any questions.

Sister Bridget found the head nun in her office, and told her in detail about Cathy's family predicament.

"Sister, that is unfortunate for them, but I will not tolerate such appalling behaviour - in the chapel of all places. If I let this matter go, all the girls will think they can do as they like. I have sent for Cathy's father, he should be here shortly. Cathy Corway will be suspended for one week."

"Don't you think that's a bit harsh Mother?" Sister Bridget replied, shocked to the core.

"No, I do not Sister, and should you not be in class yourself? Don't you have other pupils to attend to?"

Sister Bridget knew she would not win this round, so she excused herself and turned to leave.

"One minute Sister. Where is Cathy Corway?"

"She's in the outer office, I asked Sister Francis to make her a cup of cocoa and look after her, while I came to see you."

"Cocoa, she's having cocoa? She should be in St Luke's with Father Muldoon confessing her disgusting behaviour today," the nun said viciously.

Sister Bridget opened the door quietly, she was furious with her superior.

The head nun halted her again. "One more thing, will you please send Pauline Dutton to see me, immediately."

***

Jimmy Corway was puzzled. *Where the hell was Mary?* He had been in Galway at a trade show for the past four days, only returning late the previous night. That morning he had risen early and left for his office at six am, so he hadn't spoken to his wife because he didn't want to disturb her.

It was Friday and Mary was always home on a Friday. She hated the hustle and bustle people created as they converged everywhere in the town at the weekend. Friday was her baking day. She always baked her own bread and cakes, she didn't believe in shop-bought. She was a member of the old school.

On his way to the convent, Jimmy did an about turn and decided to stop in at home first. The nun could wait for a few more minutes. When he pulled into his driveway, he was surprised to find all the windows closed, despite the warm mugginess of the day. Knowing there had been a spate of petty thefts in the area lately, he assumed Mary was taking no chances. The key wasn't in the front door lock, where it would normally be. No smell of freshly baked bread, the house was still.

He looked at the message pad by the phone and found nothing, no message to inform him where she was. Then he thought she might be down the road with Mrs Cummins. The old lady hadn't been too well lately and her family couldn't give a damn about her. The seven children she had given birth to, all lived abroad, and she was lucky if she received a Christmas card from any of them. Her husband Ben had passed away over 20 years ago, so Mary liked to keep an eye out for her.

He looked through the pop up phone book Mary kept on the hall table and searched for Mrs Cummins' telephone number. Finding it, he dialled her number, but the line was engaged. *Bloody hell, is the whole of Wicklow talking to each other at the same time?* He had spent a frustrating morning trying to speak to different people and the lines were engaged for most of the time. *All right, enough is enough,* Jimmy thought aloud, *just get to the school and see what's up.*

As he turned into the convent driveway he realised, apart from school plays, parent-teacher meetings, prize giving's and sports days, he hadn't been to the convent very much. Mary always dealt with any matters which needed attending to in that area and he felt a stab of guilt. Also, he wasn't sure where to go. He hadn't bothered to ask the head nun where he was to meet her. *Just drive to the main house and stop fussing,* Jimmy told himself.

A few minutes later he parked his car outside the main entrance, proceeded up the overly wide steps towards the tall oak doors, and rang the bell.

Dong, dong, dong. *Jesus Christ, they must be all deaf in this place ... that fecking racket would raise my mother from her grave,* Jimmy said startled.

The bell donged for a long time throughout the building. He waited patiently. A good five minutes passed and nobody answered. He was considering walking around to the school so he could ask someone where he might find the head nun. He had no intention of pushing the bell again.

Just as he turned to go, the door opened surprisingly quietly. The tiniest nun Jimmy had ever seen in his entire life greeted him.

"Good morning, you must be Mr Corway," the nun said meekly.

"Yes, Sister, I am Mr Corway and I have an appointment with the Reverend Mother," Jimmy replied unsure of what he should do next.

"Mother Superior is expecting you, please come in." The little nun stepped aside and introduced herself as Sister Francis.

Jimmy wasn't sure if he should shake hands with her or genuflect.

"I'm very pleased to meet you Sister," he replied, keeping his hands rigidly by his side. He was used to dealing with workmen not miniature nuns. "Likewise, Mr Corway, will you please follow me."

"Lead the way Sister, I'm right behind you."

They walked across a wide hallway with the most highly polished wooden floors Jimmy had ever seen in his life. The thought crossed his mind that the nuns probably exercised themselves by strapping polishing cloths to their feet, and held skating contests after midnight. Abruptly, his amusing imaginations were brought to a halt by Sister Francis opening another door and asking him to take a seat. "Mother Superior will be with you presently. Once again, it has been a pleasure to meet you."

"Sister, the pleasure has been all mine, I can assure you."

Jimmy was glad Sister Francis was leaving as he was afraid that if he sneezed hard, he might damage her.

As the little nun closed the door behind her he remembered something from the past. He remembered Cathy telling him how she felt when she was led to her classroom in junior infants, all those years ago. He didn't really understand then, but he did now. He felt closed in.

He walked over to the window and looked out at the rose garden, a splendid sight. *So this is where the old bat stands each morning, watching, waiting.* Then he heard footsteps approaching and Mother Superior entered in all her glory.

"Good morning Mr Corway. Will you please sit down?"

"If you don't mind Sister, I would rather stand," Jimmy answered in a guarded tone.

"Mr Corway, I will remind you for the last time, will you please address me as Mother and NOT Sister, and if you want to stand, then do so," the nun said indifferently and continued. "I will come straight to the point. Cathy has committed a serious offence of gross misconduct," the nun announced vindictively.

"Gross misconduct, what did she actually do? Is my daughter in one piece?" Jimmy demanded to know.

"Mr Corway, please sit down. I'm getting a creak in my neck looking up at you."

Jimmy sat down reluctantly on the chair opposite her. "Now, Mother, for the second time, will you tell me what exactly has my daughter done, and by the way, where is she?" He could feel his patience ebbing.

The nun folded her hands and told him in detail about Cathy's outburst in the chapel.

He couldn't believe his ears. "You had me worried sick. I thought something serious had happened to her, plus I had to drive over here at short notice to listen to this nonsense," Jimmy's voice was rising, not a good sign.

"I can assure you Mr Corway, this matter is not nonsense as you call it. It is very grave indeed." The nun's voice was starting to rise also.

"What in God's name do you want me to do about it right now?" Jimmy asked.

"Mr Corway, in view of the gravity of the situation, which we obviously have opposing views on, I have no alternative but to suspend Cathy for one week, effective immediately."

"Suspend her, suspend her you say? Well, that is a good one if ever I heard it. What you have just told me is completely out of character for my daughter. Did it ever occur to you to analyse the situation before passing sentence?" Jimmy was furious at the nun. He paced back and forth in front of her desk.

"Mr Corway, we have certain standards in this school. Cathy's behaviour is totally unacceptable," she said to Jimmy's pacing form.

"Totally unacceptable, gross misconduct. I'll give you totally unacceptable … ah, forget it. Where exactly is my daughter? I want to see her now," Jimmy demanded.

"Very well Mr Corway, you shall do so." The head nun rose slowly from her chair, excused herself, and marched out of her office.

Jimmy was spitting fire. *Why did Cathy behave like that? She was in top form before I left for Galway.* He turned around as the door opened and the head nun entered with a miserable and swollen-eyed Cathy. The nun sat down again.

"Dad, I'm awful sorry," Cathy wailed. She was so relieved to see her father she burst into tears.

"Hush now, hush. Nothing can be that bad, hush." Jimmy wrapped her in his arms. "Looks like you have an unscheduled week off school. You've been suspended for a week." He was in a bit of a quandary; he couldn't handle female tears, young or old.

"What do you mean?" Cathy asked, confusion written all over her face.

"We'll talk about it later. I think we should both go now and leave the Mother to get on with her praying, or whatever she prefers to do." Jimmy didn't want to stay another moment in the presence of the head nun, he was afraid of what he would say next. He took his daughter's hand, bade the nun a polite farewell, and promptly left her office.

Sister Francis was waiting for them by the front door.

"Cathy pet, don't worry. It's only a storm in a teacup. This time next week, some other unfortunate girl will have done something much worse." The tiny nun tenderly said to Cathy.

"Maybe you're right Sister. Th ... thanks." Cathy replied.

"I am right, you'll see soon enough."

"We'll be off now Sister and thanks again," Jimmy said, grateful to be leaving.

"Have a safe journey and God bless you both." Sister Francis replied oozing genuine warmth.

Cathy just nodded and walked down the steps to the car. Jimmy followed her.

They drove in silence, each deep in their own thoughts. When they were nearly home, Cathy blurted out, "dad, mum's going to kill me and she's not well you know."

"No she won't love. That would be a mortal sin and your mother would never commit one of those," he replied, pretending to ignore the last part of what his daughter had said.

Mary was pottering around in the front garden when they pulled into the driveway.

"Dad, she's going to have a canary, I know she is."

"Listen Cathy, I want you to go straight up to your room. I want to have a chat with your mother and she's not going to have any canaries at all." Jimmy knew Mary would be upset when she heard their daughter had been suspended, but Cathy's suspension didn't bother him that much. The reason she'd been suspended was ridiculous, gross misconduct indeed.

"Come on inside Mary love, we need to have a chat." Jimmy said to his wife, his voice loaded with concern.

"What's going on, why is Cathy home from school? Is she sick?" Mary said facing her husband, her back ramrod straight.

"No, she isn't sick, just a bit upset, that's all. I'll make us a pot of tea and then I'll fill you in. Cathy tells me you're not well." Without waiting for an answer, Jimmy headed for the kitchen.

Mary's heart felt like lead. She had wanted to confide in her husband, but she didn't want to worry him unnecessarily, not until she received the final test results. She couldn't have told him over the phone while he was in Galway. When she went to bed the night before, she took a sleeping tablet and didn't hear him come home.

When she woke up, she was still quite groggy and he had already gone to work. Now, here he was at home in the middle of the day with Cathy, and he wanted to have a chat. *What had Cathy told him?* Mary now had deep regrets about telling her daughter of her illness. She now knew she shouldn't have said anything until Jimmy returned from his trip, but Cathy had been so insistent; she wanted to know about the phone call she'd overheard. At the time, Mary felt she had no other choice but to explain her phone conversation to her daughter. It was only fair. It was the right thing to do. *I should have waited, I should have said nothing.* She didn't know Cathy was in the house when she was speaking to the doctor.

Jimmy fumbled around the kitchen, while his wife silently studied her husband's form. Jimmy watched her out of the corner of his eye. When Mary realised the kitchen door was open she walked over and closed it.

All of a sudden, she felt dizzy and put her hand out to steady herself on the kitchen dresser. Her mouth went dry. The kitchen swayed in front of her. Immediately Jimmy was by her side and took hold of her firmly. "What is it my love? What's up?" He felt a trickle of icy cold sweat slide down the middle of his back. Goosebumps rose on his arms. "Mary, Mary, Mary, I've never seen you like this. Come and sit down love. Sit down and talk to me."

Just as quickly as it had arrived, Mary's dizzy spell passed, and she regained her composure. "Jimmy there's something I need to tell you."

"Fine love, fine, but sit down here first. You're very pale you know."

They both sat down side by side at the kitchen table. Mary took her husband's hand in hers and held it tightly saying nothing. She studied his hazel eyes, the same hazel eyes which caught her attention when she met him nearly 20 years ago when she was a young girl. She loved those eyes and now they were cloudy with concern.

"Mary, what's wrong? "Jimmy asked in a shaky voice.

Pulling herself together, she started to speak, and told him that a little while back she went to see Dr Kennedy. She told him about the intermittent but irritating pain in her side, and she thought it might be a rumbling appendix.

"What did he say? Do you have a rumbling appendix?"

"Jimmy love, Dr Kennedy examined me thoroughly and assured me my appendix is fine. We talked for a while and then he insisted I see a gynaecologist in Holles Street Hospital."

Mary's eyes never left her husbands face and Jimmy remained quiet.

"He made the appointment himself, there and then and ..."

"Why didn't you tell me about any of this?" Jimmy blurted out. He felt excluded.

"I wanted to tell you, but what was the point of making a mountain out of a molehill? What was the point of worrying you until I had all the facts?"

"Facts, what are the facts Mary? Jesus, woman, you are ill and you didn't even bother to tell me. I have to be told by our daughter. By the way, she's been suspended from school for a week." Jimmy slipped that bit of news in without thinking.

"She's been suspended. What on earth for?" Mary asked.

"I'll tell you later. When are you going to see this gynaecologist?" he demanded abruptly. The words came out harsher than he had meant.

"I saw him two weeks ago," Mary answered in a precise and firm tone.

"What did this gynaecologist say to you? What's his name?" Jimmy was becoming edgy.

"His name is Dr Lanagan and ... and ... and he found a problem with my ovaries."

Jimmy tried to speak, but Mary raised her hand to silence him, and quickly continued. "He did a few tests and a biopsy. It was a simple procedure performed under a local anaesthetic and I never felt a thing."

"Ah, Mary, why did you keep all of this from me? I should have been there with you. Do you ... do you have the results yet?"

Lowering her voice, she told him the test results were positive.

Jimmy felt like a big eejit. He must have been going around with his eyes and ears closed.

"They were positive Jimmy." Mary said again sadly. She felt like her heart was going to break.

"Positive, they were positive of what?" Jimmy's voice had risen more than a few octaves.

"Cancer, Jimmy," Mary answered, exhaling deeply.

"Cancer? You can't have cancer; there must be some kind of mistake." He tried not to raise his voice but he couldn't help himself, he was totally shocked.

"Jimmy, there is no mistake. We have to be realistic about this, for Cathy's sake as well as our own."

"Holy God, what's to be done? Tell me the truth, don't hold anything back." Jimmy felt weak, his hands were visibly shaking.

Mary decided the more direct she was the better; she had to take control of the situation. "Jimmy, I have to have a hysterectomy."

"You have to have a hysterectomy. When Mary, when do you have to have this done. When do you, do you ..."

"Tomorrow Jimmy. The surgery is scheduled for the following day." Mary felt like crying but she held herself together, she had to. It was all so sudden, he didn't know if he was coming or going. His wife had coped with all of this alone, and he thought she only had a touch of flu.

"We'll get through this Mary, love, I know we will. You're a strong woman. I don't know what I'd do without you." Jimmy thought he was losing his mind.

Earlier that morning, Mary had gone over to visit her friend Celia Dutton. She wanted to make arrangements with her for Cathy to stay over until she came home from the hospital. She swore Celia to secrecy until her husband came back from Galway. She didn't want to send Cathy off to stay with one of her brothers, they all lived in or around the north side of Dublin, and Jimmy's only sister Imelda lived in London. Mary's mother Alma Daly had moved into St Rita's old age home nearly 10 years ago. She was in the very advanced stages of Alzheimer's. They had tried to look after her themselves, but Alma's illness had been advancing quickly, and she was a danger to herself.

Even though Jimmy had fitted childproof locks to all the doors and windows, Alma frequently managed to escape, and had often been found wandering around Bray Head, stark naked. She'd sit on the kitchen table and demand Cathy play *Bloopers* with her, and none of them knew what the game called *Bloopers* was. She'd run a bath for Cathy three or four times a day, and often couldn't remember if she was putting her in or taking her out. The resulting confusion left her tearful and very agitated.

Dr Kennedy took them aside and advised them that it would be far kinder for Alma to live in St Rita's. There, she would have care and attention 24 hours a day, and it would enable them to lead normal lives themselves.

As Mary's father had abandoned them for a younger woman when she was 16, (none of them had seen him since, or wanted to). Jimmy's parents had passed away in a freak car accident when he was 23. It was natural for Mary to turn to her friend Celia for assistance. She didn't fill Celia in on all the details, she only told her she would be gone for about a week or so. Celia addressed Mary's health matters with a quiet, but genuine concern and didn't fuss. Instead, she reassured Mary that she was more than happy to have Cathy stay over, for as long as was necessary.

***

"Cathy, we have a week off school together. Mother Fecking Superior has suspended me as well. She's not right in the head. Her brain's turned into a bloody marshmallow. It's all the holy water she keeps splashing on herself. My mum says you're going to stay with us while you're mum's in the hospital," Pauline gushed to her friend over the phone.

"Yes, I know, but why did *you* get suspended? What did you do?"

Cathy was astonished to say the least. "Honestly, I don't know," replied Pauline. What did your mum and dad say?"

"Oh, you know mum. She's annoyed in her own way, but not much. Dad doesn't know yet. He's not coming back until tomorrow. Listen, what time will you be coming over?"

"Dad's dropping me off at about eight this evening. Jees, Paul's, mum is going into hospital tomorrow. Everything is just awful."

"I know Cathy, look, everything will be fine, you'll see. Hey, we can go over to the stables tomorrow and spend the day there. We can spend the whole week there. Now that's a bonus," Pauline tried to reassure her friend.

"Suppose so, but what are we going to tell Paddy?"

"The truth Cathy, we will tell him the truth. Now, get your stuff together and get over here," ordered Pauline.

Seven

Paddy was surprised to see the girls' cycle into the yard.

"What's up here? Have you two been expelled?"

"No Paddy, we've just been suspended for a week," Pauline answered before Cathy had time to open her mouth.

"All right, what did the pair of you do?" Paddy asked with a smile.

"Nothing really, Mother Superior has a bee in her bonnet again, and Cathy is staying at our house for a while, because her mum is going into hospital today. She has to have an op." Pauline winked at Paddy and he knew not to ask any further questions for the moment.

"Paddy, what can we do to help?" Cathy asked.

"Well now, why don't you both go and find Tony, he should be down by the arena with the new mare. He'll find plenty for you to do." Paddy excused himself; he had a phone call to make. He wanted to phone Jimmy Corway.

Just as he entered the yard office, the phone rang.

"Hello, Murphy's Equestrian Centre, Paddy speaking."

"At last. Good morning to you Paddy. It's Jimmy Corway here, I tried calling you several times last night, but the phone was continually engaged. Are the girls there?" Jimmy asked sounding slightly flustered.

"Jimmy, hello to you. The bloody phone has been out of order for a few days now. It was finally fixed sometime this morning and the girls are here, they arrived a few minutes ago." Jimmy briefly explained the current situation concerning his wife, while Paddy listened quietly. He didn't know much about women's ovaries, but he did know that when a mare had any kind of ovarian problems, it usually spelt trouble.

"Jimmy, do you mind if I make a suggestion?"

"Fire away, Paddy."

"It might be a bit easier on you and the girls if they stayed here for the week. They are due to stay over next weekend anyway and Mrs Byrne is in a bit of a fluster because she's short staffed right now. Two of her staff are off sick with the flu, and she'll keep the girls out of any mischief. They can stay in the guesthouse."

"Ah, Paddy, that's very kind of you, but Celia might be offended."

"No, she won't be. Paddy, you couldn't offend Celia Dutton if you tried. What time is Mary going in at?"

"I'm going home to fetch her in about an hour."

"Well then, I won't keep you any longer."

"You know Paddy, staying over with you would be just the ticket for Cathy, and it would be more pleasant for Pauline too. I don't think she's going to be very popular with her father when he finds out she has been kicked out of school for a week. You know what Sheamus can be like."

Sheamus Dutton owned a local accountancy firm, and he didn't like his schedule being upset at all. He liked everything to be just so. Sheamus always stuck to a rigid pattern in everything he did. His wife Celia never stuck to a pattern at all.

Jimmy often overheard Pauline complaining about her father's rigid ways, while Celia just let everything wash over her like water off a duck's back. She never seemed too bothered by anything.

"Right, no more said. Jimmy, you attend to Mary and I'll phone Celia."

"You're a good man Paddy Murphy. Oh, Paddy, I don't think Mary told Celia everything just yet, so mum's the word, okay."

"Right, now away with you Jimmy, leave Celia to me, and try not to worry. Give Mary my best. Bye for now."

"Thanks Paddy. I'll call you later."

Paddy phoned Celia and she thought his offer was perfect. When her husband had phoned the previous night, and she told him about Pauline's enforced week long break from school, he blew his top. She knew there would be an uncomfortable atmosphere in her home, and she was afraid that it would upset Cathy more than she was already.

Celia had three sons older than Pauline, and none of them, according to Sheamus, caused half as much trouble as Pauline did.

When Mary originally asked Celia if Cathy could stay over, neither girl had been in any trouble at all, not that it mattered to Celia; she welcomed Cathy at any time. She wasn't bothered that Pauline was suspended. What was the point in getting all upset? Getting upset wasn't going to reverse the head nun's decision.

But Pauline's suspension mattered to Sheamus. He had bellowed at his wife that he was paying good money for Pauline to attend the convent school, and was the nun going to refund him a week's school fees? He also told her he would give the nun a piece of his mind when he got home.

"You know Paddy, Sheamus can be a bit pig-headed at times," Celia admitted openly.

Paddy was aware of that fact. He wished Celia well and said goodbye. Then he went in search of the girls to tell them about the change of plan.

Cathy and Pauline found Tony exactly where Paddy said he would be. Tony thought it was hilarious that the girls weren't allowed to go to school for a week. They didn't tell him about Cathy's mother though.

Tony had been working for Paddy for five years and he was his head groom. He had a wonderful talent with horses, but he couldn't keep any news to himself. Cathy thought it would better to say nothing to Tony about her mother. If they did, it would be all over the town by the morning, and Cathy knew her mother would hate that.

Paddy met up with the girls on the way back to the tack room. Tony had asked them to exercise Johnjo and Copper over the cross-country course, and they didn't need to be asked twice. He told them about the change of sleeping-over arrangements. Pauline was immensely relieved to hear she wouldn't have to put up with her disapproving father for a while, and Paddy's plan would keep Cathy's mind occupied also.

When they reached the tack room they put both their names on the activity board, Paddy had strict rules about riding cross-country. Everyone, liveries included, had to write the name of the rider, the horse they were riding, and the time they left the yard on the blackboard. (The blackboard was supplied).

Safety was very important to their mentor. He knew the dangers that could be encountered out on the course, as well as the joys.

Paddy decided to join the pair himself, as he could do with the exercise and he could give the girls a bit of instruction as well.

The girls were pleased with the extra news, Paddy was an excellent teacher. He was good fun also.

Tony passed the trio as they were leaving the yard. He was leading the new mare back to her paddock.

"How'd she go Tony?" Paddy enquired.

"Like a dream Paddy, no resistance at all. She's settling herself in here just grand," Tony answered cheerfully.

"Good news, but will she be ready for the weekend?" Paddy enquired.

"I don't see any reason why not, she's very trusting and canny," Tony replied.

"Excellent, that's excellent. Now, we'll be gone for about an hour or so," Paddy informed him.

"Very well, enjoy yourselves," Tony said with a smile and continued on his way.

Paddy turned his attention to Cathy and Pauline. "All right you pair, let's get some decent work done. Pauline, your down-hill approach needs some work, and Cathy, you're not getting off lightly either. I'll lead you into the water jump and please remember to breath."

After a short and thorough warm-up they rode towards the first fence. The trio jumped it perfectly. The next fence was a small but tricky arrowhead.

"Okay, Pauline, you go first. Remember plenty of impulsion, ride light," Paddy instructed.

Pauline approached the fence, but four strides from take-off she turned Johnjo away. She wasn't straight enough. Her second attempt was picture perfect. Paddy was pleased with her youth- ful sensibility.

Pauline was developing a good technique. She frequently practised riding straight lines and obtaining the correct bend when she worked any of the horses belonging to the yard.

Paddy and Cathy popped the arrowhead without any problems. Paddy wanted the girls to enjoy themselves and he ignored some of the minor faults he saw. He wasn't going to waste time either, so when they approached the water jump, he rode through first, and ordered Cathy to follow close on his heels.

"Paddy, you make it look so easy," Cathy said exasperated.

"Cathy, it is easy. You make it difficult. You put the brakes on by not breathing properly. You tense up, and Copper senses it immediately. Look at the way you jumped the last combination. You had maximum control, with a good flowing line in between each jump. Try the water again, look up, keep your balance, and ride slower."

Cathy did as she was told and everything went well.

According to Paddy, all she needed was a bit more confidence.

They finished off at a downhill fence, not Pauline's favourite and Paddy let her go first. Pauline remembered his instructions. Support your horse, ride with control, slip your reins, slow down and sit up on landing. She approached the fence and jumped it reasonably well. Paddy was pleased enough.

"All right girls, let's head back. Then we'll go and get your gear from home."

Paddy had informed Mrs Byrne earlier on during the morning, that the girls would be staying over and he also told her about Cathy's mother. She had shushed him away, telling him she would handle Cathy. She was a bit worried about Mary, but she didn't let on. Overall, she was delighted the girls would be staying with her. Not just to help out, and she badly needed help right now, she was very fond of the pair of them, and she enjoyed their company. However, she told Paddy the guesthouse was fully booked, so the girls would have to stay in her cottage. She had more than enough room and she didn't mind. For some reason it hadn't occurred to Paddy that the guesthouse might be fully booked, there was several vacancies yesterday. When the girls finished up in the yard, they went up to the guesthouse.

"Now you two, later on, Moira will need a hand in the restaurant, she has a tour bus coming in for an early supper, so off you go and get changed. You know where my cottage is. You're both sharing the back bedroom. Shoo, away with you, and behave yourselves," Mrs Byrne told them firmly but nicely.

She had already told her daughter that the girls would be over to help her later on in the afternoon, and she also let Moira in on the news that Cathy's mother had gone into hospital to have a *woman's problem* seen to. Moira was used to her mother's ways, so she paid no real heed. She was looking forward to having the girls help her out. The new chef in the kitchen had turned out to be much more of an expert than she had given him credit for, she had no problems there. But she was short of waitresses.

"Moira, I've only served meals to my relatives before now, and that's only when they come around at Christmas and so on," Cathy said in a worried voice.

"Just pretend that the customers are your relatives and you'll be fine. I'll take the meal and drink orders. All you two have to do is bring the food to the tables, nothing really fancy. I'll let you know when to clear away. We'll just play it by ear," Moira replied comforting her.

"Ah, Cathy, stop being such a worry wart," Pauline jibed. She wasn't a bit bothered about helping in the restaurant. Nothing really bothered Pauline at all.

The tour bus arrived on time and the restaurant filled with a varied age group of people, the youngest was about seven and the eldest was an elderly man heavily dependant on his walking stick. According to Pauline, he was ancient, and she whispered to Moira that his skin was so wrinkly it needed ironing. Moira enjoyed Pauline's sense of humour and she smiled to herself as she greeted her guests.

Once they were seated, Moira took the drink and meal orders, and between the three of them, the drinks were served without any disasters at all. Cathy started to relax.

Pauline was listening to two of the children discussing the menu.

"I want a hamburger, but I don't see one on this menu," a young boy said.

"Look here, it says a beef patty served with fresh green leaf salad. That's more or less a burger," the man seated beside him pointed out.

"Why don't they call it a burger like normal places?" the child grumbled.

"They expect you to be able to read and understand things. Honestly, why are you always so brain dead? Why do you have to be such an eejit all the time?" the older girl opposite him said nastily.

Moira sent Pauline on her way, reminding her that it was incorrect to listen to customer's conversations. She approached the table Pauline had been eavesdropping on. "If there's something that you would like that's not on the menu, I'm sure we could make an arrangement with the chef," Moira intervened.

"I don't like salad, but I would like a burger," the boy told Moira politely.

"Then a burger it is and no salad. Would you like chips with your burger?" Moira asked the boy.

"Yes, please, lots of them," the boy replied.

"Lots of chips it is then, no problem," Moira told him.

"You're a pig," hissed the young girl opposite.

Moira took all the meal orders with the help of the girls and with the exception of one steak being slightly rare, everything went well.

When the last of the plates were cleared away, Pauline and Cathy were exhausted. They both agreed that waitressing was hard work, and they would never look at a waiter or waitress in the same way again.

Moira thanked the girls for their help and she sent them off to relax. She could handle the rest of the customers on her own. Cathy and Pauline didn't put up any argument.

They spent the rest of the evening helping Mrs Byrne in the guesthouse, and when Paddy strolled in through the kitchen door as he usually did at around nine-thirty, he found two very tired, but happy girls having cocoa with his housekeeper.

"Pauline, there was a phone call for you earlier on from a John Clancy. I clean forgot to tell you about it, sorry," Paddy said apologetically.

"Oh my God, I forgot about him. He must think I'm a right bitch," Pauline replied bluntly. "Paddy, I know it's late, but may I use the phone, please?"

"No prob's, but check with Mrs Byrne first. This is her domain," Paddy said giving Mrs Byrne a friendly wink.

"I think you might have a bit more privacy if you used the phone in the reception Pauline. Off you go." Mrs Byrne smiled broadly.

"Thanks, Mrs Byrne. Oh, is there a phone book out there? I'll have to look up his number."

"Yes love, it's beside the phone on the reception desk." Mrs Byrne was still smiling.

"Wait up Pauline. I expect the pair of you to be up bright and early tomorrow, we are going out over the cross-country course after first feed," Paddy told them.

Pauline was already halfway through the doorway. She turned around. "Oh Paddy, that's great. By the way, thanks again for having us stay over with you and Mrs Byrne." She rushed over and gave him a hug.

"Enough, enough, Pauline you'll ride Flint, and Cathy you'll ride Johnjo tomorrow." Paddy smiled at the girls and wandered off to the restaurant.

On most nights, Paddy and Moira shared an after work drink together. Mrs Byrne didn't question her daughter's feelings for Paddy, and she would never ask Paddy, about his feelings for her daughter. But, she felt there was something brewing between them. She had liked Paddy from the first time she had met him, all those years ago. Secretly she thought he and her daughter would make a perfect couple. But, she wouldn't play cupid; she knew when to stay quiet. She also knew that if anything was going to happen between them, it would, in its own good time.

As soon as Pauline had finished her call to John Clancy, Mrs Byrne sent the both of them off down to her cottage, with strict instructions there was to be no shenanigans. The girls just smiled; they were tired. Each had a long shower and literally fell into bed. Just as they were dozing off, Cathy remembered Pauline's call to John.

"Hey, Pauls, what was the phone call all about?"

"Ah, Cathy, the poor guy was really upset. He phoned me at home last night. After all, I did ask him to, and my thick-headed stupid moron of a brother told him I was out. I'm going to kill Neill when I get to him."

Pauline quickly forgot her brother. "John's coming over here tomorrow night to have coffee with me in the restaurant. Would you believe it? John Clancy and I are having coffee together," Pauline said sleepily.

Cathy ignored that last part of Pauline's answer. "Why did he do that? Why did he say you were out?"

"Who the hell knows? But I'll find out. You know, I'm sure that eejit brother of mine has a mental problem and I bet it's from playing with himself all the time." Pauline turned over in the bed and muttered goodnight to Cathy.

"But Pauline ..."

"Cathy, shut up and go to sleep, I'm wrecked."

Cathy did shut up, but she tossed and turned for a long time before she finally fell asleep. Pauline just snored quietly beside her.

The next morning the girls rose early. They helped Tony and the lads feed the horses. Paddy took care of his adored mares himself. While the horses ate, Cathy and Pauline had breakfast in Paddy's cottage. He ate most of his meals in the guesthouse or in the restaurant, but he liked to cook his own breakfast and he cooked extra for the girls.

Over breakfast, the three chatted about the clinic, which was scheduled for the coming weekend. They discussed in detail what they were going to work on out on the course that day. Paddy wanted the girls to be occupied, especially Cathy.

Eight

A friendly nurse took Mary to a four-bedded ward and told
Jimmy to wait outside while she settled his wife in. Jimmy dutifully complied. Then she asked Mary to change her clothes and
slip into bed. Mary was nervous but did as she was asked.

When the nurse finished admitting her, she allowed Jimmy to
rejoin his wife, apologising because she could only allow him to
stay for a few minutes, as it was not the official visiting time.
She whispered the matron could get a bit stroppy if she found
visitors in the wards outside the official times. Jimmy understood and thanked her.

Jimmy looked down fondly at his wife. She looked so small
and helpless; his heart went out to her. Mary was acutely aware
of his distress, so she suggested it would be better all round if
he went home. Jimmy was reluctant to leave, but he was
decidedly uncomfortable and he felt out of place. Kissing her
lightly on the forehead and with false joviality, he said that by
this time to-morrow, it would be all over.

Jimmy drove home in a daze. He didn't go straight back to his
office, he went for a pint at Flemming's instead. Father Muldoon
was nowhere to be seen and he was relieved. He wouldn't be fit
company for the Father right now.

Padraic, the barman, greeted him warmly and automatically
served him with a pint of Guinness. While he was drinking his
pint, he remembered he hadn't phoned Celia yet. Not being a
man that downs a drink in one go, Jimmy left the remainder of
his pint behind him on the bar. Padraic called after him. "Is
there something up Jimmy?" Padraic wasn't being nosey, he
wasn't the type, but he had noticed when Jimmy came in that
he seemed a bit agitated.

"No, Padraic, everything's grand. I forgot to do something,
that's all."

He went home and phoned Celia who was relieved to hear
from him. He told her Mary was fine and Celia reassured him
she wasn't in the least bit put out about the girls staying with
Mrs Byrne. She also told him to stop his worrying.

The house was eerily quiet. The only other sound, apart from
the clock ticking away to itself in the kitchen, was the new cat
called Phantom. He was meowing pitifully at the back door.
Phantom had arrived out of nowhere, like cats tend to do, about
two weeks previously. No one knew who owned him, so Cathy
had adopted him willingly. Jimmy let him in and fed him.

Oh Mary, I miss you. I never pray, but I'm going to now. Jimmy
got in his car and drove to St Luke's.

He sat in a pew beside the statue of the Virgin Mary; he thought it was somehow appropriate. He sat for a time, but he didn't pray in the conventional manner, he just sat and allowed his thoughts to do the work for him.

Father Sheehan came in to lock up the main doors, and when he saw Jimmy sitting alone, he silently approached him.

"Hello Jimmy," the priest said quietly.

"What ...Father, you put the heart cross ways in me. I was in a complete world of my own," Jimmy answered the priest in a shaky voice.

"Is there something I can help you with?" Father Sheehan asked kindly.

"Not really Father, only himself up there knows what's going to happen." Jimmy glanced at the cross behind the main altar.

"Do you want to talk about it Jimmy?" the priest enquired.

"If you don't mind Father, I'd rather not at the moment. I don't want to seem rude, but it's late, and I'd better be on my way."

"Very well, but remember, I'm here at any time, day or night."

"Thanks, Father. I'll remember that."

The two men shook hands and Jimmy went home to his silent house and Phantom. He knew it was late, but he couldn't resist the urge to phone the hospital, he didn't think they would mind. When he was finally put through to the correct ward, he asked the nurse on duty how his wife was, and she told him she was sleeping soundly as they had given her some medication. She suggested he try to get some sleep himself. Jimmy knew he was in for a long night.

He phoned the hospital several times throughout the next morning, and each time he was assured his wife was fine. The last time he phoned they told him that Mary had received her pre-medication and she would be going into theatre shortly. Jimmy couldn't concentrate on his work so he drove into Dublin and wandered aimlessly around St Steven's Green.

After an hour or so, he couldn't take the pressure of not knowing what was going on, so he went to the hospital. The ward sister told him Mary was still in theatre, but he was very welcome to wait in the visitors' lounge. She offered to get him a cup of tea and he accepted gratefully.

Two hours went by before a doctor came into the lounge and introduced himself as Dr Lanagan.

"Mr Corway, I'll come straight to the point. I'm sorry to have to tell you this, but your wife's condition is far worse than we suspected," the doctor said briskly but with a fair amount of compassion.

"Worse than you suspected, how much worse?" Jimmy's voice trembled.

"Mr Corway, we removed Mrs Corway's uterus and her ovaries, but the cancer has already spread to her pancreas." The doctor sat down beside him.

"What are you telling me doctor?" Jimmy was terrified.

"Mr Corway, your wife is very ill. She is going to need extensive and aggressive chemotherapy and the sooner we start the treatment the better. However, we cannot start the chemo for some weeks because she has to regain some of her strength after the procedure she's just been through." Dr Lanagan allowed Jimmy a few moments to absorb what he had just said.

"Is she going to die? Am I ... are we ... we going to ...to lose her?" Jimmy asked trying to stay calm.

"Frankly, Mr Corway, I can't answer that question. It all depends on how she responds to the therapy."

"Does, does she know yet?" Jimmy's voice was breaking.

"No, Mr Corway, she's still sleeping but I wanted to let you know our immediate findings as soon as possible."

"Can I see her please?" Jimmy asked in a voice that he did not recognise as his own.

"Of course you can. However, she is not in the same ward; we thought it would be more convenient for the family if we moved her to a private room. Now you can come and go as you like. I will get one of the nurses to show you the way. Mr Corway, your wife is in good hands." The doctor stood up to leave. He patted Jimmy solidly on the shoulder before he turned and walked out of the lounge. Jimmy sat frozen in his chair. *Mary has cancer in her pancreas. No, there has to be some mistake. Mary said they had found a problem in her ovaries and she was going to have a hysterectomy. She had the operation today. They suspected she only had a bit of a problem with her liver. Isn't that what she said?*

Jimmy heard his name being called from somewhere.

"Mr Corway, are you all right, Mr Corway, can I get you a glass of water? You've had a bit of a shock, my name is Matron Brody. I'll be here to guide you and if you have any questions, I will be glad to answer them to the best of my ability."

What is this woman blabbering on about? Jimmy thought as he stared blankly at the nurse in front of him.

The matron poured him a glass of water and handed it to him. Jimmy's eyes didn't seem to be focusing. He let the glass slip through his hand and it shattered on the floor. Then he heard a voice saying, "Can I see my wife please?" It didn't sound like his voice. The voice spoke again, "Can I see her now?"

"Certainly, Mr Corway, I'll take you to her presently."

"I said now!" Jimmy demanded in a voice which he defin-itely didn't recognise as his own.

"Mr Corway, calm down, please. If you come with me I'll show you to Mrs Corway's room. As I've said before, if there are any questions ..."

Jimmy interrupted her. "Yes, nurse, I have questions to ask, but firstly, I want to see my wife and I want to see her now."

The matron was used to the abrupt manner of patient's family members when they were given unexpected and bad news about loved ones. She paid no heed; it happened all the time. She wanted to comfort him and explain about his wife's disease. However, she could see he was not yet ready to understand the gravity of his her illness.

"Right, let's go there now Mr Corway, we won't delay any longer. Your wife was still sleeping when I popped in to see her only a short while ago and she'll probably stay sleeping for a few more hours."

Jimmy walked with the matron down what seemed like an endless corridor. They passed lots of heavily pregnant women, some walking around, and some sitting on chairs. A woman on a gurney in obvious labour was rushed past them. Jimmy felt out of place. Then they stopped at a door.

"Here we are Mr Corway. This is your wife's room. Ah, she's awake." The matron walked over to Mary's bed, picked up her chart and studied it carefully. "How are you feeling Mrs Corway? Are you still feeling nauseous?"

"Just a little," Mary replied weakly.

"We can give you something for that. The doctor has written you up for Maxolon, and you are due an injection shortly. It should help," she told her kindly.

There was another nurse at Mary's side and she introduced herself as Fiona. She told Jimmy she would be looking after his wife exclusively during the day. Then the matron's bleeper sounded in her pocket. "You'll have to excuse me. If you need me, just ask one of the nurses to page me and I'll come immediately," she said, meaning it.

Jimmy didn't even hear her. He had eyes and ears only for his wife. The matron understood; she knew how important it was for the family to get to grips early with a potentially terminal family member. It was all part of the healing process.

Mary raised her head when she heard her husband's voice. "Jimmy love, come and sit beside me. You ... you look tired," Mary said groggily.

Jimmy was afraid to touch his wife because she had tubes and drips everywhere. He pulled himself together and lifted her right hand since it was the only part of her that seemed to be free from any paraphernalia. It felt cold and clammy.

"Mary, what have they done to you?" he said in a strangled voice.

"Don't fret Jimmy, I'm, I'm fine," Mary said weakly before she slipped back to sleep.

The nurse said his wife would be in and out of consciousness for most of the evening, but he was welcome to stay as long as he liked. She showed him where the call bell was and told him that she would be in and out to check on her, but he wasn't to hesitate to ring should he need anything.

Jimmy sat on a chair beside Mary's bed and held her hand while she slept. Mary slipped in and out of consciousness just like they said she would. The nurse did come in and out frequently and she told Jimmy it was important to monitor Mary's blood pressure, as it was routine procedure after surgery. She adjusted the flow in Mary's IV, emptied her catheter bag, and explained that the doctor had inserted the catheter because it would be easier on his wife. She wouldn't have to use a bedpan.

Jimmy didn't leave Mary's side. He stayed holding her hand for many hours. He must have nodded off himself because he was awoken gently by a nurse saying, "Mr Corway, I'm going off duty now. Is there anything I can get you before I go? A cup of tea and a sandwich perhaps? You've been here for a long time."

"Eh, no ... no nurse, thank you, I'm fine. I'll have to go myself. I need to collect my daughter. She'll be anxious to see her mother and I didn't realise it was so late."

"If you're sure there's nothing I can get you, I'll say good-night. Nurse Beryl is assigned to look after Mrs Corway for the night shift. I'll see you tomorrow. Bye for now." The nurse turned to leave.

"Nurse, before you go, do you think that my wife is sleeping excessively?"

"No, Mr Corway, it's very normal for patients to sleep for long periods after surgery. It's the anaesthetic you see. It affects each patient differently. She'll be more alert tomorrow. May I make a suggestion?"

"Certainly, nurse."

"Don't bring your daughter in to see her mother tonight, wait until tomorrow. She'll be in better form by then."

Jimmy looked at his wife. "I think you're right. Cathy will be disappointed, but I think you're right."

"Mr Corway, please call me Fiona."

"Oh, well then, Fiona it is, and my name is Jimmy."

50

"Goodnight Jimmy, I'm glad you've decided not to bring your daughter in tonight. It's for the best."

Nine

Cathy was agitated. "Where is dad? He should have been here hours ago."

Mrs Byrne tried to comfort her, but she was having none of it. Pauline suggested she phone the hospital herself, but Cathy was hesitant.

"They won't give me any information," she answered Paul-ine snottily.

"Maybe you're right, but stop pacing around. You're making me dizzy."

"Where is he Pauline? What's keeping him? He said he'd collect me at six o' clock, and it's now past eight."

"Let's go down to the restaurant, we'll see him drive in from there." Pauline couldn't handle Cathy for much longer, she wanted to distract her.

"No, I'm staying here. You go if you want."

"Cathy, don't be silly. Have a bit of cop on, will you?"

"Cop on? What the hell do you mean?"

"I'm sure there's a good reason for your dad being delayed."

"He's not delayed, he's late." Cathy replied, close to tears. She had been moody like this all day. Pauline rolled her eyes to heaven. She knew from old that the best thing to do when Cathy became like this, was humour her. "I'm going to the guest lounge to watch television, are you coming?" Pauline asked.

"No, I'll stay and help Mrs Byrne with the remaining wash-ing up." Cathy snapped back.

"Please yourself then. Mrs Byrne, do you mind if I watch television for a while?"

"Go ahead love ... Cathy's just on tender hooks, don't mind her," Mrs Byrne whispered in Pauline's ear.

A short while later Cathy heard her father drive up. She knew the sound of his car well. She shouted up the stairs that led to the ground floor and the TV lounge, "Pauline, my dad's here, see you later."

"Cathy, for God's sakes, don't yell like that. There are guests upstairs. Do you want them to think we're having a fire drill or something? Anyway, it's not very ladylike is it?" Mrs Byrne reprimanded her.

"Sorry, Mrs Byrne, I forgot. Dad's here, I'll be back later, okay?"

"You go on love and give my regards to your mother."

Jimmy was outside talking to Paddy and Cathy nearly ran him over.

"Dad, what kept you? I've been waiting for ages. Come on now, visiting time will be over," she said sharply and went over to the car.

"Cathy, hang on a minute," her father said wearily.

"Why?"

"Your mother is fast asleep and she's likely to stay that way for the rest of the night. Let's give visiting a miss tonight."

"Oh, that's nice, that is. You've been with her probably all day and I was left here. Dad, I want to go and see mum, please."

"Cathy, it's not a good idea to disturb her tonight."

"Disturb her? You make me sound like a cleaning maid in a hotel."

"Don't be cheeky and stop behaving like a spoilt brat," Jimmy wasn't up for one of his daughter's tantrums right now, his thoughts were elsewhere. Cathy saw the concern in his eyes. "Dad, is mum okay?"

Jimmy thought he had prepared himself for that question, but he couldn't answer her.

"She's not, is she?" Cathy said quietly.

"No pet, she's not too well at the moment. The surgery went on a bit longer than expected. We'll both see her tomorrow evening. She ... she needs to rest. She needs her sleep." Jimmy was exhausted himself. "Cathy, I'm going to go home now, it's been a long day for all of us." Jimmy couldn't face his daughter's searching eyes.

Mrs Byrne approached the pair and picked up on the situation immediately. "Come along Cathy, like a good girl. Your father is tired and he doesn't need any back talk from you." She had to be firm; it was the only way to deal with the matter.

"Mrs Byrne, it's not fair," Cathy was determined to have her way.

"No, it's not fair Cathy, but that's the way it is. Give your dad a hug and come on back to the house. It's cold out here and you're shivering."

"Mrs Byrne ..."

"Now Cathy, don't Mrs Byrne me." She was taking no nonsense. She had always thought Cathy was a little bit spoilt, but her heart went out to her. She didn't know everything about Cathy's mother's medical condition; but she did know it was serious, judging by Jimmy's face.

"Paddy, why don't you and Jimmy go for a pint? Jimmy looks like he could do with one. I'll take care of Cathy."

"Take care of me. My mother is ill, not me. All I want to do is see her and I've been waiting all day."

"Well, a few more hours won't kill you. You heard your father; your mother needs her rest, so behave yourself. Now, come back to the house with me this minute. Paddy, take Jimmy for a pint." Mrs Byrne was more than firm now.

"I think you're right, Mrs. Byrne," Paddy said, agreeing wholeheartedly with her. He could see well enough that Jimmy was highly distressed, but he didn't think a public bar was the place for him right now. Not everything was sorted out over a bar counter, despite what some thought. Paddy suggested they go down to his cottage instead. Jimmy thought of the lonely house awaiting him and he accepted Paddy's offer after Mrs Byrne had ushered a furious Cathy back to the guesthouse.

The two men sat by the fire in Paddy's small but comfortable sitting room, and Paddy offered Jimmy a glass of whisky and Jimmy downed it in one go.

"Steady on, man. You'll be on your ear if you keep that up." In all the years Paddy had known Jimmy he'd never seen him down a drink like that before.

"I needed that one Paddy, believe me." Jimmy sat back in the chair and was silent for a while. "Paddy, do you mind if I use your phone? I'd like to check up on Mary."

"It's all yours. I have to make sure the tack rooms are locked. I'll leave you alone for a bit."

"Thanks, Paddy, I won't be long."

Jimmy spoke to the night nurse who was looking after Mary and she reassured him she was doing as well as could be expected. Jimmy remembered what the matron had said about answering any questions he might have. He asked the nurse if it would be possible for him to see the matron in the morning. The nurse asked him to hold on for a moment, as the matron was close by. She was still at the nurse's station. Paddy waited.

"Good evening, Mr Corway. How are you coping?" the matron asked in a professional but motherly voice.

"Well, matron, I've been better, I can honestly admit that. I was wondering if we could meet early tomorrow morning."

"Of course we can. Would you be able to come and see me in my office at nine o' clock? If that is not convenient, we can arrange an earlier or later time. It's your call Mr Corway," the matron answered, hearing the distress in his voice.

"Matron, nine o' clock is fine, thank you. Now, is my wife awake and how is she?"

"She's still sleeping intermittently, but that's absolutely normal. She was in theatre for quite some time. I'll tell her you phoned. I'm sure that will make her happy and I'll see you in the morning. Now try and get some rest yourself."

The matron didn't want to prolong the conversation. She knew that many patients and relatives could get the wrong end of the stick over the phone. "Mr Corway, my office is on the ground floor. The hall porter will show you where it is."

"Thank you, until tomorrow matron. Goodnight." He hung up the phone sadly.

Paddy came back a few minutes later and Jimmy thanked him for his hospitality, excused himself and went home. Paddy wasn't the type to push for information; he would wait for Jimmy to bring him up to date in his own good time.

Jimmy had a sleepless night and he had to resist the urge to phone the hospital over and over again as he didn't want to be a nuisance. He waited until seven the next morning. He was told Mary was fully awake and she had managed to eat a light breakfast. Jimmy's heart missed a beat with relief. He now knew the meaning of the words *lifting the weight off one's shoulders.*

Then he phoned his secretary Sandra at her home and told her he would probably be in the office sometime later on during the day. Sandra was full of enquiries regarding Mary.

Jimmy told her she was as well as could be expected. Sandra didn't question her boss any further. She didn't like the sound of as well as could be expected at all; but she knew her boss kept his private life very private.

She hoped he wouldn't mind her telling his customers that Mrs Corway was in hospital for a few days and that was the reason why he wasn't available at present. What else was she supposed to say when they wanted to speak to him? "Don't worry about a thing. We have everything under control. Give Mrs Corway my regards and I'll see you, whenever. Bye for now Mr Corway."

"I'll do that Sandra, and thanks for holding the fort."

He phoned Paddy on his office phone and he was redirected to Paddy's cottage. When it rang beside him, Paddy picked it up. "Morning, Paddy Murphy speaking."

"Good morning Paddy, is Cathy around?"

"Yes, Jimmy, Cathy is right here. She's having breakfast with Pauline and me. I'll put her on to you right away."

Jimmy thanked Paddy. Cathy, overhearing the conversation didn't need a second invitation. She practically grabbed the phone from Paddy's hand.

"Hi dad, I'm sorry for the way I behaved last night, truly I am. Are you okay? You looked pretty worn out. How is mum, how is she doing?" she couldn't get her words out quick eno- ugh.

"I'm grand pet, and last night is long forgotten, don't mention it again." Jimmy felt a huge rush of affection for his only daughter who had been mightily pissed off with him. His heart felt heavy. He was no longer in control of, or even in the company of, the people who meant the most to him.

"Dad, how is mum? Can I see her today? I have to see her today." Cathy was feeling more than a little apprehensive.

"Of course you can see her today pet. I've just phoned the hospital and she's fully awake. She even managed to eat a small breakfast, isn't that good news. We'll see her together tonight. I'll collect you at six, okay?"

"That's what you said last night."

"I thought we agreed that last night was all forgotten about?"

"Hmmm, you're right. I'll see you at six then and don't be late. Dad, I love you more than you'll ever know," she blew a kiss into the phone.

Paddy and Pauline didn't mean to eavesdrop but they couldn't help it as Cathy was right beside them. They just smiled at each other. When Cathy hung up the phone, she devoured the remainder of her breakfast and while she was pulling on her boots she announced, "Well, you two, there's work to be done around here you know. Let's get on with it then. By the way, mum is doing fine. I'll be seeing her tonight."

***

Jimmy arrived in good time for his appointment with the matron. He was lucky; he found a parking place very near the hospital entrance. The hall porter ticked him off his list, and escorted him to the matron's office. Thankfully, he didn't have to wait for very long as the matron arrived a few minutes later.

"Good morning Mr Corway. I can see that you haven't had a good night's rest."

"Matron, I've had easier nights in my time. I haven't been up to see Mary yet. I thought it would be better to wait until we've had a bit of a talk."

"Very wise Mr Corway. I've asked Dr Lanagan to join us. He'll be here presently."

"Has something happened? Earlier on I was told Mary had eaten a light breakfast."

"And so she did Mr Corway, so she did. Don't alarm yourself. Dr Lanagan wants to explain all his findings to you personally. He is busy with his ward rounds right now, but he should be finished soon. I think it would be better time wise, if we went up to the visitors' lounge and waited for him there."

Jimmy didn't argue.

As they got out the lift, they saw Dr Lanagan walking towards them. He greeted Jimmy warmly and the trio entered the lounge.

"Mr Corway, I'll explain exactly what our post-operative investigations have uncovered, and what we would like to do for your wife," Dr Lanagan said kindly.

"Don't hide anything from me, please doctor."

"No, Mr Corway, I wouldn't dream of it."

Dr Lanagan explained that the initial smear test performed on Mary, unfortunately came back with hot spots. The matron told him to speak in plain English as she could see Jimmy was already having trouble understanding medical jargon. Dr Lanagan apologised and continued. "Mr Corway, your wife's test proved positive. We found malignant cells on her cervix, which is the neck of her womb. We decided, as a precautionary procedure, to perform a biopsy on her ovaries. We found extensive cancer cells present there also. That was the main reason for our decision to operate in the first instance. We removed her uterus and both of her ovaries. Are you following me so far, Mr Corway?"

"I think so doctor," Jimmy wasn't sure if he was or not.

The doctor continued, "While we had your wife in theatre and under anaesthetic, it was easier for us to perform a more detailed examination. We suspected she might have problems in or around her liver, but we did not expect to find a tumour in her pancreas. Her pre-operative amylase levels were not alarmingly high so we sent samples of the tumour to our laboratory and the results came back positive."

"Is that why she was in theatre for so long?" Jimmy asked in a horrified voice.

"Yes, Mr Corway. That was one of the reasons."

The matron interrupted tutting at Dr Lanagan and explained that the surgeons had removed Mary's womb, and they had to remove her pancreas also. "Mr Corway, this means your wife is going to develop diabetes."

Jimmy cut her short. "She'll develop diabetes? But that's nothing nowadays, with the proper medication she'll be fine," Jimmy said feeling relieved.

Dr Lanagan took over the conversation again. "No, Mr Corway, unfortunately the cancer has spread to her liver also and we cannot remove her liver until we have found a suitable donor. She will need a transplant. That is why we are concerned about her at the present time as compatible donors are nearly impossible to locate." The doctor lapsed into silence.

"Go on doctor, tell me what you can do," Jimmy wiped the sweat from his forehead with the back of his hand.

"Mr Corway, as I explained to you yesterday, your wife will need extensive chemotherapy, but, we cannot perform the treatment in this hospital. Therefore, I would like to move her in approximately two weeks to the Rosebank Clinic in Cork. The oncology unit there is far more advanced than anything we have here in this particular hospital. We'd like to put her on the list."

"What list is that, doctor?" Jimmy's mind was in uproar.

"The human organ transplant list, Mr Corway."

Jimmy didn't know what to say. Then the doctor's bleeper sounded and he went over to the phone on the wall and dialled his call number. He spoke for a short while and then he turned his attention back to Jimmy. "I'm very sorry Mr Corway, but I have to go. I have a patient waiting for me in theatre. The matron will explain anything you don't understand. Matron, will you see to the necessary paperwork required for Mrs Corway please?" He shook hands firmly with Jimmy and he was gone.

The matron had a very high regard for the doctor, both as a physician and a surgeon, but she wished he would brush up on his bedside manner. She explained to Jimmy about the possible side effects of radiation therapy and the possibility that they might never find a compatible donor. She went on to explain the adjustments they would all have to eventually make. Jimmy hardly hearing her, asked her how much of the truth he should impart to his daughter.

"Well, Mr Corway, in a situation like this, sometimes ignorance is bliss. It's early days yet and your daughter is young. Cathleen is her name, am I correct?"

"Cathy, Cathy is her name, and she's 13. She thinks she's all grown up, but she's not. She's very emotional at the moment."

"That's more than understandable. Now, normally, I do not advocate holding the truth back from family members. But, in this case, I think it would be better to say very little to her. Your wife will have to go to the Rosebank oncology unit for chemotherapy and we have no idea how she is going to respond to the treatment. So I suggest you tell Cathy about the chemotherapy, but don't go into details about her liver or pancreas, not just yet. Tell her the operation was a success and tell her the chemotherapy is a post-operative precautionary measure."

Jimmy thought the matron was a wise woman. "Matron, you're right. There's no need to fill Cathy's head with more than she can grasp. Does Mary know about the extra findings yet?"

"Yes, Mr Corway, she does. Dr Lanagan and I had a chat with her earlier on, and she took the news remarkably well."

"That's Mary for you matron. She's a strong woman. She has the heart of a lioness and she'll lick this. You wait and see." Jimmy was trying to convince himself.

"With the grace of God she will. By the way, we are restricting her visitors to you and your daughter only, just for the time being. She needs her rest and too many visitors can exhaust a patient. This way, no other visiting family members or friends will feel offended or unwanted."

"You know best," replied Jimmy sadly.

Nurse Fiona arrived with a cup of tea. "Hello again, Mr Corway, your wife is doing quite well and she's looking forward to seeing you. She might seem a little bit groggy from the pethidine we are giving her to help with the pain, but it's quite routine after major surgery."

"Thank you, but I won't have any tea right now. I would really like to see my wife." Jimmy was polite but determined. He'd had enough advice for the moment.

"No problem Mr Corway, come along with me. I was just going back to check on her myself. I've given her a bed bath, she's quite alert despite the pethidine, and she has a roomful of flowers and cards. She must be a very popular woman."

"She is indeed. Now what's your name again? Ah, I remember, it's Fiona, isn't it?"

"Yes, Mr Corway, it's Fiona and your name is Jimmy, isn't that right?"

"You are right, Fiona, my name is Jimmy and our daughter's name is Cathy."

"I know, Mary has told me about your daughter. She's big into horses I gather?"

"She sure is. She sure is."

Mary was half-sitting up in bed looking decidedly uncomfortable when Jimmy came in with the nurse. The nurse asked Mary if there was anything she needed and when Mary assured her she was fine, she left the couple alone.

"Mary, I've been so worried about you, you've had the heart crossways in me but you look a lot brighter today and there's even a bit of colour in your cheeks. Last night you looked like death warmed up."

Jimmy looked around the room which was full of flowers and cards. He was finding it hard to connect with Mary's eyes.

"Where did all these flowers come from? Who sent all of these? Your room looks like a garden centre."

"Jimmy, will you stop blabbering on about the damn flowers. A kiss would be nice." She was strangely amused at her husband's obvious discomfort and she didn't know herself who half the people were who sent her flowers, fruit baskets and cards.

"Mary, I'm afraid I'll hurt you. You have so many tubes and things hanging out of you."

"No, you won't hurt me," she reassured him, wanting to comfort her husband. She knew he was having difficulty coping with everything on his own.

Gingerly, he hugged his wife before he sat down on the chair that had been his resting place while he kept his vigil over her the day before. "Matron wants to restrict your visitors for a while, except for me and Cathy that is."

"That's fine by me, how is Cathy?"

"She was a bit upset last night because she couldn't come in to see you, but, when I spoke to her on the phone this morning, she sounded better. I'll bring her in tonight."

"I'll look forward to that." Mary was tired and felt extremely weak, but she didn't let on to Jimmy.

They discussed the conversation he just had with Dr Lanagan and the matron, and Mary agreed they would tell Cathy only minimal details. It would be better if she thought the surgery went as planned. She would understand about the chemotherapy. Yes, they would tell her she had to have it as a precautionary treatment. Under no circumstances was anyone to be told about the other complications, particularly Cathy.

Jimmy asked Mary if she thought it was a good idea for him to ask his sister Imelda to come over, she was due to come for a three-week visit the next month anyway. Mary wasn't sure; she didn't want to upset any of Imelda's plans. Imelda owned her own recruitment agency in London and she was a busy woman.

Jimmy cut her short muttering he would find out how the land lay. He knew as soon as Imelda was told about Mary's illness, she would most probably be on the next plane. Then he examined the get-well-cards Mary had received and he looked at the ones attached to the flowers too. The majority of them were from his customers.

How the dickens did they know Mary was in hospital. Ah, Sandra, that's how. He made a mental note to have a word with her when he got back.

Jimmy seeing his wife was tiring, reluctantly told her he would go off for a short while and he would come back later on with Cathy. Mary was already dozing. She didn't hear him so Jimmy left her room quietly.

Sheamus Dutton arrived home at lunchtime that day, and he demanded to speak to Pauline. Celia told him matter-of-factly that she was down at the stables.

"Down at the stables. Have you finally gone out of your mind Celia? She gets herself suspended from school for a week and you let her go riding." Sheamus was furious.

Celia ignored her husband's arrogant annoyance and changed the subject to Mary. She told him as much as she knew, and skirted over why Paddy suggested that Cathy and Pauline stay over at the equestrian centre. She didn't tell him how relieved she felt that Pauline wasn't staying at home at the present time. Eventually, Sheamus calmed down, but he grounded Pauline for a month with no exceptions and Celia just sighed.

Jimmy returned to his office and gave Sandra an earful about releasing private family information out to all and sundry.

Sandra defended herself. She didn't know what to say to people when they asked where he was. He hadn't told her not to say anything. Anyway, it's not as if Mrs Corway is dying or anything. Hadn't he realised that people would think it was a bit strange if she said she didn't know where he was?

Jimmy apologised and went up the stairs to his office. Sandra's defensive words had stung him like a hornet. Then he phoned Imelda and he was put through to her after a short wait. After the customary exchanges between brother and sister, Jimmy revealed in full detail the true extent of Mary's condition. He asked her if it would be possible for her to come over a bit earlier than she'd planned.

Imelda agreed to come over immediately and she was annoyed with him for not telling her about Mary earlier. He explained that he couldn't have told her about something he had been kept in the dark about himself. She ignored the last bit of what he said and reassured him that he was not putting her out at all, not even a little bit, and she could do with an earlier than planned vacation.

They agreed to speak to each other later on that day and Jimmy felt much happier. Cathy was a mature girl for her age, but she couldn't be left alone all the time, and it wouldn't be fair to expect Mrs Byrne to look after her for much longer. He also had no idea how long Mary was going to be down at the Cork clinic. He would cross that bridge when he came to it.

***

Jimmy collected Cathy at six as previously planned. They hardly spoke to each other on the drive to Dublin. An unrequited silence existed between father and daughter; both of them enveloped in their own separate thoughts. Jimmy wasn't sure about anything anymore and Cathy just wasn't sure.

While parking the car he told her that her mother had a nice room all to herself.

"That's a bit of good luck, she does like her privacy and she'll sleep better in a room on her own. At least she won't have to listen to you snoring like a fog horn beside her for a while." Cathy jibed at him, she didn't know why.

"That's a good one that is. A fog horn, huh? I don't snore that bad do I?" Jimmy smiled. He was missing her sorely but he knew she was better off at Murphy's for the time being.

"Dad, you could make some real extra money renting yourself out to special effects at Ardmore Studios. The sound department would be delighted to have access to such a talented man as yourself."

"Thanks, Cathy, you're very kind. Now, let us get into the hospital and let us go quickly, it's starting to rain again. Where's your jacket?"

"Dad, stop fussing."

When they reached the hospital entrance, Cathy momentarily stopped and looked around her. "Jeepers, this place is huge. Which way do we go?"

"This way pet, we'll take the lift. Your mother's room is on the second floor."

At the nurses' station, they saw Fiona and the other day nurses in consultation; they were busy handing over patients to the night staff. As soon as Fiona saw Jimmy and his daughter approaching, she stepped forward and introduced herself to Cathy. With an experienced eye, she looked at her father who nimbly stepped back and mouthed the word *no*. Fiona was content with his decision to keep his daughter in the dark. She looked at Cathy and thought, *this pretty child couldn't possibly understand about her mother going off to Cork for treatment, treatment which was going to play havoc with her immune system. She has to be protected from the truth for the time being. After all, her mother doesn't want her to know the full extent of her wretched disease.* Fiona respected her patient's decisions and willingly followed them.

***

Jimmy was amazed at his daughter. She chatted away as if nothing was wrong, and didn't ask any awkward questions at all. Mary responded to her daughter in the same way. They watched *Coronation Street* together on the small TV that was nearly hidden from view by more flowers, which had arrived during the day. Cathy told her about her debut as a waitress and she chatted to the night nurses', whose continual presence was felt everywhere.

Jimmy raised an eyebrow to Mary and she just shrugged her shoulders. Either Cathy didn't really know her mother was extremely ill, or she was blocking it out. Jimmy feared it was the latter.

Mary abruptly asked them to go home when her assigned night nurse came in with her pethidine injection. She was tired out. She wanted to be alone. Since she'd been admitted to the hospital she hadn't had any time to think. There was always some nurse or doctor asking her how she was. She didn't know how she felt, but she knew she was angry, very angry.

But she didn't show her anger to her family; they had enough to worry about. The injections made her horribly nauseous and light-headed. When she asked why, she was told it was a relatively normal side effect so she needn't worry. She was worried; the side effects of the medication clouded her ability to think straight, and at this point in time, straight thinking was needed. Frustrated, she swiped a basket of fruit from the bedside locker and hissed, *how can anybody voluntarily become a drug addict? How can anyone want to feel like this over and over again?* Glancing at the flowers strangers had sent her, she suddenly felt scared. The eerie feeling she was the lead actor in a movie of her own funeral engulfed her.

***

Cathy's next few days passed in a hectic flurry. During the day she helped exercise the horses, she worked alongside the stable boys in the yard, she helped the instructors with the younger children and she helped Mrs Byrne to clean the guesthouse. She also pestered Moira about teaching her bar duties. Tony kept her busy also. Paddy had given him instructions to do so and Cathy wanted to be kept busy.

Ten

"I'll be back at lunch time, okay?" Pauline said to Mrs Byrne.

"All right, love, and good luck to the pair of you," Mrs Byrne smiled at Pauline's departing figure. Pauline was nervous about her ballet exam and she didn't need to be. Sonia Smith, her ballet teacher, was the daughter of Mrs Byrne's good friend Ria Smith, so she had first-hand knowledge of Pauline's progress throughout the grades.

Sonia regarded Pauline as her top pupil and held her in high esteem. When Pauline had first started dancing she was a bit on the clumsy side, but that didn't last long. From early on, Sonia saw her natural graceful movements and her ability to balance. She recognised her defined style just waiting to be unleashed when her body developed a little more.

Pauline didn't believe in losing. When she rode in competition, she rode to win. Sonia overheard her saying to Sheila Keating that 'you don't win second place, you lose first.' Sonia liked that attitude in her pupil.

"Thanks, Mrs Byrne. I'll be off, bye," Pauline said as she hopped up on her bike and cycled away from the guesthouse. She passed Paddy as he came out of the mares' stable block.

"Ah, you're off then ... break a leg." Pauline had amused him the night before when she became flustered about today's ballet exam. She only remembered the exam over supper. She had completely forgotten all about it.

Then she had gotten herself into an awful tizzy and gave Cathy a dressing down for not reminding her.

Cathy couldn't care less. She only endured her ballet classes for the sake of her mother. Her only true interest lay in horses. She was totally consumed by them; she lived and breathed for the day she could own one herself.

Riding other people's horses was fine, she wasn't ungrateful or anything, but owning her own horse was her ultimate goal.

"Paddy, don't say that. If I do, I won't be able to ride Flint for you at the weekend and that would be horribly unfair. I'll be back by lunchtime. Cheerio," Pauline said as she cycled out of the yard and straight into a large muddy puddle.

Paddy heard her swear loudly, but he paid no heed. Cathy had left a few minutes earlier in a more dignified manner.

Paddy just laughed to himself. The night before they chatted about what Paddy called this *breaking a leg business*. Cathy explained it was only superstition, as apparently it was bad luck to say good luck to a performer going out on stage. He knew sailors were superstitious, but he didn't categorise dancers like that. Some things he knew and some things he didn't need to know.

Pauline checked from around the corner to see if her father's car was in the driveway. He sometimes worked from his den at home, and it was only eight-fifteen in the morning; he could still be there. Satisfied that his car was nowhere to be seen, she dumped her bike in the backyard and went into the kitchen.

"Hi mum, I'm home. Where are you?"

Celia was upstairs making the beds. "Up here, love. What are you doing here?"

Pauline charged up the stairs two at a time. "I had to come home to get my ballet stuff. I have a bloody exam today," she said breathlessly

"Gosh, I'd forgotten about that. Pauline, please don't use bad language. You're in enough trouble with your father as it is."

"Sorry, Mum. What did he say? What's he going to do? Is he going to do anything?"

"Pauline he was livid. He eased up when I told him about Mary, but he's grounded you for a month. How is Mary by the way?" Celia was as vague as ever.

"He's grounded me? But Mum, that's not fair. It wasn't my fault--"

"Maybe it wasn't, but he's made up his mind and that is that. I asked you about Mary. I haven't heard anything from Jimmy since Monday night. I didn't want to phone as he might think I was being nosey."

"Cathy say's she's doing fine, but I'm not too sure ... I don't think Cathy has been given all the facts. And Mrs Corway has to go to Cork for chemotherapy, all the way to Cork. Apparently they have a new clinic down there which specialises in post-operative treatments. Well, that's what Cathy said."

"Yes, I read something about that place a couple of months ago. I think it's called the *Rosarybank Clinic* or something like that. It's meant to be state-of-the-art, very modern."

"Mum, it's called the Rosebank Clinic. Maybe it is as you say state-of-the-art, but why does Mrs Corway have to go all the way to there? Surely, they can give her whatever treatment she needs here in Dublin. Cathy says it has a specialised oncology unit and she muttered something about not asking for a steak in a fish restaurant. She wouldn't say another word after that, so I didn't push her. She seems to have closed in on herself."

"Yes, I remember now, they do have a specialised unit there, but it's mainly for severe cases, terminal cases, if I remember correctly." Celia's voice drifted, she had said too much.

"Jees, mum, you don't think Mrs Corway might be term-inally ill do you? You don't think she's going to die do you? Do you think Cathy knows and she's not saying anything?"

Pauline felt guilty because she had been quite sharp at times with Cathy over the last few days.

"I don't know any more than you do. They are probably sending her there because it's more up to date, than anything that's available in the Dublin. Let's not make assumptions, okay?"

Celia sensed the truth, and if Cathy had said nothing to Pauline so far, then she didn't know the truth herself. She made a mental note to phone Jimmy; if he thought she was being nosey, then so be it.

"Now, enough of what we don't know. Don't you think you should get ready for your exam? It's half-past-eight." Celia wanted to steer her daughter away from the subject of Cathy's mother's shrouded illness.

Just then Pauline's brother Neill burst through the back door shouting, "Mum, I forgot my rugby gear. Can you give me a lift back to school? I'll not make it back in time."

When Pauline heard her brother's voice she bristled hotly and met him on the stairs. "You're a little bastard, you know that?"

"No, I'm not. Mother is standing right behind you and she can verify that I'm not one, can't you mum?"

Neill was surprised to see his sister home, and even more surprised she was calling him names.

"Pauline, what have I told you about your language? I won't remind you again, is that clear?"

Pauline ignored her mother. She wanted to scratch her bro-ther's eyes out.

"Mum, John Clancy phoned me on Monday night and dip-shit here said I was out, and I was up in my bedroom with Cathy all evening. John was very upset because I'd told him to phone me."

"Stop all the bickering this instant. Pauline will you go and get ready? Neill, find your rugby gear and get into the car, or you will walk back to school and face the music for being late." Pauline trounced past her brother and hissed. "You'd better apologise to John, otherwise dad might find out about a certain incident, a compromising incident, involving a particular girl and a filthy boy in the cinema last weekend."

"How'd you find out about that? You wouldn't tell would you?"

Neill and Fiona McLoughlin had been caught snogging in the back row by the usherette. The usherette was actually an old lady who had recently moved to the town with her spinster daughter. No one knew much about them, but she had created a huge fuss and told the extremely embarrassed young couple to leave immediately. Pauline thought Fiona had very bad taste, but that was Fiona's business.

"Oh, yes I would you shit-head."

Celia had heard enough arguing. "Pauline, go and get ready. I'll drive you to the parochial hall when I drop Neill off; you know Miss Smith will have a hissy fit if you're late. Neill, come with me. Your rugby bag should be in the downstairs closet. I'll be in the car, and hurry up,"

Celia hated it when her children fought. Neill gave his sister a look that would turn milk sour.

"Sometimes I hate you Pauline Dutton," he grabbed his bag from the closet and left.

Pauline headed for the bathroom. She wanted to have a quick shower; her legs were covered in mud. Now that her mother was going to drive her to the parochial hall, she had a bit more time to spare. She only needed ten to fifteen minutes warming up before her exam, so she would have enough time to try and do something with her hair as well.

Cathy went home, cuddled Phantom, and gave him an extra helping of his favourite tinned food. The poor fellow must be feeling lonely. She'd been gone all week and her father wasn't really a cat person, and she had no intention of turning up for her exam; she couldn't be bothered.

She went into her mother's room, picked up one of her jerseys, and held it close to her face. She wanted to smell her perfume. She knew her parents were holding something back from her. She wasn't that stupid, but she couldn't bring herself to demand the full truth. She sat down on her mother's bed and cried until she had no more tears left.

Eleven

Pauline was in top form when she got back to the yard. Her exam had gone very well and she was quite pleased with herself. She went to hunt down Cathy.

"Paddy, have you seen Cathy? She didn't turn up for her exam. I don't know where she is. Tony, have you seen her?" Pauline was worried.

"Whoa, slow down a bit there. Gather yourself together." Paddy said stopping her in her tracks.

"Maybe she's up with Mrs Byrne," Pauline said hopefully.

"No, she's not, I've just come from there myself," Tony told her.

"Okay, maybe we should try her house?" Paddy suggested.

"Good idea. Can I use the phone Paddy?" Pauline asked.

"Go right ahead. You know where it is."

"There's no need to, here she is now," Tony piped up.

Cathy came into the yard as if she hadn't got a care in the world.

"Hi there, why are you all staring at me?"

"We're not staring at you. Why did you bunk out of your exam?" Pauline demanded.

"Pauline, leave it, would you." Cathy wanted to ride, not undergo an inquisition.

"Fine, I will then, but you've pissed Miss Smith off, big time." Pauline snapped at her as she went off in the direction of the tack room.

Cathy ignored her and said to Paddy, "Will we put the flags and numbers on the fences now, or in the morning?"

"The two of you can do it now, we might be a bit strapped for time tomorrow," Paddy answered warily. He didn't have time for squabbling young girls; he had too much work to do.

He wanted to try his new mare out, over a few of the junior fences, but he wasn't sure if he had the time. He'd been working her over the last few days in the indoor school, and he was pleased with her progress. Being a young horse and very green, Paddy had no intention of pushing her too quickly.

"Oh, Paddy, you did want me to ride Johnjo, didn't you?" Cathy asked expectantly.

"Yes, I did, and ride him for the whole weekend. He's gone a bit stale in the school, he needs a break. Will you ask Pauline to come over to the office for a few minutes please?"

"Sure I will. I'm actually going to have Johnjo all to myself for the whole weekend. You're a wonderful man, Paddy Murphy."

"Hmmm," was all Paddy said in reply.

Cathy found Pauline and told her that Paddy wanted to see her. Pauline ambled over to the office. "You wanted to see me Paddy?"

"Yes, I did. I've asked Cathy to ride Johnjo over the coming weekend. He needs a break from the school. You can ride Whisky, but try to keep him off any hard ground. I don't want to put shoes back on him for another couple of weeks, okay."

"Sure, and thanks Paddy. I'll look after him. Don't worry."

"I know you will. Now off with the pair of you. Get all the flags and numbers up now, there is more rain coming in and it'll be dark in a few hours."

"We're on our way. I'll put our names on the board right this minute. See you later, and thanks again."

Pauline and Cathy did as they were asked, and they finished in good time. On the way back to the yard they chatted as if nothing had happened between them earlier on.

Cathy told Pauline she wouldn't be visiting her mother that night, as her father was tied up in Dublin for most of the day.

Her aunt Imelda was arriving from London on the seven o' clock flight, and he wouldn't have time to come back to collect her, before he was went to the airport.

"Imelda is coming over today? I thought she wasn't expected until next month." Pauline asked in surprise.

"Yeah, she is. Apparently, she had to change her plans. She's some business stuff she needs to sort out here over the next few days,' explained Cathy.

"I like Imelda, she's fun," Pauline replied.

"Yeah, she's a good sort. You always know where you stand with her, and she knows her own mind, that's for sure."

The weekend passed in a flash. Paddy always liked to end his clinics with an informal competition. He liked to have every- one go home, after they had put what they were supposed to have learned to the test.

On the Sunday afternoon, the water jump seemed to have the most casualties. Cathy was secretly pleased about that.

Patricia Faircolm, the snooty young woman whose horse Dubba was in livery with Paddy, fell off at the water jump, and was nearly trampled by her competition partner. Cathy felt she deserved it, as she insisted against Paddy's advice that she needed to wear spurs.

Pauline had exercised her horse on the previous Thursday, and he did not need them at all. She tried to tell her that, but her advice was also ignored.

Miss Snooty approached the water jump, and her approach was completely wrong, so she dug her spurs viciously into

Dubba's sides. The poor animal got such a fright; he took off through the water as if a firecracker had exploded behind him. This was most uncommon, as he was usually a gentle and willing horse. Miss Snooty toppled backwards and landed hard in the deepest part of the water. She was livid.

Tony retrieved her horse, and told her that she could walk back to the yard. He didn't care if she raised hell. She didn't deserve to ride back; he told her she could go and stuff herself.

Hell has no fury like a woman scorned, was an understatement. When she finally arrived back on foot, she was soaked to the skin and freezing cold. She cornered Paddy and she let him have it.

Tony hadn't earned the title of head groom for nothing. To be given that title by Paddy, he had to be pretty damn good, and Paddy had complete faith in Tony's judgement. He was running a business, but, he would not permit any bad-mouthing of his staff members. He dismissed her as if she was a piece of bothersome tumbleweed.

"My grandfather will hear of this disgraceful behaviour," she spat venomously at him.

"I'm sure he will, Miss Faircolm. Now excuse me please, I have other business to attend to," Paddy answered her politely but firmly.

Paddy had known Major Faircolm since he was a young lad, and they had always gotten on extremely well. Paddy didn't really want to take his granddaughter's horse in as a livery in the first place, but he did it as a favour to his old friend.

Having no luck trying to cause havoc with Paddy, she turned on Tony and accused him of being insensitive to her needs. She demanded to know why he didn't send one of the lads out to collect her in the jeep. He told her that none of his lads were taxi drivers, they were stable hands, or was she so stupid that she missed that bit.

"My grandfather will have you fired, you insolent piece of shit." Then she flounced off to the car park.

Tony shouted after her, "The only piece of shit around here is the one that's stuck between your flappin' ears."

Her grandfather had already heard about it. He was in Paddy's office when his granddaughter was screaming like a banshee at everyone. Patricia was the only one who didn't know he was there. The Major was glad someone had been able to put his spoilt granddaughter in her place. He loved her, but she could get a bit trying at times, and she needed someone to take her down a peg or two.

The weekend came to a close with no further mishaps. Both girls packed up their belongings and Tony said he would drive them home. It was too late for them to cycle, plus, they had to return to school in the morning, and they were both worn out.

Patricia Faircolm removed her horse from Paddy's yard the next day, and no one was sorry to see her go, but Paddy was anxious about Dubba because she had re-employed her old groom to look after him on a full-time basis. The same groom she had fired two months before, because she thought he was unreliable. He was unreliable, because he was drunk most of the time, but no one else would work for Miss Faircolm. No one half-decent would consider the position, and that's why the Major asked Paddy to take Dubba into livery in the first place.

Twelve

Pauline and Cathy were about to enter the locker rooms when they heard a familiar tapping on the sentinel's window. They looked up, and there she was giving them the signal to come to her office.

"What does she want?" Cathy wasn't in the mood to deal with the head nun this morning.

"I don't know, but we're going to find out, aren't we?" Pauline looked up at the nun's sour face and shrugged.

"Come on then, let's get this over with," Cathy suggested feeling miserable.

They changed their shoes, hung up their coats and went reluctantly to Mother Anastasia's office.

Cathy knocked on the door and they were told to enter. The nun was still standing by the window.

"Good morning Mother and how are you today?" Pauline greeted the head nun pleasantly enough.

"I'm very well, thank you, Miss Dutton. I trust you both have learnt something advantageous during your week of suspension," the nun asked, full of her own importance.

"Yes, yes we did Mother, we did indeed." Pauline answered.

"I'm very glad to hear that, and what exactly did you learn?" The nun cocked her head to one side, folded her arms and waited.

"Oh, we learnt how to jump a downhill fence properly and Cathy has finally mastered the water fence, thanks be to God." Pauline replied raising her eyes to heaven.

Not wanting to miss an opportunity, Cathy took over. "And Mother, we also learnt how to be barmaids and waitresses and Pauline can pull a wicked pint of Guinness now. It was great fun, thanks for giving us the opportunity." She couldn't help stick that bit in.

Mother Superior was not impressed at all, and before either girl could continue any further, she ordered them to get out of her sight and go to class.

"Jees', Pauline, did you see her face? I thought she was going to have a seizure," Cathy giggled.

"Pity she didn't, we'd be far better off without her. She's just an evil rotten old bitch," Pauline replied in a harsh tone.

"Ah well, let's get to class. We don't want to piss any of the other teachers off, not on our first day back." Cathy replied.

They did get to class on time, and as it was Monday, English was the first period.

Sister Bridget welcomed them back warmly. The other girls were quietened sharply by the teacher; she told them they could catch up on all the latest gossip at the end of class, not during it.

"Girls, two weeks ago I asked you to write a poem as part of your English homework. What I didn't tell you was that the best poem will be read by its author, to the entire senior school, in honour of Mother Anastasia's feast day. That is tomorrow."

The girls started mumbling to each other.

"Silence, please. I did have a hard time deciding the winner, but I did eventually decide, and I can assure you it wasn't easy. Pauline Dutton, will you come up to the front of the classroom please?"

Pauline did as she was told.

"Pauline, I want to congratulate you on a fine piece of work. You will have the honour of representing the First Year English class on stage tomorrow and well done. If you have any questions, see me after class." She asked Pauline to return to her seat and she told the rest of the class to open their grammar textbooks at chapter nine.

Pauline was mortified. She wasn't a public speaker but she wouldn't let Sister Bridget down. She planned to practise her poem in the privacy of her own bedroom, and practise it until she had it word perfect. She liked writing poetry and short stories. She had entered a writing competition the previous year which was sponsored by a local newspaper, and she had won first prize. Her wardrobe contained a box full of her writing attempts.

The next day the entire senior school, pupils and teachers gathered in the assembly hall. A single row of chairs was arranged neatly in front of the stage for the teachers to sit on. Mother Superior was given the centre one. The pupils sat in the usual places on the gallery.

When everyone was settled, the first girl took her position in front of the microphone. Nervously, she recited her composition 'Which Way'.

Pauline was next in line and took her position on stage without any problem. She looked at Mother Superior, the nun had such a disapproving and withered expression on her face, and she made her feel sick. Not wanting to disappoint Sister Bridget she gave herself a mental shake-up and commenced.

Dreams
Your dreams are precious
Don't let them fade
Go show the world

Of what you are made
Our dreams are the foundations
That set your hopes free ...

The word free stopped Pauline in her tracks. She looked at Sister Bridget who smiled brightly back at her, then she looked at the head nun. She had her arms folded and she wasn't even listening, she was talking to Mrs Walker, the science teacher. She did look up at Pauline briefly, and she flicked her hand at her as if she was an annoying insect.

Pauline saw red. *I'll show you, you old crow.* She shuffled her papers around and found what she was looking for.

"Sorry about that. I was reading the wrong poem. I'll continue now."

I woke early one morning
The earth lay cool and still
When suddenly a tiny bird
Perched on my window sill
He sang a song so lovely
So carefree and so gay
That slowly all my troubles
Began to slip away
He sang of far off places
Of laughter and of fun
It seemed his very trilling
Brought up the morning sun
I stirred beneath the covers
Crept slowly out of bed
I gently shut the window
And crushed his fucking head

The hall was so silent you could have heard a pin drop. Then one girl started to laugh, followed by another, and before long the entire senior school, including some of the teachers, were in fits of laughter. Mother Superior stood up angrily and rang the bell on the edge of the stage.

"Silence, silence, I say."

No-one heard her; no one wanted to. She rang the bell again.

Then she screamed, "Silence, silence, or you will all be put in detention for the entire day next Saturday."

This brought the requested silence throughout the hall, although a few snorts could still be heard every so often. Sister Bridget didn't know what she should do. *Oh, Pauline, you are in for it now.* Pauline was about to leave the hall when the head nun grabbed her roughly by the arm.

"Take your hand off me, you, you wagon." Pauline spat through gritted teeth.

"How dare you speak to me like that, you brazen hussy."

"Oh, I dare, I dare to speak to you any way I want to. You're nothing but a miserable old frustrated cow."

The nun lifted her hand and slapped Pauline hard across her face. "Get your ..."

Pauline stopped her and shouted, "Shut up, just shut up and let me get the hell out of here. I won't stay in this poxy fucking school for another minute." She returned the slap hard, and stormed out of the hall without a backward glance.

The head nun was decidedly shaken. No student had ever spoken to her like that before, much less slapped her. She regained her composure and ordered the remaining girls to go back to class, and then she left the hall and went straight to her office. Pauline's parents were sent for immediately.

Pauline refused point blank to return to the school and plead her defence. She told her father he could do as he liked. She wasn't going back there ever again. Celia stayed quiet as Sheamus was causing enough of a rumpus on his own, so they went to the convent without their daughter. Mother Superior knew Sheamus from old and she had a cheque all ready and waiting for him. She was refunding the school fees he had paid in advance. She had expelled Pauline.

Sheamus ranted on like a crazy bulldog with a wasp stuck up its ass, roaring about what was to be done with his daughter and Celia calmly suggested they send Pauline over to the Templeton College for Young Ladies in Galway. At least nuns didn't run it. Mrs Cronin, who worked with her at the new meals on wheels project, had told her all about it. Her own daughter was a past pupil and she had been very pleased with the results her daugh- ter attained.

Sheamus fumed on about the extra expense, but eventually he listened to his wife. Celia usually stayed in the background letting Sheamus make most of the decisions, but not this time. They had been married for 20 years and never once, in that time had she raised her voice to her husband. She did now. Sheamus was told clearly, that if he didn't stop making everyone's life a bloody misery, he could get the hell out, and go and live with his bloody bank account.

Pauline was proud of her mother. She had allowed Sheamus to treat her like a doormat for far too long. Her mother was making a stand.

Pauline was accepted to the college and Celia drove her there a week later. She decided to book herself into the Galway Arms Hotel for the weekend, as Pauline might need her nearby for a day or two, just while she was settling in. Secretly, she didn't want to be separated from her daughter.

Pauline managed to settle in reasonably well. She was determined to make a go of it; she didn't really have any other option. Mother and daughter had made a pact. Pauline promised her mother she would behave herself and Celia promised her daughter she would never allow Sheamus to treat her like a dogsbody again.

Cathy was horrified that her best friend was not going to be with her on a daily basis, even more horrified when she realised they would only be together during school holidays. The girls promised to write regularly and phone each as much as possible. It was all they could do.

***

Mary was not recovering as well as the doctors and nursing staff had hoped for. She had developed unexpected complications and battled to recover enough strength to combat the effects of the surgery. Septicaemia was diagnosed in her blood, and the resulting high fever added additional strain to her already overtaxed heart. Despite the administration of antibiotics, the offending bacteria remained unresponsive to treatment. Mary went into a massive cardiac arrest. The doctors and nurses tried valiantly to save her, but their efforts proved futile. Mary Corway was declared officially dead at ten-past-eleven on October 2nd 1981.

Thirteen

Imelda delayed her return to London after Mary's funeral; her brother and niece needed her. She was two years older than Jimmy, but she felt motherly towards him. Her heart was heavy for him and she felt he needed her guidance and support.

Mary's death had hit Jimmy extremely hard and Cathy had not shed a single tear since her mother had died. Imelda knew the day was coming when she would cry, and she wanted to be there for her. Her friend and business partner Rachael Malone was managing Imelda's side of the company in her absence. *ImRa Staffing Solutions* was their chosen name for the company. She encouraged Imelda to stay with her family in Ireland for as long as she was needed.

Imelda and Rachael initially met when they both started work at a large recruitment agency in London.

As soon as Imelda finished high school, she enrolled in an intensive secretarial course and qualified in record time with a typing speed of 85 words per minute. Her shorthand and computer skills were just as impressive. She hated the constraints of small Irish towns and villages, where everyone knew your business. She wanted to spread her wings. She registered with an employment agency in Dublin that specialised in overseas placements and they were very impressed with her from day one. They liked her drive and her need to improve herself.

It wasn't long before they offered her a position in London as a receptionist with the sister company Execupro. Imelda willingly signed a two-year contract with the agency and headed for greener pastures.

She was free.

She found life in London quite different from the life she had known in Ireland, but she soon settled into it. Part of her contract agreement included the use of a two-bed roomed furnished flat in St John's Wood. It was only ten minutes walking distance from her office, so she had no need of transport, public or otherwise. This was a huge financial saving.

She was very lucky to get the flat in the first place. Normally company-owned accommodation was highly coveted and virtually non-existent. However, even with the rent being subsidised, she still found it a bit steep. She asked the agency if they knew of anyone who would be willing to share with her. Her supervisor introduced her to Rachael Malone.

Rachael had recently started working for Execupro in the creditors' department. At the time, she was still living at home with her parents, and she had to commute daily for over an hour each way. She needed to find alternative accommodation as soon as possible.

The two women hit it off right from the start and without any further delay, Rachael moved into the flat the following weekend. She brought a flurry of bean-bags, life-sized posters of Sean Connery, her collection of feather boas, (which she never wore but couldn't be separated from) and a very old baby grand piano. She didn't know how to play the piano which her eccentric granny had given to her on her 18th birthday. Learning to play it was very high on Rachael's *must do someday* list. Imelda enjoyed her scattily pleasant personality.

From then on, there was never a dull moment; the flat never seemed to be empty. There was always someone coming or going. When they both shared the same lunch hour, they would go home for a bite of something to eat and have a freshen-up. Some of the other girls in the office would often join them.

Before long, the girls were coming over in the evenings as well. They found it handy to shower and change clothes before going out for a night on the town together. Some of the guys in the office also dropped in frequently, mainly on the weekends. They were like one big happy family.

Boyfriends came and boyfriends went. Neither one wanted to get into a serious relationship, so between them they man- aged to acquire a varied collection of boyfriends, some good, some not so good.

Imelda was with the agency for approximately six months when she was offered a promotion in the recruitment consult-ancy section. She accepted the position and the increased salary happily. Two years later, she qualified as a fully-fledged Exec-upro Recruitment Officer.

The company was expanding rapidly and so was Imelda's individual client database. Her consistent thoroughness, and dedication to her work, did not go unnoticed.

Before long, one of her regular clients, a large catering company named *Diner's Delight,* approached her with a pro-posal. She had been working with them for some time already, taking care of their temporary and permanent staffing needs. They asked her to work for them exclusively, and, she could choose her own assistants.

From the beginning, Imelda and Rachael had constant dreams of opening their own recruitment consultancy. They both saw the window of opportunity and grabbed it with both hands. They decided to offer *Diner's Delight* a counter proposal.

The company owned many small satellite offices throughout the country, and one in particular situated near Piccadilly

Circus. This office was a constant thorn to them; it was practically non-productive. Imelda suggested they allow her to use the premises rent-free for a period of 24 months. In return, she and her partner would handle all the casual staff needs, and management requirements, at a reduced fee. This fee would be exactly half of what they paid Execupro.

Many meetings later, the proposal was finally accepted, the deal was done and ImRa Staffing Solutions was born.

Rachael invested a considerable amount into the newly formed company. This came from monies she had been left by her now late grandmother. Imelda matched the figure with the money she had inherited from her parents.

With very little persuasion, two of the girls from Execupro joined them. Sandy was from the permanent staff section and Trudy from the temporary staff desk. They employed Rachael's younger sister Tammy as the receptionist/girl Friday. She had just completed her course at a secretarial college and she jumped at the chance they offered her. Luke Harvey offered his services as operations manager, and they both accepted him willingly.

Execupro was mightily pissed off with the pair of them. Apart from the arguments over trade restraints and the stealing of top employees and clients, they told them they would never make a go of it. This was not the right thing to say to two young ambitious women. Of course they had to vacate the company flat immediately.

The Piccadilly Diner's Delight premises were housed in a quiet side street with a reasonable amount of private parking space. This in itself was a bonus as parking in the area was highly sought after. The building was a Victorian two-storey, old and spacious. They didn't realise just how spacious it was until all of the catering equipment and stores had been moved out.

The top floor consisted of four airy rooms, an ancient bathroom and a small scullery. They converted it into a comfortable two-bed roomed apartment. The ground floor had three large rooms and another kitchen and bathroom. They divided the largest room into three smaller ones. One was to be used for the reception area and the other two for interviewing lounges. The remaining rooms were used for the general offices.

While the conversions were being carried out, both women moved into a boarding house in St John's Wood. As they were fully conversant with the city's underground transport system, they weren't bothered by the hassle of commuting back and forth.

When the renovations were completed and the elegantly hand-painted sign *ImRa Staffing Solutions* was put in place over the main door, both women hugged themselves in anticipation of new-found independence.

They were a success right from the start. Within the 24 months originally specified, they were able to put an offer to Diner's Delight to purchase the premises. The catering company accepted the offer as they had recently decided to downsize and relocate to the South of England. It was advantageous to them.

Imelda and Rachael were not put out by the company's decision to relocate. They were leaving behind four Diner's Delight outlets still open. They asked ImRa to manage all the administration and staffing requirements.

With many other large clients on the books, ImRa grew from strength to strength.

Fourteen

Pauline hated her new school with a passion, but she had made a promise to her mother and she intended keeping her side of the bargain. She missed Cathy and the horses dreadfully. She'd been home once with the school's special permission for Cathy's mother's funeral, and she was due back home for the term break the next day.

Her mother called her regularly on the pupils' dormitory phone, much to the disgust of Sheamus. He regarded the additional phone bill expensive and unnecessary. Celia reminded him of her previous warning that if he didn't like it, he could move out and live with his bloody bank account.

Sheamus didn't mention the phone bill again. Celia had won another round with her stingy husband. She was looking forward to her daughter coming home, and she was looking forward to spending some real quality time with her. Sheamus could go and stuff himself. She was going to have an enjoyable get together with Pauline and with no expense spared.

Her sons approved of her new attitude and they respected her for it. Initially they had rebelled because each was given chores around the house to be completed correctly and without any moaning. It freed Celia up to do some of the things that she liked to do. She only had one recrimination - why hadn't she made a stand years before.

***

Imelda had to return to London for a few days and she asked Jimmy if Cathy could come with her. Cathy was starting her school holidays the next day and Imelda thought it would do her good to get away for a while; she was concerned for her niece.

Cathy had taken to sitting in her mother's chair by the fire in the kitchen most evenings, in exactly the same position that her mother had, when she was alive. She tried to make the same scones her mother used to make, but her efforts were less than successful. The scones resembled a bunch of inedible hockey pucks. She valiantly tried to tend to the rose bushes that Mary had lovingly cared for, but they no longer thrived like they used to.

Jimmy could see Cathy wasn't coping, not that he was coping well himself, and Imelda was right; a short trip away could do her a world of good.

They would only be gone a few days, so what would be the harm?

Cathy phoned Pauline that evening. "Pauls, how's it going?" Cathy asked animatedly.

Pauline was spending a boring evening far away in Galway. The school exams were over and there was nothing much to do. She was delighted to hear from her friend, and even happier that she sounded more like her old self.

"Guess what? I'm going to London tomorrow for a few days," she bubbled down the line.

"Jeepers, Cathy, how long will you be gone? When will you be back?"

"We're only going for three or four days. We're booked on a flight tomorrow morning and I think our return flight is on Monday night. I'm not sure though. I'll have to check."

"Who's the we?" Pauline enquired.

"Me and Imelda. She's to go back to London to sort out some business problem or something." Cathy replied, trying not to be too vague with her information.

"What are you going to do while Imelda is at work?" Pauline wanted to know all the details.

"I think I'm going to help Tammy with filing and stuff like that. Sounds boring."

Pauline had met Tammy when she accompanied Rachael to Cathy's mother's funeral, and she had liked her a lot. "Tammy's really nice; you'll have fun, but is that *all* you're going to do?"

"No, Imelda has made some plans for Saturday and Sunday. It's supposed to be a surprise, so I don't know exactly what we are doing."

"But, Cathy, I'm coming home tomorrow and I was looking forward to meeting up with you and going riding." Pauline stopped because she realised she was sounding selfish.

"Haven't you been riding in Galway at all?"

"Are you nuts? Dad would have a fit if he had to fork out any more money. He moaned enough about the fees he had to pay Paddy while I was still at school in Bray. He'd never agree to pay for riding lessons here."

Pauline's mum had laid down new ground rules, but she couldn't work miracles.

"Cathy, before I forget, have you seen John Clancy lately?"

"No, I haven't seen him in ages. Why?"

"He phoned me a few times and he wants me to go out to dinner with him, soon. Soon like tomorrow night."

"Go out to dinner? Flippin' hell, isn't that a bit formal?" Cathy burst out laughing.

"Yep, it is, but that's the way John is. Will you shut the feck up please? I don't see what is so bloody funny. Will you phone him for me, I've got no money left?"

"Phone him and say what exactly?" Cathy giggled. The thought of Pauline and John Clancy having dinner together amused her highly.

"Don't get all difficult. Just tell him I'll call him when I get in tomorrow. No, tell him he can go ahead and book a table wherever he wants. Gosh, imagine Cathy, he wants to book a table! Damn it, you're going away and I don't really fancy spending tomorrow night at home with bloody Dad going on and on about the price of everything; and my pack of feckin' eejit brothers and their mates are going away on some kind of guy thing with the school."

"What kind of guy thing? And I'm *not* phoning John Clancy for you. Do your own dirty work."

"Don't be a thick dip-shit all your life. I can't phone him, I'm broke, remember."

"Pauls, what am I supposed to say to the guy? *Hi John, Pauline Dutton's private social secretary here. You can go ahead and make arrangements for your night of passion. She's given you the green light.*"

"Just call him, ask him to phone me. Is that asking too much?"

"All right, but don't get all stroppy. I'll phone him, but you haven't told me where your brothers are going."

"I'm not really sure. Mum says it's something to do with bonding. They're going camping. I ask you, at this time of year. The only bonding they'll be doing is zipping their little dicks up in a sleeping bag after smoking copious amounts of joints."

"Don't be stupid, Pauline. None of them smoke pot."

"What bloody planet are you on? Of course they do, and so do I."

"You smoke pot? Who are you? And what have you done with Pauline Dutton?" Cathy was genuinely shocked.

"Don't be such a goody-two-shoes all the time. Shit, I have to go. Phone John please. Enjoy London, and I'll see you when you get back. Bye, miss you."

"No worries, I'll phone him right now. See you next week, enjoy your dinner. Bye."

Pauline hung up the phone. Wendy Watson her dormitory housemother and history teacher, was beckoning her.

"Yes, Miss Watson, you wanted me?" Pauline liked her history teacher a lot, as she treated all the girls' fairly and equally.

"Pauline, will you meet me in the reading room in ten minutes? I want to have a word with you." Miss Watson was smiling at her pupil as she walked along the corridor beside her.

"Is something wrong, Miss?" Pauline looked her teacher straight in the eye, as if butter wouldn't melt in her mouth.

"That remains to be seen. The library, in ten minutes, okay. I have to turn on the outside lights and lock the doors, but I won't be long."

"Ok, I'll see you there in ten minutes." Pauline wondered what her teacher wanted her for. She went to the reading room and waited. She was waiting nearly 20 minutes before Miss Watson finally joined her.

"Sorry, for keeping you waiting. I was waylaid by some of your classmates."

"That's okay Miss Watson. What did you want to see me about?" Pauline asked expectantly.

"Well now, Pauline, come and sit down over here." Miss Watson indicated to sit on the chair beside the electric fire. The fire was permanently on, as the reading room was always freezing, even during the summer months. They both sat down together and Miss Watson spoke first. "I'd like to read something to you. The author has decided to remain somewhat anonymous."

"But, Miss Watson we're having a party." Miss Watson interrupted her.

"This won't take long, just be patient."

Miss Watson opened a folder, and to Pauline's horror, took out her written and unsigned interpretation of the assignment she had completed on 'Alternative Eastern Practices' and began to read.

Feng Shui

Feng Shui is the ancient Chinese practice of increasing good fortune by influencing the whereabouts and characteristics of the cosmic energy called Qi.

It is said that a home or office, which is laid out according to Feng Shui principles, will make the inhabitants rich and blissfully happy.

Unfortunately, the art, or science of Feng Shui is sometimes practised by charlatans who just simply make it all up, increasing their own good fortunes and creating a strong threat to the gravitational pull of the earth as well.

Examples:
Your sex life can be enlivened by the introduction of fish into your living room.

Piranha's can look very attractive in an aquarium in your home. If it's too much trouble to look after the live fish, slip a small can of anchovies into your pocket. That should work just as well.

Always keep the toilet seat down.

Toilets are very negative. Don't have one in your home. If you must have a toilet, don't decorate it with pictures of the Pope. This will play hell with your internal waterworks.

Large flowing water features inside your home will increase your good fortune.

Maybe they would look attractive, but do sleep with a snorkel beside your bed, and have the plumber's telephone number handy. A word of caution, artisans don't like being called out in the middle of the night.

Never have two outside doors facing each other.

If both doors are open at the same time on a windy day, the resulting draft could allow all your positive energy to be blown away, and pro- bably end up unwanted and confused in your next door neighbour's house.

All furniture should be placed in strategic areas of your home to increase good fortune.

The compass points are north, south, east and west. If these points happen to change, the weather office will contact you.

The five elements are water, fire, and earth, metal and wood.

The alternative elements are beer, cigarettes, chocolate, rock music and X-rated movies.

Burning aromatic candles bring yang qualities into a home.

Yes, they will. Particularly if you forget about them and there's no smoke alarm installed.

It's really, really bad Feng Shui to have two mirrors endlessly reflecting each other.

There's a strong possibility that they might create a black hole in space, and suck your living room into a parallel universe.

Skylights allow good spirits to escape.

If you must have them, don't sit under them. When a clatter load of burglar's happens to be running along your roof, they might fall in on top of you.

Miss Watson couldn't continue any further because she had tears running down her face. Pauline sat in silence while her teacher continued to laugh. Eventually she gained enough composure to speak. "Pauline, you have a wonderful talent for writing. Your English teacher Miss Mooney was called away unexpectedly to deal with a family emergency yesterday, so she asked me to speak to you about your writing abilities."

"I'm not in trouble, am I?" Pauline had visions of being expelled *again.*

"No, Pauline, you're not in any trouble, far from it. Miss Mooney would like to put your name down for the creative writing course, which starts next term. As I said, you have the talent, it just needs polishing."

"Miss Watson, I love writing and I'm, I'm glad you app- rove." Pauline replied, stuttering slightly. She was ecstatic, they liked her writing!

Fifteen

Paddy phoned Jimmy and asked him to join him for a pint. He wanted to run something by him. Jimmy was feeling lonely; he was missing Cathy and Imelda. He wished he had gone to London with them, but he wanted Cathy to have some time away with Imelda. A girlie weekend was how Imelda had described it. Get her away from all her recent troubles.

He accepted Paddy's invitation and suggested they meet in the Esplanade Hotel instead of the local pub. Kind as people were, he didn't want to listen to any more commiserations. They arranged to meet at seven o' clock.

Paddy was already in the hotel bar, talking to a small group of people when Jimmy arrived. He politely excused himself from them and joined his friend.

"Evening, Jimmy, it's good to see you again." Paddy greeted Jimmy warmly. He enjoyed his quiet and solid company.

"Paddy, it's good to see you too. Let me get you a pint. That one looks a bit flat."

"Ah, I've just ordered thanks. You *do* still drink Guinness don't you? Or will I change the order?"

"No, that's all right, Paddy, Guinness will be fine thanks. Shall we sit down by the window? It seems a bit quieter over there."

"Good idea. It's a bit crowded in here. I'll be right over."

Paddy collected the drinks and joined his friend by the window overlooking the sea. They sat comfortably together, just two old friends chatting about nothing in particular. Paddy asked how Cathy was getting along, as he hadn't seen her in the yard much lately. Jimmy told him about the trip to London and Paddy agreed that a break away would do her the world of good.

"Jimmy, it's Cathy I wanted to speak to you about." Paddy chose his words carefully. He was testing the waters.

"Oh, okay. What's on your mind, Paddy?"

"How would you feel about Cathy owning a horse of her own?" Paddy looked his friend in the eye, while he waited for him to answer.

"I never really thought about it. She's never asked me to buy her one."

"Jimmy, I'm not interfering but she needs something to focus on, especially with Pauline out of the picture, if you know what I mean?"

"It's been hard for her Paddy, with Mary gone and Pauline off at the boarding school in Galway. She misses both of them, you know." Jimmy spoke with sadness.

"That's why she needs something to focus on, as I said earlier."

Paddy continued, "You know Major Faircolm, over at the manor, don't you?"

"Yes, I do, but not very well. Why?"

"Jimmy, listen up. His spoilt brat of a granddaughter has upped and gone to live in Florida. Apparently, she met some sort of American attorney when he was on holiday over here during the summer. Two weeks ago, she packed her bags and joined him in Miami and she left her horse in the so-called care of that drunken sot Reilly."

"I don't understand Paddy. What's this got to do with me, or Cathy?" Jimmy was puzzled.

"Well, the Major wants to find a new home for her horse, Dubba. He wants him to be taken care of properly and he's asked me to find him a decent and caring home, with an equally decent rider. Cathy fits that bill."

"Are you suggesting I buy this horse for Cathy?"

"No, Jimmy, that's not what I'm saying. The Major doesn't want to sell Dubba; he wants to give him to the correct person. He doesn't want any money for him." Paddy watched Jimmy's body language.

"Ah, Paddy, I couldn't just accept the horse for Cathy for free, now could I?"

"Jimmy, Dubba is a young horse, with very good conformation, he's an excellent jumper, completely bomb-proof and he's exactly right for Cathy."

Jimmy sat thinking, and Paddy didn't disturb him. He gave him time to absorb what he had just said.

It was not every day a chance like this came up, and Paddy knew the horse was absolutely perfect for Cathy. The Major wouldn't hear of money changing hands for his granddaughters horse. He told Paddy he would feel like he had betrayed Patricia if he sold Dubba.

In truth, Patricia Faircolm had betrayed her grandfather, by treating Dubba in such a bad way. He was heartbroken when she moved to Florida. She was off to marry a Yank that he or his wife, had never even met. Apparently, Mrs Faircolm was so upset she was swallowing copious amounts of Valium, washed down with frequent helpings of brandy, disguised as iced tea. She was fooling no-one. The Major feared his wife might end up in a home for the bewildered in the very near future.

Paddy liked the Major; they went back a long way.

"You know Paddy; you've caught me completely by sur- prise. I have to think this over." Jimmy didn't want to seem ungrateful, but owning a horse was a big responsibility, he wasn't sure that Cathy was ready for such a task.

"Not a problem. Can I get you another pint?" Paddy was glad Jimmy hadn't dismissed the idea completely.

"Yes, Paddy, I'll have another pint, but I think it's my round." Jimmy stood up and went over to the bar. He noticed Moira Byrne sitting with the group of people that Paddy had been talking to when he first arrived. She caught his eye and smiled.

He remembered how Moira and her mother had been absolute bricks when Mary died. They handled all the catering for the funeral and they wouldn't allow Jimmy to do a thing. He wouldn't have known where to have started anyway.

Jimmy always thought Moira was a sensible and attractive young woman, any man would be lucky to get her. *Were Moira and Paddy an item?* His thoughts were interrupted by the barman handing him two fresh pints. When he had paid the young man and left him a decent tip, he returned to his friend.

"There you go Paddy, get that down you."

"Thanks Jimmy."

The two men sat in silence enjoying their pints.

Jimmy watched the wave's crash over the breakwater. He always liked the sound of the sea, it calmed him inwardly. He remembered all the Sunday walks on the esplanade he used to share with his wife and daughter. He smiled at the memories of the journeys up to the crow's nest on the rickety cable car for Sunday lunch. Cathy used to love the cable car; she would laugh loudly and pretend she was flying. *Stop it man, don't do this to yourself. Have a bit of cop on.* He would never forget all the happy days they shared together, but now was not the time for rem- iniscing.

"Paddy, where is the horse at the moment?" Jimmy didn't know one end of a horse from the other, but he felt he should at least see the animal before coming to any decisions.

"He's stabled in my yard, enjoying being back and having the company of other horses. He used to be in livery with me a while ago, but Patricia Faircolm had a bit of a misunderstanding with Tony, so she removed him." Paddy smiled at the memory of Patricia storming into the yard soaking wet, with mascara running down her face and covered from head to toe in mud. She was absolutely furious when Paddy didn't take her side.

Jimmy interrupted Paddy's memories. "Paddy, let me sleep on this, okay? Lord, look at the time, I promised to phone Cathy at eight, she'll be waiting on me. Does she know anything about your ... suggestion?"

"No, she doesn't know anything about it at all. She's hardly been to the yard since Mary died." Paddy let his words drift off.

Jimmy pretended not to notice. "Right, I'll say goodnight to you Paddy. We'll talk soon, and thanks for thinking about Cathy. She's very fond of you, you know."

"Fair enough." Paddy felt slightly embarrassed as he got up to leave.

"Oh, Paddy, will the horse be able to stay at your yard, Cathy couldn't exactly keep him in the back garden now could she?"

"Of course he can. We'll make a plan."

Jimmy left the hotel, and Paddy returned to the group he had been talking to earlier. He stood beside Moira and slid his arm protectively around her shoulder. He wanted to steal her away from her friends and ask her something. What he wanted to say wasn't for the ears of the other members of the group. Quietly, he asked her to join him for dinner, at the new seafood restaurant that had recently opened by the harbour.

Moira thought it was a great idea. She wanted to check out the opposition, so to speak.

They had been going out together for nearly a year, but they kept the relationship quiet. After all, they did work together and theoretically, Paddy was her boss.

Paddy drove in silence to the Captain's Table restaurant. As Moira was getting out of the car, Paddy halted her. "Moira hang on a minute, wait a second or two."

"Sure, what is it? You're very quiet." She studied his face in the dull interior light of his car.

Paddy took her hand. It felt so small, soft and smooth in his weather-beaten and calloused one. "Moira, will you marry me?" Paddy was afraid to look at her in case she rejected him.

"Paddy Murphy, I thought you'd never ask me. Of course I will, and I would be honoured to be your wife."

"You mean it? You really mean it?" Paddy couldn't believe his ears.

"Yes, Paddy, I mean it. I've loved you since the first day I met you."

***

Jimmy phoned his sister as soon as he got home, but Cathy wasn't there. Imelda told him she had gone to the movies with Tammy. Apparently, the two of them were getting on like a house on fire and Jimmy was pleased with that news. His daughter was growing up and he had to accept it. He was glad she was out enjoying herself. When he told his sister about Paddy's suggestion, she thought it was a wonderful idea.

"Jimmy, she's wanted a horse of her own since ... since, well since forever."

This news was more than a surprise to Jimmy. "She's never ever said anything to me about owning her own horse." He

90

wondered just how much he didn't know about his daughter's life, he certainly didn't know about her wants and needs.

"By the way, she's going to have her hair cut tomorrow. You don't mind do you?" Imelda asked carefully, knowing her brother loved Cathy's long red hair and might be reluctant about the makeover.

"If I did, would it make any difference?" Jimmy replied feeling a bit left out.

"No, it wouldn't actually, but it would be nice for her to know that you approved." Imelda had a slight trace of sarcasm in her voice.

"Well then my dearest sister, as long as she doesn't come back looking like one of those punk-rocker types, it's fine."

"Never fear, she had her ears pierced yesterday but the tattoo will have to wait until she's older."

"She's had her ears pierced? What would Mary say?" Jimmy replied in a muted voice.

"Jimmy, Mary is no longer with us. You have to allow Cathy a certain amount of freedom, for her sake, and your own."

"I know, I know, I'll talk to you tomorrow evening. Perhaps my daughter might be available to speak to me then." Jimmy was feeling like he was on a desert island.

"I'll get her to phone you in the morning. Tammy and her friends are going to a new-age play tomorrow night, and they asked Cathy to go with them."

Imelda's words bit into him hard, *no longer with us.* Mary will never be with us again.

"Fair enough Imelda, that's fine."

"Jimmy, please stop worrying. By the way, the horse would be a marvellous early birthday present for Cathy. Remember, she is going to be *14* next February. Night, brother."

"Bye for now." Jimmy hung up the phone quietly and wondered where all the years had gone. Once again, he thought it seemed like only yesterday when he strolled along the seafront with Mary and Cathy snuggled up in her pram. He looked at his reflection in the hall mirror, and heard a voice shouting furiously inside his head. *When will the pain go away, when will the hurt stop hurting? When ... when ... when?*

***

Jimmy arranged with Paddy to view the horse the following day. Paddy laughed to himself, because Jimmy made it sound like he was previewing a prospective purchase. Perhaps a piece of furniture or an item at an auction. They agreed to meet at two o' clock.

The next day Jimmy stood staring at Dubba.

"Jimmy, he's a beautiful animal." Paddy said as he ran his hand down the horse's dark flank. Jimmy's knowledge of horse-flesh was extremely limited, but anyone could see that Dubba was a stunning horse.

"There's an added bonus, he comes with a saddle and bridle, day and night rugs, travelling gear and a hand-crafted engraved leather head collar. He also comes with a lead rein, the likes of I've not often seen before." Tony added this information freely as he strolled up the centre aisle of the stable block, leading a handsome grey gelding.

Jimmy greeted Tony and then just stood looking at Dubba. The horse had a kindness in his eye which he found hypnotic.

"Paddy, I think Cathy is a very lucky girl." Jimmy said smiling broadly.

"God works in mysterious ways. Cathy deserves him, he's a flippin' good horse and they were made for each other. They'll be perfect together." Tony said as he put the horse he was leading into the adjacent stable.

"Tony's right. Let's go over to my office and we'll have a chat."

"Fair enough. Lead the way." Jimmy patted Dubba and silently welcomed him to the family.

Dubba whinnied softly as Paddy slid the bolt into place on his stable door, and fastened the padlock carefully.

"Why is he padlocked in?" Jimmy enquired.

"Dubba's turned into a master escape artist. He can slide that bolt open quicker than you can say Houdini." Paddy was laughing.

Over a cup of tea, the two men discussed livery rates and they came to an amicable and reasonable agreement. Paddy was quite insistent that over the weekends and during the school holidays, Cathy should take care of her new horse herself. He also suggested she should take part in some of the lectures on stable management along with his apprentices. Jimmy thought Paddy was on the ball.

***

Cathy and Imelda landed in Dublin airport at seven-thirty the following Monday evening. Their flight had arrived on time, and Jimmy waited patiently in the arrival's hall. As the arriving passengers filtered through, he searched the sea of faces. Then he spotted Imelda in the distance with a young lady beside her. *Where's Cathy? Good God that is Cathy. She looks so, so grown up!* He realised with a pang of trepidation.

Eventually, when Cathy saw her father, she ran up to him and bubbled, "Dad, did you miss me? We had such a brilliant time we went to ..."

Jimmy interrupted her. "Wait up, who are you, do I know you?" he asked, teasing her.

"I take it you approve of her new look Jimmy?" Imelda said amused.

"Approve? I think she looks beautiful." Jimmy was beaming at his daughter.

"Hello, have I suddenly disappeared into another universe?" Cathy butted in loudly.

"Ah, Cathy love, I'm sorry. You look so different, so pretty. I nearly didn't recognise you." Jimmy hugged her so tightly he nearly took the wind out of her.

"Thanks dad, the ugly duckling went to London and a swan came back, huh?" Cathy was embarrassed by her father's public display of affection, especially since the boy she had been chatt- ing to on the short flight, was walking towards them.

"Excuse me. I'll be back in a minute," she announced to both. She marched across the hall to meet the boy. They chatted for a bit and then he boy was gone.

Jimmy looked at Imelda and she shrugged her shoulders. Her eyes said *leave it be; ask no questions and you'll be told no lies.*

Deciding to keep his mouth shut, Jimmy picked up the bags and led the way to the car, with Cathy chatting incessantly.

Imelda walked alongside the pair in silence.

Sixteen

"Hi Pauls, we're back. How's it going at your end? I've loads to tell you. Guess what? Dad didn't even recognise me at the airport." Cathy gushed out, bursting at the seams with all the news she had to relate.

"Slow down, will you. Have you just got in or what?" Pauline knew Cathy was coming home today, Mr Corway had told her the night before. He also told her about Dubba and Pauline was thrilled for Cathy, a little jealous perhaps, but genuinely happy for her friend. If Dubba had been offered to her, she would have had to refuse. Her father would never have agreed to pay the livery fees. Even her mother couldn't swing that one.

They planned a surprise 'unveiling' of Dubba in the stables the next day. It was imperative Cathy didn't speak to anyone else, just in case someone let the cat out of the bag. Imelda was under strict orders to monitor all incoming and outgoing phone calls.

They needn't have worried. When Cathy finished speaking to Pauline, she showered and went straight to bed. She was happily exhausted.

***

"Right, Tony, she'll be here in half an hour, her dad's bringing her over. Imagine, he actually let the air out of the tyres on her bike and hid the pump because she wanted to cycle over on her own. You know, it's hard to think of Mr Corway doing something like that now, isn't it? But I'd say Imelda had a hand in that idea." Pauline was blabbering on to Tony as she gave Dubba the final once over.

"Well, somebody had their thinking cap on then, didn't they?" Tony answered her smartly.

Tony had clipped Dubba the day before; he now sported a very elegant hunter's clip, which suited him really well. Paddy didn't want him to be fully clipped out because Dubba wasn't only an expert at opening stable doors; he was pretty darn good at divesting himself of his field and stable rugs as well.

He instructed Tony to clip just enough off, so he wouldn't lose condition through sweating, while he was being schooled. His mane and tail were expertly pulled by Pauline, and she groomed him until he shone. Between the pair of them, the horse that had previously stood in a field all alone and neglected, was transformed. He now looked a picture of beautiful equine elegance. The final touch was an A4 sized card that Pauline hung around his neck, it read:
Hi Cathy

My name is Dubba
I belong to you now.
You are my new owner.
Shall we go for a ride?

They had him tacked up and ready to go, and he waited patiently for his new owner to arrive. He had tried to remove the invitation from around his neck, but his efforts at equine contortions failed, so he ignored it, and munched away happily on his hay instead.

Jimmy pulled into the stables' car park and let Cathy out. "Bye dad, see you later and thanks for the lift. You know what? I should have gone back riding sooner. Love you." Cathy blew a kiss at her father and scooted off to find Pauline.

As she entered the main yard, she heard a raucous wolf whistle coming from the feed room and blushed bright red.

Tony waylaid her. "Well now, would you look at the get up of Miss Corway? Pauline told me ye had your hair cut and I must say it looks mighty good. It really suits you. Eh, are ye busy tonight?"

"Ah, feck off Tony, the lads are staring at me."

"Well of course they're starin' at ye. Ye go off to London lookin' one way and ye return lookin' like a fancy miss from one of them pricey magazines." Tony never missed a chance to tease.

"Give over Tony. Have you seen Pauline? Is Paddy around?"

"Yeah, you'll find them both in the stables with the new gelding."

"The new gelding? Pauline never said that Paddy bought a new horse."

"Didn't she? It must have slipped her mind. Come along, I'll show him to ye."

Tony was already walking towards the stable block.

"Is he a livery or did Paddy buy him for the school?" Cathy, as usual, wanted to know everything immediately.

"He's a livery." Tony was saying no more.

"Where is he?"

"He's in number four."

Cathy approached the stable where Dubba was waiting for her. "But why is the top door closed?" Cathy was puzzled. This was not normal practice in Paddy's yard.

"Ah, Paddy just wanted him to have a bit of peace and quiet for a few hours, just to let him settle in like."

"Then we shouldn't disturb him, should we?"

"Go ahead, have a quick look at him. He's a good peace of horse flesh and he's a quiet mannerly lad."

Curiosity got the better of her and she undid the top bolt. She noticed a padlock on the ground but she didn't pay much heed to it, she was more interested in meeting the new addition. Then she slid the bottom bolt and opened the door. There was Dubba in all his glory with his hindquarters staring her straight in the face. He didn't even turn around.

"Tony, why is he tacked up? I thought you said Paddy wanted him to have some quiet time?"

Tony shrugged his shoulders and replied, "Am I supposed to know everything? Paddy must have changed his mind. Here, stand back and I'll take him out. Will ye go and get me a hoof pick?"

"Sure, but the word please works wonders, you know."

"Okay, will ye please get me a hoof pick?"

Cathy retrieved the requested pick from a grooming kit at the far end of the stable block and when she turned around, there was her father, Imelda, Mrs Byrne, Moira, Pauline and all the stable staff standing beside the beautiful horse with some- thing around his neck.

"What, what's going on?" she said startled. She still hadn't clicked.

Her father was first to speak. "This horse has a message for you. Come over here and read it."

Cathy slowly approached Dubba and read the sign around his neck. She got as far as *I belong to you now* and she read no more. The walls closed in around her, her mouth watered and she started to shake. Paddy was quick off the mark and he caught her just as she nearly passed out.

She didn't actually faint, she just wobbled. As she gathered herself together, somewhat embarrassed, she heard Tony saying cheekily, "Ah, she's fine. It's the new hair do, that's all."

Cathy recovered quickly and she was all over Dubba like a rash. "He's mine? He's really mine?" She was afraid to believe it.

"Yes, Cathy, he belongs to you now. You do like him, don't you?" Her father asked with a huge grin on his face.

"Like him? He's stunning. But when did you decide ...?"

"The details can wait. Why don't you take him out for a ride and get to know him?"

"Oh, dad, I love you, you're the best." She flung her arms around her father's neck and nearly strangled him with a hug. Then she turned her attention to Dubba. "And you, you are the most wonderful, most stunning horse in the world, and you're all mine!"

Pauline opened a stable door opposite the one Dubba had been hidden in, and led out a grey gelding also tacked up. She had to shout above everyone else because they were all talking at once. "Come on wobbly-guts, let's go riding."

Cathy stopped in her tracks. "Who are you calling wobbly-guts?"

"If the cap fits, wear it." Pauline answered her and burst out laughing.

"Okay, Pauline Dutton, I'll show you. You jump the down-hill and I'll navigate the water fence. We'll soon see who the wobbly-guts is then, won't we?"

"You're on. Let's get going." Pauline mounted her horse and started to walk towards the gate that led to the cross-country course.

Cathy hugged her father once more, she was deliriously happy. She jumped up on Dubba with ease, and followed after Pauline, talking continuously to Dubba.

Everyone was happy to see Cathy so alive.

***

Moira's mother was driving her crazy. As soon as she'd been told about Paddy's marriage proposal, she immediately started planning her daughter's wedding.

At first Moira was happy to allow her mother to commence with the wedding arrangements. She didn't want to burst her bubble. She let her dither on for a while.

Paddy and Moira wanted a small wedding with just a handful of their closest friends and family with them, but her mother was turning the whole affair into a circus.

"Mum it's our wedding, or has that point slipped your mind? We do not want to invite half the flippin' parish. You haven't been off the bloody phone for a week now." Moira knew she was being bitchy, but she had to bring her mother down to earth.

"Moira, you are my only child and I'm not having anyone saying that we skimped on anything."

"Mum, I'm going to say this for the last time. No big wedding reception, no guest list resembling a phone book, no ten-foot-high wedding cake and we don't want, or need to hire the Shelbourne Hotel's Conference Centre."

"Right, you tell me where you are planning to stage this minute wedding reception then?"

"The restaurant here will do just fine."

"Holy Mother of God, you can't be serious. It only seats 30 people."

"Exactly mum. Now give over."

"Moira, be reasonable. What will people say? What will they think?"

"Mum, another word out of you and we'll elope, I'm not joking."

Paddy wanted to build a bungalow for them out in the far paddock, the same one that Stubbs used to graze in. Moira thought it was a wonderful idea and the site her husband-to-be suggested was beautiful. The house would stand surrounded by old oak and copper beech trees. The river would run through what would be the end of the garden. To Moira, it was almost a surreal setting.

They couldn't live and eventually raise a family in Paddy's cottage in the yard, not with half the equestrian fraternity of Wicklow trouncing through it day and night. They had thought about living in the house Paddy owned in Brittas Bay, just until the bungalow was completed, but Brittas was a good hour's drive away and it would be too far to commute on a daily basis. Paddy began his yard duties at five-thirty in the morning and Moira was frequently in the restaurant until well after midnight.

The builder gave them an estimated time of six months, weather permitting, for the completion of the new house. They decided to brave the cottage once they were married, which they planned to be by next February 14.

Paddy agreed that a few new ground rules regarding the cottage 'visitors' would have to be put in place. Moira knew the 'visitors' rules wouldn't last long, but she didn't mind. She wasn't really bothered at all. She would live anywhere with Paddy. However, she had to control her mother.

***

Jimmy saw less and less of his daughter now she had a horse of her own. He wasn't surprised when she asked him if she could give up ballet, she had lost all interest in dancing after her mother died. The added loss of her partner Pauline, whose dancing days had abruptly ended once she had been relocated to Templeton College, didn't help either.

His daughter was happy and contented with her horse, and that pleased him no end.

Jimmy was lonely but he was careful not to show it openly, he couldn't. He threw himself into his work. His business dealings had become his only distraction. He worked longer and longer hours. Unless he was physically and mentally exhausted, he would stay wide-awake for most of the night, deep within his memories. He hated sleeping alone.

When his sister suggested removing Mary's clothes from the wardrobes and cupboards because she thought it would help him with closure, Jimmy became so furious with her that she left well enough alone. He actually told her to mind her own bloody business.

Imelda never mentioned it again.

***

Imelda and Rachael had been planning to open a branch of ImRa in Dublin for over a year. Although it was a bit early for them financially, they decided to go ahead. Imelda really wanted to be based predominantly in Ireland.

She continued to live with her brother and niece. They depended on her and she couldn't abandon them. Painstakingly, she improved Cathy's cooking skills and with her help, Jimmy's ability to iron a shirt became acceptable, not perfect, but acceptable. They all got along surprisingly well.

Rachael understood Imelda's feelings and she encouraged her friend and business partner, to start looking for suitable premises in Dublin and get the ball rolling.

Flying time from Dublin to London only took 55 minutes, which made both cities easily accessible. Between the two of them and their growing number of staff members, they could easily manage another branch. It would be hard on the bank balance, but extensive research had shown them that a new branch in Dublin would be feasible and profitable.

Seventeen

1985

Cathy, at 17, was about to complete her last year in school and in a few months' time she would be writing her final exam's. She was madly in love with Dubba and her boyfriend who she had been seeing for the past six months, came in a close second. His name was Peter Wallis.

His family had relocated back to Ireland from South Africa eight months before. His father Bradley, was a pilot and his mother Shona, was a flight attendant. They left Ireland to work for South African Airways three years previously. His mother had never really settled in Cape Town as she strongly disagreed with the apartheid regime, and constantly hankered after her own kind. When her husband had first suggested they imm-igrate to South Africa, she hadn't realised how badly the political climate would affect her.

Shona, being Shona, voiced her opinions whenever she had the chance, this resulted in the family's movements being closely monitored by the South African authorities. It was definitely time to return to the home country.

Aer Lingus advertised positions for flight and cabin crew in a local Irish newspaper and when the news filtered through to them, they applied without hesitation.

The Wallis's applications were accepted and they were offered very attractive salary packages which included generous relocation costs. They sold their property in the Cape and purchased a house in Greystones, not far from Bray. Peter was enrolled with the 'Christian Brothers' and they all settled into their new life easily.

Shona was a free agent again. She could speak openly and live her life without feeling threatened.

Pauline and John Clancy had been a solid item since their formal dinner date. Everyone was surprised that Pauline had fallen for John and even more surprised that they had stayed together for so long. They were so different in many ways. They actually had a lot in common, but to an outsider, it was hard to see. Pauline was the wild one and John the quieter of the two.

John's older brother Michael had advanced quickly through the ranks as a working jockey with flying colours. He now owned his own small racing yard adjacent to Paddy's Stables. And for John's 16th birthday, he bought him a four-year-old thoroughbred called Shutsy.

Michael bought the horse for a song as he was absolutely useless on the racetrack, but he had the temperament to become a nice riding horse.

Pauline rode Shutsy more than John did, but Michael didn't mind. When Pauline was home at school holidays, she would ride Shutsy out with Cathy and Dubba. They would go for long hacks through the pine forests. The girl's favourite ride during the summer months entailed taking a packed lunch with them. When they reached their favourite spot beside the lake, they would remove the horse's saddles and tether them safely on a long lead rein. Then the two girls would eat their lunch at a leisurely pace and they often enjoyed a spot of sunbathing while the horse's relished on the lush green grass.

It was by the lake that Cathy first met Peter. He had strolled through the woods with John. John knew exactly where to find the girls and he wanted to use the opportunity to introduce Peter to Cathy. Peter was immediately taken with Cathy and she thought he was gorgeous.

At first, they dated infrequently, but it didn't take long before they were like the proverbial peas in a pod. The circle had widened. Cathy no longer felt like the odd one out. She was no longer the three in three's company. She had a real boyfriend of her own, and it felt good about it.

Peter had no real interest in horses; his particular passion was with motorbikes'. His parents had purchased him a Honda 250cc when he turned 17. Initially, his parents were convinced that every time he drove off they would never see him alive again.

Peter proved them wrong. He nearly always drove sensibly. He had only had one accident to date, and it had not been his fault. He had caught the front wheel of his bike on the tow bar of the neighbour's car as she reversed out of her driveway. The car escaped unscathed and Peter's bike only suffered some minor damage.

Nobody was hurt so his parents let it go and from then on, the neighbour reversed her car a lot more carefully. Peter had frightened the life out of her. The poor woman thought she had killed him.

Cathy's father had expressly forbidden her to ride pillion with Peter and she didn't, at least not when he was around. She would meet Peter away from her house and out of her dad's sight, but she was caught out on more than one occasion. Jimmy's customers often relayed sightings of the young couple roaring down the dual carriageway, or wherever else their prying eyes captured them together. It caused a lot of friction between father and daughter at first, but eventually Jimmy got used to the idea.

***

"Listen, Pauls, I've got brilliant news. Dad is going to London with Imelda at the weekend, and I'm going to have the house all to myself," Cathy told her friend excitedly.

Then both girls sang out in unison, *"FREE HOUSE."*

"Pauls, lets have a party."

"Cathy, that's a smashing idea. When are they going?"

"Are you deaf? I said at the weekend. They're booked on a special-offer-type thingy to discover London's theatre scene or something, leaving on Friday and coming back on Sunday."

"When did you find this out?"

"Just now, Rachael phoned Imelda. Some client or other gave them the tickets as a Christmas pressy' or bonus, whatever."

"Is this Imelda's latest attempt to broaden your dad's social life?" Pauline found it amusing that Imelda still tried to get her brother interested in other pastimes, besides work.

"Yeah, she doesn't give up easily, now does she? She means well though."

"Yeah she does. Listen I'll see you this evening. I have to go into Dublin with mum this morning. She wants me to help her with some Christmas shopping. You know what she's like. It'll take up the entire day and shit Cathy, I've an atrocious hang-over. How's your head?" Pauline enquired; silently wishing Cathy would speak a little quieter.

"Not too bad now but when I woke up I felt awful," Cathy replied truthfully. She had been extremely drunk when she came home in the early hours of the morning. The party they had been at had turned out to be a lively affair. "It was a good night though, wasn't it? What time did you and John get home?"

"Don't know, but the bird population was just waking up. Who cares? Hey, I have to go, talk later, bye." Pauline hung up the phone abruptly, her mother was calling her.

***

Jimmy had reservations about leaving Cathy on her own while he went skiving off to London's West End. Imelda told him he was being stupid as Cathy wasn't a child anymore and she blatantly refused to take no for an answer. He was coming with her and that was that.

Jimmy knew he would never hear the end of it, so he agreed reluctantly.

Cathy assured him she'd be perfectly fine. Pauline would stay over with her and they would look after everything. She accused him of being a boring old fuddy-duddy fossil.

Cathy phoned Peter and his mum answered the phone. She told her he was still sleeping but she would wake him up with pleasure as she also wanted to speak to him.

Shona was not at all happy. She had just received an unexpected call from the airline. They needed her to fill in for another long-haul attendant who had come down with a particularly bad case of malaria.

Normally, emergency call outs didn't bother her, but this time it did, she was on official leave. Leave that she had put in for last Christmas. A virulent dose of flu was plaguing the airline staff and half the country to boot, so she couldn't turn them down.

Cathy said she would phone back later as Peter would probably be in a grumpy mood and he wouldn't remember the conversation anyway. Shona agreed with Cathy on those two points. Her son's social life was worrying her, but she didn't have time to think about it just then. She would broach the subject regarding his inability to study when she got back.

Her husband was flying the Miami/Rio/London route over the Christmas season and was of no use to her, so she would have to deal with Peter on her own, as usual.

Later that evening the four friends met up in the Wimpy on the seafront to discuss the up-and-coming Christmas bash.

Pauline's day with her mother had been hectic and her hangover stubbornly lingered on.

Earlier on, Cathy had *borrowed* a bottle of vodka from her Dad's drinks cupboard and disguised it in a plain brown paper bag. As they were still under age, she was careful not to be caught pouring healthy tots into the glasses of coke. Before long, all the hangovers were magically cured and another boozy evening was launched. The bottle of vodka didn't last long.

The waitress gave them some peculiar looks and reminded them there was a minimum ordering rate after eight o' clock and three orders consisting of four cokes did not qualify. She wanted to get them out as they were getting a bit rowdy. She didn't mean to be rude, but if her boss discovered four teenagers drinking on the premises she would be in serious trouble.

Peter suggested that they go back to his house. There wasn't anyone at home and they could watch the videos that his dad brought back from his last trip. They agreed to meet up there in an hour as Pauline wanted to go and find her 'pal' who supplied her with marijuana and when John weakly protested because he didn't like her smoking that stuff, Pauline ignored him. She wasn't going to be stopped. He had one of two choices - like it or lump it.

John lumped it and shut up. They both took a detour by 'The Monks' shabby house down by the harbour. He insisted on going with her. Pauline could be annoyingly stubborn at times. John thought those people were very shady characters. He became even more pissed off when she wouldn't allow him to come inside. *She* insisted that he wait outside as 'The Monk' had promised her a further 24-hour extension on her credit, he was going to supply her with something new. This, she didn't want John to know about.

Eighteen

For the party, the girls had packed away the valuables in Cathy's house, just in case. As both of them were practically broke, they agreed not to buy each other Christmas presents. They would spend their limited funds on party eats instead.

Peter raided his mother's pantry and his father's drinks cabinet. He hoped they wouldn't notice.

John brought his music collection. He couldn't sneak any munchies or alcohol out of his house, his mother would have immediately copped on. Instead, he persuaded his brother Michael to buy him a decent quantity of booze.

Michael had been a bit on the wild side when he was younger and he didn't agree with his younger brother's early drinking, but how could he stop him? He knew John would find alternative means of getting provisions so he decided to save him the trouble.

Pauline's mother was working hard preparing for her own Christmas party and she wanted it to be well remembered, especially by her husband. He maintained it was a waste of good money to give the neighbours' a night out at his expense, but she liked entertaining and didn't care two hoots how he felt.

When the girls told her they were having a few friends over on Friday night, she vowed to keep it to herself. She didn't see any harm in it, and she promised to make them some nibbles.

***

All the preparations were finished and the four friends expected the guests to arrive about ten o' clock. By eleven o'clock, the house was still empty. Pauline started blaming Cathy and Cathy started blaming everyone.

"John, who did you invite?" Cathy demanded.

"Just a few of the lads from school and so on. You didn't give us a lot of time now did you?" John answered defensively.

"Ah, that's brilliant, just fecking brilliant," Cathy retorted and she flounced off towards the kitchen to pour herself a drink. As she left the room she shouted back, "Anyone want some A-L-C-O-H-O-L?"

Pauline was sitting on the back doorstep smoking a joint.

"Shit, Pauls, where is everyone? Feck it, let me try some of that."

"Hello, is this a new Cathy Corway before me? I thought you didn't approve."

"I don't, but I might as well try something different. This so-called party is a complete flop."

"Relax, will you? You worry too much. Here you go, inhale deep and hold it in for as long as you can."

Just a short while before midnight, the doorbell rang. John answered it. Five guys he didn't know stood on the doorstep shivering. Three were wearing bike leathers.

"Hi there, Sandy invited us. We brought some booze. Is there any food? We're bloody starving." Before John had a chance to answer, they brushed right past him as if he wasn't there. He didn't know anybody called Sandy.

A few minutes later, the doorbell rang again. Standing on the step were two couples John did know and they were freezing. It was bitterly cold outside.

"What kept you? Come in, come in," John said with relief as he opened the door wider.

After that the bell continued ringing, so they left the door open despite the biting wind. By twelve-forty-five, the house was bursting at the seams with a variety of party animals, some of whom appeared sober, and some definitely not.

Cathy ended up sitting in the kitchen sink with a bowl of crisps between her knees. She was oblivious to her surroundings and just wanted to stuff her face silly.

Peter was pissed out of his mind, but he was trying to talk some lads into moving their bikes because they had parked them on the front lawn. He didn't get very far as they wouldn't listen to him, so he shrugged and gave up. He stumbled through the packed house in search of Cathy; he hadn't seen her for a while.

Sheila Keating waylaid him and he stopped to talk to her. She was wearing a very short skirt and a very tight boob tube. *Boy does she look different out of school uniform,* he thought lecherously.

Looking over Sheila's shoulder, he saw Cathy glaring at him. She had prised herself out of the kitchen sink to find out who the hell let the skanky-looking creeps in, especially the one in particular who had been attempting to chat her up. He had told Cathy he was from Brazil and he was skilled in the art of lovemaking. Apparently, in his eyes, she was a goddess and should be worshipped. Cathy told him he was nothing more than a scumbag and in her country, he would most definitely work on the docks. She didn't expect to see Peter with his arm glued around Sheila Keating's waist. Peter swore he didn't know how his arm got there.

Cathy was having none of it. She turned her anger on Sheila. "If you want to go around wearing a skirt. Actually that's not a skirt, it's a fanny pelmet. Oh, just go somewhere else and stay away from my boyfriend you cow bag."

Sheila shrugged her shoulders unperturbed. To add insult to injury she winked seductively at Peter suggesting that she would see him later on. This outraged Cathy even further.

"Don't say a word, not a word you bastard. If you want to flirt, go right ahead. But do you have to do it in front of our friends and with the village bicycle? Jesus, Peter, she's not called 'the dartboard' for nothing. As a matter of fact, she could suck a golf ball through a hosepipe. Now piss off."

The music suddenly stopped and the house was plummeted into a deafening silence.

"Hello, boys and girls, now where's Pauline Dutton?" The stunned silence remained. "Ah come on now lads and lassies, I know she's here somewhere, or do I have to find her meself?" A man's deep voice shouted.

Silence prevailed. "One more time, where is Pauline Dutton?" The man's voice said again, this time even louder.

Michael Clancy had just arrived and he had intended his visit to be short and sweet, but when he heard what was going on, he stepped up to the man. He knew him from way back and he despised him. He knew his name was 'The Monk' and he also knew what his business dealings entailed.

"Excuse me, but this is a private party and I think you and your lads should leave," Michael suggested to 'The Monk' in a non-aggressive tone.

"Ye think we should leave. Did ye hear that lads?" 'The Monk' stepped closer to Michael.

The lads surrounded him. "Yeah, we heard him, Monk. He wants to show us the door, ha, ha, ha."

"Now, listen here rasher legs, I'll leave when I'm good and ready. And a little word of advice, mind your own fuckin' business. Go on back to your gee-gees like a good little lad and get out of me fuckin' way. Where is the little bitch? She owes me money and I want it NOW." 'The Monk' yelled at no-one in particular.

Michael held his temper. He hardly ever resorted to violence. "You're upsetting people Monk, this is a private party and I didn't see your name on the guest list."

"Oh, didn't ye, eh? Well, it's on the VIP list laddy. Now move it. Outta me way."

Pauline was listening to the scene unfold from upstairs. A short while earlier she had gone up to Cathy's bedroom to snort a line of coke from the supply 'The Monk' had given her. *Jesus Christ, what's he doing here?* She still owed him money. He had supplied her three days ago and she was supposed to have paid him yesterday. Nervously, she shouted down the stairs.

"Monk wh … what's up? Why are you … you here?"

"Ah, there ye are me little beauty. Nothin's up, now is it? We're just performin' a bit of debt collectin' that's all."

"Monk, this isn't a good time. Can we talk about this later?"

"It's not a good time, is it not me sweety? I think you're havin' a very good time at my expense. Don't ye agree lads?"

Michael intervened. "You heard the young lady. This is not a good time, will you all please leave."

"You again? Shut your fuckin' mouth or I'll shut it for ye."

"Right, if that's the way you want it we'll let the authorities handle this. John, get up off your arse and call the cops."

"No need to, they're here already," John said in a horrified voice.

The crowd separated as two burly uniformed police officer's strolled into the hallway. They had been cruising by, as Cathy's dad had asked them to keep an eye on the place while he was away. He hadn't mentioned anything about a rowdy get-together in his absence.

From her vantage point on the landing, Pauline thought the scene downstairs looked like a rehearsal from a play depicting a demonic parting of the Red Sea.

"Evening all and what have we here?" Sergeant Molloy addressed everybody in general.

"Sergeant Molloy, it's always a pleasure to see ye. We're just havin' a quiet little family get-together in view of the season and all," 'The Monk' said through thin lips and tobacco stained gritted teeth.

"It doesn't look friendly to me. Mick, turn on the lights," the sergeant ordered.

I don't believe this, Pauline mouthed to Cathy's upturned pleading face.

The silence was broken by the scurrying sounds of the other guests stuffing beer bottles anywhere that was immediately available.

"Ah, Cathy, does your father know about this gathering of the clans?" Sergeant Molloy asked kindly enough.

Cathy's stomach churned. "I think I'm going to be sick." She didn't have time to get through the crowd, her stomach reacted violently and she threw up on the floor, right in front of the sergeant.

"This party is over," the sergeant informed the shocked party dwellers.

"Right, let's go. It's time you were all tucked up in your own beds. Move along now," the assisting officer ordered, changing into his crowd control mode.

"And what do we have here?" The sergeant said coldly, picking up a butt from an overflowing ashtray. "Mick, call for back up. Nobody is going anywhere."

Nineteen

'The Monk' was arrested on the spot, for possession of illegal substances. The sergeant decided to deal with his accomplices later. He already had a large group of intoxicated minors on his hands and not enough manpower to deal with the situation effectively. The lads could wait, he had his kingpin exactly were he wanted him, in custody.

The four party hosts were taken to the police station for questioning by two young female officers. The other guests were given a firm talking-to about under age drinking and sent off with a solid warning.

The police doctor was called to take blood samples from the four detainees.

Pauline tested positive for cocaine, marijuana and alcohol. She had forgotten about the other line of coke she had shoved into her jeans pocket in her panic earlier. She was charged with possession of, and flagrant use of illegal substances, plus under age alcohol consumption.

Cathy and Peter tested positive for marijuana and alcohol. They were charged with under age drinking and illegal substance abuse.

John's blood test contained no illegal substances, just a small amount of alcohol. He was congratulated on his sensibility and immediately released with a stern, but reasonably friendly warning. But he wanted to stay with Pauline as she was terribly frightened, so the sergeant permitted him to sit with her for a while.

As Cathy's father was out of the country, the sergeant was in a bit of a quandary as to what he should do with her. He didn't want to keep her at the station overnight because her father was a friend of his, but he was going to detain Peter. He didn't like, or trust him and he knew both his parents were away somewhere, probably overseas.

Michael came to Cathy's rescue. After a brief discussion with the duty officer and the sergeant, he was permitted to sign her out on bail.

The sergeant trusted Michael. He'd had his run-ins with him when he was younger, but that was in the past. Michael was a good lad, he still had a few wild moments but he was a decent chap nevertheless.

Assuring the sergeant he would look after Cathy, he drove his sorry looking brother and Cathy home to his parents' house. His mother burst into tears when the night's revelries were recounted to her.

How would she live this down? What would the neighbours' say? Where did she go wrong? What had she done to deserve this? She cuffed John hard on his ear and told him to get up to his bed; she didn't want to look at him. *How could he associate with drug addicts, and drunkards?*

She ensconced Cathy in the spare bedroom as if she was something untouchable.

Cathy didn't care. Her stomach was rolling around like a rough sea and she felt horribly sweaty. She barely made it to the bathroom before everything erupted in an acidic volcano. Afterwards, she lay down on the bathroom floor and cried.

John heard her sobs and his heart went out to her. He knocked on the bathroom door. "Cathy, are you okay?" No answer, so he knocked louder.

"Cathy, answer me, are you okay?"

Eventually, Cathy opened the door. She looked a fright. Her face was literally green and her hair was matted with vile-smelling vomit down one side.

"John, get back to your room. I will deal with Cathy Corway," his mother roared from the top of the stairs.

John did as he was told. He couldn't do anything else.

"Cathy Corway, if your poor mother could see you now."

Cathy weakly interrupted her. "Mrs Clancy, please leave my mother out of this."

Mrs Clancy just tutted and shook her head. She gave her a voluminous nightdress, a pile of towels, and told her to have a shower.

When the duty sergeant phoned Pauline's house later that night, Celia answered the phone. She came to collect Pauline on her own and she was furious. Pauline had never seen her so angry. She didn't think her mother was capable of such wrath.

"Pauline, get into the car and don't open your mouth, or I swear I won't be held responsible for my actions. You have gone too far. How could you do this? No, don't answer me."

"Mum ..."

"I said don't open your mouth."

"Mum, I can explain."

"Apparently, you'll be explaining yourself to the magistrate tomorrow morning, and I hope you are happy with yourself."

"Mum ..."

"Shut up, Pauline."

Celia physically shook with anger and mortification. Her daughter had been arrested on drug related charges and she was to appear in the magistrates' court tomorrow morning at ten o' clock.

She had been released with a hefty bail; Sheamus was going to have a fit.

Michael collected Cathy at six o' clock the following morning. He took her home and let her change her clothes. He now sat at the back of the courthouse alongside Pauline, and her mother. Her father refused to have anything to do with her, and John was nowhere to be seen.

Peter sat with Cathy and the social worker Mrs Coughlihan who had been hurriedly assigned to all three cases. Peter's parents had been contacted by the airline, and his mother was flying in on the eight o' clock flight from London later that evening.

As Peter had spent the night in the station, Mrs Coughlihan kindly drove him home earlier to shower and change before the proceedings got under way. He was in a sorry state, and terribly hung over.

She wasn't given a lot of time to assess her new cases but she did the best she could under the circumstances.

Due to the staggering amount of seasonal offenders, an emergency session had been arranged in the local courthouse for the Saturday morning. This was not normal practice, but the station barracks could not handle all the additional riff-raff, defending drunken-driving charges, public disturbances, theft and other offences that always multiplied around the Christmas season.

The extra session did not please the Magistrate at all, and when Mrs Coughlihan asked him to have her adolescent cases postponed, her request was denied. The Magistrate told her resolutely that he would deal with them today.

While the proceedings got under way, Pauline, Cathy and Peter sat in silence.

Eventually their turn came and Cathy's name was called first.

"How old are you Miss Corway?" The Magistrate asked her sternly.

"I'm ... I'm seven ... seventeen, you ... your Lordship," Cathy answered. She was completely petrified.

The Magistrate looked over his glasses, patiently ignoring her misuse of his title. He muttered something, but no-one actually heard, as he was reading the charge sheets.

Cathy stood frozen to the spot. All of a sudden, he bellowed, "As this is your first offence, which I am taking into consideration, you will serve two months' community service, to be completed at the local D.S.P.C.A. I hope that the plight of unfortunate and neglected animals will help show you the error of your ways. Clerk, I will hear the next case if you please."

It was all over, just like that!

Peter was given a similar sentence. Then the Magistrate read Pauline's charge sheet, took off his glasses and stared hard at her.

"Miss Dutton, you have very serious charges laid against you. What have you to say for yourself?"

"No ... nothing ... Your Worship. I have nothing to say." Pauline's words nearly choked her.

The Magistrate studied her further. Eventually he spoke, very slowly and very clearly. "In view of the gravity of the situation that you have unashamedly put yourself in, and taking into consideration the fact that you are a minor, I can refer you to be tried by a higher court. Alternatively, you can choose to be sentenced by this court. What do you say Miss Dutton?"

All Pauline heard was the words higher court. *Oh God, I'm going to be sent to prison.*

"Miss Dutton, the court requires your decision." The Magistrate bellowed out not seeing Mrs. Coughlihan's attempt to attract his attention. "Miss Dutton, do not waste the court's time, your decision, please."

Pauline stared at him for a short time longer and then she stuttered, "I ... I think I wou ... would prefer you to sen ... sen ... sentence me."

The Magistrate put his glasses back on, folded his hands over and over as if he was trying to dry wash some imaginary filth from them and said, "Miss Dutton, you will be removed from my courthouse for further psychological evaluation and this case will be postponed until I have studied the relevant reports." Then the Magistrate turned to his clerk. "Mrs. Coughlihan is the defendant's social worker, is she not?"

The court clerk checked his paperwork and answered, "Yes, Your Worship, she is indeed."

"Very well, and I presume she is present in court?"

The clerk looked up and saw the social worker standing beside a now white-faced Pauline. "Yes, Your Worship, she is here."

"Please call her forward. I want to speak to her in my chambers. You can announce a recess for 30 minutes."

"The court calls Mrs Coughlihan, State Social Worker to the Magistrate's chambers. Court will resume in 30 minutes."

***

Pauline's evaluation proved that she had developed a serious drug dependency problem. She was committed to a state rehabilitation centre for a minimum of 12 weeks, effective immediately. Her parents were dumb founded - especially her mother.

Jimmy was horrified with his daughter. It took Imelda a while, but eventually she calmed her brother down.

In her opinion, Cathy should also spend some time in a programme. She thought her niece had never openly grieved for her mother, and she felt she had some underlying issues to resolve. She suggested she spent some time in 'Belvedere Heights' in London, after she had written her final school exams.

Jimmy was doubtful at first and once again, he wished Mary were by his side. He needed her opinion. Deep down he felt his sister was right, but if Cathy did not co-operate, there would be no point in sending her anywhere.

Peter just disappeared. It was as if he never existed. When Cathy tried to contact him, his mother told her he had been sent to a boarding school in England. She refused to give her any further information.

Cathy was sure Peter would get in contact with her sometime soon. But he didn't. She felt very let down and heartbroken. She had no one to turn to, Pauline had been immediately whisked off for her evaluation straight from the courthouse. She had not seen her in nearly two weeks, and Pauline's family continued to be very tight lipped about the matter.

Cathy turned to her solid and always understanding friend, her horse Dubba. He never passed judgement on her and he was an excellent listener.

Twenty

Cathy found her final exams tough going, but she passed them reasonably well. She agreed to visit 'Belvedere Heights' for a week, and participate in the course they offered on 'Discovering the True Self'.

Initially, Cathy wanted to strangle Imelda, but to her surprise, her visit to the clinic was extremely pleasant and beneficial. She stayed on for six weeks. Her career evaluation and summary showed she should seek a future in the tourist/hospitality industry. Her psychologist suggested she should seriously take into consideration the option of becoming a flight attendant

Cathy had never even thought about a career in such a field before. She had previously been considering a career in equine science, much to Paddy's delight, but the lure of far-off places caught her imagination wholeheartedly.

Imelda and her staff investigated many airlines and 'Shamrock Air' seemed the logical answer. She would be based in Dublin and could move into the spare bedroom of Imelda's flat in Swords.

Imelda only used her flat once or twice a week, the remainder of the time she stayed with her brother in Bray. She hadn't any particular 'special' man in her life. Her only other prominent commitment, besides her family, was her company ImRa. Therefore, the new living arrangements suited all.

Jimmy was happy with the way things were turning out, and Cathy thought the idea of having her own place in Dublin was extremely liberating.

When she applied to 'Shamrock Air', she found she matched the criteria.

Min 5'3" in height.

Outgoing, enthusiastic and friendly.

Eligible to work in Europe, with an unrestricted worldwide pass- port.

Clear and confident communicator.

Fluent in English and Irish.

Physically fit and able swimmer.

Eighteen years of age.

She was accepted for the pre-selection training course in Dublin.

It was an extensive course, consisting of five weeks in the classroom combined with a period of flying under supervision. In addition to her comprehensive training, she received courses in safety and emergency procedures, customer service, first aid, personal development and grooming. Her progress was closely monitored by the airline and she was assessed at each stage. Eight weeks after completion, she received a letter from the airline offering her a contract.

She accepted happily. Cathy had been given wings.

As she didn't have any rent to pay (Imelda wouldn't hear of it) and she had no need to buy a car just yet, because the airline provided a staff drop-off and collection service within the Dublin area, Cathy knew she could survive financially, if she was reasonably frugal.

Owning her own car would have been the icing on the cake, but her meagre salary was prohibitive, and Dubba's monthly livery costs drained her budget considerably, but she managed. Not only did she have crew wings, she still had her beloved Dubba.

Cathy found her first year challenging and personally rewarding. She enjoyed her new-found independence, but the Dublin/Shannon/London route bored her; she hankered after places and countries further afield.

Her second year saw her embark on routes to North and South America.

Dubba, unfortunately, had to take a back seat. He remained in livery at Paddy's, but livery was expensive. Paddy ran a business, not a charity, but he did reduce his livery fees by half. In return, Cathy permitted him to use Dubba in the riding school. She wasn't happy with the arrangement at first, but at least she would be able to keep Dubba in the manner that he had become accustomed to.

Her thoughts of rekindling her relationship with Peter had long fallen away. After her terrifying appearance in court, the entire family had moved, and Cathy didn't know where they went. They just upped and vanished. It was as if they had never existed.

On a rare three-day holiday in Miami, Cathy discovered the world of scuba diving. She had felt guilty about taking the holiday in the first place, Dubba usually came first, but if she didn't use up her free staff flights, she would lose them.

On her return to Ireland, she was rostered for the next seven weeks on the Dublin/London/Paris route. One morning while waiting in the staff lounge she saw an advertisement in the newspaper announcing a scuba-diving club in Dalkey, just outside Dublin which was starting a new six-week training course.

Immediately she put her name down and started her training the following Wednesday. It was during this training course that Cathy met Kevin Cassidy. He worked as an aircraft engineer with 'Aer Lingus' and a voluntary scuba-diving instructor with the Dalkey Scuba Diving club.

During the twice-weekly training sessions (one hour dedicated to theory, and the other pool training) Kevin watched her closely. Cathy didn't notice him in the beginning, but she did notice him six weeks later when she was taking her one star diving test.

One of the disciplines, which had to be passed 100 percent, was swimming the length of the pool underwater on a single breath. Cathy hated chlorine in her eyes and when it was her turn, she dived in and kept her eyes firmly shut. She swam the length of the pool but she did it in a ziz-zag fashion. When she spluttered to the surface, she was no more than six inches away from the finishing rope. Taking several gasps of air, she saw Kevin Cassidy with a huge watermelon grin on his face and he was signalling her to go back and start again.

The rescue diver in the pool told her she didn't complete her pool length in the specified time.

"Ah, come on now," Cathy replied, complaining bitterly.

He wasn't interested in her protestations. "Have one more try and this time keep your damn eyes open."

Fuck you, thought Cathy as she returned to the other end of the pool. Taking three very deep breaths, she dived in once more. This time she kept her eyes open and reached the rope effortlessly and well within the time allowed.

"Well done. Now if you had kept your eyes open on your first attempt, you wouldn't have had to repeat it," Kevin said cheekily.

"Did I pass?" Cathy wanted to know.

"Yes, you did."

"Thanks," she said, as she flounced off to the showers.

The following weekend had been scheduled for the trainees to experience their first open-water sea dive. The entire group was booked into a small diving hotel in Hook Head, all part of the course, and one experienced diver was allotted two trainees for the duration of the weekend.

Again, Dubba pulled at her heartstrings, but she had to complete her first proper dive.

Cathy had thought the equestrian fraternity polished off beer quickly enough, but these people put them to shame. On the Friday night the bar games started with 'row the boat' selected first. To save any unnecessary laundry, the participants, mostly trainees, were advised they should play topless. One girl stupidly complied.

Brainless cow, how could she be so thick? Cathy thought. She remained an observer. The girl was so drunk she was embarrassing.

The next morning before the pre-dive briefing, her senior buddy partner told the girl he was not allowing her to dive because she was clearly and disgustingly hung-over. The girl reacted by protesting violently to the dive master Keith Lowry, who was also the owner of the dive school.

"Discipline my dear girl, if you can't be trusted to stay reasonably sober the night before a dive, how can you be trusted as a diving buddy? Plan a dive and dive the plan. You are not a child, so stop behaving like one," Keith Lowry answered her smugly.

"And you can talk, you randy fucker. You didn't say that last night when you plied me with drink in an effort to get into my knickers, now did you?"

She knew she was being childish but her disappointment was worse than her hangover.

"The difference being, I am not a trainee my dear girl," replied Keith even more smugly. That did it, she'd had enough. "Oh, rev up and fuck off, Mr Wonderful."

Cathy actually liked Keith as an instructor, even though he thought he was he was God's glorious gift to all women.

Later on back in the bar, Kevin defended him. "He's right. We're not babysitters, we're dive instructors."

Cathy silently agreed with him.

They had another casualty later on. Another trainee hit the dust, literally. He drank so much he convinced himself he could fly like Superman. Somehow, he managed to launch himself out of the tiny window in his third-floor hotel room. Occasionally, alcohol does have some benefits; his only injury was a dislocated shoulder.

The big tough dive instructors', Kevin Cassidy included, collectively decided it would be safer if they brought the now sorry-for-himself trainee to the emergency department in the nearby hospital. They tried, pissed as farts, to put him in someone's car and bumped his injured shoulder so hard they managed to put it back in its place. Due to the 'instant fix', the trainee forgot all about his attempted flight, plus its painful consequences and promptly headed straight back to the bar. The glorious instructors' ignored the fact, that besides the shoulder injury, he might have suffered a serious concussion. Needless to say, he was not allowed to dive the next morning either.

Later than evening, more bar games commenced and Cathy went into the snooker room in search of a sober partner.

Kevin followed her. "What's up? Is the company not good enough?" He was delighted he had cornered her on her own. However, he was wrong, they were not alone. The 'wonderful' Keith Lowry was out cold underneath the snooker table snoring quietly. He acquired the nickname of 'pocket' that night and many photographs were taken of him in various positions, some with adornments.

Cathy became snotty with Kevin about the one rule for *you* and one rule for *us* syndrome. When Kevin replied *we are the experienced divers remember*, Cathy slapped him.

A big mistake on Cathy's part.

In the back of the hotel car park, there was a huge water trough, the divers used it to rinse off their equipment and it was always kept full to the brim with fresh cold water.

Kevin, still smarting from Cathy's slap, decided she needed a little cooling down. When she reappeared in the bar after her episode with him, four burly male divers pounced upon her. They carried her kicking and screaming out to the car park and dumped her in the bath. It was an unusually cold summer's evening and the water was freezing.

Cathy's roommate Meranda Quigley had her room key and reception didn't have a spare. But Meranda wasn't in the hotel. She was in the next village with one of the other trainees. Kevin felt guilty when he saw Cathy shivering, and offered her his own room key so she could sort herself out.

Cathy accepted it gladly.

When she opened the door to Kevin's room she was outraged. His room was far superior to hers. It had an en-suite bathroom. Her room didn't have one at all. *Well now, Mr. Experienced Diver... to hell with you,* Cathy thought locking the door. She moved one of the beds solidly up against it and enjoyed a long hot shower. She borrowed a clean tee shirt from a bag haphazardly flung on the floor. It came down to her knees but she didn't mind. She was dry and she was warm. Then she climbed into the spare bed and went to sleep.

As she was used to catnapping on different aircraft, the ensuing racket later on outside on the landing, didn't bother her in the slightest and she had an excellent night's sleep.

At six o' clock the next morning, she tiptoed back to her allotted room, wearing only the borrowed tee shirt and a smile.

Meranda eventually opened up for her saying sleepily, "What the?"

"Don't ask, don't say a word."

***

On returning to work the following Monday, Cathy proudly showed the other crewmembers her 'Irish Underwater Council

Club' Diver Certificate and logbook. Some were genuinely impressed and avidly questioned her; others showed polite disinterest. Cathy didn't care; she was happy and proud of herself.

But her route was disappointingly unchanged. Yet again, the Dublin/London/Paris was her schedule for the next four days.

When she flew back to Dublin the following afternoon after having an unscheduled overnight stopover in Paris, her supervisor grounded her for two weeks for not following airline regulations.

Apparently, she had breached a strict safety precaution, by not informing the airline she had been scuba diving prior to recommencing duty. She was sternly reminded about regulations that stated she was required to leave a 24-hour window between her last dive and her next embarkation. Even though her officially stamped logbook clearly showed her dive date, duration and dive depth, it was of no use. Her supervisor was adamant, she was in the wrong. She penalised her with a 14-day suspension without pay and there was nothing she could do about it, except appeal. She didn't bother arguing any further.

Twenty-One

Imelda was in the kitchen when Cathy let herself into the flat.

"Well, hello there stranger. I'm making coffee, would you like a cup?"

"Oh yes, please. You won't believe what's happened to me."

"What? What's going on? Are you off-duty?"

"Yep, I am, for the next 14 days."

"What do you mean?"

"Let me get changed and I'll fill you in."

"Right, don't be long; I have a meeting in an hour."

"No worries, I'll be quick."

Cathy returned wearing a pair of jeans and a tee shirt. She had quickly removed her make-up and her hair was brushed casually back from her face.

Imelda was sitting by the window and she thought Cathy looked beautifully fresh and vibrant. *Where had all the years gone? It seemed like only yesterday when she accompanied me to London and now look at her.* "Here's your coffee, what were you going to tell me?"

"I've been booted out of work for the next two weeks."

"Booted out of work?" Imelda immediately launched herself into her labour-consultant mode.

"Calm down. I'm actually glad. I've two weeks to spend with Dubba and I can go scuba diving as a club diver and not just as a trainee."

"Scuba diving, booted out of work? Lord, Cathy, when was the last time we had lunch together? And when was the last time we had a real good gossip?"

"Yonks ago, Imelda, yonks ago."

"Fair enough, I think we should go out to that new Italian place up the road, the one I keep hearing about. We'll have a long lazy lunch and a catch up, okay."

"Great idea, but don't you have a previous appointment already?"

"I do, but I'll reschedule."

Cathy and Imelda decided to walk to the restaurant since it wasn't very far. As soon as they were comfortably seated and their orders taken, they settled back with a glass of wine.

"Now tell me, what the hell is going on?" Imelda asked her niece in her usual protective manner.

Cathy told her about her diving weekend and her so-called breach of safety regulations.

"Hmmm, are you going to appeal?"

"Don't think I'll bother. I'm due for a promotion evaluation shortly and I don't want to rock the boat."

"It's your decision. I'm not going to try to persuade you one way or the other."

"Thanks, but the truth will eventually come out."

The waitress bringing the starters interrupted them. Cathy had ordered baby green peppers stuffed with smoked salmon, mushrooms and garlic. Imelda had ordered minestrone soup, her favourite.

"Look at it this way. I've two weeks to ride. Hmmm, these taste wonderful, how's your soup?"

"It's good, really good. Talking about riding, when was the last time you saw Pauline?"

"You know what? I haven't heard from her in about six months."

Imelda studied her niece's face for a moment. "Is she in college?"

"I don't know what she's doing. Anytime we make plans to meet, something always comes up."

"Globetrotting plays havoc with your social life, doesn't it?"

Cathy ignored the jibe. "You know, I feel guilty."

"Why?"

"She's my friend Imelda, and she's had it tough over the last few years and I miss her."

Imelda stayed quiet.

"Ah, here comes our main course."

One glass of wine turned into two and then three. Neither was bothered. They had walked from the flat so they stopped counting. Cathy amused Imelda no end with her description of the experienced divers and their so - called professional be-haviour.

"What's happening with you? Are you still seeing that doctor type?"

"No, I'm NOT," she answered nearly snapping Cathy's head off.

"Jees, sorry I asked." Cathy was studying her aunt's body language. Imelda was decidedly agitated. She had been dating a biologist for nearly two years. What she did not know at the time was that he was married to two different women and she was just another bit on the side. Now she was about to be involved in a very messy court case. She discovered the truth a few months ago when both wives contacted her and asked her to meet with them. They had only found out about each other recently and they wanted to find out if Imelda had any children as they had seven between them!

Imelda felt sorry she had been so sharp with her niece. She knew she didn't deserve it. "Sorry Cathy, I didn't mean to be so abrupt, that relationship wasn't meant to be, and I'm still a bit sensitive about it, that's all."

"It's okay. Any time you'd like to talk. Tell you what, let's go mad and have some dessert." Any worries about *once on the lips, forever on whatever* was forgotten about. They ordered a calorie-laden boozy dessert followed by Irish coffees. Imelda's disastrous relationship blended into the past, where it belonged.

***

Cathy planned to stay in Bray for her two-week sabbatical, to be close to Dubba and spend some time with her father. When she got home the house was empty, except for Phantom. He was in his usual spot on his cushion in the kitchen and he was so delighted to see her, he ran painfully up her leg.

"Phantom, now you know you shouldn't do that, you beautiful naughty cat. Dad has you spoilt. Come on, I'll feed you."

After playing with Phantom for a while, she changed her clothes and walked at a leisurely pace through the town, stopping to speak to some people and hurriedly ignoring others while she made her way to the stables.

"Look what's just walked in lads, a vision of pure beauty," Tony said doing a mock bow as Cathy walked towards him.

"Give over you idiot, come here and give me a hug. I feel like I haven't seen you in years."

Never the man to miss a chance, Tony did as he was asked. *Hmmm, this filly certainly gets better with age.*

"Is Paddy in his office?" Cathy enquired, disengaging herself from Tony's arms.

"Nope, he's standin' right behind ye, glarin' at me." Tony let her go when he saw the look of *do not even think about it* in Paddy's eyes.

"And what do we owe the pleasure of this unexpected visit?" Paddy said. He was genuinely happy to see her.

"I have some time off that I didn't expect and I thought I'd come over and spend it with my most favourite people. How are you? How's Dubba? How's Moira?"

"Nothing changes, the same Cathy asking a mouthful of questions all in one go."

"Oh, go on with you, tell me all the news. Tell me all the gossip, please?"

"I'll do nothing of the sort. I have better things to do than stand around here gossiping," Paddy replied smiling warmly at his former student.

"Please yourself, Mr Murphy. By the way, is Dubba booked for anything this morning? I know I should have phoned first,

123

but I wanted to surprise you. Can Tony come out on a hack with me?"

"No, I don't have Dubba booked for anything. And yes, Tony can go out on a hack with you. You have three horses left to exercise don't you Tony?"

"Yeah, I do, but Dubba's not one of them," Tony replied carefully.

"Tony, I'll be riding Dubba, you thick," Cathy said as she turned and walked towards the tack room.

Paddy stopped her. "Cathy, Dubba's on box rest."

Cathy immediately turned to face him. "Box rest, why?"

"He pulled a ligament the day before yesterday larking about in the paddock with the other geldings'."

"Not the same one as last time?" Cathy couldn't keep the disappointment out of her voice.

"Yes, the same one. The vet was here before breakfast to scan one of the mares and he had a look at him. He has suggested six weeks total box rest and I agree with him. Sorry."

"Poor Dubba. It's going to do his head in standing for all that time."

"Can't be helped, the damage is done. Ride out with Tony. As I said, he's still a few horses left to exercise today."

"Ah thanks, Paddy, that would be great, but I'd like to go and see Dubba first. You never told me how Moira is."

"Why don't you ask her yourself? She's in the stable with her new Connemara."

"No, I'm not, Paddy Murphy, I'm about to ride my new Connemara, and his name is Kisses. Hello stranger, where did you pop out from?" Moira said to Cathy.

Cathy didn't get a chance to answer her.

"Ah Moira, now don't go riding, not in your condition," Paddy was almost pleading with his wife.

"Paddy," Moira said sternly.

Cathy looked from one to the other. "Moira, Paddy, are you two?"

Paddy stood ramrod straight, every bone in his body oozing pure pride. He walked over to his wife and put his arm around her protectively. "Yes Cathy, Moira is pregnant. Isn't it great? Can you persuade her not to ride, at least not until the baby is born? I'm not having much luck."

"Jees, congrat's ... congratulations. This is marvellous news. When's the baby due?"

"Late December. Now come on, let's ride before my darling husband blows an impenetrable bubble around me and deposits me in a padded cell for the duration of this pregnancy." Then she kissed her husband fondly on the cheek and told him to stop fussing.

"I've lost again. Will you two at least allow Tony to ride out with you?"

"That we can and will do, husband dearest," she replied un- abashed to her very proud and very concerned husband.

With Dubba relegated to box rest, Cathy didn't feel too guilty about concentrating on her new-found sport, scuba diving. Later on that evening, she arrived at the dive club foreshore for the pre-dive brief. Only one other diver from her training group had joined up, and both of them felt slightly awkward. Once the brief was over, everyone drifted off to make his or her final preparations.

Her money was tight, but the club provided a reasonably priced equipment rental facility for new members. It suited her perfectly.

Cathy loved kitting up. The anticipation made her smile. She savoured the moment that nearly all new divers enjoy, the experience of being there for her first dive as a bona-fide club member. Maybe when she had 100 dives under her belt, being there might become dull, but right now, it was awesome.

Kevin Cassidy was allocated as her buddy for the dive and he helped her into her relatively unfamiliar equipment.

"Don't worry; this time next month, you'll be donning your gear like an old hand. Now show me your dive signals," he said in a friendly and professional manner.

They both went though the pre-dive checks together and then climbed into the inflatable.

"Kevin I've just realised. I'm scared."

"Don't be ashamed of that Cathy. If you weren't a bit scared, I wouldn't dive with you. Always have respect for the sea. It's never very forgiving. Take care of your equipment and re-member your training. If you are not sure about anything, don't be afraid to ask. We all have to start somewhere. Relax, you'll be fine, you dived really well in Hook Head," he gave her an engaging and reassuring smile.

Cathy was glad she was buddied up with Kevin. He was firm, very experienced and patient.

"It's a beautiful evening. The conditions are near perfect so it should be a pleasant dive," Kevin said to her as they cast off.

It was more than pleasant. Apart from having a bit of trouble getting back into the inflatable, Cathy enjoyed herself immense-ly.

The divers usually met for a few pints afterwards in the Dalkey Island Hotel and Kevin asked her if she would like to join him. Cathy accepted happily.

Before she knew it, it was eleven o' clock.

"Kevin looked at the time. I'd better go."

"Time always passes quickly when you're enjoying your- self," he answered looking directly into her eyes.

Cathy held his eyes and silently agreed.

"Can I give you a lift home?"

"Ah, that's okay. I borrowed my father's car. That's why I'd better get going. He worries over nothing."

"I don't blame him. Can I see you again?" he asked hope- fully.

"You know something, Kevin Cassidy? I'd be delighted."

She gave him her mobile phone number and the flat number in Swords.

Kevin gave her his mobile number and his direct extension in the hangar at the airport. He walked her to her car, kissed her lightly on her forehead and returned to the hotel bar for a nightcap. The other lads gave him a bit of a hard time about hitting on the greenhorn. He ignored the harmless banter, being lost in his own thoughts.

Ironically, he was also on two weeks' leave and the two became inseparable. They spent every day together and when Cathy introduced him to Dubba, he discovered he did not share her passion for horses. An animal that size with four dangerous feet and a mouthful of teeth he could do without.

He showed her his favourite dive sites and they shared some memorable dives.

They had been an item for just over two months before Cathy introduced him to her father. Jimmy immediately took to him but he did have one concern, Kevin was seven years older than Cathy.

Imelda bluntly told him he was being stupid. He therefore said nothing to his daughter. She wouldn't have listened any- way.

***

A year later, they were married in Enniskerry church amid a variety of friends and a small contingent of relatives from either side of both families.

Cathy arrived at the church with Imelda as her maid-of- honour in a beautiful horse drawn-carriage provided by Paddy and Moira. To her disappointment, Pauline was nowhere to be seen. Cathy had wanted Pauline as her second bridesmaid, but she turned her down. Cathy was angry, hurt and very dis- appointed.

As Jimmy walked down the aisle with his only daughter on his arm, he felt Mary's contented presence all around him. His little girl was about to become a married woman and his late wife approved.

The wedding reception was held in the Roundwood Inn. Kevin's mother only stayed a short while, feigning a sudden bout of sciatica. In reality, she could not handle the fact that her son was married. He would no longer be available to run after her every beck and call. She didn't really get along with Cathy as she thought she was far too young to be a proper wife to her only son.

The newlyweds didn't notice her early exit.

On the other hand, Bill, Kevin's father, liked Cathy from the beginning and he was delighted to have another daughter in the family. Kevin's two younger sisters' thought their brother was a lucky man to have Cathy as a wife. He'd had a lot of girlfriends in the past, but considering they worked as au-pairs in New York and hadn't spent a lot of time with Cathy, they both agreed that none could hold a candle to her.

Imelda wanted to give them a wedding present of her flat in Swords. They refused graciously. They couldn't accept such an extravagant gift. Instead, she sold it to them for the same price she had paid for it some years previously.

She had no real need for it as she lived most of the time in Bray with Jimmy and the living arrangements between brother and sister suited them both.

***

The newlyweds settled into married life easily.

Cathy received her promotion and was now flying long haul most of the time. Her new status entailed a fair deal of separation from her husband who was often away on trips himself. They both understood the aviation industry so they accepted the situation. Life together did have some irritations though.

Kevin's mother had the annoying habit of popping in unannounced, much to Cathy's frustration. She always claimed she was just passing by and in her eyes Cathy could do nothing right.

"Goodness Cathy, those curtains could do with a wash you know and the garden looks like a rubbish heap. I'll get Bill over to sort it out."

Kevin promised to have a word with her. "She's only trying to help," he said in his mother's defence.

Cathy reluctantly kept her mouth shut.

Bill did sort the garden out. He turned the *rubbish heap* into a peaceful shrub-filled retreat, complete with a tasteful water feature that Cathy found pleasantly soothing.

Cathy's new route was Dublin/New York/Cairo. She had just returned from a particularly tiring flight and wanted to get home and relax. She was grateful for the crew transport that dropped her home quite promptly without too many detours.

When she opened the front door and heard noises coming from the kitchen, she thought Kevin was home. She threw her bags down on the floor in the hallway and rushed to meet her husband. Instead, she found her mother-in-law in the kitchen wearing her apron and her rubber gloves. She had the contents of the kitchen cupboards all over the worktops. "Mrs. Cassidy, you gave me a fright. What are you doing here?"

"Ah, Cathy, hello dear. I didn't expect you home so soon."

"That is quite evident, Mrs. Cassidy," she answered trying hard to contain her anger.

"It's Maggie, call me Maggie. Mrs Cassidy sounds so formal, now doesn't it. After all, you are family now, aren't you?"

"Hmmm ... Maggie is Kevin home?"

"No dear, he's at work," her mother-in-law answered and turned her attention to the cooker.

"Yes, he should be ... eh ...eh ... how did you get in?"

"Oh, I had a key cut from the spare one on the hall table. You don't mind, do you?"

"You did w-h-a-t?"

"Cathy dear, you both have such busy lives and this kitchen is in a sorry state. I thought it could do with a bit of a spring-clean. I've had the carpets shampooed so be careful where you walk, they might still be a bit damp in places." Cathy couldn't believe her ears. She was livid.

"Mrs. Cassidy, this is my kitchen, my carpets, my home. How dare you take it upon yourself to have a key cut and?"

Her mother-in-law interrupted her sharply. "Cathy, every man is entitled to a nice clean and tidy home, and my son is no exception. Your house keeping skills are somewhat youthfully limited."

"Mrs. Cassidy, I'm very tired. I think it would be better if you left."

"Excuse me Cathy, did I hear you right?"

"Yes, you heard me right. You heard me perfectly well."

Mrs Cassidy looked her daughter-in-law up and down.

"Nonsense, I'll be out of your way as soon as I give this cooker a good scrub. You should really line it with tin-foil."

"Mrs Cassidy, Maggie. The cooker is fine the way it is. Anyway, it's Kevin's turn to clean the oven."

"Don't be silly Cathy. Kevin has never cleaned a cooker in his life."

"Well, he does now. We share everything, including all the household chores."

"Cathy, Kevin has a very responsible job. You, you can't expect him to, to clean the cooker," her mother-in-law spluttered incredulously.

"Mrs. Cassidy, we both have responsible jobs and I want you to leave my cooker, my kitchen and my carpets alone. Mind your own bloody business." Cathy felt like time had stopped and silence permeated the kitchen.

Eventually her mother-in-law broke the horrible stony and uncomfortable silence. "Well, I've never been spoken to like that by anyone ever before. I will gladly leave your kitchen alone and I will never cross this door again."

"That's fine by me," Cathy replied physically shaking.

Maggie tore off the rubber gloves and brushed roughly past Cathy heading towards the bathroom. When she came out she put on her coat, collected her handbag and with obvious disgust, left without a backward glance.

Cathy stayed rooted to the spot. A few minutes later, the doorbell rang. She opened it to find her mother-in-law standing there, white faced.

"Mrs Cassidy, Maggie?"

"I have forgotten about my husband. He is in *your* garden tending to *your* flowerbeds. Please tell him I have gone home to where I am appreciated. Here is your key. I'll have no need of it anymore," she turned and left again.

Cathy went outside to her small but beautiful garden. Bill was engrossed in his work. He hated being retired and he usually kept himself busy doing odd jobs for his neighbours. On his allotment, not far from his own home, he grew an abundance of vegetables and experimented with unusual seedlings. He was delighted to see Cathy but on closer inspection, he saw she had been crying.

"What's up with my favourite daughter-in-law? What has you so upset?" Bill asked with concern written all over his face.

Cathy told him about her *words* with his wife.

"Begorra, I didn't know she was inside. I slipped in by the garden gate about half an hour ago. Don't fret, she doesn't mean to be pushy, it's just her way. Is there any chance of a cup of tea?"

Cathy felt sorry for her father-in-law, he looked extremely embarrassed.

"Of course there is and I have some of those biscuits you like so much."

"You're a good girl, Cathy Cassidy, one of the best."

While they were drinking their tea, the phone rang. It was Pauline. Cathy was thrilled to hear from her. She mouthed to Bill *won't be long.*

Bill excused himself quietly. He had two daughters of his own and knew only too well what *won't be long* meant.

He went back to his gardening.

"Jesus, Pauline, it's good to hear your voice. Where have you been? Where are you right now?" As usual, Cathy had loads of questions to ask in one go.

"I've just arrived in Dublin airport. Mum's here to pick me up. Can we meet up later on tonight?" Pauline asked her friend a bit warily.

"You're in the airport? Where have you just come from? Of course, we can meet up tonight. Why don't you come over to the flat right now? I'd love to see you. I've loads to tell you. We've loads to catch up on," Cathy was gushing again.

"Wait up girlfriend. Mum wants me to have lunch and do a bit of shopping with her, but I can ask her to drop me off at your place afterwards. Is that okay?"

"Okay. It is more than okay, it's brilliant. Just hurry up. I can't wait to see you."

"Right then, I'll be over at five or thereabouts."

"Great, it's a beautiful day. We'll have a barbecue in the garden. Oh, you're still a vegetarian aren't you?" Cathy remembered Pauline's eating habits had habits of their own.

"Sort of, I'm still off red meat, but I do eat chicken and fish. So don't go to any trouble, all right. See you about five. I'd better go, mum is waiting. Bye for now."

Cathy held the phone to her ear for a while after the line went dead.

Twenty-Two

Pauline had had a rough time over the last years. When she was removed from the court to the 'State Rehabilitation Centre' for further evaluation, she refused to believe that she was a drug addict. However, the psychiatrist assigned to her case disagreed with her. His findings were without doubt, complete and conclusive. His patient Pauline Dutton was definitely dependent on chemical substances.

Pauline's father had practically disowned her, but her mother eventually did come around and she stood by her.

When Pauline was admitted to the centre, she was supplied with two pairs of pyjamas, two tracksuits, two tee shirts, two pairs of socks and one pair of slip on shoes. She was allowed to keep her basic toiletries and her own under garments, but under wired bras were confiscated.

Pauline thought she had been dumped into the death row section in a bizarre twilight zone.

Initially, she was admitted to the locked wing where all new patients spent the first days under close observation and on the fifth day, the withdrawal symptoms set in. She felt like she was dying and began to think that the twilight zone staff might be right after all. She finally admitted to herself that she was suffering from more than a tummy bug. Her councillors were sympathetic, but there was nothing they could do to relieve her stress except give her plenty of psychological and moral support. She had to ride it out.

Cathy tried phoning, but she wasn't allowed to speak to her. When she tried to visit, she was turned away. At the time, the receptionist explained politely that any communication with the residents was not permitted until the centre deemed them fit enough to handle outside distractions. Cathy received no information from Pauline's mother or brothers either – as it turned out, they didn't know much anyway.

Pauline spent a total of ten days locked in. When she was regarded stable enough, she was moved into the main section. Colin, her psychiatrist, suggested he accompany her on an orientation tour of the centre's facilities because sometimes the move from the secure area was a bit daunting for new residents.

They started with the occupational therapy department where about 30 patients were busy with different projects. Colin introduced her to the therapist on duty.

"Pauline this is Sadie. She'll guide you through your sessions and remember they *are* mandatory," he said in an advisory but not derogatory tone while watching her reactions closely.

"Pauline, I'm very pleased to meet you. I hope your stay with us will be a pleasant one. We can guide and help you, but the speed and success of your rehabilitation will depend entirely on your co-operation with us."

Pauline had visions of being taught how to make an endless amount of wicker baskets and macramé stuff to be sold later in the twilight zone's flea market.

"I'll do my best Sadie, I want to get out of this place as soon as possible, believe me," Pauline replied, meaning what she said.

"That's the right attitude to have. I will see you tomorrow. We will give you until then to settle in and make friends with the others. I'm sure you will enjoy your occupational therapy sessions; it can get quite lively in here at times. Now, please excuse me I have to get back to my patients." Sadie gave her a dazzling smile and returned to her basket weavers.

Get quite lively in here at times, Pauline didn't think so. Making macramé plant hangers, lampshades and weaving baskets didn't appeal to her; writing did. If the odd cough or sneeze, which came from the happy and lively participants, were anything to go by, her sessions with Sadie would be far from stimulating.

"Colin, how many residents are actually in this establishment?" Pauline enquired almost tearfully.

"Altogether, there are 74. You were extremely lucky to get a place here you know. Our other centre houses over 200 patients so do not waste your time here. Learn to live with your addiction, face up to it and overcome it. We will talk after lunch. Do you want to see your room before we continue?"

"Yes, I would thanks."

"Fair enough, lunch is at twelve-thirty sharp and the dining room is the last door on the left at the end of this corridor. Ah, here's Melanie, she's your room mate."

A girl with greasy purple hair that looked like it had bats reluctantly nesting in it, sauntered up to them.

"So, you're the new druggy?" Purple Head enquired, as she looked Pauline up and down.

"Melanie, be nice," Colin chided as his bleeper shrieked in his pocket. "Sorry I have to go. Melanie, will you look after Pauline? Please show her where her room is. Something's come up and I have to go."

"Yeah, sure I will Colin, no prob's." Melanie replied, still eyeing Pauline up and down.

"Thanks Melanie. Pauline, I'll see you at lunch," Colin said as he rushed off in the direction they had come from.

Some orientation tour, thought Pauline. "Melanie, my name is Pauline not d-*r-u-g-g-y* and I would like you to remember that, please."

"Wow, touchy touchy, aren't we? Come on. The female royal quarters are on the next floor. Hurry up; they give us fucking shit if we're late for meals."

Pauline followed the purple greasy head to a bedroom on the next floor.

"Welcome to your suite, Princess. I see the dragon has brought your stuff already."

Pauline wasn't impressed with her sleeping quarters. They were even worse than the locked ward. The room contained two beds and two bedside lockers. On one bed, there was a box that contained her permitted personal belongings.

The solitary mirror that was bolted to the yellow and white wall had fine wire mesh over it. The only other adornment in the room was a pair of faded yellow curtains.

"The dragon? Who are you talking about?" Pauline asked her new and decidedly scruffy roommate.

"The dragon ... that'll be Margaret, she's the ward supervisor. You'll meet her soon enough. Oh, the bathroom is across the hall," Melanie replied stiffly.

Pauline ignored her and launched herself at the box, which contained her belongings and began searching through the meagre contents.

"Hey druggy, put your stuff away later because we'd better get down to lunch."

Pauline spun around and reminded her roommate yet again, that her name was Pauline and not druggy.

"For fuck sake Princess, don't be so sensitive. If it's any consolation, I was hauled out of Spain by my old man and dumped in here four months ago. And I am a drug addict and I have been one for years," Purple Head announced.

"You ... you have ... have been on drugs for years?" Pauline stuttered, not sure how else to reply.

"Yep, since I was about ten and I'm 24 now."

"Fourteen years and you're still not clean?" Pauline gasped.

"I never really wanted to be clean before. It's not that difficult to overcome drug addiction," Melanie replied, sound- ing full of herself.

"It's not?"

"No, Princess it's not."

"But, but ...

"The point you are stupidly missing is, that overcoming drug addiction is easy. It's the decision to decide or simply put, deciding to give up is the hard part," Melanie informed her while she scrutinised her purple hair in the wire-clad mirror.

"And have you decided to give up?"

"Yeah Princess, I have. Aren't I special?"

Giving up drugs is easy, it's deciding to that's not ... that's the hardest part, Pauline said to herself. She looked at Purple Head with new eyes. Then for the first time she noticed her rounded abdomen and stayed silent.

Melanie followed Pauline's gaze and put a hand protectively on her swollen stomach. "Yeah, I have a bun in the oven and it's this little package that made me decide to give up the shit. Now come on, it's lunchtime."

"I'm not hungry. I think I'll have a nap," Pauline said glancing around the dismal room once again.

Purple Head just laughed. "No one is allowed to miss meals without permission, and you only nap when they tell you to. Let me give you some advice; don't argue with them, you won't win. Come on for fuck sake, I'm supposed to be looking after you and I'm not losing any of my hard-earned privileges because of you."

They reached the dining room and Purple Head announced, "Everyone, this is Pauline, the new druggy. She's visiting us for a while."

Some looked up and nodded, others ignored her totally.

Colin came up behind them and told Melanie to sit down and then he showed Pauline where she should sit. Purple Head sat at another table, much to Pauline's relief.

The table Pauline had been shown to had about 20 people seated around it, only two of them were female. A fat man on her right was shovelling food into his mouth at an alarming rate. He introduced himself as Mick.

"Hi," Pauline replied looking at him with disdain.

"What are you really in for?" Mick asked her.

"Drugs," she replied with a would-you-believe-it expression on her face and she couldn't resist asking him what he was in for.

"Alcohol," he answered gloomily.

"Oh," was all she managed to say in reply.

"Drugs," a male voice said behind her. She spun around and thought she recognised the face that belonged to the voice. She was sure she had seen him in 'The Monks' house down by the harbour. Her skin felt like millions of needles were pricking her repeatedly and she started sweating profusely.

"Are you all right?" a voice said somewhere close by her. She didn't answer; she just sat still and wished she was invisible.

A fat woman plonked a plate of what looked like pasta and meatballs in front of her. Pauline stared in horror at the sorry-looking sludge.

"Excuse me, I can't eat this. I'm a vegetarian."

"So what's that got to do with it?" The woman snarled back at her.

"I don't eat meat."

"That's tough. You'd better start."

"I beg your pardon, there must be some mistake," Pauline replied, acutely aware of many eyes on her.

"Beg all the pardons you like, I don't care if you eat it or starve," the woman said and stomped off towards what Pauline presumed was the kitchen.

Pauline was starving, but she couldn't bring herself to eat the mush swilling around on the plate. She stood up and silently called them all a pack of low life's and left the dining room. As she flounced through the door, she practically knocked over Colin in her haste to get out. He had been watching and listening. He told her to follow him to his office immediately, which she did reluctantly.

"Pauline, sit down," Colin said to her, with definite firmness in his voice.

She momentarily stared at him before sitting on one of the chairs in front of his desk.

"Pauline, we don't cook special food for anybody. While our patients are in the admission ward, we sometimes make an exception." Colin spoke sternly.

"But I'm not asking for special food. I'm a vegetarian, I don't eat red meat. That's all."

"A lot of people who come here have certain eating disorders and it's very important they learn to eat what we give them," Colin told her.

"I understand, but that's only for the anorexics, bulimics and the overeating people."

"No Pauline, everybody gets the same food. You know, I'm worried about you."

"Worried about me, why?"

"Because you're primary addiction is to drugs and you may well have an unhealthy relationship with other substances. You may get the drug addiction under control but you might become addicted to something else, like alcohol or food."

"Okay, I come in here to get treatment for my short bout of drug abuse and by the time I leave, I'm an alcoholic and an anorexic. Brilliant."

"Not quite."

"So what am I supposed to eat?"

"Whatever we give you. No arguments."

"You sound like my father."

"Do I?" Colin studied her quietly.

"Yes, you do, and he wouldn't eat that slop that was put in front of me either."

"Pauline, just co-operate. Don't turn your stay here into an extended one."

Colin reiterated to her that while she did dislike meat, she had to learn to accept some things in life and changing her culinary preferences was one of the ways to start.

At the time, Pauline thought he was demented but she wanted to get the hell out of the twilight zone and if changing her eating habits scored her brownie points, she would comply.

In her first group therapy session for new arrivals, Pauline learned about the points system. The same points system or privileges earned which Melanie had mentioned on her first day out of the secure wing.

Pauline thought the so-called points system was draconian to say the least. Residents were required to help out, not only in the kitchen and garden, but the laundry as well. In return, they would be allotted points, which would earn them the required amount to receive visitors and make phone calls.

Pauline earned none for the first seven weeks as the thought of washing other people's bed linen disgusted her highly. Pulling up weeds, scrubbing floors and peeling potatoes didn't rate much either. She didn't particularly want to see or talk to any of her family or friends, not even Cathy. The staff tried to encourage her to move on and up, but she was stuck with a bad case of self-chastisement combined with a massive dose of guilt.

Apart from not wanting to see her family or friends, she didn't want to talk to any of them on the phone either – she didn't trust herself.

In her occupational therapy sessions, Sadie the always-smiling therapist insisted she participate in the regular activities because manual dexterity, in her mind, was important. Pauline thought Sadie was a basket case herself. Sadie told her if she wanted to write stories or poetry she could, but firstly she had to take part in the prescribed activities set down by the centre. Writing was to be done in her own time. And write Pauline did, long into the lonely nights because sleep only came to her for very brief periods. As Purple Head ignored her most of the time and slept like the dead, Pauline put her thoughts, fears and dreams down on paper, witnessing many sunsets and sunrises whilst doing so.

She thought her group therapy sessions sounded like the confessions of the utterly deranged and she had to attend them three times a day. However, at each session she learnt a little more about the reasons why some people resorted to drugs, alcohol, developed eating problems (there were various kinds) and became sex addicts.

They did this to overcome the myriad of problems they encountered and felt unable to face without the false help and brief release these so-called 'destructive time out' measures afforded them, at a serious price.

She did encounter a few altercations, one in particular which came to vicious blows when an obese male inmate on garden duty alongside her had the irrepressible desire to have a 'feel' at her boobs and in the process, practically ripped her tracksuit top clean off.

Afterwards, Pauline was outraged further as she was given double cleaning duties for a week and all because she had the temerity to defend herself. The groper ended up in the secure medical wing needing several stitches over one eye and she was expected to apologise to him when he felt better. Pauline feared she would kill the fat bastard if he came near her again.

The other was not so physical, but a definite infringement on Pauline's limited amount of privacy. It happened in one of the group therapy sessions that Purple Head was late for because she had to visit her gynaecologist beforehand. When she arrived back, she slunk in as slinkily as a pregnant woman could slink, looked at Pauline devilishly and sat down opposite her.

Instantly, Pauline knew she was up to something, but what? She had grown somewhat used to Melanie's snide and often bloody-minded remarks, so she steeled herself and retreated into a world of her own making. It was that particular world Colin and his team were doing their utmost to get in to.

The usual spats which broke out between the members of the group were quite normal and encouraged in a controlled way. Then it was Purple Head's turn to give her opinion on what was being discussed at the time.

She grunted her way onto her feet and started reading giddily from a small notebook, which looked very familiar to Pauline. 'French men are renowned for masochism and womanising. They are totally insecure leaders and lovers. They all think they have a 1,000 ft high phallus, resembling their beloved Eiffel Tower. Take a look at Napoleon for instance'.

Pauline lurched forward screaming, "Where did you get that? That's my private stuff; give it back you dyed hair whore."

An inmate quickly grabbed her and held her in a vice-like grip. Purple Head ducked behind the session leader and continued, "Wowee guys, you have to listen to this bit. 'She admired his well developed chest covered in dark brown hair that narrowed to his flat stomach leading to more dark hair from which his member reared up confident as a conductor's baton raised for action.'

"Melanie, I swear I'll kill you, you bitch," Pauline screamed and tried to kick her way out of her captor's strong arms.

"Pauline, you will do no such thing, you will SIT DOWN. Daniel, let her go and Melanie, if what you are reading is Pauline's property please return it to her immediately," the session leader barked at them all.

Purple Head sauntered over to a quivering Pauline, handed her the notebook and said, "Loved the lesbo bit Princess. Why don't we get it together? How about sometime tonight?"

Some members of the group egged Purple Head on and others sat in silence.

Pauline, now free from Daniel's restraining arms, grabbed her notebook and ran from the room slap bang into Sadie. "Pauline, what on earth?"

Pauline didn't answer her; she headed straight for Colin's office, burst through the door demanding that she be allocated a new roommate this very day.

Colin sat her down after chastising her for not knocking and told her categorically that she was to sort out her differences with Melanie and stop running away from anything and everything that rocked her little world.

"Rock my little world? Colin, that's ridiculously unfair, she's a thief and you are condoning her actions. Jesus, she looks like her own experiment. No, a filthy pantomime hen's arse would be more appropriate," Pauline flung back at him with pure unadulterated hatred shooting from her eyes.

"And what makes you so perfect Pauline?" Colin asked sitting back in his chair watching her body language.

"Perfect, I'm not perfect but I do care about other people's feelings and I respect the privacy of others. That fucking hen's arse wouldn't know how to spell the word privacy. Colin, my writing is my private affair and it's not to be bandied around in bloody group therapy."

"Pauline, the day you entered these doors you gave up all rights to privacy. This is not a hotel, it is a state rehabilitation centre and if you choose not to co-operate with us during your stay here, the next step my dear girl, is prison."

"Ah, come on Colin, get a grip." Pauline stood up and walked over to the bulging bookcase covering one wall from floor to ceiling. She studied the contents of the shelves while she tried to regain some composure.

"Prison, yeah Colin, that's a good one that is." Colin's words had hit her like a thunderbolt.

"Pauline, I do not have the time to discuss this with you now, the resident who has an appointment with me is waiting in another wing. I suggest you go and book your own appointment through the proper channels as set down by the centre's etiquette rules."

"Centre etiquette rules? Sure, I'll do that doc, but before I go, answer me this ..."

"Pauline, I will answer any question you put to me when you have a proper appointment. Rules in this establishment are not made to be broken. We will talk soon, I promise."

"But ..."

"Proper channels Pauline. I am now running late, please excuse me."

Pauline's stay lasted 16 weeks before she was deemed responsible enough to return to the outside world. She was released after her mother signed a personal guarantee that she would attend weekly group therapy sessions. On the other hand, her father wanted to pack her off somewhere, anywhere that he wouldn't be reminded on a daily basis that his daughter was a recovering drug addict.

Celia thought her husband was behaving ridiculously. Pauline had made a mistake and she had to live with the consequences for the rest of her life, but she didn't have to be continually punished for it.

Pauline's eldest brother Joseph agreed with his mother. He had recently qualified as a junior architect and had just moved into his own bed-sit in Sutton. It wasn't in a fashionable part of Dublin but it was all he could afford on his salary. Nonetheless, it was his, and it allowed him to put some distance between himself and his whisky-tippling father, whom he never really got along with at all.

Pauline's relationship with her father was difficult to say the least, so he asked her if she would like to move in with him until she got back on her feet. She would have to sleep on a sofa bed because the bed-sit was small, suitable only for one person really, but that didn't matter to Pauline. She accepted his offer gratefully.

She joined the 'Greater Dublin Literary Society' with the help of the rehab' centre, where she attended various writing courses and completed her final school exams. To help pay her way, she worked as a waitress in a small but popular Italian restaurant, just off O' Connell Street.

Celia insisted that Sheamus provide her with an allowance until her financial status improved. However, as usual, anything which separated Sheamus from his beloved cash upset him greatly. Pauline's income was more than adequate in her father's eyes and it was pathetically paltry in her mother's.

Celia made sure her daughter did not starve by supplementing her income from her housekeeping money.

Pauline felt ashamed and she tried very hard to make the most of things, but her life had changed irrevocably and she was having a tough time dealing with the issues her drug dependency had created.

Every time Cathy managed to contact her, Pauline always made some excuse as to why they couldn't meet up. She felt guilty because she had dragged her best friend into the sordid world of drugs. Cathy tried to convince her otherwise, but Pauline was extremely angry with herself and deliberately kept her friend away. She felt she had to, to allow Cathy to get on with her own life and not be bothered with a recovering junkie's problems.

A year later, she fell 'off the wagon' and that was when Cathy lost nearly all contact with her. They did meet up now and again, for what Cathy later described as token chats and Pauline had met Kevin briefly on more than one occasion, but she continued to remain distant.

However, she did show her face at Cathy and Kevin's engagement party, but only stayed for a short while. When she was introduced to Kevin's father, she liked him immediately. But, when his mother was introduced to her, she backed away. Maggie had looked at her as if she was something to be scraped off the sole of her shoe.

Pauline didn't envy Cathy a prospective mother-in-law like that; she didn't envy her at all.

Then she disappeared altogether.

Twenty-Three

Kevin's mother phoned him at work and they endured a painful conversation. She recounted her confrontation with Cathy to him word for word. Kevin told her that his wife had every right to be annoyed. How would she like it if she came home to find Cathy cleaning her kitchen? How would she like it if she came home to find Cathy had had her carpets shampooed?

His mother was astonished he didn't take her side and she became petulant. However, unbeknown to Kevin, she reluctantly agreed deep down that he had a valid point.

Cathy was in the garden when Kevin arrived home earlier than she expected him. He wrapped her in his arms and told her how much he loved and missed her.

"I've missed you too and I'm off for three days. Oh Kev', we can spend some real quality time together. Can you take some leave?"

Kevin slipped his arms from around her and held her by her shoulders. He looked deep into her expectant hazy green eyes. "Ah Cathy, I wish I could, but I have to go to Morocco on the eight-thirty flight tonight. I've a bloody engine change to do and I can't put it off."

"No, Kevin, tell me you're joking," the disappointment in her voice was heavy.

"I wish I was Cathy, believe me I wish I was," he answered, truly meaning it.

"How long will you be gone for?"

"Not long, four, maybe five days, providing we don't run into any new problems." He hated upsetting her but he couldn't help it.

"Well then, we'd better make hay while the sun shines," Cathy said with a twinkle in her eye.

"That, I like the sound of." Kevin lifted her effortlessly into his arms and threw her gently over his shoulder. "Right, let's make loads of hay and create lots of sunshine." He ignored her playful protests and carried her into the bedroom, depositing her gently on the bed.

"Kevin Cassidy, you're incorrigible but I love you."

They were interrupted by the doorbell ringing.

"Who the hell is that?"

Kevin wanted to ignore it and so did Cathy, then she remembered Pauline was coming over.

"Oh my God, Kev', that must be Pauline. I forgot to tell you she was coming over. Your wanton hay and sunshine distracted me."

Straightening her clothes, she rushed into the hall, pulled the door open and Pauline nearly choked her with a hug.

"Lord, Cathy, it's good to see you again, you look wonderful. Married life suits you no end."

"Oh, Pauline, it's great to see you too. Kevin, look who's here." All her lusty thoughts disappeared with the arrival of her best friend.

Kevin hurriedly adjusted his trousers and thought about lots of freezing cold water before making his way into the sitting room.

The two women were already in an animated conversation when he casually strolled in knowing it would be nearly impossible for him to get a word in edgeways, but he was happy for Cathy. He knew she'd missed her friend sorely as she highly valued the friendship.

"Pauline, I must say you're looking well. Whatever you've been doing with yourself suits you," he said, hugging her warmly.

"You're not looking too bad either you know," Pauline answered him coquettishly and winked slyly at Cathy.

Cathy just laughed at the pair of them.

"Kev', will you light the barbecue? It's such a lovely evening; it would be a shame to stay indoors."

"Your wish is my command," he replied walking away, leaving the pair gabbling to each other.

He wasn't sure if he would have time to have supper with them, he had to be back at the airport in three hours. Nevertheless, he busied himself with the charcoal and smiled broadly when he heard their laughter drifting out to him.

Once the fire looked like it had taken, he went to pack his bag.

"Cathy, do you know where my epaulettes are?" Kevin shouted from the bedroom window. They had gone into the garden to soak up the afternoon sun.

"You'll find them in the top left-hand drawer of the tall boy."

"Thanks."

A few minutes later he shouted, "Cathy, do you know where I put my credit card, the one I use for trips?"

"It's in the drawer in your bedside locker. You put it there yourself, remember?"

"Right, so I did, thanks."

"Come on Pauline. Give me a hand will you? I'd better get supper on. What would my wonderful mother-in-law say if I sent my husband off to Morocco on an empty stomach? Everything's prepared. I just need you to give me a hand to carry it outside."

"Okay, tell me what to do and you can regard it as done," Pauline replied. She was finally at ease with herself and was determined to close the chasm she had created in their friendship. She knew she had treated Cathy shoddily and swore inwardly she would never do it again. Nevertheless, right now, was not the correct moment in time to start mending fences.

When Cathy had finished fussing around, they settled themselves comfortably in the garden again. Once Kevin was finally organised he left his small bag by the door in the hallway and rejoined the women in the garden.

Cathy who was never able to figure out how he managed to travel so light asked, "Have you got everything packed?"

She hated helping him get ready for a trip as she felt like she was encouraging him to go. She knew it was silly but she couldn't help herself.

"Yeah, I have, I think."

She decided she had better check. It was a good job she did, because he hadn't packed any socks or sunscreen.

Satisfied her husband's bag contained the necessities; she returned to the garden, adjusted her chair in the late sunshine and relaxed.

"Right, ladies, can I get you a glass of wine?"

"Mmmm, yes please, sounds good," Cathy replied lazily.

"Pauline, would you like red or white?"

"White, if you please kind sir," Pauline answered.

"Right then, two glasses of white wine coming up." Kevin walked inside to pour the drinks.

Cathy was worried. She wasn't sure if Pauline was supposed to be drinking; that was why she hadn't offered her any wine herself.

Pauline leaned forward and whispered. "It's okay. I'm a recovering drug addict not an alcoholic."

Cathy felt embarrassed, an emotion she was not used to experiencing where Pauline was concerned.

"Pauls, I didn't mean to ..."

"Forget it, okay," Pauline said gently.

Kevin returned with the drinks and then sat in the chair opposite his wife. The sun caught the highlights in her red hair and he thought she looked so beautiful his heart felt like it was about to burst with pride.

"Well now, am I going to put the chicken on to cook, or is it going to magically cook itself?" he asked trying to get a rise out of them.

"Give over will you. Just put it on the charcoal. The coals should be ready for cooking by now. By the way, what did your last slave die of?" Cathy playfully pushed her husband out of the way and started cooking.

"No, you sit down. I can do this, I'm not helpless you know." Kevin insisted.

Cathy looked at Pauline and the two smiled at each other. Kevin's insistence on being the executive chef-of-the-day amused them. Pauline didn't know him very well, but she could see he was madly in love with Cathy and she with him. She was happy for her friend and was glad she was in their company.

All too soon, it was time for Kevin to go. Earlier on, he had phoned for a taxi, he wanted to leave the car at home for Cathy. He didn't want her to drive him to the airport, as she'd laid into the wine with Pauline and was enjoying herself.

When the taxi arrived, Cathy didn't go outside to see her husband off, she hated saying goodbye. She stayed in the garden with Pauline. Kevin understood; he felt the same about goodbyes himself.

Later on, not wanting to be separated from her friend as well, Cathy asked her to stay over, but Pauline politely refused. Cathy became increasingly insistent. Pauline, realising she couldn't win, phoned her mother. After a short chat, she told her she was fine and upon hearing the slight annoyance in her mother's voice, she reminded her she hadn't seen Cathy for a long time.

Celia told her that she hadn't seen her daughter for a long time either. Pauline decided to end the conversation feigning supper was ready and promised to call her later. She didn't want to prolong the conversation since she didn't want her mother to cotton on to the fact that she'd been drinking. She wasn't a child any longer, but her mother insisted on treating her like one, and it drove Pauline crazy. *What harm can a few glasses of wine do? Drugs created the problem, not booze.*

They talked long into the night. Pauline chatted on and on about her new job as a junior freelance journalist with a funky magazine in London. She told Cathy about her fall from grace as her mother had described it, when she lapsed back into the world of drugs. She apologised profusely for missing her wedding day.

Cathy let her ramble on and on. It was as if a sluice gate had opened up.

It was close to midnight when she told Cathy that 'The Monk' was about to be released from prison; she also told her about her frequent nightmare's that he was coming after her for being instrumental in his arrest and consequent jail sentence in Mount Joy Prison.

"It was John Clancy who tipped the police off that night," Pauline blurted out.

"John Clancy tipped them off, but why?" Cathy cast her mind back to the night she had been arrested and shuddered at the memory.

"I don't know why he did it and I've never asked him either. Cathy, he never even phoned me once, not once." The anger in her voice was tangible and Cathy picked it up immediately.

"Pauls, it's all in the past now. Try leaving it there."

"That's fine for you to say. You didn't spend months in a lunatic asylum, did you?"

The wine had loosened her tongue and she was becoming a little belligerent, but Cathy wasn't going to allow her to pass the blame. She had to make her take responsibility for her own actions.

"I didn't snort coke did I? I did spend some time in residential therapy myself. Jesus, Pauline, you have no idea how much I've missed you. Have you any idea how many times I agonised about your whereabouts? Why, why did you have to disappear without a bloody trace? How could you betray our friendship like that?"

Cathy was extremely happy Pauline was home but she had to clear the air. She had kept her views to herself for long enough. She had kept the hurt inside for too long.

Pauline looked at her, looked straight through her and said, "Sorry."

"Sorry, is that all you're going to say?" Cathy's voice was rising.

"Listen to me Cathy, I had to stay away. I caused enough trouble for you in the past and I didn't want to be the cause of any more. You see, I still had a few demons to deal with, demons that might have affected you. I made some huge fuck-ups and I wasn't having you involved any further, not until I got things sorted out so to speak."

"And are you sorted out, are you?" Cathy demanded, watching Pauline's every move.

Pauline stood up, walked over to the window and stood staring at her reflection.

"Pauls, answer me. Are you sorted out? Have you buried all your demons? I need to know."

Cathy waited for her friend to answer but Pauline stayed silent. She continued staring out through the window, staring into the darkness beyond.

"Pauls, don't give me the cold shoulder."

Pauline turned around to face her. "Oh, Cathy, I'm not giving you the cold shoulder. I was lost in thought for a few minutes, that's all."

She moved over, sat by her side, and changed the subject away from her bygone demons. "Tell me, whatever happened to Peter Wallis, do you ever see him?" Pauline asked, looking down at the floor.

"No, I've haven't clapped eyes on him since the day of the court case. You know, I used to think he was wonderful, bloody marvellous in fact. Looking back, he was always self-opinionated and shallow. Sometimes you think you know a person really well, but Peter Wallis had many hidden agendas."

"What do you mean?"

"Ah Pauls, you remember what he was like. He was plain bloody selfish. Even then, he had an eye for the girls. Don't tell me you never noticed?"

Pauline had, but she kept her thoughts to herself for the moment. When they were teenagers, Cathy often wore blindfolds regarding some issues and Peter Wallis was one of them.

"What happened to him?" Pauline asked again.

Cathy turned her mind back to a time she really wanted to forget about. "Pauls, I'm not really too sure."

"Ah, come on now ..."

"Listen Pauls, at the time I had to buckle down and study for finals with Mother Superior and everyone else watching my every move. Anyway, I never saw him again after the court case, he was sent to a boarding school somewhere in England and, after the exams were over, I went to 'Belvedere Heights'. By the time I got back, his family had moved to Canada. Well, that's what I was led to believe. Shortly after that, I started working with 'Shamrock Air' and I just forgot about him."

"I'm going to be honest with you Cathy, I never liked him. I'm glad you split up with him, so let sleeping dogs sleep their bloody heads off. Put him behind you forever. You have a wonderful husband who adores you and I couldn't be happier for you."

Cathy studied her friend's eyes. She saw the depth of true deep honesty pooled in them. "Thanks, Peter Wallis is well forgotten about, you brought him up not me. While we're on the topic of relationships, do you know that John Clancy got married last year?"

"John Clancy is married? Should I care? I pity the bride. Who did he marry?" Pauline replied, trying not to show that she really cared.

"Do you remember Fiona McLoughlin?" Cathy asked carefully.

"Of course I do. Nooo, he didn't marry her, did he?" Pauline was astonished.

"Yep, he did and they moved to Australia, to start up a sheep or cattle ranch, something like that. Apparently, he has relatives over there."

"Well, wonders will never cease. Fiona McLoughlin was always a sly little bitch, they deserve each other."

Pauline became distant again. John had hurt her deeply. Even though she had tried hard to put him behind her, something stayed with her, something stayed in the recesses of her mind, something called revenge. But she didn't mention this to Cathy.

Since her release from rehab' she attended many counselling sessions and the advice, which was repeatedly given, was to forget about him and his betrayal. She knew her counsellor's were right, but someday, somehow, she would get her own back. That she was determined to do.

"Pauls, you never answered me. Have you sorted yourself out? Are you done with drugs?" Cathy asked again.

Pauline looked gob smacked for a few seconds.

"Yes, Cathy, my drug taking days are over. Well over."

The conviction and determination in Pauline's voice satisfied Cathy. "Pauls, you've paid dearly for your mistakes and I've paid for mine. Let's just get on with our lives. Put all memories of John Clancy, Peter Wallis and 'The Monk' far away. Promise me you'll never disappear again. I couldn't handle it."

Pauline looked crestfallen and Cathy continued, "Look here girlfriend, yesterday is well gone and tomorrow has yet to come. There's nothing to be gained by dragging all that shit back into our lives again. Now is there?"

"No, there's nothing to be gained, I agree. But, I'll never forget, I can't forget," Pauline said even more distantly.

"I'm not asking you forget completely. I am asking you to move on. Move on and use that period in your life as a learning tool, nothing more."

"Some learning tool," Pauline replied.

"For the last time, forget about that part of your life. For God's sake, Pauline, forgive yourself."

"When did you get to be so philosophical?" Pauline asked.

"Ah Pauls, enough of this doldrums stuff. Listen up. I'm off for three days. Why don't we go out to the stables tomorrow? It's been ages since we were out there together and you haven't seen Moira and Paddy's new baby yet, have you?" Cathy suggested, trying hard to turn the mood around.

As far as she was concerned, they were reunited and their friendship had remained intact, despite the rocky times behind them.

"No, I haven't seen the baby yet. They had a little girl didn't they? I heard Moira had a miscarriage quite late in her first pregnancy and it affected her badly. Am I right?"

"Yes, you're right, she did miscarry and it did affect her badly, very badly. But they have a healthy little girl now and she's beautiful."

"How old is she?"

"Two, her name is Casey. I want to have one just like her some day."

Pauline laughed at the thought of Cathy playing the little mummy bit. "Yeah, let's do that. It will be good to see the old crowd again. By the way, how is Dubba?"

Cathy downed her wine. "He's back out at grass."

"Why?"

"Remember his ligament injury, the one that put him out of action shortly after I got him?"

"Sure, but that was a long time ago."

"I know, but according to the vet it never really healed properly. To cut a long story short, eighteen months ago he went lame again. He spent weeks on box rest but it didn't make much of a difference, so we turned him out to grass for another six months and he seemed fine. Then we brought him back into work gently, but the tendon gave out again and now he's back out at grass. It's such a bloody nuisance."

That didn't sound too good to Pauline at all. She knew tendon injuries sometimes never healed properly and she took the direct approach.

"Will he ever come sound again?"

"Good question. That bitch Patricia Faircolm must have ridden the shit out of him when he was a youngster."

"Yeah, she did ride him hard when we knew her," agreed Pauline.

"Yep, she did and we don't know what that drunken eejit of a so called groom did with him when she took him away from Paddy's. Anyway, I think we should go to bed, I'm beginning to see two of you."

"I'm pretty bushed myself," Pauline replied. She didn't think she would sleep much, but she could see that Cathy was exhausted.

Twenty-Four

Imelda's business was now very high profile. She was often photographed at the races, gallery openings and theatre first nights. She dressed very well and always looked terrific. Over the years, she had plenty of suitors and the odd lover but no-one special in her life. None, who mattered enough to make a real difference in her personal albeit staggered love life.

She had her own way of doing things and could never imagine herself as a married woman with a load of snotty nosed kids hanging around her day and night. Her career involved a lot of travelling and she didn't need any of the distractions that a husband and children would inevitably bring along.

When she was in Ireland, she stayed with her brother. He didn't want her to stay anywhere else. He enjoyed her company, even if it was infrequent. They had been very close since they were children and time had not changed anything between them.

Jimmy also led a quiet life as far as the opposite sex was concerned. However, now and again, he attended the odd business function with a different female on his arm each time, but nothing ever came of it. Even though Imelda and Cathy encouraged him to develop some kind of a relationship, he doggedly refused to let go of Mary's memory. They didn't expect him to forget her, none of them could or would, but they wanted him to move on. Her father had become set in his ways and Cathy feared he would remain that way for the rest of his life.

Imelda organised a local woman to come in three morning's a week to handle the housekeeping chores as Jimmy was hopeless at them himself. At least the washing and ironing was done regularly and the grocery shopping. The woman she employed was a widow herself, so she was glad of the extra money.

Some time back Cathy had persuaded her father to take up golf, but he spent most of his time on the green swearing at his putter and ranting about the amount of golf balls he went through.

He had three branches of *Corway's Electrical* now, which kept him busy enough. His work had become the main factor in his life.

***

Just as Cathy and Pauline were leaving the flat both suffering from hangovers, the phone rang. It was Imelda.

"Well hello stranger. Long time, no speak," Cathy said smiling rather painfully.

"Yes, it's been a while. How are things on your end?"

"Fine, they couldn't be better but to tell you the truth, I've a terrible hangover."

Cathy's head felt like the entire *St Patrick's Day* parade was marching in one ear and out the other.

"Good night, was it? Imelda asked.

"Yeah, it was actually and guess who's standing right beside me, equally hung over I might add?"

"Father Christmas?"

"Funnee. Pauline's here. She flew in from London yesterday."

"Ah, let me guess. The pair of you stayed up most of the night gossiping and drinking copious amounts of vino?" Imelda answered slightly concerned but happy the pair were together again. She knew how much Cathy missed Pauline.

"Yes, something along those lines. Where are you?"

"I'm in the Dublin office. What are you doing tonight?"

"Nursing my sore head and I'm never ever drinking again."

"Famous last words. Why don't you and Pauline join me for supper tonight?"

Cathy instantly perked up. She always enjoyed her little get togethers with her aunt. "That sounds good, let me check what Pauline is doing."

Pauline thought the supper invitation was a wonderful idea, she really liked Imelda.

"It's fine with her, where will we meet, and at what time?"

"Lorenzo's at seven-thirty?"

"What's this thing you have for Italian food? Let's try the new Japanese place in Blackrock. Kevin is away so I have the car all to myself. We were just on our way out to the stables for a few hours, so I will be able to get back here to change first. I'm sure you wouldn't want to be seen among high society with myself and Pauline covered in horse slobber."

At the time Imelda could not have cared less if her niece and Pauline both arrived together wearing raunchy suspender belts, stockings and little else.

"Right you're on. It's in the shopping mall isn't it?"

"Yeah, it is. Will you book a table or will I?"

"Leave the arrangements to me. If there are any problems, I'll phone you on your mobile. Oh, how is the new Murphy edition? Are they getting any sleep?"

"She's as good as gold and she's gorgeous."

Imelda found it hard to believe that any baby was as good as gold. Babies scared her. "Glad to hear that, please give them my regards. See you at seven-thirty. Have fun and don't forget to take your mobile phone with you. I tried to phone you on it earlier, but as usual, it was off."

"Sure, but you know I hate the bloody thing. I can't get used to it. I feel like such an eejit talking on it."

"Yeah, I know. When I bought my first one, I felt the same, now I can't be without it. Take it with you and turn it on. Phone you later, bye."

"Bye Imelda." Cathy rooted through her handbag, found her phone only to discover that it was indeed turned off. She pressed the on button and to her relief, the battery had four bars of power left.

They took the scenic route out to Bray. Cathy wanted to show Pauline where the new refurbished dive club was. It was a beautiful day and the sea was like a pane of glass.

"What's it like down there in fishy land?" Pauline loved swimming, but the thought of scuba diving did not rank very high on her list of future accomplishments.

"Oh, Pauls, it's wonderful. You have no idea of the peace and tranquillity below the surface. The colours are amazing."

Pauline envisioned amazing colours all right. The kind created by the nuclear power plant on the North West coast of England, which polluted the Irish Sea with its waste.

"Isn't the water freezing?"

"A little bit at first. I can manage about an hour or so before it really gets to me. Our last dive together in the Killary estuary nearly froze me to death."

"Hmmm, but I'm sure its fun getting all nice and warm again with Kevin afterwards, huh?"

"Pauls, you're terrible."

"I know, but you love me."

***

The car park was practically full when they pulled up at the yard.

"Looks like business is booming," Pauline remarked.

"Yeah, Paddy's doing very well for himself and the restaurant has been refurbished. It is very chic. Moira has done wonders with it. Shit, why didn't I think of it before, let's have supper here tonight instead of the Japanese place?"

"Good idea, we have to support our local community now don't we? Let's see how the land lies first though, by the look of the car park, half of Ireland's riding fraternity is already here," Pauline replied.

"Oh, I'm sure it'll be fine. I'll phone Imelda later and see how she feels."

On the way to the office, they passed a group of riders going into the indoor arena. They sounded French.

"Jesus, Cathy, did you see that little weed looking at you? He practically stripped the clothes off your back with his beady little eyes?"

"Yeah. The ugly fecker, when he looks in the mirror I'm sure his reflection ducks."

"You're cruel, Cathy Corway."

"No, I'm not. Just imagine how his mother must feel. She probably fed him with a slingshot when he was a baby. And, I'm Cathy Cassidy now, dimwit."

"Charming, Cathy Cassidy, you have such a way with words."

Another group approached them and Paddy was riding alongside the leader. He reined his horse in expertly.

"Well now, what a nice surprise," Paddy said smiling from ear to ear.

"The pleasure is all ours. Are you going out cross-country?" Cathy asked with a touch of envy in her voice.

"Yes, we are. I've a group of French visitors over for the week and they think they know it all," Paddy replied keeping a careful eye on his departing pupils. "Moira's up in the house, why don't you pop up to see her. I'd better catch up with that lot. Do hang around for a while?" He rode off in a controlled collected canter.

Tony spotted them and he wandered over.

"Hello, you two. Now is me imagination runnin' riot, or do I see the fair Pauline Dutton standin' in front of me?"

"The one and only Tony. How are you doing?" Pauline replied smiling warmly.

"I'm doin' just fine, now that you're here. I was just about to make meself some coffee. Would ye like some?"

"Yes please." They both said together.

1"Come into the office then and no dawdling. I don't want me lads gettin' distracted by ye. Now do I?"

"No fear of that and we're right behind you," Pauline answered and gave him a playful shove.

While Tony busied himself fiddling with the coffee things, Cathy asked him about Dubba.

"Cathy, I'd rather ye spoke to Paddy about him," Tony sounded sharper than he intended to.

"Why, he is okay isn't he?"

"Look, Cathy, it's not me place ye know."

"Tony will you please answer me."

"Okay, okay, don't get your drawers in a twist. Now, this is only me own opinion ye understand?"

"Yes Tony, and I hold your opinion in high regard, you know that."

"Right then, I'm goin' to be straight with ye. It'd be better if ye never rode Dubba again. His tendon is buggered, it's fin- ished."

Cathy just stared at Tony.

"That's a bit drastic isn't it?" Pauline piped in.

"Maybe, but it's only me own opinion as I said. Look, he's already been blistered once and confined to his box for six weeks, right?"

"Yes," agreed Cathy.

"Then he was put back out to grass, right?"

"Yes Tony, he was and he's out at grass again."

"Me point exactly. We brought him back into work very slowly and his tendon blew up again. Cathy, we've had him out for months and there's not much improvement."

Cathy stayed silent, so did Pauline. They both knew deep down Tony would never have said what he did if he did not completely believe it.

"Here's your coffee, ye look like ye could do with it."

They drank the coffee in silence and then Cathy said in a muted voice. "Thanks, for the coffee Tony, we'd better get over to see Moira now."

"Okay, see ye both later on," Tony replied, knowing he'd upset Cathy and silently wishing he'd kept his mouth shut.

Dubba's paddock was on the way to the bungalow and Cathy asked Tony for some carrots as she had forgotten to bring some herself.

"Jake should be in the feed room, he'll give ye some gladly. Cathy, I'm sorry I'm the bearer of bad news to ye."

Cathy just nodded.

They passed the sand arena where a group of teenagers were being put through their paces. One girl in particular was having trouble keeping her horse straight, through a grid of staggered cavaletti. Pauline made some remark but Cathy didn't hear her. She'd seen Dubba in the distance and whistled to him. When he heard her voice he raised his head to listen and on her second whistle, he came cantering towards her. He stopped in front of her with an expectant expression on his face implying, *and where are my carrots.*

Cathy fussed over him while he munched away contentedly. On closer inspection, she found a considerable amount of heat in his tendon and it looked slightly bowed. He didn't seem to be too bothered by it.

"Pauline what do you think?"

Pauline slid two fingers down the back of his lower leg and applied pressure to the dodgy tendon. Dubba flinched and pulled his leg sharply away.

"I hate to say this and I'm no vet, but I think Tony might be right."

Cathy turned her attention back to Dubba.

"You great big lummox, we'll get you fixed up, somehow."

Dubba, hearing some other horses returning to the stables gave Cathy a gentle and familiar snort before he trotted off without a care in the world. He had to see what his equine friends had been up to. The fact that it had started drizzling didn't bother him in the slightest. Cathy shrugged her shoulders. "Come on, let's see what Moira's up to."

Moira saw them coming up the rear driveway from the kitchen window. She was pleased to see Pauline with Cathy as she hadn't seen her for ages. She watched the two friends happily chatting away despite the rain.

Moira was a bit lonely. She was finding the constraints of motherhood challenging. She missed her freedom. Anytime she wanted to do anything for herself, she couldn't. She had to put her daughter's needs first.

Her mother said she was suffering from postnatal depression (she had read about it in a magazine and now she regarded herself as an authority on the subject).

"You two are a sight for sore eyes. Come, get in here out of the rain," Moira gushed at her two unexpected visitors.

"Moira, you look great. Motherhood obviously suits you and the house is fabulous," Pauline said.

"Yeah, the house is nice and I'm sure it looks better than I do."

They ignored her reference to her appearance. Moira had always pushed compliments away.

"Where's the baby? Cathy says she's gorgeous."

"She is, when she's asleep," Moira answered moodily.

"Ah, come on now, every new mother finds it hard in the beginning, don't they?" Seeing the look on Moira's face, Pauline wished she'd put her brain in gear before she'd opened her mouth.

"Suppose they do," Moira muttered.

The baby started crying in another room.

"There she goes again, just like clockwork. She sleeps for about 20 minutes and then she's off again. Come on, I'll introduce you to Casey, the loudest baby in the whole of County Wicklow."

She took them into the elaborately decorated nursery where her daughter was screaming her head off.

"She certainly has a pair of healthy lungs. Can I pick her up?" Pauline asked.

"Be my guest," Moira answered.

Pauline went over to the cot, picked up the red-faced little girl and instantly fell in love with her. Within seconds, Casey stopped crying.

"Oh Moira, she's beautiful. Look at her tiny little fingers, her cute little nose."

"How did you do that?" Moira asked puzzled and slightly jealous.

"Do what?"

"Stop her crying."

Pauline didn't answer; she was too engrossed with the little bundle of perfection in her arms. She was utterly fascinated with her.

"Let's go and have a cup of tea. Bring Casey through will you Pauline?"

"It'll be my pleasure, won't it you little beauty," Pauline answered, still studying the baby's extremities.

While Pauline played with Casey, Moira made the tea. She was about to sit down with the girls and her now silent daughter when Paddy came into the kitchen shaking himself off like a puppy.

"Hi you lot, it's coming down in buckets outside and ..."

"Paddy, just have a look at what you've done. Are you going to clean up the mud you've just walked in?" Moira shouted at her husband.

"Ah, I'm sorry, I'll get the mop," Paddy said apologetically and he went towards the scullery.

"Don't bother. I'll do it myself."

Cathy had never seen this side of Moira before.

"Paddy, can I talk to you about Dubba?"

"Sure, but it'll have to be quick. Come into the den."

Paddy confirmed what Tony had told her. However, he didn't agree that Dubba's tendon was finished. He had one last trick up his sleeve. He told her he wanted to try him on com- frey."

"What's that?"

"It's a herb sometimes known as knitbone. I've had trouble locating it in dried form, but I've finally tracked down a supplier up in Antrim and I'm expecting a delivery of it early to- morrow."

"How does it work?" Cathy was all ears.

"It's a powerful anti-inflammatory. Combined with cider vinegar, garlic and devil's claw, it just might sort him out. I'll have to bring him back in on box rest for a month or so, in order for the herbs to work. He is too bloody nosey out in the pad- dock. He keeps running around like a colt."

Cathy agreed with him about Dubba's continual adolescent behaviour. "He'll hate being kept in, but we have to try," she looked at Paddy for reassurance.

"I can't guarantee it'll work, but I've had good results with it in the past. I just wish I could have tracked it down sooner," he said looking at his watch. "Sorry Cathy, but I have to go. Clients to look after, you know."

"Paddy, I don't want to delay you but what's up with Moira? I've never seen her so, so down."

"Baby blues," Paddy said quickly. "She'll be fine in a few weeks, don't worry lass. Worry is interest paid on trouble before it comes due. Have to go, bye." He hurried off.

Cathy returned to the kitchen. Moira was sitting by the fireplace with Pauline and Casey. The baby was fast asleep in Pauline's arms.

"Your tea's gone cold. Shall I make you a fresh cup?" Moira asked, sounding calmer.

"No thanks, I'm fine honestly."

"Looks like Pauline has missed her calling. She seems to have a way with Casey," Moira said moodily.

"Moira, when was the last time you had a night out?" Cathy asked.

Moira rolled her eyes towards heaven. "You know Cathy, I can't remember."

"Well, we're having supper Japanese style with Imelda tonight. Why don't you join us? We'll have a girls' night out."

"I'd love to, but we've a full house at the moment with the French contingent and they are a bit of a handful. Another time maybe," Moira replied with a dejected tone in her voice.

"Okay, how about we have supper in the restaurant here instead? I know it'll be a bit of a busman's or a bus woman's night out for you Moira, but it would be great for us all to have a natter and catch up."

"Ah, come on Moira, say yes, don't be a spoilsport," Pauline said backing Cathy up.

Moira looked at her sleeping daughter. "To hell with the froggies, you're on. I'll phone Charlotte, she often helps me out. She was marvellous when I was in hospital giving birth to madam over there. I'll be back in a few minutes. Oh Cathy, put the kettle on will you? You look a bit harassed yourself."

She came back a few minutes later looking more relaxed.

"Charlotte's agreed to step in for me, she was quite pleased actually. I'll leave Casey with my mother. She normally looks after her while I'm on duty."

"Wonderful, I'll get in contact with Imelda," Cathy replied, rooting through her handbag once again. *Jesus, I must sort this bag out, it's becoming a health hazard.* She found her phone and called Imelda.

Imelda was all for it. It would give her a chance to check the restaurant out; she was always on the lookout for new venues to entertain her clients. She could kill two birds with one stone.

**

Cathy dropped Pauline off at her mother's house. She didn't go in with her, she wanted to get home and have a snooze. Her jet lag was catching up with her.

When she got home, she phoned her father at his office. Her hangover doggedly lingered on and the thought of driving back across Dublin late at night made her feel even more tired. She would stay in her old room in Bray tonight.

Sandra answered the phone. "You've just missed him, but he should be back in about an hour. How are you?"

Cathy cut her short; she wasn't in the mood for one of Sandra's long enquiring conversations. "Just tell him I phoned and I'll call him later."

"Can I give him a message?"

"No, its okay Sandra, I'll phone him back. Bye."

All of a sudden, a wave of nausea overwhelmed her. *Hell, drink doesn't agree with me.* She lay gratefully down on her bed.

Then she was disturbed by the sound of her handbag ringing. For a second she thought she'd lost her mind. *It's that bloody mobile thing again.*

By the time she retrieved the phone it had stopped ringing. Not really bothered, she snuggled back down underneath the covers. Then the phone beside her bed shrilled, it was her father.

"Of course I don't mind if you stay the night here, this is still your home too, you know."

"I know that dad, but I wanted to check with you first. You might have made plans of your own."

"Don't talk daft. It'll be great to have you here. I was talking to Imelda a short while ago and she mentioned that you're going out for a night on the town."

"Yeah, the three of us are going out to Murphy's restaurant."

"The three of you?"

"Yep, Pauline, Imelda and myself."

"Oh, I didn't know Pauline was back. I met Celia a few days ago and she never said anything."

"She only got back yesterday."

"Fair enough, do you want me to collect you?"

"No, it's okay. I have the car."

"Okay pet, I'll see you later on."

"Sure dad. Love you."

"Love you too, bye."

157

Twenty-Five

"Cathy, it's good to see you. You're looking very well. Bloom- ing, would be more accurate. Come into the kitchen. I haven't laid eyes on you in such a long time," Celia said leading the way down the hall.

"Thanks, Mrs Dutton. You look good yourself. Is Pauline ready?"

"I think so. I'll give her a shout."

"No need to," Pauline said as she walked into the kitchen dressed to kill.

"Don't you think that skirt is a bit too short for a young woman of your age?" Celia asked.

"Mum, young is the operative word and I'm not in my dotage yet you know."

"Well, don't bend over or you'll show everyone everything."

As usual, Celia was at a loss for words when it came to her daughter's choice of wardrobe.

"You fuss too much mum. See you later and we shouldn't be too late," she replied kissing her mother fondly on her cheek.

"Let's get this show on the road, Mrs Cassidy."

"Nice seeing you again, Mrs Dutton."

"A short and sweet visit, but it was nice seeing you too, even if it was only for a few minutes. Have fun."

"We will, see you later."

They heard a key in the door and Pauline's father came in. He always came home at seven-fifteen, regular as clockwork. Whisky o'clock.

"And where do you think you're going, dressed like that?" Sheamus growled.

"Hi, dad, delighted to see you too. Come on, Cathy, we'll be late."

"Pauline you will not ..."

His wife interrupted him, "Sheamus, your supper is ready."

"Celia, she's not going out dressed like that."

"Sheamus, your supper is ready and it's ready n-o-w."

Cathy and Pauline were already halfway down the driveway.

"I need a drink," Pauline said with definite urgency in her voice.

The restaurant was fairly full when they arrived. Imelda was sitting at the bar talking to Moira and Paddy.

"Well now, would you look at the pair of glamour girls arriving? If that's Cathy Corway and Pauline Dutton, I must say they clean up well don't you think?" Paddy said as he pulled two bar stools out for them.

"Moira, your husband is such a gentleman, you should be very proud of him," Pauline shot back.

"Someone has to be, don't they Paddy Murphy?" Moira answered.

"Suppose they do. Now I have to be off, some of us have work to do," Paddy replied smiling broadly.

"Hmmm, we know, overworked, underpaid," Moira said in his ear and kissed him on the cheek.

"Can't you stay and have a drink with us?" Cathy asked him.

"Are you crazy? I'd be totally outnumbered."

Paddy turned to the barman. "Paul, you'd better keep an eye on this bunch. They might get a bit rowdy and lose the run of themselves."

"Never fear boss, I'll keep them under control," Paul replied winking at Paddy.

"Fair enough, I'll be off then. Enjoy your supper girls. Oh, Moira, don't worry about Casey. I'll bring her down to the house when I'm finished with that lot." He nodded at his dining French students and squeezed his wife's hand.

"That'll be grand Paddy, but make sure you wrap her up warmly. The night air isn't good for her."

"Moira, give over. Your mother will have her swaddled up so tightly that a gale couldn't get at her if it tried. Just relax and enjoy your night off."

"Paddy is right, Moira, stop fussing and I think you need a refill," Imelda said. Seeing Moira was extremely tense, she signalled the barman.

Paul hadn't taken his eyes off Pauline since she'd walked in, and he was over in a flash.

"What can I get the ladies to drink?"

"I'll have a large whisky and water please. My father would turn anyone to drink," Pauline muttered.

Paul pretended he hadn't heard the last bit.

Imelda glanced briefly at Pauline; she knew her father continually gave her a hard time.

"Coming right up, and what would the other lady like to drink?" Paul said, still eyeing Pauline's long slender legs.

"I'll just have a mineral water for the moment please," Cathy replied.

"And Moira, will you be having another?" Paul asked.

"Sure, Paul, I will."

"Am I invisible or something?" Imelda said as she waved her empty wine glass in the air.

"The same again?" Paul said apologetically.

"The same again, thank you young man," Moira replied and leaned over to Cathy saying quietly, "Still feeling muzzy?"

"Just a tad," Cathy answered, hoping she sounded better than she felt.

"Moira, I wouldn't have recognised the place. It looks super," Pauline remarked as she looked around her.

"Thanks, it's more functional this way and much more practical. But I can tell you, I had my work cut out for me getting Paddy to agree to the renovations."

Moira had opened up one of the outside walls and it now led out onto a tiled balcony via large double-glazed doors, which commanded a superb view of the paddocks and the river. It gave the guests the alternative of eating and drinking *al fresco* if they chose to, and the balcony had become a popular watering hole during the summer months.

It also afforded her the opportunity to add the necessary wheelchair access, which she felt, had been omitted as an over-sight when the original plans had been drawn up.

She had partially separated the bar from the main restaurant with a simple but effective semi-circular wall of fame. All the horses who had gained achievements in the equestrian centre to date were immortalised in acrylic by a young man who lived locally. As a boy, he had been paralysed by a freak hunting accident on his pony. Although he couldn't ride any more, his paintings were his way of staying in contact with the equines he dearly loved. Stubbs had been his first commission and he had painted him from an old photograph. Paddy thought the likeness was remarkable.

The old stonewalls had been lined from floor to ceiling with aged knotty pine. In the attic of the house, Paddy owned in Brittas Bay, Moira had found a pile of old tapestries depicting various hunting scenes. Most of them were hopelessly moth-eaten but a few were presentable enough for display. They found a new lease on life on the pine walls.

The stark chandeliers had been replaced by softer lighting, which gently brought out the sheen in the heavy autumn-coloured velvet drapes that hung across the glass wall over-looking the indoor arena. During horse shows, they could be pulled back for spectator enjoyment.

On the decorator's advice, the ceiling panels had been re-moved to expose the heavy wooden beams, and muted spot-lights had been dispersed at random between them.

The semi-circular chairs were made from light oak and Moira had them recovered in deep maroon leather. They matched the oak tables beautifully. Moira hated table clothes, instead, she used maroon place mats with the name Murphy's Restaurant and Equestrian Centre embroidered on them in bronze-coloured thread.

The fireplace had caused a slight bit of consternation between Moira and Paddy. He said it was a hazard, but with the help of the local fire chief, Moira won her case. It was created from the granite stone blocks that had been discarded when the original stable block was rebuilt. It was shaped like a large horseshoe with a seating area on either side, constructed lovingly from railway sleepers by a local carpenter.

The tiled floor was covered over with a deep shag pile carpet in a muted mustard colour with a slight green fleck in it.

Moira's love of plants was tastefully evident. Her strategic placement of large ferns and miniature date palms created a warm and friendly atmosphere.

"Why don't you all go ahead and order? I reserved a table by the fire for you. I need to check on something," Moira said before she disappeared through the kitchen doors.

Paul handed them the menus. "Ladies, can I get you another drink?"

"Oh, I think we could manage another one," Imelda answered.

"Same drinks all round?" Paul asked, now studying Pauline's legs.

"Yes, thank you, the same again and I think you should top Moira's glass also."

A short while later Charlotte took the food order and they moved over to their reserved table. Moira joined them once again and promised she would leave the restaurant in Char- lotte's capable hands. They were determined to hold her to her word. A few minutes later, the starters arrived.

"Cathy you're very quiet. Don't tell me you're still hung over?" Pauline asked.

"No, I'm fine, just a bit tired. I hope I'm not coming down with something," Cathy fibbed.

"How was your last trip?" Moira asked. She didn't need to enquire about the food as they were all eating with gusto.

"Actually it was fun. We had a good bunch of passengers and a parrot. I wonder where the poor thing is now," Cathy said, more to herself than anyone else.

"Did you say a parrot?" Moira and Imelda said together.

"Yeah, somehow a passenger managed to smuggle a little 'Sun Conure' on board."

"Oh, come on, how could that happen?" Imelda asked.

"He carried it on board in his hand luggage," Cathy replied matter-of-factly.

"But surely security would have noticed?" Imelda said with a lift of her eyebrow.

"Well, he managed to get on board with it, so security slipped up somewhere," Cathy answered.

"Start from the beginning. How did a parrot get on board your flight?" Pauline demanded to know.

"Okay, but can I have a glass of wine? I think the gingered chicken and melon has cured my hangover. And Moira, it was really good, my compliments to the chef."

"I'll let him know. Now back to the parrot." Moira was starting to relax.

Cathy settled back in her chair. The trio wanted to hear her explanation.

"The flight of the 'Sun Conure'." Cathy laughed.

"Yes, go on, tell us." Pauline urged.

"Right, hold your proverbial horses, will you. Oh, Moira, do you have a bottle of Merlot in stock by any chance? "

"Yes, we do, I'll get Paul to open a bottle." Moira went over to the bar and placed Cathy's order. On her way back, she was waylaid by a couple of regular customers.

"Now see what you've done with your *have you any Merlot?* She's supposed to be on a night off." Pauline chastised Cathy.

A few minutes later Moira sat down with them again. "Sorry about that, your wine is on its way. Ah, here it is."

Paul opened the bottle with an exaggerated amount of testosterone flourish. When he had poured it, he reluctantly went back to his bar duties. He found Pauline much more interesting than any of his other female customers.

"Pay no attention to him, he's new and harmless but he does think he's a bit of a ladies' man. Now, can we hear about this sun bird before our main course arrives?" Moira asked and made a mental note to have a word with Paul about his unnecessary forwardness.

Cathy continued once more. "We were getting ready for take off. The passengers all embarked without any fuss at all. Usually someone is in the wrong seat or there's not enough room in the overhead bins for their duty-free, whatever, the usual stuff. But we had no prob's anywhere and we took off on time." Cathy stopped to take a sip of wine. "Mmmm, this wine is good."

"Here, have the bottle. What airport? Which country?" Pauline asked sliding the wine bottle across the table at the same time.

"Cairo, Africa."

"I know where Cairo is. The parrot, what about the bloody parrot?" Pauline was becoming impatient.

"Keep your knickers on, Pauline."

"Jesus, it's like trying to get blood out of a turnip. Will you tell us about the damn parrot? We can't read your mind, you know." Pauline pushed her gently on the arm.

"Where was I?"

"You'd just taken off or something along that line." Imelda reminded her.

"Yeah, well, we were about five hours into the flight and most of the passengers were sleeping. That's one of the plusses with night flights. Anyway, Cody and I were in the rear galley having our supper when the attendant bell rang in row 129 and I went to answer it. The passenger, I forget her name, told me that something in the overhead bin didn't seem quite right. We were speaking quietly until the man sitting beside her woke up. He looked very uncomfortable and he wanted to know if something was wrong. Then he became very agitated. Now I'm thinking we have a bomb on board, honestly I did."

The waitress interrupted politely. She asked Moira if they were ready for the main course. Moira asked her to wait for a few minutes.

"Go on Cathy, continue." Moira encouraged.

Cathy did as she was asked.

"I told her I'd have it checked out and she happily sat down again. Cody was the head steward on that flight so I informed him that a passenger thought there was something suspicious in the overhead on 129 etcetera, etcetera. Cool as a cucumber, he sauntered up the aisle to have a word with her. She told him it wasn't her bag but she had definitely heard some weird noises coming from that bin. Without any prompting, the male passenger piped up that the bag was actually his and he could explain. I'm standing behind Cody trying to remember the emergency procedures I'm supposed to follow, just in case, but I couldn't remember a thing. My mind went blank. Cody asked the male passenger to describe the contents of his hand luggage. The man stayed quiet so Cody asked him again. Honestly, he looked like he was about to start crying. I didn't know what to think. He told Cody he was sorry for any trouble that he might be causing and he admitted openly that his bag had a parrot in it." Cathy finished her wine.

"Can we get another bottle please?" she said to the waitress standing close by.

"Anyway, Cody brings the guy and his bag down to the rear of the aircraft and sure enough, inside was a small wooden box containing a live and very forlorn looking little bird. How he got it past security I still don't know. Then Cody told me to stay with the passenger while he went up to the cockpit. The poor fellow, his name was Johann, was very upset. He told me he had the

163

bird for over six years and he didn't want to leave it behind. He was being transferred to London or something like that. I was so relieved he only had a bird in his bag and not a couple of pounds of explosives. I could have kissed him. To cut a long story sideways, the parrot was put behind the observer's desk in the cockpit and Cody reassured the female passenger that everything was fine. He told her the bag contained a battery-operated toy parrot and there was nothing to be concerned about. Are we going to eat at all tonight?"

Moira signalled the waitress to bring the main courses. "Is that it? What happened to the guy with the bird? Was he arrested?" Moira asked.

"I think he was when we arrived at Heathrow, but ..."

She was interrupted by the French visitors noisily preparing to leave. One of them came over and thanked Moira on the group's behalf for her hospitality and he complimented her on the cuisine.

Then their own main course arrived and they were temp-orarily distracted by the urge to satisfy their appetites. Pauline wanted to hear the rest of Cathy's flight with the parrot so she urged her on.

In between mouthfuls, Cathy told them that the captain was a grumpy old fart. He had ranted and raved about security breaches, lack of competence and FAA regulations. "I always thought his hair looked strange but I didn't realise he was wearing a toupee."

"How did you find that out?" Imelda asked gob-smacked.

"James, the co-pilot, called me up to the cockpit. Shall we have Irish coffees afterwards?"

"I think that's a good idea, but shall we finish our meal first?" Moira said, laughing silently to herself at Cathy.

"Yeah, okay, but the grumpy old fart had fallen asleep."

"The grumpy old fart? You mean the captain. He'd, he'd fallen asleep?" Pauline was nervous enough about flying and she didn't like the idea of the captain sleeping on the job at all.

"Yep, out for the count, fast asleep in noddy-land." Cathy was used to flight crew having a quick naps on long-haul flights. To Pauline, the whole prospect of sleeping captains' was appalling.

"Anyway, the bird managed to escape," Cathy said, gulping down more wine.

"Are you for real?"

"Pauline, shut up," Imelda and Moira said together.

"Yes, I'm for real, the bird escaped. Listen here, when I opened the cockpit door it was sitting on the old fart's shoulder nibbling away on his toupee or wig, or whatever you call it. The little blighter had actually pulled it sideways off his head and down over his right eye. You should have seen the expression on James's face, it was classic."

Pauline had to butt in again. "James, is he the other pilot?"

"Pauline, you said you'd stay quiet." Imelda reminded her.

"Sorry, I won't say another word all night."

Cathy continued, "Jees, it was a hell of a job getting the little devil back in his box. Imagine a bird that small eating his way out through a plywood box. He nibbled away at the hinge until he'd made a tiny little hole and squeezed himself out. James didn't notice anything until he saw it landing on the old fart's shoulder."

"And they say statistically, flying is the safest mode of transport," Moira said. She was enjoying herself.

"Statistically it is. Anyway, that's enough of my trolley-dolly stories. Moira tell us about motherhood?" Cathy couldn't help but ask, as Kevin was keen to start a family.

"It has its ups and downs, like anything else, I suppose."

Cathy could hear from her tone she wasn't going to get much information out of her, so she dropped the topic.

The coffees were served by Paul, who made such a fuss that Moira shooed him away, much to his disgust.

"Pauline, the magazine you work for in London, what's it called?" Imelda asked.

"It's called *Coffee Break*."

They all laughed. Pauline didn't mind. It wasn't the first time the magazine's name had been criticized.

"No, seriously, that's what it's called. They like the name; nearly everyone has the same reaction that you all do. They think it advertises itself or something like that. The guy's in advertising are a bit weird."

"What do you write? Give us an example." Imelda was curious.

"I write short stories. The magazine publishes three or four of them a month, along with human-interest topics, wacky competitions, crosswords and ... all that sort of stuff."

"Come on, don't be shy. Tell us what you wrote last."

"Ah, it was a bit silly."

"Well, they wouldn't have printed it if they thought it was silly. Now would they?" Cathy enthused.

"Tell us, please," they all said together.

"Okay, okay, okay, give me a sec." Pauline leaned back in her chair while she decided which story to tell them.

"Right, this story is more of a long winded kind of a joke really, I'm going to give you the condensed version."

"Okay, what's it called?" Cathy asked as she finished her glass of wine.

"A Moral in the Story." Pauline answered.

"Pauline, wait a sec," Moira interrupted.

"Charlotte, can we have four Irish coffees' please?"

"Sure, four Irish coffees' on the way," Charlotte replied.

"Sorry Pauline, please go on," Moira was all ears.

"Okay, now I don't want any criticism from anyone, especially you Cathy Corway." Pauline threw a scrunched up napkin at her friend.

"My lips are sealed and it's C-A-S-S-I-D-Y not Corway."

Pauline didn't answer her and started telling her story.

"Miss Ryan, a young and enthusiastic primary school teacher recently qualified from college, gave her class of lively six-year-olds a homework assignment, which would involve a certain amount of family participation.

Over the coming weekend, they were to ask their parents to tell them a short story with a moral to it. None of them were quite sure what exactly a moral was, so she set about explaining the word to them. One little individual thought she was talking about a knitting pattern because she often heard her mother saying one plain, one moral.

Miss Ryan thought the assignment was a good one. Her students' knowledge would be broadened with the help and co-operation of their families and she was quite pleased with herself.

The following Monday morning, her students' waited eag- erly to tell their tales, and each child was convinced that his or her story was definitely the best.

Eventually, Miss Ryan asked Mary Connelly to stand up and tell the class her story. Then she sat back in her chair and waited patiently for the little girl to gather herself together.

Nervously, Mary stood up and started her tale.

"Well, Miss, my dad has hundreds of chickens. Now the hens lay many eggs, but out of every three eggs that they lay, one is a dud and we only get two chicks. That's what dad calls them - duds. The child stood still and stared at her teacher.

"Thank you, Mary, will you tell us the moral to your story?" Miss Ryan prompted.

"Oh, don't count your chickens before they are all hatched completely out," Mary replied, beaming at her teacher.

"Very good, thank you, you can sit down now."

A wave of hands shot up in the air. Miss, Miss, me, me, me.

"Children, quiet now, please. Peter Mooney, will you tell the class your story please?" Miss Ryan asked the boy.

Peter stood up, pushed his chair backwards and it toppled over.

"Sorry Miss."

"It's okay Peter, relax, take your time," Miss Ryan soothed.

The boy sorted himself out and started to tell his contribution.

"My dad's a chicken farmer as well, but he sells the eggs." Peter announced indignantly as he cast a sideways glance at Mary Connelly before continuing. "He was bringing all the eggs to market one day and he had a bit of an accident, his van drove into a pot-hole. It was a huge pothole, right in the middle of the road. Anyway, all the eggs fell over, and a lot of them got broken. They made a huge gooey mess."

Miss Ryan smiled warmly at him. "Peter dear, the moral to your story?"

"Right, Miss, don't put all of your eggs in, in the, in the one basket Miss."

"Excellent Peter, thank you. You can sit down and slowly this time."

Imelda smiled to herself. She thought Pauline was a born storyteller. Cathy wanted to order some dessert. Pauline told her she needed to be de-wormed and Moira suggested the Pavlova.

"Did your mother make it?" Pauline asked.

"Yes, she did. She likes to keep her hand in."

"Well, if Mrs Byrne's Pavlova is on the menu, I want two portions. It's always scrumptious," Cathy said.

"See what I mean? Moira, call Tony, I'm sure he'll have a spare horse de-wormer in the feed room." Pauline quipped.

"Very funny, Pauline, very funny," Cathy said, smiling.

Charlotte was dispatched for three portions of the famous Pavlova.

"Come on Pauline, finish the story. Don't pay any attention to the bottomless pit beside you," Imelda said. She ordered cheese, crackers, and a glass of port.

Moira suggested that they all have some port, as it would round off the meal nicely.

"Shall I continue or not?" Pauline asked Imelda.

"Please do, some people have left their manners at home, you know."

"Thanks, I'll go on then?"

Imelda nodded in agreement.

"As I was saying before I was rudely interrupted. Miss Ryan was deciding which one of her eager little pupils' she would choose next, when she noticed Tommy Maher was about to burst, so she asked him to tell his story. She was a bit nervous where Tommy was concerned. He wasn't a bold child, but, if anything went wrong in the classroom, or in the school playground, Tommy was sure to be involved.

Tommy was delighted he'd been chosen next. He stood up carefully, looking his teacher straight in the eye.

"Miss Ryan felt a slight shiver run down her back. She knew where Tommy was concerned anything was possible. Her gut instinct had kicked in big time. Tommy glanced around the class. Once he was satisfied that he had everyone's attention he started his story.

"Well now Miss, my Uncle Pat was a pilot during the war. One day he was sent on a big important mission, a really huge mission Miss. He had to rescue three presidents from some place in America. They'd all been arrested by another country. But the aeroplane he was flying in got itself into a big problem and the pilot told him he'd have to jump out. Now, all Uncle Pat had with him was his parachute, his bottle of whisky, his machine gun, and a big knife."

A distinct silence surrounded the classroom.

"He jumped out of the plane and his parachute opened with no problems at all. He was happy about that. Dad said that sometimes they don't open you know. Anyway, while he was parachuting down, he thought it would be a good idea to drink his whisky, just in case the bottle got broken when he landed, you understand.

Now, he's enjoying himself, he's looking all around him, and he's feeling happy. Then he looks down again and he notices he's another problem coming up very, very quickly. You see he was about to land in the middle of a hundred of the enemy guys'. They weren't the ones that had the president's though, those ones were miles away. Anyway, he landed safely enough, and the bad guys' surrounded him and guess what he did then?"

Not one child in the classroom said a word, so Tommy continued. "He shot 70 of the enemy guys' with his machine gun and then he ran out of bullets. So, he killed another 20 with his knife but the blade went blunt. Then, he lost the complete run of himself and he killed the other 10 with his bare hands. 100 bad guys' to kill on your own is a lot you know."

"And what is the moral to your story, Tommy?" Miss Ryan asked him with a fair amount of trepidation.

"Ah, sure, that's simple Miss. You don't mess with Uncle Pat when he's been drinkin'."

Pauline was given a round of applause. She hadn't been aware that a few of the other dinner guests had been listening in on her story telling.

Imelda was highly amused. *Pauline fits the bill exactly. She's a perfect candidate for that new job.* She made a mental note to have a chat with her the next day.

"Pauline Dutton, you're the limit. What else have you written? I must subscribe to *Coffee Break*," Moira said as she wiped the tears from her face.

"No, enough is enough. No more talk about my work. Are we having a nightcap?"

"Imelda, I think you and I had better take this one home soon or we'll be pouring her into the car." Cathy giggled.

"And this one nominates Cathy C-a-s-s-i-dee for the sobriety award of the evening. What time do you close Moira?" Pauline enquired.

"Whenever, the night is still young."

"A woman after my own heart. That's what you are Moira Murphy."

Paddy heard them before he saw them and his heart leapt when he singled out his wife's laughter. She sounded like her old self. He had come in through the yard door just as Paul was locking up the main entrance by the car park.

"Seems like the party's in full swing in there," Paddy said to Paul.

"Sure does. Shall we join them?" Paul answered with a glint in his eye.

"Paul, I think it's meant to be a girls' night out."

"Fair enough boss, but will you join me for a pint at the bar? The place is empty except for the four rowdies, and I don't think they'd notice if the devil himself decided to ride past them on the back of a rhinoceros."

"A pint. That sounds good. I want to have a quick word with Moira anyway. They sound well oiled up."

"They are, but what the hell, all of them are having a good time, and there's nothing wrong with that, now is there?"

"No Paul, that's for sure. Pull two decent pints of the black stuff and I'll be right over."

"Two pints on the way boss."

"Did you lock up downstairs?" Moira asked Paul as he passed her on his way back to the bar.

"I did indeed, and I found your husband lurking around in the shadows."

"I would hardly say I was lurking around Paul. You've an odd way with words."

Moira looked up when she heard her husband's voice. "There you are Paddy. Come on over here and join us. We're just about to have a nightcap. Where's Casey?" Moira looked around concerned.

"Now don't fret, your mother is keeping her for the night, and that, my dear wife means, you can have a few extra hours in bed tomorrow morning. Charlotte is coming in to help with the breakfast rush, so you've nothing to worry about."

"I'd better phone mum, Casey might need something,"

"She has everything she needs, so give over. You're having the entire night all to yourself and there's no other woman in this fair country that I know who deserves it more than you do."

"You're a good man Paddy Murphy," Moira said to her husband.

Pauline butted in. "Paddy, where have you been all night? And before you say anything, we're all getting taxi's home."

Twenty-Six

Cathy woke up to the sound of someone knocking. She didn't know where she was for a few seconds, then, looking around her, she remembered she was in her old bedroom in Bray.

"Cathy, wake up, Celia Dutton is on the phone for you," her father said, knocking loudly on her door.

"Hang on, hang on a second dad. I'll be right there," she jumped out of bed and threw on her old dressing gown.

"Sorry, what did you say?"

"I said Celia Dutton is on the phone, she's looking for Pauline. Do you know where she is? She didn't come home last night."

"She didn't ... what time is it?"

Jimmy checked his watch. "It's seven-thirty. Go and speak to Celia, don't keep her waiting any longer, she's very worried."

Cathy looked at her father through bloodshot eyes and dashed past him into the bathroom. Her stomach lurched. "I'll be right back; I need to go to the loo."

"Oh, oh fine then but hurry up," Jimmy replied.

She came down the stairs feeling a bit liverish. Her father was sitting rather dejectedly on a chair in the hall beside the phone.

"Where's Imelda, maybe she knows where Pauline is?" Cathy asked.

"Imelda was up and gone with the lark's. I dropped her off at Murphy's just after six. She left her car over there last night," Jimmy said wearily.

"I don't know how she does it. She survives on the absolute minimum amount of sleep."

"She's always been like that. Are you okay? You're as white as a ghost."

"I'm fine. I must have eaten something that didn't agree with me."

"Sure Cathy, it must have been something you ate, or drank perhaps? I told Celia you would phone her back."

Cathy was white-faced, she felt terrible. "Right, I'll do that now."

"Her number is by the phone on the notepad," Jimmy told her as he paced up and down the hall.

Cathy's hands were shaking as she dialled the number, her stomach was decidedly unsettled, Celia answered on the second ring.

"Pauline, is that you?"

"No, Mrs. Dutton, it's Cathy, sorry I kept you waiting."

"Don't worry about that. Pauline didn't come home last night and she didn't stay with Joseph either. Do you know where she is?"

Cathy momentarily froze. "Eh, eh, Mrs Dutton, we all shared a taxi home. We had a bit too much to drink. We thought it would be safer to leave the cars behind."

"Pauline was drinking? She's not supposed to drink. She can't drink, she's in recovery. Oh my God, where is she?"

"Calm down Mrs Dutton, I'm sure there's a logical explanation."

"Cathy, just tell me when was the last time you saw her?"

"Mrs Dutton, the taxi dropped Imelda and me off here and then Pauline and Paul continued on."

"Who's Paul?" Celia's voice was rising.

"He's the barman at Murphy's. He shared the taxi with us last night."

"What kind of a person is this, this Paul? Is he a respectable man?" Celia demanded.

"I don't really know him. Actually, last night was the first time I'd met him." Cathy felt a strange sensation in her chest, like a lift that had plummeted out of control to the pit of her stomach.

"Do you have this Paul person's telephone number?" Celia asked with a frantic tone in her voice.

The lift in Cathy's stomach went wild. She experienced a myriad of emotions; guilt and shame mingled with anger and resentment. She didn't know where Pauline was. She had visions of Pauline being shacked up and stoned out of her mind with the likes of 'The Monk'. Then she felt guilty for thinking like that.

"No, I don't have his number, but I'll get it for you. I'll call you back shortly"

***

It took Pauline a moment or two to realise she wasn't in her own bed. Then, it all rushed back to her. The taxi, the sex with Paul, and worst of all, she was still in his bed.

In her head, she sat bolt upright, tore at her hair and screamed. *How could I?* In reality, she lay quiet and still. Her senses had returned with the daylight and she was in the horrors.

Trying not to move, she carefully opened her eyes. Someone was still beside her. It was Paul.

Like a caged animal, her brain lurched hither and tither wondering where her clothes were. She bitterly regretted letting Paul make love to her.

172

Why had she gone to his flat in the first place? She had certainly gotten more than the promised late-night drink. Then she heard a voice.

"Morning, sexy." Paul was awake.

She pretended she was still asleep. Then she felt his arm sneak around her naked body and he pulled her closer to him. She bristled when she came into contact with his body. He had gotten lucky, very lucky with her the previous night. She instantly realised sleeping with Paul had been a terrible mistake on her part, and it would never happen again.

"Hello," he murmured to the side of her head.

She didn't answer, she wouldn't. She couldn't look at him either, so she decided to keep perfectly still in the hope he would lose interest in her. She had to get out, but she didn't want to fling back the covers until she knew where she could find her clothes.

Then the phone shrilled loudly on the bedside table.

"Don't tell anyone I'm here, don't let on, okay,"

Paul assured her, her secret was safe. He thought about not answering it but he knew it would only ring again.

"Morning, Paul speaking."

"Paul, sorry to wake you, but do you happen to know where Pauline is?" Paddy said straight to the point.

"Pauline? Pauline who?" Paul pretended to play dumb, but not a lot slipped by Paddy Murphy.

"Pauline Dutton, she was in the restaurant with Moira last night. The young woman you couldn't keep your eyes off. Apparently you shared a taxi home with her," Paddy said impatiently.

"Paddy, hang on a second," Paul covered the mouthpiece and shrugged his shoulders at Pauline.

Pauline was nearly out of control. She made a quick decision. "You'd better tell him I'm here with you. Otherwise my mother will have the special branch dragging all the rivers in search of my body."

"You're sure you want me to tell him?" Paul asked, wearing nothing more than a sly smile on his face.

"I don't want you to tell him but what choice do I have?" Pauline hissed in exasperation.

"It's your call," Paul replied.

"Paddy, Pauline is here with me. She stayed the night and she slept on the sofa."

Paddy interrupted him abruptly. "Tell her to phone her mother please. She's half out of her mind with worry." Paddy knew that Paul didn't own a sofa. His flat consisted of one bedroom, a small kitchenette and a tiny bathroom.

"Will do boss. Would you like to speak to her?"

Pauline nearly had a coronary. She mouthed the words *no, no.*

"That's not necessary. I'm sure she has other things on her mind besides speaking to me. Just make sure she phones her mother immediately." Paddy hung up without saying another word.

"Jesus Christ Paul, why did he phone you?"

"Well now, let me think. We all left Murphy's together, in the same taxi. Imelda and Cathy got out ..."

"Ah, shut up, you eejit. Give me the phone." Pauline dialled Cathy's mobile. *Cathy, please, please have your phone switched on.*

Cathy did have her phone on, and she answered it on the second ring. Kevin had just called to let her know he would be coming home the next day.

"Pauline, where the hell are you? Your mother is climbing the walls."

"That's nothing new. I can't talk now, will you come and collect me now, this instant. I'm at Paul's place."

"You're at Paul's place. The barman Paul? Moira's barman Paul?"

"Yes, the same one. Are you coming to collect me or not?"

"I'm still in my dressing gown. I'll have a quick shower and I'll ..." Pauline stopped her in mid-sentence. "Shower later. I need to get home now."

"What's the panic?" Cathy quizzed.

"Cathy, quit dithering. If it's too much trouble I'll call a taxi."

"There's no need to do that. Where does he live?"

Pauline didn't know where Paul lived and she was in his flat. She had just gotten out of his bed.

"Hang on."

Paul was sitting quietly, just smiling at her.

"How does Cathy get here? What's your address?"

Paul gave her the directions and she relayed them to Cathy who promised to come right over as soon as she had collected her car from the restaurant.

Pauline hissed at her to hurry up, again.

Cathy hung up the phone, pulled on a pair of jeans and a sweatshirt, and asked her father to drop her off. He didn't ask any questions, he just agreed.

To Pauline's horror she realised she had been talking on the phone stark naked and Paul was obviously enjoying the view. She grabbed the clothes she could find and charged into the bathroom. *Fuck it, fuck, fuck, fuck,* she said to her reflection in the stained mirror. Then she remembered she hadn't phoned her mother.

Hastily putting herself back together, she returned to Paul's love den. He was talking on the phone. She snatched the receiver from his hand and shouted into it, *he'll phone you back*. She phoned her home number and her brother Joseph answered. He'd just popped in to have breakfast with his mother as he had a client to visit in the area.

"Pauline, for God's sake, what are you playing at? Mum is doing her nut. She thinks you've been abducted."

"What's all the fuss about? I'm not two years old you know." Pauline was in her defensive mode.

"You should have let her know you weren't coming home."

"Good God, I don't believe this. Can I stay at your place for a few day's just until she settles down a bit?"

Joseph always had a hard time refusing Pauline anything but he was extremely annoyed with her. He thought she had no right to be so inconsiderate.

"That'll be okay, but speak to mum. She's standing right beside me." He handed the phone to his mother.

"Pauline, tell me you're all right. Where are you? Why didn't you phone to say you weren't coming home?" Celia was in a complete dither and very upset. Normally she took everything in her stride.

"I'm fine. I stayed the night with a friend and I didn't call because I didn't want to wake you. It was late when we left Murphy's."

"Wake me up? I didn't sleep a wink all night and your father is furious. Which friend did you stay with?"

"Mum, that's none of your business and stop treating me like a bloody child. I'm sick of it. I'm a grown woman and I make my own decisions. Find something else to do besides interfere in my life."

"Pauline Dutton, don't you dare speak to me like that. I am your mother and I will not tolerate it. You're a brazen brat." Celia handed the phone back to her son.

"Well done, you handled that very diplomatically."

"Now don't you start," Pauline answered her brother.

"Do you want me to come and pick you up?"

"No, don't worry. Cathy's on her way to collect me, but thanks anyway. I'll see you later."

"Hang on, where exactly are you?"

"Joseph, leave it. Do I question you about your social life, huh?"

"Oh for Christ sake Pauline, what's the big secret? You're not in any trouble are you?"

"No, I'm not."

"You sure?"

"Yes, I'm sure. Joseph, I can't talk now. I'll see you back at your place."

"All right, I'll leave it for now, but I won't be home for a few days. I have to sort a problem out in Limerick. Phone me when you get back to the flat please."

"Right, I'll do that. Bye"

Pauline waited anxiously by the window for Cathy to pull up. She was trying to avoid having any further conversation with Paul. She didn't want to look at him. But she had to pee, and as luck would have it, Cathy arrived and beeped the horn while she was in the bathroom.

When she was finished, she nearly choked when she saw Paul standing at the open door wearing only his boxers.

"For fuck sake, do you normally stand around in public dressed like that?" She wanted to strangle him. "Don't bother answering me, bye now." She put a blinding smile on her face for Cathy's benefit and the effort nearly popped her eyes out.

"Wait," Paul said.

"Wait for what?"

"Can I see you again?" He asked sheepishly.

Pauline's smile was fixed solidly on her face and she told him ever so politely, no, he couldn't.

She jumped into the car beside Cathy.

"Have you gone completely crazy? You look like shit." Cathy was appalled at Pauline's appearance. She had mascara smudges under her eyes, her hair was a mess, and she had a large hole in the knee of her panty hose. And, she was missing a shoe.

"Thanks a lot. Since when did you become Mother bloody Teresa's fashion guru? Will you please drive the car? He's still standing at the door." The smile disappeared from her face.

"And where am I to drive to?" Cathy asked wearily, she was feeling terribly queasy.

"Anywhere, just get away from here." Pauline could feel Paul's eyes boring into the back of her head.

"Did you phone your mum?"

"Y-e-s I did. Now drive the fucking car."

Cathy realised she couldn't take Pauline back to her mother's house, not in the physical state she was in. Her mother would probably collapse. Without any further consultation, she decided to take her home to her own flat in Swords. At least she could have a shower and borrow a change of clothes from her. They stayed silent for most of the journey.

"Thanks for collecting me, you're a good mate you know," Pauline said as Cathy parked the car outside her flat.

"Don't mention it. What are friends for eh? Come on, let's get inside. I feel like a bunch of fairies dried their wings on my tongue."

"You do look pretty pale. The after effects from last night?" Pauline said closing the car door.

"Yeah, I don't think I'll ever drink again." The lift in her stomach was searching for another floor.

"How many times have I said the same thing, but it was a good night, wasn't it."

"Yes it was and some of us had more fun than the others."

While Pauline showered, Cathy fetched some clean clothes for her and started to make some coffee, but the smell of it launched the lift in her stomach into an erratic dalliance.

As Pauline came out of the bathroom, she was nearly sent flying by Cathy's mad dash past her.

"Jesus, what's the hurry?" Pauline asked alarmed.

Cathy didn't answer her. When she returned about 10 minutes later, Pauline took control of the situation. "Come on, into bed with you."

Cathy looked sadly at her and flopped down on her bed wishing Kevin was home.

Pauline quickly showered and dressed in the clothes Cathy had left out for her. Luckily, they wore the same dress and shoe size. Then she joined a sorry-looking Cathy in her bedroom where she was curled up underneath the blankets."

She studied her friend's face.

"Why are you looking at me like that? Stop it. You are making me feel like a piece of meat on a butcher's counter."

"When did you have your last period?"

"I can't remember. You know me, I'm never regular."

"Well remember Cathy. I.U.Ds are not one hundred percent safe."

"Oh my God Pauls, do you think I'm pregnant?"

"The thought had crossed my mind."

"But I can't be. I don't want to be."

"Mrs. Cassidy, I think we should find out. Come on, go and have a shower and I'll pop down to the pharmacy and get one of those home pregnancy kits."

Without another word, Pauline grabbed one of Cathy's jackets from the hall closet and left for the pharmacy.

Cathy didn't stir. Her mind flashed back to a comment she had recently overheard between two flight attendants. '*My husband and I are either going to buy a dog or have a child. What we can't decide on, is, whether we should ruin our carpets or ruin our lives.*'

When Pauline returned a short while later Cathy was still in bed feeling miserable.

"Lazy sod, now the instructions say that. Bloody hell. According to this, you have to start peeing and then stop, then start again, aiming directly onto this plastic thingy. Then you wait for three minutes. Blue means negative, red means positive."

"Pauline, I'm not pregnant. I'm hung over."

Pauline was taking no nonsense from her. "I've bought the thing now. Go, just go and use it."

Cathy thought Pauline was over reacting. "Give me that leaflet thing, I'll read it myself." She studied the instructions through watery eyes. "It's a guide to pelvic floor exercises, and it also has the added bonus of diagnosing if one is pregnant or not. I'm not going to hear the end of it until I actually pee on this thing, am I?"

"Nope, you're not."

"Right then, I'll be back." She slouched off with the offending plastic object in her sweaty palm.

The phone rang and Pauline ignored it. She was anxious that it might be an advance team retained by her father to track her down and carry her off to rehab land.

"Who was on the phone?" Cathy asked when she came back with the pregnancy test in her hand.

"I didn't answer it. Feck it Cathy, what colour has that thing turned?"

"It's red."

"Red, did you say red? Let me see it."

"Yep, you're absolutely right, it's red. The test is positive. You're going to be a momma. Oh, Cathy this is great."

Cathy burst into tears and Pauline was at a loss for words.

A few minutes later, she was calm enough to speak. "Pauls, I don't want to be pregnant. I'm not ready to be a bloody mother yet."

The phone rang again.

"Oh, Pauls, answer it," Cathy said through great big hiccupping sobs.

Not wanting to admit her own fears about the impending hit squad, Pauline reluctantly answered the phone.

"Hello, this is the Cassidy residence. How can I help you?"

"The Cassidy residence. Who is this?"

Pauline recognised Maggie's voice and mouthed across the room, *it's your mother-in-law.* Cathy turned even paler and slid an imaginary knife across her throat.

"It's Pauline Dutton, Mrs Cassidy. How are you this fine morning?"

"Very well, thank you. I would like to speak to Cathy if you please and tell her to hurry up. I have a luncheon appointment."

What a snotty bitch, Pauline thought.

"Cathy's not here Mrs Cassidy. She just popped out to buy a bucket of condoms, or something along that line. Kevin should be home soon and you know how Cathy likes to be organised." Pauline heard the sharp intake of Maggie's astonished breath.

"I'll ...I will call her back later on."

"I'll tell her you called. I'm sure she'll be awfully disappointed she missed you. Bye now."

The line went dead; Mrs Cassidy didn't answer her. *Sanctimonious old cow,* thought Pauline.

"I can't believe you said that. She's probably bolted straight off to the church to say 900 Stations of the Cross and 300 novenas."

"Ah, it'll give her something to talk about over her luncheon. You shouldn't let her get to you."

"That's easy for you to say. Listen, I'm going to make an appointment with a doctor and I'm going to do it now. I think that test is faulty." Cathy had done her maths and she realised she was over a month late.

She found the number of a local doctor's surgery and the receptionist told her she could come along right away. There was no need for her to make an appointment, the practice worked on a first-come first-served basis. Cathy was glad about that as she didn't have a regular doctor since Dr Kennedy had retired over a year ago. The only real need she had for a doctor since she married was to have her I.U.D. fitted and that had been fitted in the woman's clinic. Any other minor ailments were attended to by the airline doctor.

***

Upon her arrival at the surgery, Cathy filled out the necessary new patient registration forms. Then she took her seat in the waiting room alongside Pauline and she fidgeted like a child while she waited for her name to be called. There were only two other patients ahead of her. Nevertheless, the time crawled. Eventually her turn came.

"Mrs Cassidy, will you follow me?" The receptionist asked her. She led Cathy into a consulting room and introduced her to Dr Pricemore.

The doctor was young, attractive, and female and she had an engaging smile. Cathy warmed to her.

"Mrs. Cassidy, it's a pleasure to meet you. Would you like to take a seat?" Dr Pricemore asked her pleasantly.

"Thanks, I will." Cathy normally hated doctors' surgeries and hospitals. Anything to do with the medical profession in general made her uneasy, but the woman sitting in front of her made her feel relaxed.

Dr Pricemore read briefly through her details. "Now Mrs. Cassidy, how can I help you?"

Cathy told her about the home pregnancy test and the doctor agreed they could give a false result. She asked Cathy many questions about her health in general, and then asked if she had brought a urine sample along. Cathy hadn't thought to bring one.

"That's fine, don't worry. I'll give you a specimen bottle and maybe you could give me a sample now?"

"Sure I can. But, how long will I have to wait for the results?

"The urine test will give us a result in a few minutes."

Cathy was relieved to hear that. She went off to the loo with her sample bottle and when she returned, Dr Pricemore took her offering without batting an eyelid. She sat down and waited, neither spoke. The minutes ticked by like hours for her.

"Well, Mrs. Cassidy, congratulations are in order, you are definitely pregnant."

Cathy was crestfallen. She had convinced herself that the home kit was faulty and the whole pregnancy issue had been blown out of proportion.

"You don't look very happy about the results. Is there a problem with the father perhaps?"

Cathy stared at her for a few moments and then replied, "A problem with the father. No nothing like that, he'll be delighted. He'll start buying cigars for the entire country as soon as he finds out. As a matter of fact, my husband is very keen to start a family."

"But you're not happy about the idea yourself?"

"Don't get me wrong, I want to have children. Not just right now. I'm not ready to be a mother."

Dr Pricemore understood Cathy's concerns. "Mrs. Cassidy, we'll get you ready. Will you pop up on the examination couch? I want to give you a quick once over."

Cathy removed her shoes and lay down robotically. She was far away in another land, the land of Holles Street Maternity Hospital where her mother had died. She remembered the vast amount of pregnant woman who seemed to be institutionalised there and the muffled screams she had heard coming from distant places within the hospital. She was working herself up into a panic. She was brought back to reality by the doctor taking the blood pressure cuff off her arm, at the same time telling her she was going to take a blood sample for some routine tests.

"Hmmm, sure, yes doctor, that's okay. Can you tell me when

the baby will be born … due?"

"I'll estimate the date for you in a minute. Let's finish up here first," she answered Cathy professionally, but kindly.

"What's the blood test for exactly?"

"Oh, nothing at all alarming. I just need to determine your blood type, Rh stats, and blood count etcetera."
Cathy had no idea what Rh stats were and didn't bother to ask.

Dr Pricemore took the blood sample efficiently and Cathy hardly felt a thing. Then she asked Cathy to join her at her desk. When Cathy was seated in front of her she asked her a few more questions while she studied a chart.

"If the date of your last period is accurate, your baby will be due the last week of February. You are approximately 10 weeks pregnant."

"Ten weeks pregnant." Cathy exclaimed and went cold.

"Give or take a few days. The exact period of gestation can only be determined accurately by ultrasound, but that will come later on."

She gave Cathy a prescription for folic acid tablets which she instructed her to take every day and she gave her a booklet entitled 'First Pregnancy Questions and Answers'.

"One last thing Mrs Cassidy, do you know your husband's blood group?"

Cathy couldn't remember what type Kevin was.

"It's not important right now. You can let me know on your next visit. Can you come and see me next week?"

"Sure, I'll do that. Will I make an appointment with your receptionist?"

"Appointments aren't necessary. I'm on duty every morning from nine-thirty to twelve-thirty. Congratulations again, this time next week you will have adjusted to your good news and you will be feeling a lot happier."

Cathy hoped she was right.

Pauline was chatting with the receptionist when Cathy reappeared from Dr Pricemore's consulting room.

"Well then, are you pregnant?" Pauline was hopping around with curiosity and anticipation.

"Yes, I'm 10 weeks gone."

"Ten weeks. Oh my God, we're having a baby." Pauline hugged Cathy and started fussing like a mother hen.

"Come on mum-to-be, let's get you home. You need to rest. You need to do something. I can't believe it, 10 weeks pregnant. Cathy, you are going to be a mum. Can I be the godmother?"

Twenty-Seven

Kevin was going to be a father and he was ecstatic. He tried to persuade Cathy to give up work right there and then. He wanted the best for his wife and unborn child; he wanted her to take things easy. Cathy was having none of it. She refused to become a stay-at-home mother. That role she might agree to when the baby was born, not before.

Shamrock Air reassigned her to ground-hostess duties and she hated the position vehemently. It bored her to tears. Dealing with difficult passengers in-flight was one thing, but dealing with them on the ground was another. Nevertheless, she stuck to her guns.

When she was approaching the seventh month of her pregnancy, Kevin was headhunted by *Beta Air*. The main core of the company concentrated on the repair and leasing of aircraft engines. They offered him a competitive salary package, which was just over triple the amount he was receiving from *Aer Lingus*. As *Beta Air* was relatively new, Kevin investigated the company thoroughly. When he was satisfied the position was a viable one, he resigned.

Aer Lingus, were upset and disappointed, he was highly regarded in his field. They offered him a counter offer but he refused. He wanted to experience new fields. His new job would entail a lot more travelling, but that didn't bother Cathy too much. She was used to short separations from her husband. Within specific areas of the airline industry, it was common-place.

However, Kevin refused to take on any assignments outside the country until his son or daughter was born. He wanted to be with his wife when she gave birth to his first child and *Beta Air* were more than happy to comply with his initial requests.

When Cathy reached full term and there was no sign of her going into labour, she became intolerably ratty. She had given up work six weeks before and she was fed up heaving herself around everywhere. She couldn't remember the last time she saw her feet from an upright position and was mightily pissed off.

Kevin was convinced all women actually lost their minds when they became pregnant. He had tried; work permitting, to accompany her to her gynaecological visits and pre-natal classes. He read everything he could lay his hands on regarding first pregnancies, labour and the father's participation therein. But, Cathy bewildered him. One minute she was the epitome of sweetness and pie and the next she was a ranting banshee.

Cathy's gynaecologist told them that first-time mothers often exceeded the expected due date and pregnant women in general suffered from various hormonal pendulum effects. This they knew already and it didn't do anything to help Cathy's mood swings.

Nonetheless, it was an exciting time for them both. Kevin and his father turned the spare bedroom into a beautiful nursery. They removed the small featureless window and replaced it with a much larger one that allowed the sun into what was beforehand, a rather dingy room. They constructed a built-in wardrobe with an ingenious baby-changing station alongside, complete with its own mini bathroom.

Cathy and Pauline spent many happy and sometimes agonising hours selecting the correct furniture. The nursery contained everything that a baby could possibly need.

Kevin had felt a little left out in the furniture-shopping part, but he didn't mind. However, the baby car seat and stroller had to be given the once over by him, before the final decision was made.

At one stage, they had considered moving to a house in the country, but they liked the flat. They had done a lot to it and it was their first home together. It was situated on the ground floor and was very suitable to raise a young child in. They put the idea on the back burner for a while. Moving to a new house would come later on.

Cathy was overdue by nearly three weeks and her gynae-cologist became concerned because her blood pressure had risen to an unacceptable level. He advised admission to the nursing home the following day for inducement.

Cathy was thrilled her pregnancy was finally coming to fruition. Kevin was relieved and a bit disappointed. He had entertained glorious visions of frantically but calmly driving across town through red traffic lights, with his young wife in the early stages of labour.

Cathy laughed at his visions. *How could he be frantic and calm at the same time?*

At ten o' clock, the following morning Cathy was ushered into the theatre at *St. Michael's Nursing Home* to have her water broken. She had been told the procedure was a simple one and virtually painless. It wasn't. To Cathy it felt like a mutant family of party-going manic scorpions had crawled up inside her. She was about to tell the doctor to push off and leave her alone, when all of a sudden, she experienced a feeling similar to an elastic band popping inside her, followed by a warm rush of fluid gushing out of her body. The membrane had finally given way.

The doctor inserted an intravenous drip into the back of her hand and told her everything looked good.

A short while later the nurse who was escorting her back to her room told her she had seven children herself. Cathy thought the nurse was gone in the head.

Kevin was waiting anxiously for her. He hadn't been allowed into the theatre, but he was assured he could to stay with his wife during her labour and birthing. With his help, Cathy managed to settle herself down, and 20 minutes later, she experienced her first labour pain. It was a mild one, but Kevin panicked and rushed out to summon help. A nurse returned with him and routinely checked Cathy over. She reassured her all was well and she would be back in a short while. Ten minutes later Cathy had another pain, it was much stronger than the first, catching her off guard.

When the nurse came back, she examined Cathy internally. She told them the baby was in a bit of a hurry to meet the parents.

"Do you mean the baby is about to be born?" Kevin blurted out.

"No Mr. Cassidy, your baby won't be born for a while yet. Your wife has a bit of a way to go. Later on I'll give her some pethidine to help her."

"Pethidine ... drugs. I'm not giving my baby drugs," Cathy said appalled at the nurse's suggestion.

"Fair enough, Mrs Cassidy. Now relax and remember your breathing techniques." She adjusted the flow from Cathy's IV and went off about her business.

For the next two hours, Cathy's pains came regularly, ten minutes apart. Then things started to speed up, her contractions jumped to three-minute intervals.

Kevin babbled on about the dives he planned for them when the baby was born. He reminded her that she'd soon be able to ride Dubba again.

Cathy hadn't any interest in his dive plans or Dubba, she told him to shut the hell up.

"Ah, Cathy love, don't be like that."

"Don't be like w-h-a-t? You get into this bed and give birth to this bloody baby then."

Kevin didn't answer, as he didn't know what to say.

A new and stronger contraction flooded her body and she demanded that Kevin do something, got someone, anyone. He didn't have to. The nurse came back and busied herself with Cathy's charts while another contraction started a powerful rippling wave of pain through her patient.

She muttered some words while she checked Cathy's blood pressure.

"Is everything all right nurse?" Kevin asked, nearly crushing Cathy's hand in his anxiety.

"Everything is fine."

"Fine, is that what you call it? I call it fecking agony."

Another contraction much stronger than the last one started and to Cathy, it seemed to last forever. "Enough, enough of this crap, give me the drugs and give them to me now!"

The nurse told Cathy she was going to move her to the labour ward because her contractions were coming quite close together. She would give her an injection there.

"Labour ward, is the baby coming?" Kevin asked. He was trying very hard to be calm.

"No Mr. Cassidy, your wife isn't about to give birth just yet. I want to bring her into the labour ward so we can monitor her more closely."

"Hello, excuse me, but have I disappeared into another dimension? I'm the one in bloody labour here. Shit." Another contraction hit her hard. "Pethidine, give me the pethidine, give me any bloody drug available. Give me them all."

"Mrs Cassidy, hang on for a few more minutes until we get you set up in the labour ward," the nurse said as she unhooked the drip from its stand and clamped it tight.

"Hang in there, and my other choice is?"

"Cathy love, is there anything I can do, is there anything I can get you?" Kevin felt like a helpless buffoon.

"Yes, get this damn thing out of me." Cathy wasn't a happy puppy. She shoved Kevin's hand away roughly, as he tried to help her out of bed.

"Now Mrs Cassidy, you're only making things worse for yourself."

"How can I be making things worse? Jesus, Mary and Joseph, how do women do this over and over again?"

As soon as she put her feet on the floor, another contraction nearly flattened her. It was too much for Kevin to bear. He swept Cathy up in his arms and told the nurse to grab the IV. He was taking his wife to the labour ward himself. She was not going in a wheelchair.

The nurse didn't argue; she was well used to the angst that parents-to-be managed to get into. She had developed a fair bit of buffalo hide over the years.

"You'll be fine Cathy, think of a coral reef. Think of shoals of fish. Think of Dubba."

"Kevin, shut up, just shut up. The only thing I want to think about right now is fucking drugs."

When they reached the labour ward, a midwife connected a foetal monitor to Cathy's hugely swollen abdomen. She explained it would enable her to monitor the baby's progress more efficiently.

"What the hell is that noise?" Cathy's voice quivered.

"It's your baby's heartbeat, it's perfectly normal," the midwife reassured her.

"But it sounds so fast."

"Don't you worry about a thing. Everything is in order, just keep telling yourself that this time tomorrow it'll be all over."

"Bloody hell, I hope it doesn't go on for that long," Cathy exclaimed in horror. "I've had enough now. I've changed my mind. I want to go home. I don't want to do this anymore."

A particularly vicious contraction started which left her completely exhausted. Someone in the distance said to her, "Mrs Cassidy, listen to me, with your next contraction, I want you to push, but don't push until I tell you to."

The pethidine had kicked in, but not enough for Cathy's mind and body.

"Kevin Cassidy, this is your fault, get the hell out of here. I never want to see you again," she screamed at her astonished husband.

The doctor arrived and put his hand gently on Kevin's shoulder. His eyes said, *she doesn't mean it.* Kevin knew she didn't, but he wanted to do something to ease her pain; he was heart-scalded. But there was nothing he could do except try to soothe her with words of encouragement and reassurance. He told her how much he loved her. Cathy told him how much she hated him.

"Now Mrs. Cassidy, with a bit of luck you should be a mother in a short while," the doctor said briskly.

"Luck, short while. I'm laying here probably breathing my last breath and you're talking about luck. Kevin will you get this eejit away from me, and that other one down there, the one underneath the tent thingy, the one who thinks I'm some sort of lucky dip." She couldn't say another word; a contraction so strong gripped her so violently she felt like she was being torn wide open.

"All right, now push. Come on, give me a big push," the doctor ordered.

Cathy pushed as hard as she could. She felt like a giant sea urchin was trying to drag itself slowly out of her.

"And again Mrs Cassidy, another big push. I can see the head," the nurse told her firmly. Kevin was as white as a sheet and he felt dizzy.

"That's it Mrs Cassidy, one more push, a big one this time."

"I can't, I can't," she whimpered.

"One more Mrs Cassidy, come on now, the head's through. Come on, it's nearly over. One last push and you'll be finished," the doctor urged her on.

Summoning every ounce of strength she had left, Cathy pushed as hard as she could; she felt as if her body was being ripped in two. The pain was excruciating and she screamed.

A tiny cry, and then a louder one, penetrated her pain.

"Mrs Cassidy, it's a little boy and he has a head of black hair just like his father, congratulations!" The doctor handed the baby to the waiting nurse.

"Let me see, let me see." Cathy struggled to sit up, she was exhausted. Kevin helped prop her up and cradled her lovingly in his arms.

"Patience," the nurse chuckled as she wiped the baby and weighed him.

"He's a little bruiser, eight pounds." The nurse lifted the baby out of the scales and after she put an identity tag around his wrist, she placed him gently in Cathy's arms.

Cathy looked down at her son and a feeling of tremendous adoration swept over her for the little tiny person she held closely. "Kevin he's beautiful. Look, he's got little tiny nails and stubby little toes and long eyelashes."

Kevin couldn't speak.

"Congratulations, Mr and Mrs Cassidy, you've a fine son," the doctor said again while he washed his hands.

"Thanks," Cathy whispered. She was thoroughly engrossed with her new baby.

Kevin was filled with a mixture of emotions. One single tear rolled down his face. His wife had just given birth to a beautiful healthy baby boy and the pride he felt swelled his chest to full capacity.

"Cathy you're the finest woman in Ireland," he said proudly, his smile was taking up most of his face.

Cathy looked from her tiny son to her husband and burst into tears.

"Ah don't cry now," Kevin exclaimed in confused horror.

The nurse arrived from the nursery to take the baby away and bath him properly. She assured the new parents she would bring him back very soon.

Cathy was exhausted and didn't put up much of an argument. Kevin gathered her up in his arms and held her tightly. "I love you Mrs Cassidy."

Twenty-Eight

1996

"You can't be serious Kevin. You have been away for over 11 weeks now. I might as well be a single mother."

"Ah Cathy, I can't help it. They shipped the wrong parts out to us."

"Yeah, Kevin, and the last time you were delayed, there was a problem with the avionics and that's not even in your field."

"Cathy, please try and be reasonable."

"Be reasonable, is that the way you want me to be? Okay, I'll be reasonable. Reason this. You missed your son's fifth birthday because you were away. You missed his sixth birthday because you were away. How many wedding anniversaries have we actually shared together on the correct date? How many times have I made excuses for you to Connor, because you weren't there when something important was happening in his life? When he fell off his bike and broke his arm were you there for him? No. When he had his tonsils out, were you there to comfort him? No. When he played the part of a sheep in the school nativity last year, was his father there? No. You weren't even here for Christmas Day last year."

"Cathy, stop it, give me a break. What do you expect me to do?"

"I expect you to be a supportive husband to me and decent father to our son. That's what I expect."

"Jesus, how can you say that I'm not a supportive husband? The reason I'm out here in the first place is so you and Connor can have a decent lifestyle."

"I'll post you a gold medal for misguided achievement. What address would be the more convenient for you?"

"There's no talking to you when you're in one of your moods. Where's Connor?"

Cathy was about to blow a fuse. She hated it when Kevin turned an argument around. "He's not here."

"He's not? Where is he then?"

"I took him marlin fishing in Bolivia and the bait ate him." She slammed the phone down in its cradle.

Connor was in the garden helping his grandfather finish off the gazebo he was building. He loved helping his granddad; the two spent a lot of time together. He came rushing into the sitting room with his muddy boots in his hands.

"Was that dad on the phone? Is he coming home tomorrow?"

Cathy looked at her son's open and enquiring face. "No Connor, he's been delayed."

"Ah, Mum."

"I know love, it can't be helped."

Connor gulped. "He's staying away because he's gone off us. If he really loved us, he'd be at home like all the other kids' dads' are. It's all your fault for shouting at him. I hate it when you shout, you spoil everything." He threw his boots angrily on the ground and stomped off to his room.

Cathy was shocked by his angry words. "Connor Cassidy, you come back here."

Bill put his hand on her arm. "Cathy, leave the lad, let him cool down. He's only shaking the down out of his feathers. I take it Kevin's landed himself with a bit of overtime?"

Cathy stared at her father-in-law. He never openly interfered in any aspect of their lives before. "Yes Bill, he's landed himself with a bit of overtime, again," she replied desolately.

"Ah, Maggie used to get upset when I'd be away for long stretches for *Aer Lingus*. It wasn't easy for her then and it's not easy for you now, but that's the way it is. Kevin has hydraulic fluid in his blood and there's not a lot you can do about it. But don't ever think you're alone; you'll always have us about, you know that. Now, is there any chance of a cup of tea? There's something I need to discuss with you."

Cathy knew what Bill had just said was true, but it didn't ease her.

"Is something wrong, Bill? Has something happened while I've been feeling sorry for myself?"

"No lass, nothing's wrong, well not really. I've got myself into a bit of a pickle with Maggie, and probably with you as well. I need your help to sort it out."

Cathy went into the kitchen to make the tea.

Bill sat down and started to tell her about Maggie's fifty-fifth birthday the following week. She knew about the birthday already as Maggie had been dropping momentous hints about it for weeks. However, she didn't interrupt her father-in-law. Bill was normally a man of few words.

He reminded Cathy about the slap-up birthday bash he'd organised as a surprise at the 'Airport Lodge', but Maggie had gotten wind of it yesterday and he didn't know how. She told him in no uncertain terms it was a disgraceful waste of money. She wanted to have a party at home with her family and close friends. A party where she could serve the canapés and finger food she had raved about at a reunion function they both attended last month.

Cathy couldn't see where the problem lay.

Bill told her Maggie's knee and elbow were playing her up a lot lately and she didn't think she'd be able to do all the cooking on her own. "I opened me big mouth and suggested that you might help her." He searched Cathy's face for her reaction.

"Of course I'll help with the preparations. No, I have a better idea. Why don't we have a party for her here? I'll get Pauline over and we'll do the catering. Maggie won't have to do anything except turn up and enjoy herself."

"Begorra Cathy, I couldn't let you to go to all that trouble. No lass, I couldn't."

"Bill, you've just built a beautiful gazebo and the garden looks super. We can have a barbecue with lots of canapés and finger food. Yes Bill, that's what we'll do. We'll christen the gazebo on Maggie's birthday with canapés everywhere."

Bill didn't get a chance to dissuade Cathy because the doorbell rang, it was Interflora. They were delivering a huge bunch of red roses to Cathy from her husband. Bill was pleased with his son. Cathy didn't have the heart to tell him that Kevin always sent her roses when he was away.

Once, on arriving home, he actually openly admired them and asked her if his father had grown them on his allotment.

***

"Mum, Pauline's here," Connor yelled from the front door with a big grin on his face. He adored Pauline and he was feeling important because his suggestions where going to be included in his grandma's party arrangements.

"Yes, Connor Cassidy, I'm here and I want a big hug from you."

"Ah, give over Pauls, I'm not a little baby any more you know," Connor announced in his *I'm the man-of-the-house-when-dad's-not-here* voice.

Pauline smiled at him; he was only six-years-old and the spitting image of his father. She could already hear the sound of hearts shattering in the future.

"Well, I'm sorry and when did this happen?" Pauline said, ruffling his hair.

"What's happened?" Connor asked, looking around him.

"When did Connor Cassidy turn into this sour-pussed old man and what has he done with the Connor Cassidy who gave me a hug happily last week?"

"Mum's right, Pauls, you're nuts."

"Nuts am I? I'll give you nuts."

Pauline made a lunge at Connor and he scampered out of her reach running slap-bang into his mother. She was carrying a bundle of ironing she had finished earlier on and it fell from her hands.

"Connor, now look what you've done. Why don't you look where you're going?" Cathy chastised him.

Pauline rolled her eyes to heaven. "Hello Pauline, how are you Pauline. It's nice to see you Pauline and thanks for coming over Pauline."

Cathy looked at her friend babbling on to herself and burst out laughing. "You're a big eejit Pauline Dutton, but I love you."

"Okay I'm guilty. I'm a big eejit, aren't I, Connor?"

"No you're not. It's mum that's not nice," Connor said defending Pauline.

"Ah, I'm only joking love, you know I am," Cathy reassured him.

Connor looked at both faces and was satisfied his mum was only joking. He didn't want Pauline to start staying away for weeks on end like his dad did.

All three gathered up the scattered pile of laundry and Cathy put it away.

"Now what's been happening with the Cassidy crowd?" Pauline asked as she curled herself up on the sofa with Connor beside her. "Kevin's due home tonight, isn't he? Hey, Connor, do you think he'll have a surprise for you? I bet he will, what time is he getting ..." Pauline stopped when she saw Connor's face. She read Cathy's eyes and immediately understood the situation.

Connor slid off the sofa and slunk away, muttering he was going to play in his room.

"Sorry Cathy," Pauline said in a whispery voice.

"Its okay Pauls, I'll be back in a minute." Cathy followed her son to his bedroom; she had some damage control to perform.

Fuck you, Kevin Cassidy, Pauline said to herself angrily.

***

Maggie was sitting at her kitchen table studying a list in front of her. She'd been tickled pink ever since Bill put Cathy's idea to her. *A barbecued supper evening. How very avant-garde. This is going to give nosey Rosy Donnelly something to talk about.*

Rosy Donnelly had been one of the organisers of the reunion evening a while ago, and she had been responsible for the canapés and finger food that had been received so well. Even though Maggie had been impressed with the catering, she didn't let on to Rosy. No, she could never do that.

"How many guests are you planning on inviting? I need to give Cathy the numbers," Maggie quizzed her husband from across the kitchen.

Bill was dozing in his favourite chair by the fire. The weather had turned sour earlier on in the afternoon and he had gotten soaked. Maggie's stew had warmed him up nicely and the blazing fire had made him sleepy. He woke with a start. "Eh, what? Did you say something, Maggie?"

"I said who are you inviting to the party?" Maggie asked again.

"Oh, I, I'll leave the invitations to yourself Maggie. It's your birthday after all."

Maggie muttered something along the lines of *as usual I have to do everything myself.* She left the kitchen to phone Cathy, she'd remembered something she had wanted to mention to her earlier on.

Bill settled back in his chair. He felt a bit guilty, but he knew no matter what he suggested, his wife would find some reason to discount it. He didn't mind, it was just Maggie's way of doing things. He knew she meant no harm.

"No, Maggie, it's all right. You needn't come over tomorrow to show me how to make cocktail bacon and potato bites." Cathy bit her lip hard, her mother-in-law had phoned her three times in the past two hours and she was driving her screwy.

"They can be quite tricky you know," Maggie said importantly.

"I know they can, but rest assured, a friend of mine works as a chef in the catering division of *Shamrock Air* and she gave me a few tips. She prepares all the meals for the first-class passengers." Cathy didn't know anyone in the catering staff, but she knew full well that the mention of first-class would shut Maggie up.

"Oh, well then, you're all right on that side. Now, did you order the smoked salmon from Wrights? They don't open on a Saturday any more."

"Yes, Maggie, I ordered the smoked salmon from Wrights, and before you ask, I've placed an order with Super Quinn for the French and Italian bread." *Jesus, if this is the way it's going to be for the next few days, I think I'll call in caterers,* Cathy moaned to herself.

The more Cathy thought about the upcoming party, the more the idea of using caterers appealed to her.

***

"I'll get it mum," Connor yelled as he raced into the hall to answer the phone.

"Hello," Connor answered in his new big-boy voice.

"Hello Connor, how's my lad?"

"Dad, where are you? Are you at the airport? We're having a party next week for gran's birthday. Mum's making fancy things and something weird with fingers in them. Don't know if I'll like those and we're having a barbecue with the gazebo," he blurted down the phone to his father.

"Wait up there soldier, slow down a bit," Kevin replied, visualising his son and wishing he could be with him. He had so many of his mother's ways it amazed him. "How was school today?"

"I didn't have school today. I started my school holidays yesterday. The Christmas ones," he informed his father sternly.

"I thought you started them tomorrow. Silly me," Kevin replied, knowing he'd put his foot in it again.

"No, tomorrow I'm going to 'Bru-na-Boinne' on a school trip. It had to be cancelled last month because a lot of the kids got the chicken pox. Remember?" Connor was excited about the trip. It was to be his first one with his school.

"Oh, yes son, I remember, should be fun," Kevin fibbed, it was the first time he'd heard about it.

"Here's mum, she wants to speak to you, bye."

"Connor, I wanted to tell you ..." Kevin didn't finish as Connor had already laid the phone on the table. "Bye, son, I love you," Kevin said to no-one.

Connor went off to organise his satchel for his day tour, yet again. He was having difficulty deciding which items were necessary and which were absolutely vital. His mother retrieved the handset and greeted her husband.

"Hi, sweetheart, how are you?" Kevin said, testing the waters carefully.

"I'm fine Kev'. Look, I'm sorry I was such a bitch yesterday morning. I just miss you so much. I love you Kevin Cassidy."

"I miss you too. Forget about yesterday. Good news, I'll be in on the eight o' clock flight tomorrow night."

"You will, are you sure? The job's finished then?" Cathy had a flashback to the last time Kevin promised he would be home, only to find out at the last minute he had a change of plans.

"I'm sure, and I've taken a week off."

Cathy could hardly believe her ears. "A whole week, seven days. Kev', hang on a sec. Connor, come here quickly."

Connor came out of his room slowly with a sulky expression on his little face.

"Hurry up Connor, this phone call is costing your Dad a packet. Here, speak to him, he's coming home tomorrow and he's taking a week's leave. You'll have him all to yourself for seven days."

Connor grabbed the phone from his mother. "Dad is it true? Are you going to be on holidays with me? Why didn't you tell me before?"

"Yes son, I'm going to be able to spend a week of your Christmas holidays with you and your mother, I tried to tell you before, but you wandered off."

"Oh brill, you'll be here for gran's party as well."

Cathy interrupted her son. "Connor, you'll have to say goodbye to your dad, he's been on the phone for ages."

"Okay, bye Dad. See you."

"Bye, Connor, I love you."

"Ah, that's gooey stuff, bye."

"Well, you've certainly made his day," Cathy said happily.

"Seems so, and what about Mrs Cassidy's day?" Kevin flirted.

"Oh, I suppose I'm pleased enough, Mr Cassidy."

"Cheeky floozy. When I get back I'll have to teach you a few manners, won't I."

"I can't wait."

"Sorry love, but I really do have to go. See you the day after tomorrow. Oh, what on earth is Connor going on about? Something on the lines of fingers and parties?" Kevin asked at the last minute.

"Your mother's fifty-fifth birthday party, she's celebrating it here."

"She's celebrating her birthday at our place?" Kevin was practically speechless. "Never mind, you can tell me tomorrow, I'll phone you in the morning. Have to go, bye love."

Twenty-Nine

"Mum hurry up, we'll be late," Connor urged. He stood directly in front of her tapping his foot. Cathy's heart twanged, her son's body language childishly replicated that of his father.

"We've at least a half-an-hour to spare will you relax, and have some manners. I'm on the phone," Cathy said sternly, her eyes told her son *behave yourself or you are going nowhere.* Connor knew that look very well, he knew when he could push his mother's buttons, and he also knew when he should stop.

"Sorry about that. Right, you'll deliver first thing in the morning?"

"Yes, Mrs Cassidy, I'll have your order to you by nine o' clock."

"Wonderful, thanks Mr Brewster, bye."

"It's a pleasure Mrs Cassidy, and if there's anything you've forgotten, don't hesitate to call and I'll have it sent right over."

"Thanks again, bye."

"Okay Connor, we can get going now, and don't forget your jacket. It looks like it's going to rain."

Her son nearly ran her over her in his dash to get out the door. Cathy didn't say anything; she found his excitement infectious. "Have you got everything?"

"Yep, I have, I think."

Just like his father, Cathy thought. "Are you sure?"

"Yes, I'm sure. Stop fussing."

"Right then, let's get this show on the road."

Just as she was closing the door behind her, the phone rang. She thought about ignoring it but decided not to. "Connor love, go to the car. I'll be there in a bit."

"Ah, Mum."

"Connor go on, I'll be quick." Cathy picked up the phone wearily; the last person she wanted to speak to was her mother-in-law.

"Hello."

"Hello my darling. What are you doing today?"

"Kevin, what's up? Oh, for Christ sake, don't tell me, you have a change of plans."

"Well, yes I do, and no I don't."

"Okay, what is it this time, another engine some *Yank* has let go tits up?"

"No love, I'm in Heathrow and I'll be in Dublin in about three hours. I managed to get on a flight from Miami last night."

"Oh Kev', that's brilliant. And I thought ..."

"Well now Mrs. Cassidy, that's what thought, brought you. Listen, my car is in the workshop and it won't be ready until later on today. Can you pick me up?"

"Sure I can. What time?"

"My flight is due in at eleven-fifteen. You don't sound very happy."

"Of course I'm happy, you big lummox. Connor is waiting at the car. We were just about to leave for the rendezvous point."

"The rendezvous point?"

"His school trip, remember? That's his new word at the moment."

"Ah, sorry, I forgot, I didn't get much sleep on the plane last night."

"That's because I wasn't there to look after you."

"Will you look after me tonight?"

"If you play your cards right, I just might."

Connor burst through the door. "Mum, come on, they'll leave without me."

"Okay love, I'll be right there."

"That's what you said five minutes ago."

"Connor, don't be cheeky."

Connor left reluctantly.

"I think you'd better go, it sounds like Connor's about to burst a gasket."

"Yeah, but I'm not going to say anything to him. Let him have a nice surprise when we both collect him this afternoon."

"Good idea, I like that. Okay, see you in about three hours or so. I love you, Mrs Cassidy."

"I love you too. Now the quicker you go, the quicker you will get here, bye."

The school car park was packed with parents and many children of various ages.

"Okay pet, have a good time and I'll be here to collect you at three o' clock. Come on, give me a kiss."

"Mum, please, the other kids will laugh. I'm too old for that kind of thing, get a grip."

"Yes Connor, you are perfectly right. You're far too grown up to give your mum a kiss goodbye in public."

"Yeah, I am. I'd better get on the bus, bye."

Connor did a quick about turn. "Mum, you won't hang around and wave me off, will you?"

"Don't worry, I won't embarrass you, I promise. Have fun."

Cathy watched the bus pull out, hidden from sight in her car. When she was satisfied he was safely on his way, she drove off.

As she had a bit of time to kill before she collected Kevin and Imelda's office was on the way to the airport, she decided to chance a visit with her aunt.

She was lucky, Imelda was in, and she was delighted to see her niece. "Fancy a cup of coffee?" Imelda asked.

"Lovely, thanks."

Imelda picked up the phone and asked her secretary to bring two coffees. She also asked her to hold her calls for a while. Then she turned her full attention to Cathy. "I can't chat for long, but tell me how's the party event of the century coming along?"

"Fine, but I'm not going to have a barbecue evening, the weather forecast looks bad for the next week, so I've decided on a buffet supper instead."

"Have you told Maggie about the change?" Imelda asked carefully.

"Are you mad? She'd get herself into a complete flap. I'm not saying a word until the day before. I've already had to put her off from coming over to make tipsy tarts in my kitchen, so Rosy Donnelly won't make any unnecessary remarks about how much brandy went into them."

"What do you mean?"

"Ah Imelda, the last day-trip they were on, *Nosy Rosy* ordered tipsy tart for dessert, and when she tasted it she said at the top of her voice *they must have stood in the next room when they poured the brandy in.* Can you credit that?"

Imelda had never met *Nosy Rosy*, but she had built a mental image of the woman, and it wasn't a pleasant one. "I don't think tipsy tarts are very avant-garde as Maggie likes to say, do you?"

"No Imelda, I don't, but she wants them and she's making them herself. In her own kitchen, thank God."

The coffee arrived and Imelda thanked her secretary.

"What's on the revised menu then?"

"Oh, the canapés and the famous finger food of course. I ordered those from Gabriella's, along with a roast turkey and a honey-baked ham. That should do the trick, plus an unusual selection of salads. Pauline's going to help me prepare a risotto and a vegetable lasagne, just in case some of them would prefer hot food."

"Pauline's a good friend."

"That she is, I'd be lost without her. She really loves the job you fixed her up with, you know."

"I do know Cathy, and she's very good at it. My client is more than pleased with her work ..."

Cathy butted in. "Crikey look at the time. I have to go. Kevin's flight will be in shortly." She got up to leave.

"Cathy, wait, I have an idea."

"You do?"

"The thought just popped into my head. I know someone reliable that supplies marquees and the like. I'll organise one for your back garden, then you'll be able to light the barbecue and Maggie can have her *al fresco* evening whatever the weather throws at you."

"Imelda Corway, that's a terrific idea, we can have a barbecue and a buffet. You're incredible."

Imelda poo-pooed her niece's compliment. "Right, off you go then, go collect your husband. Leave the marquee arrangements to me."

"Imelda ..."

"Cathy, go."

***

Kevin came through the arrival gates exactly on time, there had been none of the usual delays with customs.

Other arriving passengers looked on as he swept Cathy into his arms and kissed her heartily. Neither cared, they had eyes and ears only for each other.

"Come on Mrs Cassidy, let's get out of here. I've had enough of airports for a while."

"I'm not arguing," Cathy replied as she ran her hand through her tossed red hair and slipped her other one around her husband's arm.

"I'll drive, I have to stop off at the office and collect a set of keys for someone, it won't take long, I promise," Kevin said with a sideways glance at his wife.

Cathy was too happy to argue. Usually, when Kevin went to the main *Beta Air* offices after a long trip away, someone, who needed something done urgently, always waylaid him.

Kevin parked in the staff car park and true to his word; he came back within five minutes.

"Well, Mrs Cassidy, just one more stop and then we can go home."

"Ah Kev', where are we going to now?"

"I promised a mate that I'd check up on his house. He moved his family down to Shannon and his house is empty. I promised him I would make sure all the taps are off and so on."

"Can't you do it later? I've loads to do for your mother's party and Connor will be back in few hours." Cathy's day was closing in rapidly.

"Nah, I'll check it out now, get it done and over. It's over in Ardcath just outside Ashbourne, not far," Kevin said in his persuasive tone.

"Okay, but don't stay long." Kevin just smiled.

They pulled into the driveway of a two-storey, granite fronted dormer styled house with double garages. The front garden was slightly overgrown but it was obvious to Cathy it had been tended to with loving care in the recent past. There was a second tree-lined gravel driveway, which to Cathy's eye, led off to what looked like a hay barn.

"Here we are, come inside the place is empty. Have a look around," Kevin said as he fished a bunch of keys from his pocket.

"No Kev', I'd feel like I was invading someone's privacy. You go ahead and check the place out, I'll wait here."

Kevin walked around to the passenger side of the car and opened the door. "For once in your life don't argue. Come with me."

"Okay, okay, keep your hair on."

The hallway was wide and it led into a big L-shaped lounge with huge windows and a beautiful old-fashioned fireplace.

The dining room was oak-panelled and it had connecting leaded glass doors that opened up into the most beautiful kitchen Cathy had ever seen. To her amazement, the kitchen window afforded her a perfect view of a full-sized dressage arena. She saw a stable block near the barn, the same one she had noticed when she first arrived.

"Go and have a good look around, there's no-one here," Kevin encouraged her.

"Are you sure?"

"Positive."

Cathy explored the rest of the house. There were three other rooms on the ground floor, a study, a guest bathroom and a medium sized bedroom.

Upstairs she discovered the master bedroom that had the same view she had seen from the kitchen. There was an arched wall that led into a dressing room with enough built-in wardrobes to house six people's clothing. Another door led to the en-suite. It was huge and Cathy loved the design. It had a sunken marble jacuzzi and a corner bath with matching sinks, and, to her amazement, a small sauna. She joked with Kevin that the shower was big enough to hold two people very comfort-ably. He agreed with her, muttering something about conjugal rights. Cathy pretended she didn't hear him.

There were three other bedrooms. Two of them had the basic bathroom and the third was smaller, not much more than a box room.

"Come on, have a look outside," Kevin said as he grabbed her hand and bounded down the stairs.

"Slow down Kev', please."

Once Kevin had found the correct key for the back door, they walked down to the stables. Cathy thought they were perfect. Each one was spacious and airy. All four had automatic drinking-water dispensers and fixed hayracks. The floors were concrete with solid drainage grids in front of the stable doors. To the side of the stables there was a reasonably sized feed room and separate tack room. The numerous paddocks that Cathy could see from her vantage point were correctly double-fenced.

Kevin came up behind her. "Nice place, isn't it?"

"Nice, it's fabulous Kev'," Cathy answered truthfully.

"Would you like to live here?"

"Don't ask stupid questions. I'd give my right boob to have a set-up like this, and the house is magnificent."

"Well then, my darling wife it's yours. That's if you want it," Kevin announced proudly.

"What, have you gone bonkers?"

"No, I haven't gone bonkers, as you so eloquently put it. The owner is an old mate of mine from *Aer Lingus*, and as I said before, he has moved back down to Shannon. The asking price is fair as he is selling it privately so there will be no agent's fees. All I need is your okay and then we'll let the lawyers take care of the rest."

"Kevin Cassidy, are you serious?"

"Yes love, I am. You could make a nice horse set-up of your own here. And the village school up the road has a very good reputation ..."

"Kevin, stop, let me absorb what you're saying."

"Nothing to absorb, we've always said that we'd move to the country some day and that day has come. I didn't want to say anything to you about the property before I knew for sure that it was still on the market. There was some talk about a neighbour- ing farmer buying the place, but the deal fell through."

"Oh my God, can we afford it? How much land is it on? How soon can we move in?" Cathy knew she was babbling, but she couldn't help it.

"It's on ten acres, and, yes, we can afford it. Shall I phone the lawyer now?" Kevin asked his bemused wife.

Cathy didn't hesitate. "Yes, yes, yes do."

Kevin took his phone from his pocket and phoned his lawyer, he set the wheels in motion to buy.

They re-examined the house and outbuildings. Cathy walked every inch of the land and was thrilled to find a fast flowing stream that bordered four of the paddocks.

In the barn, she discovered a tractor and a pile of uprights and jumping poles. She walked through the house twice and then a third time. The more she looked at it, the more she loved it. She felt she was in a dream. Then she remembered Connor. "Kev', it's two-thirty and Connor's due back at three. We'll have to go. We'll be cutting it fine as it is."

"Right, I'll lock up quickly and we'll be off. Boy oh boy, he's going to get more than one surprise today."

Thirty

Connor wasn't too happy at first about the idea of moving to a new house and a new school. He liked the school he was attending in Swords, and he didn't like the thought of being separated from his friends.

When he told his school friends about the move, they gave him a bit of a hard time. They said he'd become a culshee and a redneck.

He soon changed his mind when Cathy explained that Ardcath was only 40 minutes outside Dublin and it wasn't a redneck or culshee area. He'd be able to have his own dog and whatever other pet his little heart desired. His old friends could stay over at the weekends and she reassured him he'd make new ones as well. Therefore, the house move turned into a big adventure instead of a worry for him.

Kevin wanted to move in as soon as possible and the lawyers arranged for them to take up immediate occupational rental until the paperwork was finalised. He had another long trip coming up, so the sooner they moved the better. However, he hadn't told Cathy about the trip, not yet.

Maggie didn't say anything good or bad about the house purchase; her immediate concern was focused on her birthday party. When Cathy let her know that a marquee was about to be erected in her honour, she felt like a queen bee. She wanted to come around to the flat and supervise, but Kevin put his foot down. He told her straight out that the company contracted to erect the marquee, were more than competent. He also told her if she didn't stop fussing, he'd call the whole thing off.

She was annoyed at her son's inference, which implied she was being a bit of a busybody, but Bill calmed her down. It was supposed to be a surprise party, after all.

Cathy waited until the night before the party to tell her she decided to use caterers. Much to her surprise, Maggie was thrilled.

Somewhere along the line, the tipsy tarts had been totally forgotten about. Cathy didn't remind her.

Maggie's party also afforded her the added opportunity to start packing up for Ardcath. She had a busy time ahead of her.

***

There was only an hour or so to go before Maggie's guests were due to arrive. The marquee looked wonderful and apart from the risotto and lasagne, Cathy didn't have to do a thing, food wise. Gabriella's had lived up to its reputation. They laid out a wonderful spread on dry iced platters in the dining room. The bar area was relegated to the marquee and for the barbecue; they supplied marinated chicken, prawn, pork and beef kebabs. Everything was going to plan.

"What do you bet that's Maggie?" Cathy scowled at Pauline when the phone rang. Her mother-in-law was driving her crazy. She had phoned her five times throughout the day, despite Kevin's warning.

"Hello, Maggie." Cathy's tone had an edge.

"How did you know it was me, dear?"

"Just a wild guess, I suppose," she replied, trying to hide the sarcasm from her voice.

"Cathy dear, can I speak with Kevin, please? I want to check up on one last thing." Maggie sounded agitated.

Cathy threw her eyes up to heaven and made a ferocious face at the mouthpiece. "I'll get him for you, hang on." She practically threw the phone down on the table.

"Kev', it's for you. It's your mother again."

Kevin picked up the phone. "Yes mother, what is it this time?"

"Ah, Kevin, I'm sorry to worry you, but will the smoke from the barbecue come into the marquee? I don't want *Rosy Donnelly* to ..."

"No, mother, it won't, now relax."

"I am relaxed. And did the caterers ..."

"Mother, give over, will you. Everything's fine and under control."

"There's no need to be rude, Kevin," Maggie replied, miffed with her son's attitude.

"I'm not being rude. I'm busy, now I have to go. Goodbye." He hung up the phone and went into the kitchen. "For crying out loud, hand me a beer will you love."

"What's wrong now?" Cathy asked warily.

"My mother will be the death of me. She's now worried that the smoke from the barbecue will come into the marquee." Kevin was fit to burst.

"Here's your beer. Just think how happy she'll be when she gets here," Cathy soothed.

"It's not worth it," Kevin moaned. "Between her and *Rosy Donnelly*, I'll be dead from stress before this night is over"

"Let's get Rosy pissed," Cathy suggested wickedly. "You know she hasn't got a head for alcohol at all, one glass and she's singing. Do you remember the party your mother had on her last birthday? Will you ever forget her singing, 'Somewhere over the rainbow' and that was after one glass of sherry."

"Ah now, Cathy, she's elderly," Kevin said.

"I'd love to hear *Rosy Donnelly* singing." Pauline was game for it.

"And you will Pauline, elderly or not, *Rosy Donnelly* is going to have a pleasant evening," Cathy retorted.

"I'll keep her glass filled," Pauline volunteered gleefully.

Promptly at seven-thirty, Maggie arrived with Bill at her side. He looked harassed.

"It's all very nice indeed," Maggie proclaimed while she surveyed the lay out. "The marquee looks wonderful. I love what they did with the lighting. And the food looks edible," Maggie said as she scrutinised everything.

Before Pauline could say anything, Cathy pinched her hard on the back of her arm.

"Now Bill, I'd like you to greet everyone with me when they arrive, which they should be doing shortly."

"Ah, Maggie, I have to help Kevin. I can't stand at the door for the next half-hour or so."

"Well, it would be good manners," Maggie snapped at her husband.

The doorbell rang and Bill backed away silently.

"Ah, Brian and Theresa, welcome." Maggie turned on her hostess smile as her first guests arrived.

"Hello there. Can I get you a glass of sherry?" Pauline asked the first arrivals.

Cathy was nowhere in sight.

"That's very kind of you my dear girl, I'd love one," the elderly woman whom Maggie had called Theresa replied.

"Mrs Cassidy, can I get you a glass as well?"

"Well, Pauline, that would be nice. Thank you," Maggie replied, ever so graciously.

Three more guests arrived and Pauline made sure they all had drinks. Then Rosy arrived.

"Good evening Rosy," Maggie said regally.

"Good evening, to you too, Maggie. Will you excuse me for a minute, I have to go and pay the taxi driver. I wanted to make sure I had the right address before I let him go." She returned in less than a minute.

"Would you like a glass of sherry Mrs Donnelly?" Pauline suggested with a wicked glint in her eye.

"Well, thank you but no, I'll just have an orange juice."

"For goodness sake Rosy, have a sherry and stop your non- sense. An orange juice indeed," Maggie snorted.

"Here, get that into you," Pauline offered Rosy a glass.

"Thank you dear," Rosy said to Pauline and she took a surprisingly large sip.

Cathy poked her head out of the kitchen. "Pauline, get in here quickly."

Maggie didn't hear Cathy's plea for help, she was too busy receiving her guests.

"What's wrong?" Pauline's heart sank at the look of dismay on her friend's face.

"The risotto, it's stuck to the bloody pot."

"Oh crikey. I told you to keep stirring it," Pauline groaned. She inspected the risotto and the damage wasn't too bad. At least it didn't have a burnt taste to it.

"Look, we'll put it into the serving dish now and keep it warm in the oven. It'll be fine, don't panic, the lasagne is nearly cooked as well. They'll be eating soon, I hope."

Cathy returned to the sitting room, she thought she had better show her face.

"I see you didn't use a table cloth, Cathy dear," remarked Rosy.

"Not with a pine table Rosy," Maggie interjected quickly.

"Oh, but a linen tablecloth is very classy you know. You cannot beat a bit of class. But then I was reared to it," Rosy replied, smiling sweetly at Maggie.

Maggie snapped back. "Indeed Rosy, but you'd never guess it."

"I think the table is delightful and the food looks delicious," Mary Dwyer cut in diplomatically.

"Please, help yourselves to the canapés, and the bar is in the marquee," Cathy said as she scuttled back to the kitchen.

"Where is Connor? I haven't seen him in a while," Maggie asked Cathy's retreating form.

"He's outside with his dad at the barbecue, and it's not smoking the room out, as you can see." Cathy swore to herself and continued on her way towards the kitchen.

The sherry and wine had loosened tongues, and every so often, loud chuckles and guffaws would resound from the marquee. It seemed that the 20 or so guests were thoroughly enjoying themselves. Maggie was in her element.

True to her word, Pauline topped up Rosy's sherry glass at every opportunity.

Someone started singing 'Poor old Dicey Reilly she has taken to the sup.'

Rosy, not wanting to be outdone, warbled on with 'Somewhere over the rainbow.'

Cathy and Pauline both grinned from ear to ear when they passed by to join Kevin and Connor. Bill had tucked himself away in the corner with an old friend from *Aer Lingus*. The two were animatedly talking about the speed at which aircraft was developing nowadays.

"Well, that lot are having a good time," Kevin announced, as he poured them a well-earned drink.

"Mum, is Mrs Donnelly drunk?" Connor asked. He had never seen the *Nosy Rosy* behave like that before.

"No pet, she's just enjoying herself in her own way," Cathy reassured him.

"Hmmm, granny seems to be enjoying herself in her own way as well," Connor replied. Then, he changed the subject. "Dad said we're going to go and buy a puppy tomorrow. It's going to be an early Christmas present," he informed his mother.

Cathy looked at her husband. This was the first she had heard about buying a puppy the next day. Connor had wanted a puppy for a long time, but the present garden was too small.

"Kevin, tell me, what breed have you two planned on?"

"Your father's friend over there breeds golden Labradors and he says we can have the pick of the litter. They are eight weeks old and ready to go," Kevin answered and pretended to busy himself with the kebabs.

Cathy would have preferred to have waited until they had actually moved house before they added a new addition to the family, but she couldn't disappoint her son. His face was flushed with excitement. They could put up with a puppy for a little while in the flat.

Rosy started up again, *'Four and twenty virgins came down from Inverness ... and when the ball was over there were four and twenty less.'*

Maggie grabbed her aside and hissed, "Rosy, behave yourself."

"I beg your pardon Maggie, this, this is a party not a PTA meeting you know." Rosy was not impressed by Maggie's acid tone.

Kevin stepped in between the pair. "Mother, the supper is ready, will you inform your guests or shall I?"

"No son, that's fine. I'll do the honours myself." Maggie wasn't missing a chance to be the centre of attention. She tapped her wedding ring on her now empty glass. "Can I have everyone's attention please?" Maggie said in her best voice, the one she used when she answered the phone.

"Supper is being served in the dining room. Please help yourselves and enjoy."

The turkey and ham were both moist and tender. No one noticed that Cathy had slightly burnt the risotto. Pauline's lasagne was given lavish praise and judging by the empty plates afterwards, the meal had gone down a treat.

Pauline did the rounds with a bottle of port, and Connor circulated once with cheese and fruit skewers. He didn't bother doing a second round as he hated being talked down to.

Rosy had started up singing again and she didn't just accept the glass of port she was offered, she grabbed the bottle from Pauline's hand, and made a wobbly attempt to use it as a dancing partner.

Maggie was becoming infuriated. Everyone was egging Rosy on, and Rosy complied.

Pauline was in kinks.

"I think you've overdone the booze," Cathy laughed with her friend.

"She'll never live this one down. What's she singing now?" Pauline enquired

"Haven't a clue," chuckled Kevin.

"Oh, Pauline Dutton, may God forgive you," giggled Cathy.

"I think one of us should take her home," Kevin suggested.

"Don't be such a spoilsport, she might start lap dancing and really liven up the party," Cathy said incorrigibly.

"Sometimes I wonder about you." The thought of *Rosy Donnelly* lap dancing made him shudder.

Kevin eased his mother aside. "Shall I take Rosy home?"

"I think that would be a good idea, a very good idea. I'll go and get her coat," Maggie said relieved.

'*Oceans apart, day after day,*' Rosy's voice shrieked out.

"Good woman yourself Rosy," someone applauded.

"Come along Rosy, it was a great party but it's time to go now," Kevin said firmly.

"Oh, but it, it's shearly yet," Rosy slurred.

"Now Rosy, it's late," Maggie said as she helped Kevin steer her to the door.

"Just when I shwas shtarting to en ... enjoy myself. I have to ... to ...go," Rosy slurred.

When she was safely ensconced in Kevin's car and he had driven off, Maggie returned to her guests. She whispered to Cathy, "So much for class."

Thirty-One

For Cathy and her family the next few days were hectic. She was living out the article she had read in a magazine recently, about families at each other's throats due to the stress of moving house. She hadn't realised how much stuff they had gathered over the years until the packing crates started to pile up.

She sorted out what they did, and did not need. She set the *did not need* aside, she planned to give this as a donation to the *Vincent De Paul.*

Then Kevin's hoarding instincts kicked in and he promptly packed up her intended donations for removal to Ardcath, insisting they *did* need all of the items his wife was so flippantly casting aside.

Her mother-in-law whispered she could always dispose of the unwanted items at the other end. Maggie understood how Cathy felt, Bill was the same; he never wanted to throw any- thing out either.

In addition, Connor's new puppy Hank was proving to be a handful. He found the packing crates a convenient place to try and practise cocking his leg on. That particular extra Cathy could definitely do without.

Despite Connor's protestations, she locked Hank outside in the garden, where he howled his head off and then he disappeared altogether. He somehow managed to dig his way out underneath the garden gate. Connor and his grandfather eventually found him cowering behind a dumpster two streets up from the flat.

Bill put the frightened puppy in his car and without consulting anyone; he returned Hank to his breeder for safe-keeping until the move to Ardcath was over.

Connor was disgusted and voiced his opinions on the issue very clearly to his father when they returned home.

"Look Connor, you'll get him back in a few days, he's safer where he is at the moment," Kevin said in an effort to calm the waters. If he had to launch another search-and-rescue team in the midst of all the upheaval, he would go crazy.

"It's not fair, he was lonely out in the garden all by himself," Connor pouted.

"Connor, just stop acting like a brat and go and finish packing up your room. You're supposed to be helping your grandmother, not standing around sulking."

"What if he escapes from the new house?" Connor quest-ioned his father with real concern.

"That's hardly likely son, the back garden has a high wall all the way around it. If he manages to jump over it, then we will have to invent a doggy 'Grand National' because he would be a sure winner. Now get."

Connor didn't know what a doggy 'Grand National' was, but he did know by the tone of his father's voice that he had better not push the issue any further.

Cathy thought the flat looked cold and unloved when everything was finally packed up. She also felt a bit sad. She had lived in it for a long time and had accumulated many happy mem- ories, which would stay with her for the rest of her life.

The flat wasn't going to stay empty for long. *Beta Air* had readily agreed to rent the property from them on a month-to-month basis; they were going to use it for accommodation for the flight crews.

The company had grown considerably over the past few years, and they now boasted a fleet of six passenger aircrafts with another four scheduled for delivery the following year. They did offer to purchase the property, as it was conveniently located close to the airport. However, because property prices were due to increase in the New Year, Kevin and Cathy decided to hang on to it.

Kevin shared his wife's emotions, but the new house beckoned and he wanted to get his family settled in as quickly as possible.

"Come on love, let's go. We have a lot to do at the other end. It's going to be a long day."

"You're right Kevin. Did I tell you today that I love you?"

"No, Mrs Cassidy, I can't recall you doing so. I was beginning to think that you'd gone off me."

"I'll show you how much I actually love you later on tonight."

"Promises, promises."

"Wait, I want to check over the place one last time."

"Cathy, you've done that two or three times already. Any-way, *Beta Air* won't be moving in until next week. It's not as if you can never come back here again."

"Hmmm, no Kevin, I won't come back here again. This chapter of our lives is over, and we have a new one just about to start and I can't wait."

"Well then, why are you still standing here? Do I have to carry you out?"

"Well, you did carry me in."

Without another word, Kevin threw his wife gently over his shoulder and carried her out laughing.

"Come on Connor, don't stand there gawking. We're about to follow the yellow brick road," Kevin said to his son.

Connor was beginning to think his parents were weird.

***

"Well now Cathy, that's the kitchen crates unloaded and packed away. I have to be off now, but I'll come back over tomorrow." Maggie informed her daughter-in-law. "Is there anything else you'd like me to do?"

"Ah, that's okay Maggie. You've done enough already. By the way, I would never have gotten this far, sorting out this chaos, without you. Thanks a million, you've been a brick." Cathy really meant what she said. Despite Maggie's bad knee, she had worked like a Trojan and Cathy was grateful to her.

"Not at all dear, it's been a pleasure."

As Maggie drove out, Pauline drove in. She came armed with a large picnic basket filled with sandwiches, flasks of tea and coffee, two bottles of wine, a six-pack of beer and several cans of soft drinks. She dumped her food and beverage contribution on the kitchen table.

"Okay, Mrs Cassidy, where are you?" Pauline shouted at the top of her voice.

"She's upstairs having a row with the curtains," Connor told her as he rushed out the back door.

"Well, hello to you too, Connor. Have you forgotten to unpack your manners perhaps?"

If Connor heard Pauline's minor chastisement, he didn't let on, as he didn't answer her. He was in a hurry to get back to something, somewhere.

Pauline sidestepped the numerous boxes in the hall and headed upstairs.

"Cathy, Cathy, where are you?"

"I'm in here," Cathy's voice sounded muffled.

Pauline found her friend standing on a stepladder in her new bedroom trying to persuade a pair of curtains to hang properly.

"Hi, how's it going? Sorry I couldn't get here any sooner. I got caught up in work," Pauline said to Cathy's back.

"Never mind, you're here now. Will you help me with these bloody things before I take them outside and burn them?"

Connor was right; she was having a row with the curtains.

"Relax, stop stressing. You don't have to get everything done in one day, now do you?"

"No, I don't, but it would be nice to be able to go to sleep tonight without the neighbours looking in."

Pauline looked out the window. "What neighbours? The nearest house is half a mile away and I don't think they'll be able to see in. But, on the other hand, you might have a flock of voyeuristic sparrows lurking around at dawn to ..."

"Pauline, shut up, come over here, and help me take the weight of this damn curtain so I can get the last hooks in."

Between the pair, they managed to get the curtains to hang reasonably well.

"Now will the lady of the house please come downstairs and have a cup of coffee and put her feet up for ten minutes?" Pauline suggested.

"Pauls, I have no idea where the kettle is, let alone the coffee," Cathy replied grumpily.

"Well I do, so move it." Pauline steered her by the shoulders in the direction of the stairs.

"How the hell do you know where the kettle is?" Cathy wanted to know.

"I don't. I packed you a picnic basket and I know where that is, so come on girlfriend, break time."

"Okay, you win," Cathy said wearily.

Connor flashed past them on the stairs.

"Whoa there cowboy. Will you go and find your dad and grandfather? I'm sure they could do with a cup of tea and a sandwich. Pauline brought us a picnic."

"Pauls, you brought sambos. Did you make your special ones?"

"Yes Connor, I did, and I made special ones just for you," Pauline replied.

"You're the best Pauls. Can I have one now, I'm starved?" Connor pleaded.

"Ask your mum, she's the boss not me," Pauline winked at Cathy.

"Mum, please."

"No Connor, remember your manners. Wait for the others, a few more minutes won't kill you. Off you go and hurry up."

Pauline and Cathy hungrily unpacked the picnic basket together.

"Jees Pauls, you've brought enough food to feed a regiment."

"Yeah, well, I wasn't sure how many people were here, so I packed extra."

"I believe there's a gourmet feast somewhere in here, compliments of the delightful Pauline," Cathy's father said as he came through the back door with Connor, closely followed by Kevin and Bill.

"Yes, there is. Come on sit down, the lot of you. We've been ordered to take a break by Madam Hitler here," Cathy replied to her father.

Without any further encouragement, they all sat down to enjoy a well-earned break.

Connor sat on an empty packing crate, munching away on his special goody pack, Pauline had slipped quietly to him.

"I'm glad to see that someone thought about feeding the workers. My wife obviously thinks that we can survive on fresh air," Kevin said in between huge mouthfuls of sandwich.

Cathy threw a scrunched-up piece of sandwich foil at her husband.

"By the way, what *are* you all doing out there?" she asked with a curious excitement in her voice.

"Rewiring the stable block," her husband answered.

"But why, what's wrong with it?"

"Well, love, an army of rats have had an AGM throughout, and it's in a pretty bad state," Jimmy told his daughter.

"Ah, you're not serious."

"I'm very serious. I've disconnected everything so you will have no power out there for a while. But I'll send my lads over tomorrow and they can replace the whole lot. While they are here, would you like me to get them to rig up some floodlights in the sand arena for you?"

"Gosh, that would be handy. Thanks dad."

"Don't mention it; I think you could do with some lighting in the barn as well."

"Good idea."

"Me and granddad have been building a kennel for Hank, haven't we, granddad?" Connor said, supplying his particular work report to his mother.

"Yes, lad, we have. And you're a great little helper. I couldn't do it without you." Bill replied, praising his grandson.

"Mum, can we get Hank back today? Please say yes," Connor asked.

"Oh, I don't see why not. What do you think, Kev'?"

"Fine by me but ..." He was interrupted by a loud crashing sound, coming from upstairs.

"What the hell?" Kevin exclaimed.

Everybody went to investigate and Connor got there first.

The curtain rail Cathy and Pauline had hung the curtains on earlier, was in a heap on the floor. It had brought down large chunks of plaster with it.

Cathy was speechless when she saw the mess. Connor started laughing and Kevin joined in. Pauline saw the funny side of it also. Bill tried not to laugh but he couldn't help himself.

"I never liked those curtains anyway love," Kevin said, still laughing.

Cathy turned on her husband. "You never liked them?"

"No, love, I never did."

"Why didn't you tell me before?"

"Dunno, never got around to it before now, I suppose," Kevin admitted.

"Look on the bright side. It's better that this mishap happened now, and not after we've finished moving everything in," Kevin said as another chunk of plaster crumbled off the wall.

"Kevin, we have a bit more work to do than we anticipated," Bill volunteered.

Cathy didn't say a word.

"I hope you haven't moved into *Fawlty Towers*. There's no one by the name of Manuel around here is there?" Pauline giggled.

"Oh, you're so very comforting and very tactful. Pauline Dutton's bloody mouth comes to the rescue yet again," Cathy said in a strangled voice.

"Close your ears Connor, your mother's gone off her rocker," Kevin said to his son.

Connor was now convinced that his parents were weird.

"Ah dad, she's not, but can we go and get Hank now?" He asked innocently not realising his timing was not quite right.

In an attempt to avoid a showdown between mother and son, Kevin turned to his father-in-law.

"Well, I think we've gone as far as we can go *outside* today, haven't we Jimmy?"

"Eh, yes, yes we have. It's getting dark, but I'll have the lads here bright and early tomorrow morning," he replied.

"Okay, Connor let's go, but Hank has to stay in the back yard. Remember our deal."

"Sure thing, I'll get his lead. Thanks dad, you're the best."

Cathy was fit to be tied. She was standing in her new bedroom that now had a thick layer of plaster dust and crumbled mortar everywhere, and the main issue being discussed was the dog. She said nothing, she didn't trust herself.

Bill took his son aside. "Let me go and collect the pup with Connor. I think it would be wiser if you stayed here with Cathy. Anyway, I'd like to see me old mate again." Kevin agreed.

Thirty-Two

Slowly but surely over the next few days, the house in Ardcath turned into a home. It no longer resembled an explosion in an auction room.

Kevin repaired the plaster on the wall over the window in the bedroom. He selected the new curtains that now hung there. Cathy insisted he chose them. The whole curtain affair had turned into a bit of a family joke.

Every one of the packing crates had been emptied and returned to the removal company. Cathy quietly asked the driver to drop off a couple of unpacked crates to the charity of his choice.

They bought a new suite for the lounge and they furnished the dining room with an eight-place dark mahogany dining table and matching chairs they had discovered quite by chance, in a second-hand furniture shop down in the village. It was in excellent condition and the price was very reasonable, so they snapped it up. It suited the room perfectly.

Kevin's parents gave them a house warming present of new carpets throughout the ground floor (Maggie had a thing about carpets). Cathy had to admit the old ones were a bit on the shabby side.

There were a lot more alterations Kevin wanted to get into immediately, but he couldn't fit them all in. His seven-day leave was nearly over and he had to get back to work. As he had faithfully promised Connor he would take him Christmas shopping, he took a couple of extra days off.

***

It was the first time Cathy had been entirely alone in her new home since they had moved in, and she felt a bit lonely. While she was making herself a cup of coffee, she decided to give the stables just one more check. "Come on, Hank, let's go for a walk."

The puppy had settled in fine; apart from the odd accident on the kitchen floor, he was no trouble at all. The newly-built kennel was only used during the day. By night, Hank slept on a rug in the kitchen. Cathy didn't like breaking her own rules, but she agreed with Connor, he was far too cute and little to stay outside all on his own at night. When he had grown up a bit, she would review the matter.

The pair of them headed off towards the stable block. Hank couldn't make up his mind if he was coming or going and his antics amused Cathy no end.

All the rewiring had been completed along with the barn lights and the floodlights in the arena were also in place. A load of straw and hay was stacked correctly in the barn. It had been delivered the day before by the same supplier Paddy used. The feed room contained the same food mix Paddy fed his horses. The stables had all been whitewashed and the floors scrubbed down with Jeyes Fluid and left to air dry.

Kevin and Bill managed to get the old tractor running, much to Connor's delight. He sat proud as punch on his dad's knee while they raked the sand arena together. There had been a few mishaps in the beginning, but they soon got the hang of it, and the end result wasn't too bad at all.

Cathy was satisfied. All was ready for Dubba's arrival the next day.

The day Tony told her she might never ride Dubba again flashed back into her mind, and she shuddered. She'd been devastated by Tony's disclosure, but she hadn't let on to anyone; not even Pauline knew how desperate she really felt at the time. Something deep down inside her told her to believe in Paddy; she had to believe that Dubba would recover.

Paddy's herbal treatments on Dubba's tendon had worked wonders. It had taken time and loads of patience, but Paddy's cure had paid out. Dubba had continued to stay sound for a number of years now. As he wasn't a young horse any more, his days of competing were over. However, he was well able to handle long hacks out on flat ground, and Cathy was happy enough with that.

Tomorrow, he would be grazing in her paddocks and stabled in her stables. She'd have him with her day and night. To Cathy it was a dream come true.

Paddy was boxing him over in the morning and bringing his paddock mate with him. Dubba had become besotted with a scruffy-looking donkey that had been previously badly abused. Luckily, he had been rescued by the D.S.P.C.A. and sent to Paddy for safekeeping until alternative arrangements could be made for the poor animal.

Once again, Cathy counted her blessings.

Hank started barking at something in the barn and Cathy went to investigate. He was only ten weeks old and didn't know much about self-preservation. Cathy was afraid he might have cornered a rat, but she could find nothing out of the ordinary. Nevertheless, he had found something that was very interesting to him.

Just as she was about to abandon her search she heard a meowing sound coming from the back of the straw bales. She moved some aside, and found a scrawny tortoise shell cat with a litter of kittens. By the look of them, they had just been born. The mother cat spat viciously at her so she picked Hank up and brought him back to the house. She returned with a bowl of milk and some of Hank's tinned puppy food, which she quietly put, beside the new and very protective mother.

Cathy's animal family was growing.

***

"Oh mum, we've had a brilliant day. We did loads of shopping and we bought loads of new decorations for the tree. We had lunch in Bewley's and we bought Hank a new collar. We bought you a present too, but it's a surprise, so I can't tell you what it is," Connor exclaimed breathlessly as he dashed past his father who was hauling a Christmas tree behind him.

"Ah Kev', we made a pact, remember. No Christmas presents from each other this year."

"It's only something little, isn't it, Connor."

"Yeah, it is. I'm going to put Hank's collar on him now. It's got his name on it."

Kevin continued dragging the tree into the sitting room.

"Cathy, hold the tree until I prop it up with some logs."

Connor came back with Hank running around in circles. He was doing his level best to divest himself of his new present.

"I'll hold it too," Connor offered.

Cathy watched her husband doing his best to get the tree to stand straight in the barrel.

"It's too big Kevin, you'll have to chop off a few branches at the bottom," Cathy suggested.

"It'll be fine, stop fussing," Kevin replied. His hair and clothes were full of pine needles.

"All right then, make a mess of it," Cathy said, and stomped off to the kitchen to make a pot of tea.

When she was gone, Kevin got a saw. "I'll just take a few branches off the bottom, but don't tell her."

"I won't," Connor promised.

By the time Cathy came back, the tree was all ready to be decorated. She saw that Kevin had taken her advice and chopped off some of the bottom branches, but she said nothing. They spent the next half hour or so decorating it.

Hank was still running around in circles trying to rid himself of his new collar, then the Christmas tree fairy caught his eye and he ran off with that instead. Luckily, it was retrieved before he did too much damage to it. Kevin joked that their Christmas tree looked very individual topped off with a one-winged fairy.

Connor was delighted. Last Christmas his dad had been away, he couldn't get a flight back on time to be with his family for Christmas Day. He didn't get home until a few days afterwards.

"Oh, Connor, I forgot to tell you something," Cathy said.

"What?"

"Don't say what, say pardon. We have a new family in the barn."

"What kind of new family?" Kevin and Connor asked together.

"A litter of new-born kittens."

"Baby kittens, can I go and see them, can I please?" Connor pleaded.

"Wait until tomorrow," Kevin said to his son.

"Ah, dad, don't be a spoilsport."

Cathy knowing there was a strong possibility her son would try to sneak out on his own to investigate the new additions said, "Yeah dad, don't be a spoilsport."

"But it'll be black as pitch out there," Kevin replied, defending himself.

"Granddad fixed up the lights. Remember?" Connor looked at his father as if he had lost his mind.

"Okay, okay, you both win, again," Kevin replied, with a huge smile on his face.

They didn't turn all the barn lights on, as Cathy didn't want to disturb the new mother too much. The first thing she noticed was the food and milk she had left earlier was gone. That was a good sign.

She pulled a straw bale away gently and exposed a sleepy mother cat with her five kittens. She didn't spit this time; she just raised her head and started licking her new family.

Connor was mesmerised. "Can we keep them, can we?" he whispered in awe.

"We'll see," Cathy answered; she didn't want to promise Connor anything yet, because she didn't know whom the mother cat belonged to.

"Ah, mum, they're so small. Please say yes," Connor begged.

"I'll tell you what. If nobody claims them, we can keep two, but not the entire litter," Cathy replied.

"Ah, thanks, mum you're the best. Isn't she, dad?"

"I think I could agree with you on that one son."

***

Early the next morning Paddy arrived with Dubba. To Cathy's relief Dubba backed out of the horsebox calmly, which was very unusual for him, as normally he hated travelling. His donkey friend just plodded after him. Cathy led them both to the nearest paddock and let them go.

Dubba curled his top lip, smelled the air, and snorted approvingly. Without a backwards glance, he charged off like a young colt.

The little donkey looked at him as if he was stark raving mad and quietly began to graze. He had no plans to gallop around anywhere.

Paddy and Cathy watched Dubba for a while. When they were satisfied he wasn't going to attempt anything stupid, they left the pair to familiarise themselves with their new home.

"We'll have to give that poor little donkey a name," Cathy said.

Then she heard her son in the distance shouting, "Nameless, Nameless, I've brought you a carrot."

"I think he's just been christened," Paddy said, laughing at the irony.

"Yep, I think he has. Actually, Nameless suits him quite well, don't you think?"

"Aye, lass, it does," Paddy answered truthfully.

"Will you come inside and have a cup of coffee?" Cathy asked her mentor.

"No thanks, I have to be off. I've a full day ahead of me, so I won't delay. Now if you need anything, or if you're concerned about Dubba in any way at all, you only have to pick up the phone."

"Thanks, Paddy, I have to admit I do feel a little anxious."

"There is nothing to feel anxious about. You're a good horsewoman with a sensible head on your shoulders."

"Well, Mr Murphy, you're too kind," she replied, giving him a mock bow.

"Now, listen to me, you've got a very nice little set-up here, don't waste it. Use it."

"I don't intend to waste it Paddy."

Paddy took Cathy firmly by her arm. "I mean use it properly. Take in a couple of liveries. It will bring in some pocket money and the company will be good for you when Kevin is away. I can put you in touch with a couple of people on this side of town immediately. And, I want you to think about getting another horse for yourself. One you can compete on, you're wasting your talent."

Cathy was taken aback. "But, Paddy I ... I've just moved in."

"No buts, Cathy. Now I must be off. Think about what I said, and give my regards to Kevin."

"I will and thanks again. Say hello to Moira for me."

"I'll do that, cheerio."

218

Thirty-Three

Connor loudly catapulted his parents out of a sound sleep at five o' clock on Christmas morning.

"Santa's been and he's left presents. Come on, come on, come and see."

Hank had followed Connor upstairs and picked up on the boy's excitement and he was yapping his head off. Connor didn't really believe in Santa any more, but he didn't let on to his parents.

"What time is it?" Cathy asked sleepily.

"Dunno, but its Christmas morning. Come on mum, come on dad, please."

"Connor, will you shut that damn dog up?" Kevin ordered grumpily.

"Kevin, don't be such a crank," Cathy said as she slipped out of bed and put on her gown.

"Come on, Dad, you have to see."

"All right, all right I'm coming, I'm coming." Kevin's head was a bit sore. They had received a lot of unexpected guests last night. A constant stream of neighbour's had called in, they wanted to welcome the new family to the neighbourhood and wish them a Happy Christmas. A boozy late night followed, but it had been an enjoyable one.

Connor couldn't contain himself any longer. He ran out of the bedroom and bounded down the stairs with Hank at his heels, followed by his mother.

When Kevin, still half-asleep, stumbled into the sitting room a short while later, his son immediately pounced upon him. He needed assistance setting up the remote-controlled car racing set that Santa had left for him. While his father busied himself with the layout of the tracks, Connor decided to try out the new mountain bike, his other big present from his parents. Wobbling slightly at first, he cycled out of the sitting room and down the hall, gathering speed as he went and came to a crashing halt at the bottom of the stairs. Luckily, he didn't hurt himself. The bike also survived undamaged.

Unperturbed, Connor left the bike where it was and returned to see how his dad was getting on with the racing set.

"Dad, what's this bit for? Where does this go? I want to drive the red car."

Kevin looked up at his wife imploringly. "Coffee, lot's of coffee."

Cathy left the pair of budding *Formula One* drivers together and went off to make the much-needed coffee. When she returned with the rejuvenating offering, Kevin accepted the steaming cup gratefully.

Connor couldn't eat or drink a thing; he was too full of excitement. She sat quietly for a while, watching her family figure out which part went where, not even trying to interfere. She thought it was wiser to leave them to it, without any aid from a third party.

Eventually, father and son managed to construct a decent racetrack, which stretched all the way around the sitting room. A raucous and haphazard race started.

"You can't take a corner like that," Kevin exclaimed, as his son's car careered off the track.

"Yes I can. I just need more practice," Connor replied while he fetched his upside-down car from underneath the curtains.

"Not if you want to stay on the track and finish the race you can't. Let's change the hairpin," Kevin suggested.

"No, let's make the straight longer instead. We can make a tunnel with the box. Bet you won't be able to pass me in that."

Without saying a word to the driving teams, Cathy unlocked the back door. "Come along Hank let's wish Dubba and Nameless a Happy Christmas."

Dubba was still lying down when she popped her head over the door. He whinnied contentedly when he saw her, and rose slowly to his feet.

"Oh, you're a lazy lump, and a Happy Christmas to you too, my beautiful darling." She rubbed his ear fondly.

In the next stable, Nameless was munching away on the hay he had not managed to finish from the night before. He just looked at Cathy briefly and went back to his obvious favourite pastime, eating.

"Happy Christmas, Nameless. Boy you're getting a belly on you." Cathy decided there and then that she would have to restrict his diet. She did not want to have a case of laminitis on her hands. She wished he were a little bit more on the friendly side. The poor animal was covered in scars, both physically and mentally. He needed plenty of tender loving care and Cathy had an abundance of that to give him. He was fine with Connor, but he remained distant and cautious with adults, particularly men.

A cold wind whipped around her ankles and she shivered. She realised she was still in her nightclothes.

"All right you two, I'll go and get dressed and I'll be back in a jiffy to let you both out."

***

When she got back into the warm house, the sitting room furniture had been completely rearranged to accommodate yet another track layout.

"Don't you think it's time that you both got showered and dressed?" No answer.

"Hello, galley slave calling team leaders. The galley slave requests a team debriefing. Sometime like now."

"Oh, hi, mum, watch this next bit. It's going to be brilliant," Connor answered, without even looking at her.

"Kevin."

"Hold on a minute, love, will you? Connor, ready, steady, gooooo."

"I might as well not be here at all," Cathy said in mock anger.

"What did you say?" Kevin asked absently while his son passed his car on the straight.

"Got ye, told you I would," Connor shouted.

"Beginner's luck son, beginner's luck."

"Yeah, sure, dad, if you say so ... and Connor Cassidy comes down the straight ... he crosses the finish line ... breaks a new world record. Still say it's only beginner's luck, huh, dad?" Connor said triumphantly.

"Put your money where your mouth is and do it again," his father teased. Then he leaned over to whisper something in his son's ear. "Don't you think we should give your mum her Christmas present?"

Connor jumped up from his father's side and ran over to the Christmas tree. He returned with a small and beautifully wrapped parcel. "Happy Christmas, mum. I picked it out myself, but dad helped a bit," Connor announced proudly.

"Thank you, Connor. What is it?"

"Open it, open it," Connor enthused.

Cathy carefully undid the wrapping paper. Inside she found a deep maroon leather box. She lifted the lid and discovered a gold locket, and chain inside. It was obviously quite old, probably antique. Kevin stood up and came over to be by his wife's side. Cathy looked him straight in the eye. She was confused. Apart from her wedding ring and watch, she hardly ever wore jewellery of any kind.

"Open the locket, sweetheart," Kevin said fondly.

Cathy fumbled with the mechanism for a few seconds until the locket popped open. On the inside were two photographs. One was of her mother holding Cathy in her arms when she was a baby and the other was of herself holding Connor. He was no more than three weeks old. Tears stung the back of her eyes and threatened to spill out. Connor misunderstood the expression on his mother's face.

"Don't you like it, mum?"

"Oh, Connor, I think it's beautiful. I really, really do. Kevin, it's perfect."

"Dad, help her put it on," Connor said tugging at his father's dressing gown sleeve.

Cathy looked at the innocent face of her son, and not wanting to disappoint him, she handed the locket to her husband in order for him to do the honours. It nestled comfortably just below her collarbone and felt warm against her skin. For a few brief moments, Cathy thought she could smell her mother's perfume and a strange feeling of utter contentment washed over her. She felt as if her mother was close by, watching her.

"Mum, why are you crying?" Connor had spotted his mother's tears.

Kevin looked at Cathy and grinned. "Connor your mother's a great big softie. You know how she cries at the sad bits in a movie."

"But this is a happy bit," Connor replied, confused.

"Oh, she cries at them too," Kevin said.

"Do you, mum?"

"Yes," Cathy sniffled.

Cathy had a long day ahead of her. In previous years, they had gone to Kevin's parents for Christmas lunch and the following day they went out to visit Cathy's father and Imelda in the evening.

Because of the recent house move and the arrival of Dubba and Nameless, Cathy and Kevin diplomatically changed their regular plans for Christmas Day. They had invited the families and some friends over for drinks later on in the evening instead. They wanted to spend Christmas in their new home, together.

Maggie was a bit put out, she had ordered her usual amount of turkey, ham and spiced beef from her butchers. She couldn't possibly change her order at such short notice. Her daughters had phoned the previous day from Vancouver to say they were not coming home for Christmas either. They had just been offered a job together on a cruise ship, and the opportunity was too good to pass up.

Maggie let on to no-one how disappointed she really was. She hadn't seen her daughters in nearly three years. They kept in contact telephonically and wrote to each other frequently, but it wasn't the same. Nevertheless, she understood her son and daughter-in-law's desire to have Christmas Day in their new house. Kevin had been away a lot in the past few years and she knew first hand, what it was like to rear a family with an absent husband.

Cathy had just stepped out of the shower when the phone rang again. It had been ringing all morning. Friends good-naturedly phoned, wishing them Happy Christmas and congratulating them on the new house. Pauline had phoned to ask if it was okay to bring a friend over with her later on. Imelda phoned to warn her there was a strong possibility that her father might bring a female friend along with him as well. The only other information Imelda would impart about the mystery woman, was that she was a nurse.

Two of Cathy's uncles called throughout the morning. It was only at Christmas time they ever really spoke to each other and Cathy felt guilty about not keeping in contact with her late mother's brothers. She didn't distance herself intentionally from them; it just happened that way.

Her father had been unable to face them socially when Mary had passed away, his late wife's brother Thomas in particular. Thomas possessed the same eyes and mannerisms his late wife had. Jimmy could not bear to look into his eyes; they reminded him too much of Mary.

Over the years, the distance had widened and eventually, all contact had practically ceased. Apart from the odd phone call when something important happened that they should know about, they had really nothing to say to each other.

Cathy had tended to Dubba and Nameless who were content grazing away in the paddocks. Connor had helped her muck out the stables and they fed the new mother cat in the barn together. She wouldn't allow him to handle her new family but she had allowed Connor to stroke her briefly while she ate the food he gave her. He was extremely pleased with himself.

"Kev', I'm going to have forty winks. Will you keep an eye on Connor? God only knows what he'll get up to today," Cathy told her husband.

The previous late night and subsequent early morning start had caught up with her.

"Sure, I'll handle things," Kevin replied and he kissed her fondly on the forehead.

Just as she finally laid her head down on the pillow, the phone rang yet again.

"Is someone going to answer that phone or do I have to do everything myself?" Cathy yelled from the bedroom.

"I've got it. Relax," Kevin retorted.

Thirty-Four

"So, how's life in the sticks?" Pauline asked Cathy later on that evening. She had arrived early to escape from her ever-moaning father. She had brought along an intellectual type with her called Philip. He was the latest addition to the stable of Pauline's male followers.

"Don't be ridiculous, Pauline. If you had any sense of geography, you'd hardly call County Meath, the sticks," Cathy replied in a friendly manner.

"Oh, my father maintains that a mile north of Trinity is the sticks," Philip volunteered. He took a long slug from his glass of wine; he seemed to have a fondness for the grape.

"Really, and what does your father do, Peter?" Cathy asked sweetly.

"My name is Philip. My father is a journalist and he is starting a new television series soon, very intellectual, very thought provoking. He's researching it at the moment," Philip's eyes sparkled with his own importance.

"How wonderful for him Pete ... Philip. Now if you'll excuse us, I need Pauline to help me with something," Cathy said as she dragged Pauline away with her eyes.

"Where the hell did you get him from?" Cathy asked, bemused. Philip was definitely not the type Pauline normally went for.

"Ah, he's not that bad really. He gets a bit stuffy when he has a few. The hunk I was supposed to bring called off at the last minute. He had to sort out some family crisis or something. Philip is nothing more than a handy substitute," Pauline replied without a care in the world.

"Why didn't you come alone then? You didn't *have* to bring anyone with you. It's not a society evening, you know," Cathy said a little wildly.

"And how was I supposed to get here, my dear and wonderful friend? Have you forgotten that my brother had more than a slight altercation with my car and a telegraph pole yesterday?" Pauline reminded Cathy.

"Shit, Pauls, I forgot about that, how is he?" Cathy replied apologetically.

"He's grand; the car's a write-off though. He's a bloody stupid fecking idiot. I'll never let him drive my car again, that's for sure."

Cathy didn't get a chance to reply, she heard Connor shouting. "Mum, granddad Corway's here, and he has a lady with him."

Cathy nearly passed out peacefully. She made a mental note to have an urgent chat with her son about his manners. Curiosity got the better of her and she excused herself to greet her father and his guest. She would deal with Connor's manners later.

Her father kissed her warmly on the cheek and introduced her to Fiona, *his lady*, as Connor had announced to the country-side.

"I'm very pleased to meet you, Fiona," she said stiffly. She thought she had met this woman somewhere before, but for the life of her she couldn't remember where.

"Likewise Cathy, actually we have met before, but it was a long time ago," Fiona replied. She watched Cathy carefully.

"We have? You, you, do look familiar," Cathy stuttered.

"Cathy, Fiona is a nurse in 'Holles Street Hospital'," her father contributed cautiously.

Cathy gulped. The penny dropped, with a huge clang. She remembered who Fiona was. She was the nurse who had looked after her mother before she died. What was going on? First, the locket, and then the brief scent of her mother's perfume. Now, right in front of her, accompanied by her father; was the woman who was one of the last people to have seen her mother still alive.

Cathy's father studied his daughter's eyes. A momentary silence seemed to pervade the hallway.

Jimmy had been seeing Fiona on and off for a little over two years. Fiona had wanted to keep the friendship strictly on a platonic level and so did he. Despite the reluctance on both sides to allow the relationship to develop, it had. Over the past six months, they had become very close indeed.

The previous night, over a cosy Christmas Eve dinner at their favourite restaurant in Sandymount, Jimmy asked Fiona to marry him. She accepted his proposal without hesitation. The engagement ring he had placed on her finger was nestling safely on a chain around her neck. She didn't want to flaunt it in front of his daughter until she had tested the waters ahead of her.

"Sorry Fiona, where are my manners? Let me take your coats," Cathy was hunting for something to say, but she could not immediately think of anything else.

"I'll do that, mum," Connor volunteered importantly.

"Hello, my name is Connor. Are you granddad's girlfriend?" Connor asked innocently.

"Connor, how dare you?" Cathy snapped, and she felt like slapping her son.

"Connor, will you show me the new kittens? Which one is your favourite?" Pauline interjected.

"The kittens, sure, come on, they are just gorgeous. Be back soon mum, and don't worry, we won't upset the mummy cat, will we Pauls?"

"No, we won't upset the mummy cat, we promise," Pauline winked at her friend. Cathy was extremely grateful to her.

Kevin joined his wife at the door.

"Ah Jimmy, how are you? And this beautiful lady must be, if I heard correctly, Fiona. Happy Christmas and welcome to the pair of you. Come inside to the fire, it's cold out here. What can I get you to drink?" Kevin said with genuine warmth in his voice.

The next hour passed in a in a blur. The house filled up with friends and family; everyone was having a good time. Cathy joined her guests in the cosy sitting room. She curled up into a corner of the sofa. She hadn't pulled the curtains and she could see the lights of the houses in the distance.

Now and again the headlights of a car would flicker and shimmer along the higher road before disappearing into the darkness. The stars shone brighter than she'd ever seen them before. It was like a living scene on a Christmas card and Cathy felt content. She removed the locket from around her neck and looked at the two photographs inside. While she was studying her mother's face, she became aware of someone standing beside her.

"May I join you?" Fiona asked.

"Certainly, please sit down. I was away somewhere in my own world. Look at the stars. Have you ever seen them shine so bright before?" Cathy said dreamily.

Fiona leaned forward to look out of the window; she finger- ed the chain around her neck absentmindedly.

"A Christmas present?" Cathy enquired.

"Sorry, Cathy, what did you say?" Fiona was taken off guard.

"Your necklace, was it a Christmas present?"

"Oh, I suppose you could say that," she replied.

Once again, Cathy caught the brief scent of her mother's perfume. Instantly she knew what she must do. "Fiona, can you excuse me for a minute?"

"Sure, no problem, is there something I can help you with?"

"No thanks, everything is fine. There's something I have to do, but I need to find my father first."

"I'm right here, so you don't need to find me," Cathy's father said smiling down at her.

"Dad, come and sit with us," she patted the empty space on the sofa beside her.

"Well, I won't argue with you there. My feet are killing me. Damn new shoes," he groaned as he settled himself comfortably.

"Dad, Fiona."

They both looked at Cathy enquiringly. Satisfied she had their attention; she took a deep breath and continued. "When two people are nuts about each other, it's only natural that they would want to be together morning, noon and night, especially at Christmas. Would you both agree?"

"Yes, Cathy, I agree with you on that one," Jimmy replied.

Cathy raised an eyebrow at Fiona and waited for her answer.

"I agree with your father. Yes, they would," Fiona replied.

"I thought so. Fiona, do me a favour. Will you take your ring from around your neck and put it on your finger where it belongs?" Cathy said sincerely, looking from Fiona to her father.

"How did you know?" her father said in a croaking voice.

Cathy opened her locket and showed them the photographs.

"Mum told me, and I'm very happy for you both."

Cathy stood up and called for everyone's attention. "Will you all please raise your glasses in a toast to my father Jimmy Corway and his lovely bride-to-be Fiona Williams?"

***

It was getting late and Cathy was tired; it had been a long day. She wandered out to the stables; she needed a quiet place to think. Imelda saw her slip out the back door and started to go after her but changed her mind. She thought it would be better if she let her be, but when Cathy had not returned over half-an-hour later, she went to investigate.

She found her niece talking quietly to Dubba.

"Hi, I'm not interrupting anything, am I?" Imelda asked, concerned for her niece's welfare.

"Ah, Imelda no, you're not interrupting anything at all. I was just saying goodnight to Dubba, wasn't I you beautiful creature?" Dubba gave her a soft whinny in reply.

"He seems to have settled in nicely," Imelda remarked. She knew nothing about horses, but Dubba looked relaxed and contented to her inexperienced eyes.

"Yes, he has, and so has Nameless. He's still a bit distant, but it's early days yet."

"Nameless?" Imelda quizzed.

"The little donkey in the next stable. He's Dubba's friend isn't he, Dubba?"

"Oh, okay. Cathy that was a wonderful thing you did earlier on for your father and Fiona. I'm proud of you."

Cathy turned her attention away from Dubba and looked directly at her aunt. "You knew all along and you didn't say anything. Why?" Cathy questioned.

"Try to understand, it wasn't my place to say anything. Jimmy was extremely concerned as to how you would react, with Fiona having nursed your mother in her final hours. It was up to him to tell you, not me," Imelda said firmly.

"Does it matter now? I don't think so. Dad's happy, Fiona's happy, I'm happy, you're happy, everyone's happy." Cathy realised she was sounding childish. "Look Imelda, honestly, I have no problems with dad getting married again, and that's the truth. I'm fine."

"Cathy, 'F.I.N.E.' stands for freaked out, insecure, neurotic, and emotional."

"Imelda that's not fair," Cathy was shocked her aunt could think that way about her.

"Then why are you out here all alone?" Imelda asked, going straight to the point as usual.

Cathy froze. She could never hide anything from her aunt. Ever since she was a child, Imelda had been able to see right through her. She knew there was no point in avoiding the matter that was bothering her any longer.

"Kevin has to go away again tomorrow, and before you say anything, I know it's his job, and I should simply accept it. But it's hard, very hard. I put my career on hold for Connor. He deserved to have his mother with him full time for the first few years of his life. But Imelda, he'll be seven years old next February. I've wanted to go back to work for a few years now, but how can I? What kind of a person would Connor turn out to be if both of his parents were no more than fleeting apparitions in his life? When he was born Kevin's life continued on, mine has turned stagnant." Cathy had a lump the size of a football in her throat.

Imelda thought her niece isolated herself unnecessarily but she said nothing in reply, she let her continue.

"Kevin's inside pissed as a fart, and he hasn't got a care in the world. He hasn't even had the manners to tell me he's going away again. I had to find that out accidentally," she gulped the tears back

"He'll be back in a few days I'm sure," Imelda soothed.

"That's just the thing. He will not. I overheard everything on the landline extension in the bedroom. I didn't intend to listen in, but I did. He's off to South Africa tomorrow, and from what I heard, it's going to be a long stint."

"Have you spoken to him about it yet?"

"Haven't had time, he's too busy socialising."

"Well, you had better make time. I wanted to speak to the pair of you about something myself and now that Kevin is away again tomorrow, I'd appreciate it if we could have a chat tonight."

"Imelda, you won't get much sense out of him tonight. He's been laying into the brandy again."

"Can we at least try?"

"Sure we can, but let me speak to him first. He doesn't know I overheard his conversation with *Beta Air*. What do you want to talk to us about anyway? What's so urgent that it has to be discussed tonight?"

As usual, Imelda came straight to the point. "The flat in Swords, I want to make you both an offer to repurchase it. I'd like first refusal. And, by the way ..."

She was interrupted by Pauline's arrival. "So this is where you are? I should have known Dubba would be far more interesting than any of us, isn't that so, Dubba. Hey, Imelda, I didn't think you had any interest in horseflesh," Pauline said. She was in terrific form.

"Don't be so thick Pauls. I was just doing a final check out here and Imelda joined me. We were just having a chat."

"Well, you're both mad chatting out here, it's bloody freezing," Pauline said through chattering teeth.

"Wearing a skirt that short, I'm not surprised. But then again, if you've got it, flaunt it," Imelda jibed.

"Imelda Corway, you're terrible," Pauline laughed.

The three women walked back to the house together in relative silence.

When they opened the kitchen door they heard a loud male voice saying, *don't mess with Mother Nature or frigging mother-in-laws, guffaw guffaw.*

"Oh God, Philip's off. Sorry Cathy," Pauline said and scurried across the kitchen to try and shut him up.

"Philip, I think you've had quite enough to drink," she hissed as she deliberately pried the glass from his hand.

"Ah Pauline, my schweet little Pauline, I was just trying to sexplain to Kevin here that two wrongs def ... definitely do ... don't make a right, but three rights do make a ... a left."

Kevin just rolled his eyes upwards.

"I don't know what he's on about either," Pauline muttered to a relieved Kevin.

"Philip, shut up, you're making a show of yourself," Pauline spat at him.

"Ah now, see what I mean ... if at first you don't shucceed ... skydiving definitely isn't you my scheweetness."

Whatever Philip was trying to say he couldn't finish, he keeled over, flat on his face unconscious. Pauline was mortified.

"We'll put him in the study for a bit. Let him have a sleep," Kevin suggested. "Hey Tommy, give me a hand here, will you?"

Between the two of them, they half-carried, half-dragged the unconscious Philip into Kevin's study, where they dumped him unceremoniously in a chair. Without a backward glance, they rejoined the others who were all in a lively state of conscious merriment.

Thirty-Five

Cathy's loneliness was becoming unbearable. Kevin had been away for over two months and she was finding the long nights hard to handle.

Kevin phoned her every second day and she tried not to moan, but sometimes she couldn't help herself. He had no idea when he would be home, as the job had turned into a much bigger one than *Beta Air* envisaged. The company had been given a window of opportunity to open up a route from Gatwick to Freetown on the West Coast of Africa and they took it on gladly. It meant Kevin and his team had to be on call 24 hours a day.

While Connor was busy at school, Cathy rode Dubba through the numerous woodlands surrounding the area. She made friends with Susan Coleman, an older woman who lived a few miles away. She was a kind and jolly woman with twin teenage boys. Her husband Ciaran was the local pharmacist down in Ashbourne village. Susan owned Gomez, a cantank- erous and difficult horse, whom she rode infrequently.

Initially she accompanied Cathy on a few out rides, but Dubba took exception to the bad manners his equine neighbour blatantly displayed. Gomez continually tried to bite him, and Dubba had been the recipient of more than a few nasty sly kicks from the bad-tempered animal. Instead of the rides being pleasant, they turned into a continual battle of wills. Much to Cathy's relief, Susan hinted it would be better if she rode Gomez alone, like she had been doing for the past few years.

Cathy took to riding on her own again.

When school was finished for the day, Connor nearly always brought a friend or two over to play. They blasted through the house with noisy and sometimes boisterous play, and the hay barn had become a clubhouse and refuge for the often battle-scarred mountain biking team they organised.

It was when Connor went to bed at night that Cathy became acutely aware of just how lonely her life had become. She adored having Dubba and Nameless with her at all times, but they did restrict her movements considerably. She couldn't stay over in Bray like she used to. She couldn't really do anything which prevented her from returning home after dark. The animals had to be tended to, morning and evening, seven days a week.

Hank was growing fast and she tried to take him with her everywhere she could, but he was a handful. No one had claimed the stray mother cat, now named Flea, or her kittens. For the life of them, Connor and Cathy couldn't decide which two kittens to keep, so they kept the lot. All the previous rat and mouse problems ceased to exist.

A phone call from Pauline changed everything. She was in a bit of a state. The lease on her apartment was about to expire and the owner (without any previous consultation with her) had just informed her, he was selling the property to a developer. She would have to look for somewhere else to live and she had less than three weeks to find a new apartment. So she asked Cathy if she could stay with her for a short while.

It was a temporary answer to Cathy's prayers and she told Pauline to pack up and get over as soon as possible.

Pauline moved in the next day, and being a minimalist at heart, her move went a lot smoother than Cathy's had. Connor was thrilled to have her stay with them and he took his role of man-of-the-house while dad's away, very seriously now that he had two women to look after plus the cats, dog, horse, and donkey.

Pauline's job was less demanding than it had been. The mundane and time-consuming tasks she had to perform in the past, were no longer her total responsibility. In the advertising agency she worked for, she had risen through the ranks and was now head production designer, responsible for the visual design of the sets when the company shot adverts for their clients. She coordinated and delegated to a variety of departments, set decoration, construction, paint, props and sometimes wardrobe. So she didn't have to spend as much time at the office as she had in the past.

A lot of her work could be performed just as efficiently when she wasn't on set, via the internet and conferencing calls from home.

She missed the horses at Paddy's. She rode Dubba a few times but it wasn't the same. Dubba was Cathy's pride and joy and she would never take advantage of Cathy's good nature in any way.

However, Cathy had been dropping more than a few hints that she should buy a horse of her own and stable it with her. Pauline had considered the idea herself more than once, but to date, she never really had the time to devote to a horse. Now things were different. *Yes, she would buy a horse, of her own.* When she told Cathy her decision, they immediately phoned Paddy to help them find an appropriate horse, a horse Pauline could com- pete on.

Paddy told them he had a five-year-old Irish Draught gelding that had just come in, but it would suit Cathy more than Pauline. He was only 16'0" hands and as Pauline was taller, she needed at least a 16'2" minimum. Cathy was against the idea of buying a second horse for herself. She had Dubba.

"Yes, Cathy, you do have Dubba and you always will, but you can't compete on him. Think of the fun we'll have together. There's a terrific riding club not far from here, well within hacking distance. We could participate in the local drag hunts, and there's that wonderful cross-country course that was built last year near Tara. It would be just like old times."

Cathy gave Pauline a wicked smile. "You're on, we'll do it. But I'll have to check with Kevin first, he should be phoning if he's not caught up in anything, shortly."

Kevin didn't phone that night, but he did phone first thing the following morning before Connor left for school. Connor answered the phone and he was quite cool with his father. It was his seventh birthday in two days, and this was going to be the third one in a row his dad would be away for.

He brightened up considerably when his dad asked him if he could keep a secret, a secret just between the two of them. Connor whispered of course he could. He also whispered that his mum was standing close by him so he couldn't really talk secretly.

Kevin told his son he would be home the next night, in plenty of time for his birthday and they would do something special together. But, he wasn't to tell his Mum, as he wanted to give her a surprise. Connor now thought his father was the best dad in the world, still weird, but the best. He said his goodbyes, handed the phone to his mother and dashed off like a scalded rabbit to find Pauline. He had to tell someone the news.

"What was all that whispering about?" Cathy quizzed her husband.

"Ah, nothing much, just guy stuff," Kevin answered and quickly changed the topic. "Connor sounds in good form."

Cathy didn't reply to her husband's reference about their son's form one way or the other. Instead, she briefly told him about Pauline's decision to buy a horse and that she was considering buying a second one for herself. Kevin had no objections either way. He was happy for his wife. Since Pauline had moved in, she had been a lot more cheerful. He knew she was lonely, desperately lonely, but what could he do. He was lonely too.

He was under contract to *Beta Air* and with the new route in place; they needed a full-time maintenance crew stationed permanently in Johannesburg. The responsibility fell upon his shoulders to recruit and supervise the technical crew stationed there on a rotation basis. He now knew he was going to be away for six or seven months at a time, but he hadn't told Cathy or Connor that.

Pauline was using Kevin's study as a temporary home office. She had just started sifting through the new specs she had received for the latest advertising campaign her department was working on, when Connor burst through the door and shut it firmly behind him.

"Pauline, dad's coming home tomorrow, he'll be here for my birthday, it's a secret, and you're not to tell mum because it's a surprise."

Pauline was taken aback by Connor's excited outburst. "Slow down and tell me all that again," Pauline said in an effort to get him to speak more clearly.

Connor heard his mother calling him. He couldn't stand still; he hopped from foot to foot. "Dad's coming home tomorrow. He just told me he was. It's a secret and we're not to tell mum because it's a surprise."

"Oh, well then, my lips are sealed. I'll tell you what ..." Pauline stopped in mid-sentence because Cathy opened the study door a hell of a lot more gently than Connor had done a few minutes ago.

"So there you are ... will you stop annoying Pauline and come along. You'll be late for school." She opened the door wider giving her son the signal to move it. Connor scampered off, thoroughly delighted with himself.

Pauline halted Cathy's exit. "Hey girlfriend, I don't have much on today. Let's go out to Paddy's and have a look at the gelding he was talking about. No harm in looking is there?"

"Sure, I've already put Dubba and Nameless out and the stables are done, so I can go as soon as I've dropped Connor off at school," Cathy replied. The idea of seeing the crowd at Murphy's again appealed to her a lot, and the possibility of finding a new horse, appealed even more.

"What time did you get up?" Pauline queried.

"I couldn't sleep, so I got up at five to let Dubba out. He wasn't very impressed with me."

"I'd say he wasn't. Okay, you drop Connor off and I'll be ready when you get back."

"Right, I won't be long. Oh, will you lock Hank up in the yard? He's still in the kitchen feeling sorry for himself."

"No probs. I'll lock the mutt up."

Hank wasn't in Pauline's good books at the moment. He was in disgrace for chewing the heel off one of her new shoes during the night, and he had received a good slap for his misdemeanour.

When Pauline heard the front door close and the car start up, she phoned Kevin on her mobile. He confirmed Connor had not gotten his facts wrong, and yes, he would be home tomorrow for a few days. He confided in her that his stay overseas was going to last for at least another five, maybe six months, and he pleaded with her not to be in any hurry to move out. They chatted about a few other things and then she heard Cathy's car pull up in the driveway.

"Kev', I have to go, Cathy's back. We're going to look at a new gelding at Paddy's. See you tomorrow, bye." She pressed the end button on her phone and went to find Hank. He was sulking on his rug in the kitchen.

"Okay, you stupid lump, I forgive you." Hank immediately started running around her legs in obvious relief.

"Come on boy, outside and behave yourself." Pauline gave him a quick cuddle and locked him in the yard.

"Paddy, he's a beauty. What's his jump like?" Cathy asked mesmerised by the chestnut gelding she was looking at in the front paddock.

"Why don't you tack him up and find out for yourself?" Paddy suggested.

"I'd love to, thanks," Cathy said, anticipation oozing out of her.

Paddy shouted to one of his lads to fetch the new chestnut's saddle and bridle.

"By the way Pauline, there's a mare that came in last week, but she's only 6'1". It'll do you no harm to try her out," Paddy said as Cathy led the chestnut past them.

"Okay Paddy, I'll do that. Where is she?"

"Come on, I'll show you."

They walked together towards the mare's stable block.

"Why have you got her in?" Pauline asked. Paddy never kept his horses locked up, unless he had a valid reason.

"The farrier is coming to put shoes on her, but he phoned as you drove in to say he's running late, so you can take her out. Stick to the soft ground, her feet are a bit sensitive."

Paddy opened the stable door and ran his hand down the mare's spine and she nuzzled his shoulder.

"Paddy, she's a skewbald and a very pretty one at that. Aren't you, you beauty." Pauline patted the mare on her neck and received a series of contented snorts in return.

"She seems to like you. Let me take her out so you can have a proper look at her."

It was love at first sight for Pauline. The mare was beautifully marked and she was in terrific condition.

"She hasn't been ridden much lately, so she might be a bit hot. She's a good mover, nice and light. I saw her jumping last year in the welcome stakes at Cavan, and she handled the fences very well."

"She's got good strong cannon bones and a kind eye. I like her Paddy," Pauline said as she circled the mare.

"Now don't go rushing into anything. I just want you to try her out, nothing more," Paddy said sharply.

One of Paddy's lads walked past. He told him to tack the mare up, and bring her over to the main sand arena. Then they went back to see how Cathy was getting on.

She was trotting the chestnut around gently and Paddy took up his instructor's position in the middle of the arena.

"Right Cathy, at the next bend, ask for canter."

Cathy did as she was instructed and the gelding responded beautifully to her aids. His transition was perfect. Paddy put up a fence and told Cathy to pop over it. The horse jumped it with style.

After completing a few more exercises, Paddy told her to take the horse out cross-country. He asked Pauline to join her on the skewbald as the ground was good and soft out that way.

"Oh, Cathy, try him over the water fence while you're out that way," Paddy said with a twinkle in his eye.

An hour later, they rode back into the yard. Cathy was in love with the chestnut gelding and Pauline was equally im- pressed with the skewbald mare. They had tons of questions to ask Paddy and he answered them as he always did, truthfully.

"I'll tell you what. Seeing that you're both convinced that these horses are the perfect and ideal ones for you, I'll box them over tomorrow. Keep them for a week, get to know them, and if you still feel the same after that, then we'll talk further."

"Brilliant," they both said together and left Paddy's yard contented.

When Cathy phoned Pauline at her office the next day to tell her the horses had arrived, Pauline took the afternoon off. She couldn't wait to get back and see the beautiful skewbald again. Nobody would notice her absence as she was always in and out of the office. And anyway, it was Friday.

Connor was in a terribly excited mood and Cathy put it down to the arrival of the new horses. She did remark to Pauline that it was somewhat strange for him, as up to now, he refused point blank to even try to learn to ride. Pauline tactfully suggested his excitement was probably due to the anticipation of the birthday party he was having in McDonald's tomorrow afternoon.

They tacked the horses up. Paddy had sent a saddle and bridle with the skewbald as he knew Pauline did not own one, and they both rode the new arrivals in the sand arena. The skewbald had been shod but they couldn't leave Connor alone so they stuck to the facilities on site.

Both horses behaved wonderfully and they had a terrific ride, just like old times. Dubba snorted angrily when they put the new arrivals back in the vacant stables, so Cathy made an extra fuss over him and he soon settled down. Nameless paid no heed. He had no fear of horses; his only fears lay with humans.

Cathy was locking up the tack room when she heard a familiar voice; she put it down to her imagination. The wind often played tricks at that time of the evening. When she rounded the corner of the stable block to make doubly sure the bolt was properly locked on Dubba's door, she couldn't believe her eyes. Standing beside Dubba's stable as cool as a cucumber was her husband.

"Kev', Kevin ... you're home." She dropped the bucket she was carrying and ran into his arms. Pauline just had to hug someone too, so she grabbed Connor and he didn't protest. She whispered in his ear that maybe it would be a good idea if they left his mum and dad alone for just a little while.

When his parents came into the house about 30 minutes later, Connor could see his mother had been crying. He told Pauline his mum often cried when she was happy, she'd done the same thing at Christmas when she opened her present.

Pauline knew Cathy's tears were born from frustration and utter disappointment. Kevin had obviously explained that his homecoming was not much more than a fleeting visit.

Pauline wanted to leave the reunited family alone, so she tactfully made an excuse that she had to visit her mother. She was really going to stay in a hotel for the weekend. She promised Connor she would be at his party tomorrow, and tried to leave quietly. Cathy was having none of it.

"This is your home Pauline Dutton, and you are going nowhere. Going to visit your mother, sure you are. You've never been a good liar, so don't try and start now." Cathy was definite. Pauline was going nowhere.

Kevin backed Cathy up. Connor took the overnight bag out of Pauline's hand and hid it in the hall closet.

The weekend passed all too quickly. Connor had a great time in McDonald's. Afterwards, Kevin, Cathy and Pauline escorted him, and his five birthday guests to the movie *Star Wars*.

Kevin's return flight to London left the next day at five-thirty to connect with the nine-thirty flight to Johannesburg. Cathy was miserable and Connor locked himself in his bedroom. It took a lot of cajoling, but eventually Pauline persuaded him to come out to the kitchen for his supper. She had cooked his favourite, sausages and chips.

Kevin had left a letter for Cathy with Pauline; he thought he could explain the situation better that way. Later on, when she was satisfied Connor was sound asleep, Pauline handed the envelope to her friend. Cathy burst into fresh tears.

"So this is how my marriage is going to be from now on ... two-night stopovers every so often and ... and bloody letters."

"Cathy, open it, read what Kevin has to say. He's very cut up about having to leave," Pauline said gently.

"I need a drink. Would you like one?" Cathy announced in a voice that would freeze hell over.

"I'll get it, you stay by the fire. White wine, or would you like something stronger?" Pauline's heart felt heavy.

"White wine please and bring in the bottle Pauls," Cathy replied, still staring at the unopened letter in her hand.

Pauline busied herself in the kitchen trying to open a bottle of wine that was proving to be very stubborn; eventually it co-operated. She took two glasses from the cupboard and rejoined Cathy in the sitting room.

"Now, will you open Kevin's letter?" Pauline poured the wine and handed a glass to Cathy.

Cathy took a large gulp and tore the letter open. Inside were two open-return business-class tickets to Johannesburg.

"What the hell?" Cathy was confused.

"Read the letter, it will explain all," Pauline urged. She knew about the tickets; Kevin had confided in her the day before. She also had a fair idea about the contents of the letter. Cathy slowly opened up the pages her husband had written. She read them once; then she read them again.

"Pauls, Kevin wants Connor and me to come over to Johann-esburg for a few weeks." Cathy's voice croaked with emotion.

"Well, go then, I'll look after everything here. I have four weeks leave coming up soon, and I ..."

Cathy stopped her. "Pauline, how can I just up and fly off to Jo'burg? I'm not that bouncy thing from the *Magic Roundabout* you know. What about the horses, and what about Connor's schooling?"

"Connor is young enough to miss a few weeks from school, and we'll make a plan with the horses. I've just told you, I have four weeks leave due."

"But Pauline, it's not fair on you."

"Piffle, bullshit. Stop behaving like a moron. We'll make a p-l-a-n, are you deaf as well as thick? Just say you'll go. And if you hurry up, you'll catch Kevin in time to tell him the good news before he boards his connecting flight from London. It's only eight forty-five and his flight doesn't leave until nine-thirty."

Cathy sat thinking for a few minutes. She picked up the phone on the coffee table beside her, and dialled her husband's mobile number. Kevin answered almost immediately.

"Hi honey, do you fancy having a couple of visitors for a while?" Cathy said smiling broadly.

"You're coming over, you're really coming over?" Kevin sounded ecstatic.

"Yes, my darling. Connor and I are coming out to Jo'burg to be with you for as long as we can," Cathy answered, now with joyous tears rolling down her face.

"Ah, Cathy, that's the best news I've had in a long time. When are you leaving? Can you leave tomorrow?" Kevin was bubbling.

Cathy laughed. "Kev', I have quite a few arrangements to make first, but I'll be there soon."

"Hurry up and make them, I need you and Connor here with me. My life is empty without you both."

"I'll start right away. Phone me when you land. I love you Kevin."

"Each day that goes by, I love you more and more Cathy. I'll phone as soon as I've landed."

"Do that and try to get some sleep on the flight. You'll be worn out if you don't."

"I'll sleep now that I know you'll be with me soon. Is Connor excited?"

"Kev', he doesn't know yet, I haven't told him. He's fast asleep in his bed."

"Fair enough, I'd better go, my phone battery is about to die, and my flight is being called. I'll talk to you and Connor in the morning. Love you, and thanks. Tell Connor ..." Kevin's phone battery ended the conversation.

***

Pauline decided to keep the skewbald mare, she adored her. She named her Amadeus. Only Pauline would think of a name like that for a mare. The official name on her passport was *Precious Papyrus*, but Pauline preferred Amadeus. Cathy also liked the chestnut Irish Draught already named Guinea. But she decided not to make any hasty decisions about purchasing him, not just yet.

Paddy understood, he thought she was being sensible. He gave her the contact details of Shea Whelan, an old friend of his who lived locally in Ashbourne. Paddy knew him well, and he assured her he ran a reputable yard, and was extremely reliable with horses.

Both Cathy and Pauline liked Shea instantly. He had a quiet air of confidence about him, and he arranged for one of his lads to come in twice a day to muck out, attend to the yard, and the horse's needs in general.

Connor's headmaster had no problems with Connor taking time off school. A short break would not be detrimental to his education, not at this particular stage in his life. He willingly gave Connor the necessary permission, and wished them a safe trip.

Imelda offered to stay over with Pauline, as it afforded her the opportunity to have the flat in Swords repainted. Cathy's dad promised he would keep an eye on things and told her she wasn't to worry about a thing. She was to go and enjoy herself.

Connor was beside himself with excitement. Up to now, he had only ever seen exotic animals in the zoo. Very soon, he was going to see them roaming free. Kevin had promised they would visit the 'Kruger National Park' for a weekend. Not only would Connor see the animals during the day, he would hear them during the night as well. Cathy started them both on a course of anti-malaria tablets. Connor didn't know what malaria was, but it sounded important. When he told his friends he was going to Africa, they were extremely impressed. They were ready to go.

One week later at eight-thirty in the morning, Cathy and Connor were wandering around the duty-free shops in Dublin Airport. They were waiting for their flight to be called. It was the only place she could keep her son entertained, as the business-class lounge was being refurbished at the time, and he couldn't sit still.

As luck would have it, a dense fog had settled, and stubbornly refused to lift. Cathy was worried the flight might be delayed. She phoned one of her friends in the control tower. He told her the flight was delayed, but only for an hour at the most.

Three hours later, the passengers travelling on flight 745 from Dublin to London Heathrow were asked to board. Cathy tried to settle Connor down but he was too excited, so she let him be. As long as he didn't make a nuisance of himself, she was happy.

As the flight attendant donned her life jacket, during the pre-flight *in the event of an emergency announcement;* Cathy remembered back to the times she had demonstrated the same procedure herself. She smiled to herself. She missed her job, but Connor needed her on *terra firma.* She settled back in her seat and waited patiently for the aircraft to take off.

Connor was busy fiddling with his headset. "Mum this doesn't work, my radio is broken," he whispered in a disgusted voice.

"Connor, it will work as soon as we take off. Now sit quietly."

"Are you sure?"

"Yes, I'm sure."

As the aircraft taxied onto the runway, the captain told the cabin crew to arm the doors and crosscheck. Connor was nearly fermenting with anticipation. He had flown before, but never in business-class and he was feeling very important and very privileged. He tugged at his mother's arm and announced, "Mum, I'm hungry."

"Connor, you'll be given lunch shortly," Cathy answered in a firm tone.

"How soon is shortly?" Connor quizzed.

"Shortly, after take-off."

"Gotcha," Connor replied.

Cathy smiled.

Fifteen minutes later, they were airborne and the cabin crew started the in-flight service. When the flight attendant laid a small tablecloth over Connor's tray he was very impressed and he thanked her politely. He told her quite loudly that they didn't use tablecloth's at home, Cathy's smile broadened. So did the passengers sitting opposite them.

The captain's voice crackled over the intercom. "Ladies and gentlemen our weather office in Dublin has just informed us we have to divert to Shannon; due to a very un - cooperative fog surrounding Heathrow airport. We are sorry for this inconvenience and I will update you shortly."

Cathy heard the familiar rumbling of disgruntled passengers; she was glad she was only a passenger and not a member of the crew.

"Mum, where's Shannon? Is it near London?"

"No Connor, it's not anywhere near London."

"But we're supposed to be going to London."

"Yes, Connor, I know we are, but the weather has changed our plans for us, hasn't it?"

"But, mum, I don't want to go to Shannon; I want to go to Africa. I want to see dad and the 'Kruger Park'."

"Well Connor, the 'Kruger Park' and your dad will have to wait for a little longer." Cathy caught the flight attendant's eye and asked her for a gin and tonic.

"Certainly, madam, and would the little boy like anything to drink?"

"I'd like a coke, please," replied Connor instantly.

"Okay, one gin and tonic and one coke coming right up."

"Thanks," Cathy and Connor said in unison.

"Mum, how much longer before we get to Africa?"

Oh God, this is going to be a long flight, thought Cathy.

Some time later, the intercom sprang to life again and the captain announced they would be landing in Shannon airport in approximately ten minutes; he apologised again for the diversion.

"Mum, I have to go to the loo, where is it?"

Cathy downed her gin and tonic, just as the flight attendant came to clear away in final preparation before landing.

"Connor, why do you always have to wait until the last minute? Oh hell, I'll take you, come on." Cathy unbuckled her seat belt and stood up. The flight attendant informed her that they were starting short finals and they would have to remain seated. Cathy knew she was talking nonsense, but, nevertheless, she sat down again, much to Connor's dismay.

"Mum, I have to pee and I have to pee now," he said with a fair amount of urgency in his voice.

"You'll just have to hang on until we land," she told him firmly.

"Why can't I go now? I have to go now!"

"Well, you can't," Cathy said with a note in her voice that made Connor keep quiet.

As the aircraft landed, Connor forgot all about his insistence on visiting the toilet. Cathy was relieved, and she didn't remind him until they entered the terminal building. While she waited outside the toilets for him, she switched on her phone and called Kevin. Her call went automatically to his voicemail. Frustrated she phoned the *Beta Air* offices. She was told that the delay was definitely due to the weather and the reason they had been diverted to Shannon was because of the backlog of air traffic in Heathrow and Dublin.

They had no further concrete information for her then. Cathy knew she would just have to wait the weather out. There was nothing else she could do. She tried Kevin's mobile number again and this time he answered. He knew about the delay already and sympathised with her. They talked for a few more minutes before Cathy's decided she had better hang up, as the chances of losing Connor in the overcrowded airport, was high.

Eventually, at seven o' clock that evening they boarded the flight to London. Connor was tired and grumpy and so was Cathy. It had been a long day. If they were lucky, they just might make Heathrow in time for the nine-thirty to Jo'burg. If they were not, well, she would cross that bridge when she came to it.

They did arrive in London on time for their connection and when Connor boarded the aircraft, he was awed at the size of it. However, they didn't take off until nearly ten thirty that evening.

"Mum, what's upstairs?"

"Upstairs, that's first-class, Connor."

"Oh," he replied and played with the controls on his armrest for a few minutes.

"Can I go up there?"

"No, you can't."

"Why?"

"Because you can't."

"But why?"

"I've told you, upstairs is for first-class passengers only."

"You didn't say only, you only said it was for first-class passengers."

"Connor, you're getting on my nerves, will you stay quiet? Read your book."

Connor sat still, he couldn't read his book, it was in his bag in the overhead bin; he didn't want to risk telling his mother where it was, not just yet. He was supposed to have had it, and any other small item that was necessary for the flight, with him in his smaller bag under the seat.

"Would you like a pre-flight glass of champagne?" a friendly flight attendant carrying a tray of wine and juice asked Cathy.

"No champagne thanks, but a glass of mineral water would be grand," Cathy replied.

"Sure, and for the little boy?"

Cathy had visions of Connor wanting to explore the toilets again. I think he's fine, thank you."

"No I'm not. Can I have some orange juice please?" he asked in his man-of-the-house voice.

"Sure you can, here you are." The attendant placed a glass of juice in front of Connor and he immediately spilled it all over himself.

"I'll be right back with your water, Mrs Cassidy, and we'll get you cleaned up right away. Okay, Connor?" The flight attendant turned back towards the galley.

"Jeepers, mum, how'd she know our names?"

"She's very clever Connor, now settle down, please." Cathy silently thanked God she'd put a couple of changes of clothes for him in his bag in the overhead.

"Did you know all your passengers' names?" Connor asked curiously.

"Connor, please be quiet. I've got a headache." She saw the pinched look on her son's face and she felt guilty for being so sharp with him.

"If, you're a good boy, the flight attendant will bring you some toys to play with, special airline ones, very special ones."

"Cool," Connor replied, he thought that sounded brilliant.

The flight attendant returned with Cathy's water. "Mrs. Cassidy, would you care to move to another seat? The aircraft isn't full, we have plenty of space. I'm sure your son would be more comfortable in a dry seat." She winked at Connor and he gave her a huge smile back.

"Thanks, I think that's a good idea," Cathy replied gratefully. She stood up and started to retrieve her hand luggage from the bin.

"Don't worry about your luggage overhead, I'll bring that across for you, as soon as we've taken off."

"Okay, thanks." She gave the flight attendant an engaging smile and moved to the other side of the aircraft. When they were seated once again, Connor announced he wanted to go to the loo. The flight attendant was on the ball. "Its okay, Mrs Cassidy, I'll take him; we have a few minutes to go before take-off. Cathy accepted her offer wearily.

Once the seat belt sign had been turned off, the flight attendant returned with Cathy's and Connor's hand luggage, from the other side of the aircraft. Cathy thanked her and stopped her storing it overhead, she wanted to retrieve a change of clothes for her juice-soaked son.

"Okay, Mrs Cassidy, I'll leave you to it. If there's anything you need, anything at all, don't hesitate to use the call bell." She smiled broadly at Connor and promised to bring him his own personal video game player. Connor now thought he must be in the first-class passenger section. His mother had to be wrong, upstairs was probably a storage room.

Cathy opened Connor's flight bag, to her horror; she found all the clothes, which she had packed carefully, covered in ink. The packet of markers she told him not to pack had leaked everywhere. She had one of two choices; allow him to continue the flight wearing juice-soaked pants, or ink-soaked ones. She chose to leave him as he was. He wasn't complaining, he was too busy figuring out how to play the game he had selected on the small portable game machine the flight attendant had just brought him. Cathy began to relax. Connor was thoroughly occupied with the video game and the variety of complimentary toys he'd been given. She extended her footrest, reclined her seat, and ordered another gin and tonic. The orange juice incident was now forgotten.

Once they had eaten supper, Cathy settled her son down to sleep. He was reluctant at first as he was afraid he might miss something. But she was firm and Connor eventually complied with her wishes. It didn't take him long to fall asleep, he was thoroughly exhausted. Cathy watched her son for a while before she nodded off herself.

She was awoken by the intercom. "Ladies and gentlemen, the captain has switched on the seat belt signs as we are experiencing a small amount of turbulence. Please return to your seats, fasten your seat belts and remain seated until further notice. Thank you."

Connor stirred and asked sleepily what was going on.

"Ah, nothing much Connor, it might get a bit bumpy for a few minutes, that's all."

"Bumpy, that's cool. But why?" He sat bolt upright in his seat and waited for an answer.

"We're passing through a bit of bad weather," Cathy reassured him.

"Oh, okay. I suppose it must be awful windy out there. Oh look, mum, I just saw some lightning." Connor glued his face to the window.

The intercom sprang to life once again. "Ladies and gentlemen, my name is Derek Coyne. I am the first officer on board tonight's flight to Johannesburg. Due to the weather conditions, we are experiencing, and to make your flight more comfortable, we will be descending to 30,000 feet. Thank you." The intercom went silent.

Great, thought Cathy. She knew the flight would be more than a little bumpy for quite some time to come.

"Mum, does that mean we're landing in Africa?" Connor asked, dragging himself away from the window and the rather spectacular lighting bolts, which, to his mind seemed very close by.

"No, Connor, the pilot is only descending to get out of the bad weather. We've a long way to go yet."

"How much longer?"

Cathy checked her watch. "About seven hours or so. Why don't you go to back sleep?"

"Nah, I'm not tired now. Do you want to play with this game?" Connor retrieved the video game from the seat pocket and held it up for her.

"Not right now, maybe later. Do try and go to sleep. You don't want to be all cranky when your dad picks us up, now do you? "

Connor curled up in his seat and tried to go back to sleep, but he couldn't.

"Mum, I'm thirsty."

"I'll get you a drink when the seat belt signs are off."

"How long will that take?"

"It shouldn't be long now."

"You sure? Because I'm awful thirsty and I'm hungry."

"Connor, you'll have to wait."

"Okay, but can I get my book?"

Cathy bent forward to fish Connor's smaller bag from under the seat in front of him.

"No, mum, it's in the bag up there," Connor told her, rolling his eyes upwards.

"For goodness sake, Connor, I told you to keep your books and toys in the smaller bag." Cathy stood up against her better judgement and opened the overhead bin. She searched through Connor's ink-soaked bag, but the book he wanted wasn't in it.

"But, mum, it must be. It's the one we bought in Dublin airport."

Cathy rooted through the bag again and her hands became covered in ink. Satisfied the book was not there, she put the bag back and closed the bin.

"Connor, I'll be back in a minute I have to wash my hands."

"Can I come? I want to wash mine as well."

Cathy glanced at the still illuminated seat belt sign and decided to risk it. "Okay, come on, let's go."

Connor undid his seat belt and walked in front of her to the forward heads. While they were trying to walk properly in the bumpy aircraft towards the front, a passenger stood up suddenly and knocked Connor onto the passenger in the opposite seat. He sprawled across the lap of a large woman. Cathy picked her son up and apologised. The passenger just smiled.

"Connor, are you okay, did you hurt yourself?" Cathy asked, watching a flight attendant making her way towards them.

"I'm fine. Stop fussing."

"Madam, I'll have to ask you to return to your seat. We should be out of the turbulent conditions we are presently experiencing, shortly."

"Sure, but I'd like to take my son to the bathroom first, and then I might be able to get him to go back to sleep,' Cathy answered, fairly politely.

"Ah, its okay, my mum's an air hostess too. She knows what she's doing. Don't you mum?" Connor said to the flight attendant.

"I'm sure she does, but, as your mother should know, it's a little bit dangerous to go wandering around when the seat belt sign is on. Look what just happened to you." The flight attendant spoke to Connor but eyed Cathy.

Connor ignored her and scampered off to the toilet. Cathy followed him.

When they were back in their seats, the friendly flight attendant who had looked after them when they boarded the aircraft in London, came up to Cathy. "Is everything all right? Did your son hurt himself?"

"No, he didn't, he's fine. Thanks."

The flight attendant steadied herself as the aircraft hit a particularly rough pocket of air. "Glad to hear that." She turned and walked as steadily as she could back down the aisle.

"Mum, I want my book."

"Connor, I don't know where it is, go back to sleep for a few hours. When you wake up, we'll be near Johannesburg."

"I'm not sleepy, I'm thirsty," Connor said sulkily.

Cathy didn't answer him. She covered him with his blanket.

"Mum, I hope I haven't lost my book," Connor said peeping out from under it.

"I'm sure you haven't. It'll turn up."

"Hope so," Connor answered sleepily, his eyes were closing.

Cathy sat still. Before she knew it, the sun had come up. She didn't think she'd fallen asleep, but she must have. When she checked her watch, it was nearly seven o' clock in the morning and the cabin crew were busy serving breakfast. She woke Connor gently.

"Oh, hi mum, what time is it?"

"Nearly seven o' clock, are you hungry?"

Connor threw back the blanket and looked out of the window; he could see nothing but clouds. Disappointed he asked, "Mum, are we nearly there yet?"

"We've a few more hours to go. Would you like some breakfast?"

"Sure, but how many more hours have we to go?"

"Less than two," Cathy answered patiently.

"Two more hours ... I'm bored. Oh look, there is my book in the pocket thing on the seat. How did it get there?" He grabbed his book from the seat pocket in front of him, and then shuffled around on the floor for his bag.

"Connor, what are you doing?"

"I'm putting my book away; I don't want to lose it again. I want dad to read it with me."

Cathy smiled. Her son loved his father reading to him. She used to look forward to her own father reading bedtime stories to her when she was a little girl. "Good idea. It'll be safer in your bag. Now, sit up and put your tray down for breakfast. I'll put your book away."

"Okay, but how did it get ..."

"I don't know how it got there. Maybe it was there all along and you didn't notice."

When the remains of their breakfast were cleared away, the passengers started the ritual visitations to the toilets in order to freshen up before landing. Cathy knew from many past experiences that some of them could spend quite a length of time in the loo having no regard for the other passengers. Some just wandered around the aircraft wanting to stretch their legs. One man in particular stopped to talk to her.

"Not such a bad flight."

"No, not too bad really," replied Cathy. She wasn't in the mood for idle chit-chat.

"We're going to see my dad in the 'Kruger Park'," Connor volunteered.

"Really, is he a ranger?"

Cathy interrupted. "What my son means is, we're going to join his father in Johannesburg, and then, we are going to visit the 'National Park'."

"Ah, I see. Don't forget to take your anti-malaria medication."

"We did, we've been taking the malaria stuff for a while now. Haven't we, mum?" Connor announced proudly.

"Yes, we have. Come on Connor; let's see if we can tidy you up a bit."

"Are you going to stay in the main camp?"

Cathy cut him short. "I don't want to seem rude, but I need to sort my son out." She stood up and busied herself with the bags in the overhead.

"No worries, I'll move out of your way and young man, enjoy the park."

"We will, it's going to be deadly, really cool."

The passenger gave him an award-winning smile and wandered off.

"Can I help you?" the flight attendant asked as she walked past.

"Don't think so, no matter what I change my son into he'll still look a sorry sight when we land," replied Cathy.

"If we had a different purser onboard I'd take you down to the crew quarters, but the one on this flight is a stickler for regulations," the flight attendant whispered to Cathy.

"Not to worry, we'll manage. Thanks, anyway," Cathy replied meaning it.

"We should be landing in approximately 20 minutes. Hope you had a good flight."

"We did, thanks," answered Cathy.

"It was fun, but I was bored. Mum made me sleep," Connor said, not wanting to be left out.

"Well, you won't be sleepy when you land, will you? You won't miss out on anything in Johannesburg because you won't be tired, and I'm sure you'll be allowed to stay up late tonight." She smiled at Connor and winked at his mother.

As more and more passengers moved around the aircraft, Cathy decided to wait outside the loo door with her son. She had to tidy him up. She couldn't possibly parade him in Jo'burg airport looking like a mouldy orange. She had found a pair of shorts in his bag that only had ink on the hem of one leg, and a tee shirt that somehow escaped the leakage.

"What's keeping them in the loo, mum?" Connor asked impatiently. They had been standing with some other passengers for over ten minutes. Cathy made a quick decision.

"I don't know pet, but come with me." Taking his hand, she marched up the stairs to the first-class section. The 'stickler to the rules purser' confronted her. "Madam, this part of the aircraft is reserved for first-class passengers only. Please return to your designated area."

"Well, this is a medical emergency,' Cathy replied and flounced straight into the first-class loo and slid the bolt firmly. Then she proceeded to help Connor change his clothes. She brushed her teeth and freshened up her make-up. After dragging a comb through Connor's hair and her own, she opened the door to find the purser waiting outside.

"Madam, this is not appropriate. Is the little boy all right?"

"Yes, thank you, false alarm," replied Cathy and went downstairs again, unaware that the purser was hot on her heels. As soon as she sat down the purser who evidently thought she owned the airline, confronted her.

"Madam, did you have a medical emergency with your son or not?"

"Not," replied Cathy.

The woman seemed to snort or do something with her nostrils. Cathy didn't hear what she was saying because the captain's voice echoed loudly throughout the aircraft. He was telling the cabin crew to prepare the cabin for landing. The purser sauntered off full of her own importance.

"Mum, what was wrong with that lady?"

"Nothing was wrong with her Connor, nothing at all," Cathy replied trying to hide the irritation in her voice. Connor decided he had better stay quiet but he was finding it hard to do so.

Cathy was feeling really cranky. She let her thoughts drift back to Ireland and Pauline. They had been through a lot together and had endured more than their fair share of anguish, but they had survived it all, so far. She looked at her son and wondered what lay ahead for him.

Connor's voice burst through her thoughts, "Mum, look, is that Africa down there?"

Cathy leaned over and saw the parched brown savannas of the African continent below her. "Yes Connor, it is. Actually, we've been flying over Africa for many hours. You couldn't see it until now because of the clouds."

"Wow, where's the airport?'

"You'll see it very soon, don't worry."

The flight attendant passed by checking to see if her passengers' seat belts were securely fastened. Then the captain's voice echoed around her again.

"Cabin crew ... arm the doors and cross-check."

A few minutes later Connor shouted loudly, "Mum, I can see lot's of buildings, big ones."

"That's Johannesburg, Connor. We'll be on the ground in a few minutes."

"I can't wait to see dad again, can you?"

"I can't wait either.

Made in the USA
Middletown, DE
14 February 2020